THE FALL OF THE NEPHILIM

Cradleland Chronicles

FLIGHT TO EDEN

QUEST FOR ATLAN

THE FALL OF THE NEPHILIM

F
HIR

RIC

CRADLELAND **3** CHRONICLES

DOUGLAS HIRT

THE FALL OF THE NEPHILIM

RiverOak®
Good News in Fiction

COOK COMMUNICATIONS MINISTRIES
Colorado Springs, Colorado • Paris, Ontario
KINGSWAY COMMUNICATIONS LTD
Eastbourne, England

RiverOak® is an imprint of
Cook Communications Ministries, Colorado Springs, CO 80918
Cook Communications, Paris, Ontario
Kingsway Communications, Eastbourne, England

THE FALL OF THE NEPHILIM
© 2006 by Douglas Hirt

This story is a work of fiction. All characters and events are the product of the author's imagination. Any resemblance to any person, living or dead, is coincidental.

Cover Design: Lisa Barnes
Cover Illustration: Ron Adair
Map ©2006 Susan Kotnik

First Printing, 2006
Printed in the United States of America

1 2 3 4 5 6 7 8 9 10 Printing/Year 10 09 08 07 06

ISBN-13: 978-1-58919-045-0
ISBN-10: 1-58919-045-9

LCCN: 2005910802

For Rich and Rebecca

Skylight Garden

Whirl-Mag Generator

The Ark

Cross-Section showing decks

windows and
Skylight Gardens

← cat-walks →

generator

Deep Pool

Structural
Ventilation
Relief

And as it was in the days of Noah, so it will be also in the days of the Son of Man:

They ate, they drank, they married wives, they were given in marriage, until the day that Noah entered the ark, and the flood came and destroyed them all.

—LUKE 17:26–27 NKJV

Prologue

The Dawn ... of the End

Five hundred quiet years had passed, and then for only the second time within the collected memory of man, the earth shook.

Footsteps froze and eyes went wide while birds exploded from treetops and filled the sky in frenzied flight. After the spasm ceased, people had to wonder: What did the rumbling of ground foreshadow? Some claimed the earth's circuit around the sun must have shifted. Others whispered dreaded warnings that Dirgen had climbed from the depths of the sea to stalk the coastlines. And a few learned men declared with pompous self-assurance that it had only been a global hiccup deep beneath their feet.

But he knew. And he understood.

No easing of ancient stresses, no giant gas bubble of poorly digested primordial fodder working its way through a rocky intestine had shaken his kingdom.

It wasn't of the earth at all!

He recalled the dark sentences uttered eons ago that had set these events whirling into motion.

Poised in the glare of sunlight streaming through towering crystalline windows, peering out over his city ... his world, he knew.

The waking-stirrings of the Tyrant!

Clenching a fist at the crystalline ceiling of his Temple, anger tore from his throat. "I won't give them up!" His strident defiance echoed down the halls of eternity, and the still, small voice that came back at him said:

"They are mine, and I love them."

Stunned into silence ... in the midst of all his glory ... in the center of a world he had fashioned to his will, he indeed understood.

The Tyrant of Old was on the move again....

And Lucifer knew his time was running out.

1

Escape

*N*od City—somewhere outside the Oracle's Temple complex.

Noah careened around the corner of the narrow alleyway and skidded to a halt, his lungs burning, his heart hammering.

Lamech stumbled to a halt at his side. "I'm … getting … too old for this." He seemed about to collapse into a heap.

Noah grabbed his father into his arms to keep him on his feet. "Can't stop now." Fire flared in his own lungs, his legs on the verge of turning to jelly. He could only imagine how his father felt.

An instant later Thore leaped across the bright slash of daylight into the tight shadows and threw himself against the wall. He sidled up to the corner and peeked around it. "I don't see them. But they can't be far." He was breathing hard too, but Noah knew Thore would only stop because Lamech needed rest. At the moment his face bore all the softness of chiseled sparkrock, and his dark eyes were narrowed with worry.

"I don't think …" Lamech heaved in a ragged breath, "those Nephs …" his chest rose and fell, rose and fell, "much wanted to hear that."

"Maybe you just need to find a different way to say it, Father?"

Thore glanced at Lamech, but no grin cracked the tall Hodinite's brittle-stone mask.

Their big canic, Vaul, paced nervously, muscles rippling, head bent toward the mouth of the alley, ears flattened against his slick, black fur, and fighting fangs bared.

Lamech let out a heavy breath, wiping his forehead with his sleeve. "And just how would you have said it, Son?"

Noah raised his eyebrows. "I wouldn't have said it at all."

Thore reached under his cloak and the long Makir sword peaked out, but it was the fistproj that he drew. "Let's move." He took Noah by the arm.

They started down the shadowy gap between the buildings, which grew darker as the alley twisted. Noah stared at the narrow alleyway ahead and a shiver grabbed at his shoulders. Thore kept him moving.

With Noah's support, Lamech managed to keep up. Vaul stalked close at their heels, a deep growl rumbling from his chest. A thickening gloom seemed to be creeping in from all sides, and a twinge of fear caught Noah in a tightening fist. "You know where this will take us, Thore?"

"No idea."

The walls seemed to squeeze tighter as they plunged deeper into the winding gap. High overhead a broken line of blue flashed in and out of view as a zigzagging pattern of connecting bridges flickered past. Noah shot a glance over his shoulder at the alley's mouth, growing smaller and dimmer in the distance.

Suddenly the small window of light filled with giants.

"They found us!"

"I know!" Thore hadn't glanced back, but somehow he had sensed the Nephs' arrival. Noah had long ago stopped trying to figure out how the Makir's mind worked.

Thore stopped and cocked his head, listening. "In here." He kicked open a locked door, shattering the wooden jamb at the iron latch.

Noah helped his father up a single stone step. They stumbled past shadowy casks and crates, through a fragrant mixture of sweet ale and sharp biddleberry wine, to a door where Thore halted, listening.

"This way."

The door opened onto a dim hallway, and a new odor wafted down on a stale breeze.

Noah's nose wrinkled. "Thore! You know where we are?"

"One of the Nephs' barracks."

At least it wasn't that squeezing alleyway. His heart jumped at the pounding of Neph feet in the alleyway behind them.

Vaul took the lead. Thore, guarding their rear, rushed them down a hallway with doors leading off on either side. For the moment the way remained clear, and they passed through the barracks and flew out the exit.

Once outside, Noah could breathe again without gagging on the musty Neph odor. They had exited on the Oric staging ground—a paved skirt in front of the wing-sailer shed where the Oracle's star jumper fleet stood in a line.

Not far away, a wing-sailer sat on the end of the runway warming its cycler. *The Creator was with them!*

The Neph in the pilot's seat didn't notice them as they rushed for the sailer. Thore strove ahead, grabbed the startled giant by the front of his green uniform, and flung him across the pavement, then leaped behind the controls while Noah and Lamech clamored up onto the green silken wings, over the wicker sides, and tumbled into the seats behind him. Vaul sprang onto Noah's lap.

"You know how to fly one of these things?" Noah shouted above the roar of the cycler.

"Of course." He studied the controls, reached for a lever, hesitated, then pulled it. The cycler sputtered and nearly died. He hastily pushed it the other way and grinned over his shoulder. "They're not all the same."

Noah rolled his eyes and helped his father work the buckles on the safety straps as the sailer started forward.

Picking himself up off the pavement, the evicted Neph plunged after them, yelling something, but the words were lost to the roar of the cycler and racing hum of the rubber wheels as they started forward. Noah gritted his teeth and latched his fingers into the wicker coping that formed the outside edge. The giant raced after them, his long legs drawing him nearer.

"Faster, Thore!"

"I'm going as fast as it can!"

To their right, Nephs spilled out of the barracks, some swinging projers to their shoulders. Noah squeezed his eyes shut, his fingers plunging deeper into the coping's coarse weave, his surging blood pounding in his ears. And then the staccato burst of projers drowned the pounding, and splinters of wicker stung his cheek and hands. His lungs seized.

With a lurch his weight seemed to double as the sailer angled steeply upward. Noah chanced a glance. The world tilted and his stomach made end-over-end flips. Nod City sprawled below them. Gleaming walls encircling the Temple complex, shaped in the Oracle's gigantic five-pointed star, swooped into view then dropped away leaving a clear view of the Temple in its middle. Nearby, the Oracle's Image—that immense mound of baked brick that had been sculpted into the Oracle's face—stared with piercing eyes heavenward.

A deafening boom sent wicker flying everywhere. The sailer careened sharply to one side.

"We've been hit!" Thore shouted.

Noah glanced back and went to stone at the sight of the

sailer's shattered tail. His father grabbed his arm, and Vaul's attention seemed fixed upon the Oracle's Image as Thore fought the sticks.

The wing-sailer rolled skyward then plunged earthward. In glimpses, Noah watched the Oracle's Image looming larger.

His great muscles straining at the sticks, Thore somehow forced the sailer's nose up moments before it careened off the side of the Oracle's nose and then came down hard in a jarring stop.

Noah's vision whirled, his eyes flashing images of sky and ground. Exactly where on the Oracle's face the sailer had crashed was unclear as he tried to get his bearings, his view blurred by sloshing inner-ear fluid.

Somehow Thore had worked himself free of the wreckage and Noah was vaguely aware of him tugging at his straps.

"Where … where are we?" Mesmerizing golden stars burst all around him.

"We gave the Oracle a black eye. Snap out of it. They're coming!"

Noah realized Vaul was licking his face as his brain gripped the situation, his stomach teetering on the verge of violently rejecting his morning meal. The smell of burning wicker and the tendrils of black smoke rising from the shattered wing-sailer's cycler spurred him into motion.

He staggered out of the craft and stared at the long scar down the side of the Oracle's nose. That must have broken their violent descent. Wits returning, Noah turned to help his father from the belts and out of the wreckage as flames licked up the fuselage.

"You all right, Master Lamech?" Thore asked.

"Think so." His father staggered off a few paces and sagged against the Oracle's lower eyelid.

"No time to rest." Thore pointed. Far below, the Nephs swarmed toward the monument.

"Which way?" Noah cast about, scanning the ponderous stone eyeball. There seemed no way off the huge monument.

Thore was still in a quandary when Vaul took off.

"This way!" Noah grabbed his father's arm and set off after the canic.

"Not that way!" Thore shouted, but they had already climbed over the lower eyelid and were sidling along the long, sloping cheek to the end of the Oracle's embattled nose. Below, guards had reached the monument and were racing up the zigzagging steps incised in the Oracle's hair.

At the apex of the cheek, Vaul stopped. Lamech bent over, breathing hard. Noah steadied him as Thore came up behind, his fistproj drawn and ready. "We need to get off this pile, not climb it," he said as swarms of Nephs switchbacked their way ever closer.

Vaul leaped ahead, turned in front of the Oracle's nose, and disappeared. Noah drew his father along, following the canic into the dark recess of the Oracle's nostril. The deep shade momentarily blinded him. Feeling his way forward, his hand found the top of a railing as his feet tottered on the edge of a step.

Thore covered their backs while Noah helped his father. The squeezing sensation inside his chest returned as the passageway narrowed. He imagined the Nephs' hot breath burning his neck. He briefly shut his eyes and shook his head. *Not now. You can control this. You must!*

The steps wound deeper and deeper into the structure. Here and there a tiny slit let in a hazy shaft of light, but soon even that disappeared. They must be well underground by now, but the stairs seemed endless. They passed into older construction. The tight walls that brushed Noah's shoulders laughed at him and tried to squeeze out the last of what little breath was left in his burning lungs. But the sound of pursuing feet echoing down after them managed to keep the fear at arm's reach.

Now the passage was nearly black, except for an occasional panel of energized moonglass fitted into recesses in the bare brick walls. They came to a place where part of the ceiling had collapsed and a gap had opened in the wall.

Vaul leaped into the gap, barely wide enough for Noah to squeeze through.

"No. Not inside that!" Noah moaned.

Thore bent forward and peered inside, then turned to him.

"I can't do that." Noah stood firm.

Thore picked him up and shoved him through. He went rigid as the closeness squeezed him. Then the bottom of the shelf fell away and he tumbled into nothingness. The next instant he landed with a splash in a shallow pool of water. It happened too fast for him to cry out. Sitting up, he just managed to throw out his arms and break his father's downward plunge, followed by a grinding sound, Thore grunting, bits and pieces of masonry showering down and splashing. An arm flung overhead, followed by another grunt.

"He's stuck!" Lamech scrambled to his feet.

Noah and Lamech grabbed hold of Thore and with a yank pulled him through the gap. They went down together beneath the Hodinite's weight.

The blackness all around was crushing. Noah gasped as a hand clasped his mouth. Beyond the narrow gap the sounds of footsteps grew louder. Eyes stretched wide, he watched the faint flicker of shadows as Nephs rushed down the passage just beyond the wall, close enough to reach out and touch.

A Neph stopped and peered through the gap, then hurried on. Slowly the pressure of Thore's hand let up.

Noah mustered his reserves and took control of his fears. "Where are we?"

"Don't know." Thore stood.

Noah reached a hand overhead in search of a ceiling and found one at the very end of his fingertips. "Another tunnel."

From the darkness, his father's voice whispered, "The Temple site is riddled with them—from back in the days when it was being built."

"You know these tunnels?" Thore said quietly from Noah's left.

"Not well," Lamech said.

A little way off, a pair of greenish-orange eyes shone at Noah. As he stared, he became aware of a faint light up ahead, too dim to have ever been seen if even a single ray of daylight had been able to pierce through the stone monument above to ... to who knew how far underground they had plunged.

"There's a light up ahead," Thore said.

Noah felt Thore step past him. The eyeshine disappeared and the canic was at his side.

"It gets brighter up ahead," Thore said.

Groping, he found his father's arm. "Let's go." They felt their way along the wall, testing the floor as they advanced. The muscles across his shoulders contracted. He could imagine a gaping hole lurking ahead, just waiting to hurl him down into the Pit.

About halfway up a wall, a rectangle of stone gave off the faintest amber glow.

"Moonglass." Lamech brushed a hand over the old panel, cleaning off hundreds of years' worth of dust and webs. It hardly gave off any light. "At one time it would have illuminated this whole passage."

Noah remembered how moonglass used to glow all on its own, back during the early years when the magnetic veil was so much stronger.

Thore drew out his dagger and worked the blade along the end of the stone. It came loose and crashed to the floor, shattering into chunks. They each took a piece of it. In the faint light, Noah could barely see his companions, but as they crept on, his eyes became more sensitive. The ancient walls came into clearer view—the arching ceiling overhead, the cobbled floor where pools of water stood in the low spots.

Noah swept aside unseen spiderwebs that fell across his face. His panting muffled the distant plop … plop … plop of dripping water. His heart raced in the suffocating tightness. Sweat prickled and chilled his forehead. He scolded himself. *The ceiling isn't going to fall in, nor will the walls topple, pinning me so tightly I can't move my arms.*

That terrified him the most—being trapped. He tried not to imagine how it might feel being encased alive in the strangling arms of this darkness.

His father's grip tightened upon his arm. "It's all right, Noah."

Did his fear show—even in this gloom?

"There's another one up ahead," Thore announced, and presently stopped to sweep the cobwebs off an amber panel of moonglass.

"I know where we are," Lamech said quietly. "We've found our way to the tunnels deep beneath the Temple. We're in the old Temple Prison. I remember it. There are cells behind all the doors we've passed."

Noah had been too filled with fear to notice them, but now he took note of the regularly spaced doors on either side of the tunnel.

"Do you know how to get out of here?" Thore's cheek caught the amber glow, although his features remained in shadows.

"They go on and on. Levels on levels. At one time the Temple Prison held over ten thousand captives." He gave a quiet laugh. "The Lodath needed a lot of backs to build the Oracle's Temple. Prisoners make for cheap labor. It didn't take much to get thrown in here back in those days."

"Now with the Oracle's Liberties the law of the land, it seems a person can't get thrown into prison even if he wanted to." Thore's unseen wry smile was clearly visible in his tone.

Lamech said, "Except by worshipping the Creator. That will

cost you your liberty, if not your head." He went silent for a moment.

"I've heard the Lodath had ordered these passages sealed once the complex had been completed." Noah drew in a slow breath and let it out. "There is likely no way out except the way we came in."

Thore tried one of the doors. It seemed stuck.

Lamech grabbed a lever in the wall that Noah was certain he would never have spied, even if he'd been looking for it. He strained to pull it. The sound of iron grating against iron moaned down the long, black tunnel. "Now try."

The hinges had almost rusted solid, but they could not resist the muscles of a Makir Warrior. With a nerve-edging squeal, the door gave way. Noah followed them into the cell where another panel of moonglass gave off a hint of light from behind partly open wooden shutters. His foot came down on something like a stick that snapped beneath his weight. He leaped back as something clattered to the floor.

Thore held his shard of moonglass near the wall where the bones of a hand and part of an arm dangled from an iron wrist cuff. The rest of the skeleton lay in a dusty heap beneath a stone ledge. "Someone forgot to tell him he could leave."

Lamech didn't smile.

Moving around the cell, Noah discovered it was larger than it first appeared. A stone ledge ran around the cell and iron cuffs hung from chains attached to rusty rings set into the masonry. "You were in here?" The thought of being chained to the wall of this chamber choked him.

"One very much like it. I was over there, chained, and Pyir Klesc was over there, across the room."

Noah shivered and rubbed his arms. "Let's get out of here."

He turned to leave the morbid place, feeling for the door. Without warning, a golden seam of light cut through the blackness and flared in front of his eyes.

2

The Commission

*N*oah threw an arm up to shield his eyes from the light and staggered backward, bumping into Thore. The golden glow spread out, filling the ancient dungeon, and a faint, sweet aroma permeated the room.

"What in Dirgen's name?" Thore growled, reaching under his cloak.

The stone walls faded into a blue haze, taking on a faint, ghostly image. The room filled with the shapes of dark creatures that passed through the stone as if it were mere smoke. Noah startled at the sight of an imp hovering near his ear, his head bulbous and encircled with eyes.

Vaul leaped toward it. The many-eyed creature shot backward and taunted, "This crushing darkness will hold you forever, Noah! Feel how it sucks the breath from your lungs."

He backed away. His heel caught, and he fell … but something caught him and propped him back up on his feet. A tall being stood behind him, another behind Thore, and a third behind his father. Guardians! Messengers of the Creator! Then Noah understood.

Thore drew his sword and wheeled to face this new threat.

"Put the sword away, Thore." Noah sensed His nearness now. He turned back to the rift where ribbons of light were streaming out like waves of golden water.

One of the Guardians leveled a gold and ivory staff at the many-eyed creature. "To your knees. The King comes."

All around them dark beings shrieked and tried to flee. They came up short, trapped, when myriad Guardians encircled the room.

The golden light brightened. The sweet scent grew stronger, faintly lilac-like. A being came through the rift and stepped to the right. An instant later a second being emerged and stood to the left of the rift.

Cherubim!

Each held a long, golden sword, crossed in front of the rift, flames licking off the keen edges in eddies of red and orange that remained momentarily suspended in the air before slowly dissipating.

The mighty warriors of the Creator looked familiar....

The dazzling radiance within the rift brightened yet again. The rip between the two worlds stretched and widened. A portal of pure white stone coalesced from the particles of golden light. And it, too, was familiar....

In the midst of the portal blossomed a white light that grew steadily brighter, taking on the shape of a man. Noah's earlier fear gave way to fascination; icy dread changed to warm desire. As the figure grew closer, Noah sucked in a startled breath of recognition and fell to his knees.

The Gardener had returned!

His father and Thore likewise went down. No amount of physical strength could have prevented it. Vaul was already stretched out on the stone floor. From within the misty-dungeon walls, wails of despair rose and the dark creatures prostrated themselves as rebellious knees were forced to bend.

The Gardener stepped from the portal, His clothes and face filling the dungeon with holy light. "Noah. Lamech. Thore." His voice was the same as Noah remembered it, but now more commanding, more powerful as it rumbled like falling torrents. "Rise and stand before Me."

The Gardener was no longer dressed as Noah remembered Him. Gone were the simple work clothes; the trousers that had always appeared as if He'd just come from kneeling in the rich black earth of a flower bed. He stood before them as a warrior in a gleaming white breastplate and a shining pauldron on His shoulders. But He carried no weapon—and had little need of one as the words from His mouth could slay worlds!

"Master," Noah breathed.

The Gardener smiled. "Peace, Noah. Peace to all of you."

Thore's sword drooped, forgotten in his hand.

Dark beings cowered upon their knees, the lament of their tortured voices filled the dungeon. The Gardener glanced at the pitiful creatures, a deep sadness upon His face. "You may return to your master now."

Their shrieks faded away, and for the first time since entering these deep tunnels, the squeezing fear of the confinement lifted from Noah's spirit.

Vaul circled around behind him and sat down near the three tall Guardians who also had risen to their feet.

"Time grows short." The Gardener considered each of them. "You are faithful servants, and your reward awaits you, but there is much that remains to be done."

"Name the job, Master," Lamech said.

He smiled. "I know your heart, Lamech, and your works. One hundred years ago I visited Methuselah in a dream. I told him how the wickedness of man was great in the earth."

Noah knew of the dream, and the message given Grandfather Methuselah—a word of dire warning. It had emboldened his preaching ever since … especially once Grandfather Methuselah had grown too old to travel far and wide.

The Gardener glanced at him as if He had heard the thought. "It grieves Me that the imaginations of men's hearts have become evil. My sprit will not strive with these stiff-necked rebels forever. They are flesh, and all flesh is destined to come to an end. I allotted one hundred and twenty years for their hearts to turn back to Me. Yet, they have not. Evil increases, both man and the fallen Malik have chased after strange flesh."

Noah gulped. Had he not done enough? Had he failed the Gardener? "We've tried to warn the people, but the words of the Deceiver have spread far and wide."

The Gardener nodded. "That is why I come to you now. I have a commission for you, Noah, the reason you were selected from the beginning."

"Me?"

"Yes, my son. It grieves My heart that I have made man, and I will wipe man from the earth, him and all that I have created."

"All life?" What of the women and children, his family and friends? Vaul and all the creatures?

"The earth is corrupt, and it must be cleansed. The end of all flesh is before Me. In twenty years I will send water from the heavens and bring a flood upon the earth such as has never been before—the likes of which will never be seen again. I will destroy all flesh in which is the breath of life."

"You will destroy everything?" His great-grandfather, Enoch, had warned of a coming judgment by water; still he struggled to grasp the magnitude of the proclamation.

The Gardener nodded gravely. "But you, Noah, have found favor in My sight. You and your family will be a new beginning."

Noah glanced toward his father and Thore, then back. "How?"

"You will build My ark, and in My ark you will be protected from My wrath."

"What's an ark?"

"A vessel of salvation, Noah. A boat. You will build it three hundred spans long, fifty spans wide, and thirty spans high. You will make it out of gopher wood, and pitch it inside and out."

His thoughts whirled, scrambling to understand. The size was beyond his immediate grasp, but seemed immense. He tried to get a hold on what he was being told.

"Build a raised-roof section along its upper deck, a single span above the deck, and finish it with windows round about."

"Windows." He should be taking notes. He forced his brain to catch up.

"You will build but a single door in My ark, high up on the side. Within the ark, construct three levels, and corrals and pens and cages to hold each kind of animal."

"Animals? A boat for every kind of animal?" His jaw had gone slack, and he couldn't seem to crank it shut. "I know nothing of boat-building."

The Gardener smiled. "I will be with you in this, Noah." He extended His hand, and in it was a scroll. Noah hadn't noticed Him holding it a moment earlier. "The details are all here."

He took the scroll from the Gardener and stared at it.

"Lamech." The Gardener put a hand upon his shoulder. "I wish for you to keep speaking truth."

"Yes, of course."

His view went to Thore. "And you must keep a watchful eye on Noah. Once the old Serpent learns of this, he will plan his revenge. You will remain at Noah's side, the strong warrior you are."

The Makir bowed. "Yes, Master. I have sworn an oath to protect him, just as my father, Rhone, had before me."

Noah's brain reeled. A boat—an ark—all life gone....

The Gardener took a step back toward the gleaming portal of white stone. Now Noah knew why it had looked so familiar. It was the same portal that once opened into the Cradleland ... and had vanished the very day he and his family had left in the company of the Messenger, Sari'el. The two cherubs were the same two golden protectors who had stood before the Garden's entrance for over a millennium, guarding the way to the Tree of Life from the Deceiver.

"You will see Me again in the fullness of time." He stepped into the rift.

Thore said, "How are we to find our way out of these tunnels, Master?"

The Gardener spread His hands to the cherubim. "My servants will guide you." An ivory radiance enveloped Him, and He was gone.

Slowly the rift sealed itself, the golden light faded, and then only the two cherubs and the three Guardians remained. The blue haze was now quite noticeable. Looking around, Noah's skin tingled at the sight of dark creatures creeping back into the dungeon.

Silently, the cherubim started forward and the blue haze thickened. Noah glanced at his father and Thore, then followed the two emissaries of the Creator toward one of the dungeon's walls. The three Guardians followed along. Walls were no impediment, and as they strode through them, the floor dropped away and their feet treaded empty space, climbing upward.

Dark creatures hovered around them, but none dared to come close, and none offered the least resistance to their passage through the stone and earth.

With a jolt to all that he understood to be normal and natural—and nothing of the last few minutes might have been called either—Noah's head broke the surface of the ground, and the paved courtyard of the Temple complex spread out before him at eye level! Orange baked pavers shot away to the horizon of his vision. Then his neck and shoulders emerged from the ground. His chest and waist followed, and finally his legs climbed up out of the solid earth.

A pillar of smoke still trailed skyward from the Oracle's Image where the wing-sailer had crashed.

Encased in the azure glow, he had a rare sight—emissaries of the Deceiver and the Creator, many similar to the three Guardians who strode at their sides—were everywhere. Here and there some quarreled, some fought, others merely followed humans around as though connected to them in some special way. All the while, these same humans went about their business unaware of the world just out of the reach of their senses. He didn't see any Malik like the two cherubs leading them. The cherubim were quite different, and every dark spirit-creature knew it, giving them a wide berth.

It seemed but a moment and they were out of the complex, out of the city, and far along the road that ran eastward, away from Nod City.

※

The long, lazy spirals of black smoke continued to climb into the pinkish-blue sky from the monument's right eye. From his vantage point upon the long, marble balcony, high up on the sloping side of his Temple, the Oracle watched the guards scurrying about far below. In their green cloaks, they appeared small and fragile, like delicate malikwings floating upon the surface of a pond, only this pond was the burnt orange color of baked clay.

He frowned. Didn't they know it was too little effort too late? What had occurred was still a mystery, but he knew something inside the realm had shifted.

At his feet a small flock of painted goldbeaks scurried about, greedily snatching up seeds.

Where was Ekalon? The realm was reeling, and he didn't yet know the cause! First the sailer falls from the sky, and now this. What were these humans up to? His fingers flexed with impatience.

Down below, someone finally thought to haul up a hose and drown the fire. He despised the smoke, how it marred the beauty of his Temple. A frown pulled heavily upon his face and he drew another handful of seeds from a pocket, scattering them along the stone railing where two scarlet-crested green and blue Quetzals chased after them.

What did it mean, these disturbances within his realm?

He stiffened and narrowed his view toward a point upon the glazed plaza. An intrusion?

Forcing his mind past the tiles, through the intervening barriers, it came upon a boundary—something impenetrable—and he could reach no further.

So, You have entered my kingdom yet again!

"This is my world! You have no right to meddle in it!" He cringed at the outburst and looked over his shoulder. The vast room beyond the long crystalline window was empty. He hated it when he lost his temper ... so unbecoming of a god.

He concentrated on the barrier, feeling for an edge to see around, but he could find none.

Ekalon was coming. He pulled his thoughts back and turned as the air rippled in waves of heat, and space and time unzipped. Ekalon stepped through the smoldering rift and stood before him.

"High Prince Lucifer." He bowed slightly. "I have news."

He saw at once that the news Ekalon brought was not good. "The Tyrant of Old has invaded my realm. I felt Him move."

Ekalon's large, unblinking eyes showed no surprise. "In the lower chambers, Master."

"And that?" He indicated the smoldering hulk of the sailer.

"Noah, Lamech, and a Hodinite named Thore."

"Thore, son of Rhone." Rhone had thwarted his plans once before. "So, the sleeping giant awakens."

"It would seem so, Master."

"How were the chambers penetrated?"

"There was a breach in a wall beneath your Image." Ekalon cradled his black battle staff in the crook of his arm. "A recent fracture. Perhaps from the shaking we've experienced lately."

The shaking … Noah … and the Tyrant on the move again. What could it mean? "Have it sealed at once."

Ekalon nodded.

"Where is Noah now?"

"He is leaving the city."

"Leaving? Just like that? He is leaving my city and my warriors have not stopped him? He was in the realm, vulnerable. I felt it open for him!"

Ekalon stiffened at the rebuke. "Master, we could do nothing."

"Why!"

"He and the others were under the protection of," he hesitated, "cherubim."

"Cherubim?" His own kind … so close … and the Tyrant. The Oracle recoiled. No wonder the realm trembled. Like in the beginning when he had naively believed he could thwart the Tyrant's plan by merely destroying the Tree. It turned out more of a challenge than that.

He drew in a breath. His Temple had been boldly invaded. His world! Calming, he said, "Very well. These cherubs are gone?"

"Yes, Master—as far as we can determine. There was a blind, and none could draw near."

"So no one knows why the Tyrant chose this moment to return?"

He saw Ekalon's hesitation. "No, Master."

"Then we need to find out. It's time we move on Noah. He has enjoyed his freedom in Atlan far too long. Send out Seekers, learn the reason the Tyrant has chosen this moment to return. I must know!"

Ekalon bowed stiffly. The air shimmered and the rift swallowed him up.

The Oracle turned back to his Image. The smoke was but a lingering wisp in the air, the flames doused. As the sunlight streamed down on him, setting his pearlescent skin aglow, he tried to put the worrisome incident out of mind. He remembered how he had once been, how his beauty had radiated the heavenly glory, before his exile to Rahab, and then to this miserable stone infested with these creatures.

How could the Tyrant love them so?

He frowned. Whatever it took, he would regain that lost grandeur, and in doing so he would grind these miserable humans back into the dust from which they had been fashioned. He would present their ashes on a platter to the Tyrant.

Noah was again a player in the Tyrant's plan. Somehow, he had to get to him. And somehow, he would.

3

Far Port

*F*ive years later ...

The TreeTop Swift raced through forests, across rivers and lakes, around and over mountains, and even through the middle of some of them, connecting the far-flung villages and towns of the Known World in a golden web of Tubal-Cain Company bronze. It was a definite intrusion into what was once called the Wild Lands, but Lamech appreciated how it compressed weeks of travel into mere days.

Now as the slender rail crossed the border into the Longrun District toward the end of the third quartering, Lamech glanced at his suntracer. He gave a sigh and reached under his seat for the shiverthorn traveling bag, tucking the book he had been reading inside it.

He was alone in the wicker carriage. Sometimes he traveled with one of his sons, and sometimes with Mishah, but alone was how he spent most of his days since Noah had stopped accompanying him. Noah had a more important commission now, and for the last five years it had consumed all of his time. Just the same, he missed his company and looked forward to seeing him again in a few weeks.

And then he'd go home.

A vision of Mishah filled his thoughts, a lonely weight settling in his heart. He tried not to think of how she looked, saying fair journey on their doorstep, or the feel of her parting kiss. That had been two months earlier. He shook the vision from his head and sighed again. He was getting old, and old men belonged home with their wives, not rushing around the world, preaching.

The pendant carriages began to slow, the whining of the large drive wheel overhead dropping in pitch as it approached the Far Port landing platform. He buckled the bag closed and hefted it onto the cushioned seat next to him as the river came into view past the open side of the wicker carriage.

With the squeal of brakes and the odor of hot rubber, the long string of carriages slid to a smooth halt, swaying slightly as they settled above the hewn stone platform. He studied the few faces waiting near the TT terminal. Many bore the clear marks of Neph parentage. The muscles along his jaw tightened. The Deceiver's blood-pollution was a plague, though no one thought much about it anymore. He looked for Kerche's narrow chin and humped nose among the people, but didn't find them. Maybe Kerche hadn't gotten his message, maybe he was away on business?

Lamech frowned, rising from the wide wicker seat and making his way off the carriage. He paused on the landing, watching the river traffic in the soft pink light of dusk.

Once a far-flung outpost on the edge of the Wild Lands, Far Port had grown up over the years. Stone wharves had planed the river's once rugged banks into a razored line as far as he could see. Hundreds of stone piers reached out from both banks into the smooth water, like cogs in a gear, not quite meshing. It was hard to imagine how the raw-boned Far Port used to be; a tinderbox collection of wooden buildings running down one wide street. The tinderbox had burned to the ground several times, and each time the determined folks of Far Port had rebuilt it bigger and sturdier.

He inhaled the river air. The Hiddekel River once ran in torrents here, fed by the Great Falls located not far above the town. Channeling the waterway, and diverting much of the falls into the magnetic generators, had tamed and groomed the river ... emasculated it. He felt a sardonic smile cross his face as he turned, searching for Kerche.

The town certainly had loosened its belt and spread out since that day, more than five hundred years earlier, when Mishah and Pyir Rhone had overnighted here.

But even though Far Port appeared all grown-up, it was still only a bawdy frontier town—maybe even more so now, with the Oracle Liberties rampant across the land.

"Lamech!"

He turned at the sound of his name and spied Master Kerche coming up the ramp and pushing past two bullnecked, craggy-browed men. Kerche never did anything except at full throttle, and sometimes Lamech suspected the little man wore three-point blinders as well. One of the men, Lamech noted, had six fingers. The other's hands were shoved into the pockets of a dirty blue tunic. Neither were as tall as a full-blooded Neph, but there was no hiding their lineage. They scowled as he bustled past in his rolling, short-legged gait, as though walking upon the deck of a plunging ship. Kerche was a hump-nosed Kleiman—an ex-Atlander, and an ex-gatherer on a commercial seavining boat.

He grinned and stretched his arms, and gave Lamech a big hug that landed somewhere about his middle. "Lamech! Fair journey, I hope?"

"Fair, but long. Much too long." He noted with some relief that the nephlings had dismissed the Kleiman and gone back to their conversation. "I was hoping to find you home."

"Fortunate your message arrived when it did. I was planning a trip back to Atlan, but I've postponed it for a few days." His deep voice belied his short stature. But then, that was the way it was with Kleimen.

"I'm heading there myself, to see my son." He picked up his bag and they started down the ramp to the street, then crossed over to the wharf side of it and followed a paved river walkway.

"Wonderful! We can travel together!" The Kleiman beamed.

"You're not on your way back to Morg'Seth?" Kerche scrambled to keep up; one and a half steps to each of Lamech's strides.

He slowed his pace. "I'm ready to go home, Kerche, but I need to speak with my son ... in person."

Kerche nodded, understanding Lamech's meaning. Paper or magnetic messages could be intercepted. These days, meeting face-to-face was about the only way to ensure privacy. "Perilous times we live in."

"So true ... how's business?" he asked, to change subjects.

Kerche gave a short laugh. "Magnetics! Curiosities from a bygone age! Not much call for them, except from collectors, or restorers trying to renew a quaint lighting fixture, or keep an old building historically accurate. Even then, they usually energize them." He lifted his bushy eyebrows. "Energizing moonglass is what keeps me and my family in bread and keelits."

Lamech grinned. "Don't forget to eat your keelits."

Kerche chuckled.

Mistress Ela, an old Kleiman friend, used to admonish Lamech and Mishah about the health benefits of keelits. "The lesser cousin to the Tree of Life," Mistress Ela had called them up until the day she fell asleep in Adam's Bosom.

They bored deeper into Far Port's rotting core where old roads snaked between close-set buildings, built in the days before cyclarts were much in use. Here and there a few wooden storefronts stood as reminders of the town's rude beginnings. Most, however, had been replaced with stone, and some of the more recent ones were of baked bricks. The streets were still paved in cobbles, and squeezed darkly between the looming walls of the narrow shops beneath their living quarters, three and four stories tall.

Kerche's Magnetics and Novelties shop was a mere doorway with a narrow, bronze-barred display window half a span to the left, cluttered with moonglass panels and icicles. The whole street was lined with pigeonhole businesses like his.

Kerche unlocked three separate dead bolts and shoved the heavy door open. The wooden floor creaked out a long, low protest at Lamech's weight. He ducked his head beneath the moonglass dangling from the ceiling: blues, reds, golds, pale yellows, vibrant greens, and dull, muddy browns—the rarest type of moonglasses—on slender cords, each glowing a soft light.

It was like stepping into a kaleidoscope. There were long green spirals, tiny pink balls, and flat, thin olive discs that chimed in the breeze. Along every square span of wall space hung larger panels. Moonglass artwork perched on tables in fancifully carved ebony or saubor-wood stands. Among them were a few pieces crafted in the shapes of prancing unicorns, leaping dolphins, lumbering behemoths, and even swooping mansnatchers—these latter to attach to nursery ceilings, presumably to entertain, if not frighten, little children.

Lamech's senses momentarily went into color overload, and he focused on Kerche's back as they made their way toward a beaded-curtain doorway. "You must keep the family busy back home."

"They make more than I can sell ... as you can see."

Stepping through the curtain brought some relief to his eyes. They were in a short hallway, stacked with wooden crates everywhere except in front of another closed door. He noted the projer leaning in the corner near the beaded curtain.

"Look around you. It will be years before I move all this stuff. One reason why I need to return to Atlan." He shook his head and rolled his eyes, then stabbed a pudgy finger onto a button. In another part of the building, somewhere above his head, Lamech heard a muffled bell.

"Kerche?" a woman's voice asked from a metal grate set in the wall near the button.

"Who else, Slo? Master Lamech is with me."

A few moments later came the muted scraping of footsteps from beyond the door, then the clinking of safety bolts being unfastened.

"Lamech!" Slo's slim face bunched about her pink cheeks, her eyes beaming with delight as she flung her arms about his waist.

He hugged her back then looked at her. "Is it possible you are growing younger?" She was his age if not older. Even so, she was still an attractive, fine-boned, big-eared Kleiman.

Kerche grinned. "I made a wise choice marrying a mature woman."

"It's the keelits," she teased back. "Honor our house." She took his arm and tugged him through the doorway. Kerche followed behind, shutting the thick door and throwing all the bolts. Up in their living quarters, Slo towed him to the welcoming room's honor seat and saw that he was properly settled in.

"How's Mishah, and the family?" she asked.

"They are well. And your children?"

"They're just fine. They seldom come to the mainland, you know, so Kerche and I, we travel to Atlan a lot."

"Kerche said you were planning a trip."

She smiled and nodded. "I'm looking forward to a nice, relaxing visit to Deepvale again. This city gets to me sometimes. A woman can't walk the streets these days without finding trouble."

"Nor a man." Kerche shed his outer tunic, hung it on a hook, then slipped out of the holster that resided under his left arm and hung it up too. "At least we can offer Lamech a safe place to lay his head for a few days, before he continues on his journey." He huffed. "The inns can't be trusted anymore to put stout locks on their doors."

"And Noah?" Slo's eyebrows arched inquisitively. "How is he? I miss not seeing him as we used to."

A pang of loneliness ached within. "I miss him traveling with me. But I'll be seeing him in a few days."

"We can make the journey together." Kerche fell into a chair across from the honor seat.

"That would be nice," she said.

"Slo, have we any of that biddleberry ale left?"

"We do. And some goat cheese and keelit rinds." She went into another room.

Kerche took a pipe from the rack. "Noah is a good preacher. Almost as good as you, Lamech."

Lamech laughed. "Better."

"Is that pride I hear in your voice?" Kerche grinned as he settled into a chair, stretched out his short legs, and folded his arms comfortably about his well-fed belly.

"Maybe just a little." The fire of truth burned inside his son as hotly as it ever had inside of him, but their styles were very different. Noah could make inroads in places where his own forcefulness would only have thrown up roadblocks.

"I suppose a father's pride is forgivable." Kerche tapped out the pipe and filled it with fresh tobacco.

Lamech leaned forward. "Tell me, how are the Creator's Kinsmen faring here in Far Port? I hear disturbing news that the Deceiver is making life difficult for those of the true faith. Kinsmen are ending up in Nod City. Some simply disappear."

Kerche's forehead folded with a scowl. "The Oracle's darkness reaches across the Known World. Nephs are increasing like lop-hoppers, their nephlings becoming more and more common." He shook his head as he lit his pipe. "This diabolical scheme to improve man through alien inbreeding is devastating the Creator's finest fruits." He stabbed the stem of his pipe at Lamech, then at his own chest. "You and me."

"'The uplifting of man,' he calls it!"

Kerche made a sound as though he had bitten into a rotten keelit. He leaned back in his chair. "And people believe the rubbish!"

"People are easy to deceive when the truth of the Creator no longer lives in their hearts."

Kerche nodded somberly. "Someday even Atlan will fall. High Councilor Rhone can only hold out so long."

"I hope not." Atlan had been in the Deceiver's sights since Noah had found refuge there five hundred years earlier. It was solely because of the Creator's strong hand that Rhone's island nation had not only remained free of his evil influence, but also had prospered and advanced. Atlan's fleet was supreme, her weapons superior to those of the Lodath's Neph armies. Lamech frowned. How long that would last was anybody's guess. Hopefully, until the judgment. Afterward, it wouldn't matter.

"What is it, Lamech?"

He looked into his friend's concerned face. "I was thinking of Atlan."

"So far she is standing strong, unlike Far Port, and everyplace else."

"The Settled Lands are holding out," Lamech said.

Kerche puffed a cloud of blue smoke. "For now." His teeth clamped the stem of his pipe, and a long moment of silence passed as he pulled smoke into his lungs.

Lamech's mood darkened. How long before the Lodath would move on Morg'Seth and the other Settled Lands was a point of much heated debate. He thought of Mishah, concerned about her safety. But she was in the midst of their family. She was as secure with them as she could be if he were there.

Kerche stirred himself from his reverie. "I told a few of the

Kinsmen you were coming." His eyebrows dipped toward the hump on his nose. "Questions have come up recently that they want you to address. I can arrange a meeting, if that's all right with you?"

"Questions?" He put aside his concerns, suddenly interested. "Of course I'd be happy to meet with the Kinsmen. In fact, I was going to suggest it."

"I thought so." Kerche chuckled. "You never could pass up any opportunity to preach."

※

The next morning Lamech and Kerche left for the meeting with the brethren—the Creator's Kinsmen as they called themselves. It was a name that had caught on elsewhere, too.

Kerche had arranged the gathering after Lamech had retired for the night, the traveling taking a brutal toll on him, as it often did nowadays. There had been a time when he could skip from village to village, sleeping in stolen moments, eating on the run, propelled by nothing more than the truth of the Creator's story written in the stars. But his body was no longer up to the grueling schedule, his heart seemingly becoming more and more firmly anchored back in the Lee-lands of Morg'Seth with his wife and his children.

I'm just an old man whose passions have outlived his vitality.

The ancient streets were too narrow and too congested with people to allow for cyclart traffic. He enjoyed the brisk walk, having ridden so much these last few weeks, traveling the TT between villages and towns and cities. He welcomed this chance to stretch his legs and work his muscles, even though the walk from Far Port's aging inner city to the newer outskirts was quite long. He recalled when all this had been forests, but the exploding population had pushed the town's frontiers far from the river's edge where it had its genesis.

They walked with purpose. Kerche had warned him that to amble about a place like Far Port, as if uncertain, was to invite trouble. Lamech already knew this. Far Port was not much different from a thousand other places north of the Settled Lands of Hope.

Everywhere he looked showed signs of the Oracle's infestation; Nephs and generations of nephlings rubbed shoulders with humans as though they were no different. That most people were not outraged at the pollution in the human bloodline proved how pervasive the Deceiver's lies had become. Anger tightened his jaw.

"Try not to stare at them." Kerche glanced over worriedly as they hurried on.

He glanced away. Proclaiming the truth of the Creator's coming Strong Man to those with tainted blood did no good. They were part of a fallen race of Maliks; eternally lost. When the Strong Man returned to redeem fallen man, He would not—or was it that He could not?—do anything to save those who had even one drop of Malik blood in them.

"They wear the Oracle's pledge pendant, and they know that you and I don't."

Lamech nodded. "It puts them in touch with the Deceiver's realm." He understood only vaguely how it worked.

Kerche's eyes widened. "Makes me go cold inside."

A commotion ahead turned both their heads. They drew to a halt as a pair of nephlings burst from a doorway and tumbled out onto the sidewalk just ahead of them. Growling and scratching, kicking and clawing and swinging, they tore at each other like enraged hook-tooths. A crowd began to gather. Kerche cast a worried look up and down the street. Nephs and humans, and many of uncertain blood, attracted by the uproar, began to close in around them.

"We ought to get out of here," Kerche said.

The crowd cheered and booed, and Lamech heard the familiar barking of oddsmakers, seizing on the opportunity, gathering bets.

"Is there another way?"

Kerche backed away from the crowds and the combatants, toward a narrow street they had just passed. "Got to be careful. Something like this can spread and before you know it, the whole street breaks out in fighting."

They hadn't gone but a few steps down the gloomy lane when there came the crack of a fistproj, then another. They looked back at people fleeing from the street they had just abandoned. Kerche expelled a nervous breath and hurried on. Lamech kept one eye cocked over his shoulder as he tagged along at the little Kleiman's heels.

The buildings pressed closer, muting the light. Piles of rusty cans and old timbers leaned against walls; boxes crowded opened doorways where everything from crying to laughter spilled out in a confusing cacophony.

They emerged on a slightly wider street. This cluttered thoroughfare appeared at first glance to be one continuous row of festival halls, reminding him of a thousand other streets he'd seen in a hundred villages and towns. Everywhere he traveled, the scenes were nearly the same.

Here Nephs and humans prowled from one festival hall to the next, gathered in small groups, or sprawled in the gutters in a drunken stupor. Now and again one would look up and follow them with his or her glance. Kerche strode along at a determined pace, one trained into him over the years that didn't appear too rushed so as to avoid drawing attention to himself.

Finally the avenues began to widen, the milling crowds to thin, and cyclarts became more common. Lamech breathed a little easier. This section of Far Port reminded him of Nod City when he and Mishah had been newly married and on her pilgrimage to the Mother. How his anger had burned at a society spiraling into a morass of filth; forsaking the Creator. It had seemed the vilest of places in his naive youth. But that was five hundred years ago. The relaxing of moral constraints, known generally as the Oracle's Liberties, had since unshackled almost all remaining restraints. Add that to the growing numbers of Nephs and nephlings ... Lamech shook his head. How could the world become any worse?

He longed for the sanity of the Lee-lands of Morg'Seth.

4

The Creator's Kinsmen

*I*t will never work."

"What do you mean?" Noah sprang from the chair and paced the small, cluttered harborside studio jammed with wooden boat models and rolled-up scrolls crammed into hundreds of square holes. A tilted table longer than he was tall held a sheet of heavy paper with the carefully measured lines of a sleek cruiser taking shape upon it. "It has to work!"

Frustrated at hearing the same old story again, he drew to a halt in Jerl-eze's chokingly small design studio and peered a moment out an oval hole in the wall at a pair of gray kormens circling the bright blue waters of Kinsman Anchorage, collecting his thoughts. Calmer, he turned back to the placid face staring at him. Master Jerl-eze's bemused smile and wide blue-gray eyes shouldn't really have surprised him. He'd noted the look before—many times.

"All right, Master Jerl-eze, tell me why it won't work." Maybe he'd have a fresh reason? His exasperation wasn't unfounded, he reminded himself. Jerl-eze's patronizing look hadn't been the first. The project was impossible. No less than four learned Boat Masters had told him the same thing, and with nearly that same whimsical look on their faces.

The boatbuilder rocked back in his chair, pressed thinning lips together, and considered. Maybe Jerl-eze was waiting to see if he'd truly gotten a grip on his impatience. He folded his hands and placed them on his right leg, which was crossed over his left.

"The barge is simply too large, Master Noah."

But these were the dimensions the Gardener had given him! He felt like shouting! Instead, he drew in another breath and counted to five. "Too long? Too high? Or, too wide?"

"Long."

"Why does it matter how long the boat is? Can't it be built to any length?"

Jerl-eze leaned forward, hands cupping his kneecap. "The problem is not in building the structure. You can certainly build a barge three hundred spans long. Build it six hundred spans if you wish. The problem is that the first large wave you crest"—he broke an invisible stick and made a snapping sound, then casually placed his hands back in place—"it'll snap in two like a child's sugar stick."

Noah deflated. The same answer ... five different times now. It had to be true. Yet the Gardener had clearly told him the size of His ark. He might have suspected he had misheard Him, if it wasn't also written upon the scroll.

"All right. This is a problem, Master Jerl-eze, and it's why I came to you. You're The Master Boatbuilder. How do I overcome this issue? How do I make it work?" In the past, at this point in the discussions, he'd been politely but promptly rushed from the presence of previous builders. Master Jerl-eze, however, seemed prepared to explore the problem with him.

"May I ask you why you want to build this barge, Master Noah? Nothing this large has ever been attempted, as far as I know. What do you intend to haul in it? There isn't a sea on this wide green stone of ours that can't be crossed in a day or two."

"Livestock."

Jerl-eze smiled. "You can carry a lot of clucking osters in

something this large. It would be far more economical to build a barge half the size and make two trips. Have you considered that? We could easily go as large as two hundred spans. I even have drawings already made of such vessels somewhere in here." He laughed and flung open his arms in an exaggerated gesture. "You'd be able to transport half the wildlife of Atlan in it."

Noah smiled and lowered himself back into the chair that he had shot out of a few moments earlier. Half the wildlife was not what he'd been instructed to carry. "What other problems do you see in the project?"

Noting somberly that he wasn't going to consider altering the dimensions, Jerl-eze cleared his throat and leaned back into his chair—perhaps to put some distance between himself and this crazy man sitting before him.

The smile nudged a little further up one side of Noah's face. *Let him think what he wants.*

"You've provided for no means of propulsion—no cycler, no sails. You show no prow in your drawing. A box like you propose to build won't go anywhere. It will just squat down heavy in the water and stay there." His eyebrows lifted abruptly. "It will stay there very well indeed. Actually, your proportions are ideal for stability. We build barges to the very same proportions all the time, and they are as unsinkable as a log. Just smaller." He waved a hand at the rough sketch Noah had given him. "The largest ever built is a hundred spans short of this thing."

This was getting him nowhere. "In other words, you can't draw up the plans for me?"

"Not can't. Won't." Jerl-eze gave a long, patient sigh. "So, now you wonder why I won't? It's because my reputation would come into serious question. Look, even if you could build such a barge—if you could even afford it—where would you construct the thing? There isn't a dry-dock in all of Atlan to accommodate such a monster."

"I intend to build it on land."

Jerl-eze's eyes widened, sparkling with amusement. "In that case why am I worrying about its seaworthiness?" His laugh wasn't unfriendly.

"The water will come to it."

"You'll dig a canal?"

"No. Not exactly."

Jerl-eze nodded, a knowing smile touching his lips. "I've heard of you, and what you have been proclaiming. It's a judgment from the Creator, correct?" He rolled up Noah's drawing and handed it back to him. "Master Noah, I do wish you luck on building your barge, if that is what you truly believe will happen."

"But you won't design it for me?"

He pursed his lips and thought a moment. "I'll tell you what. If you figure out how to strengthen the keel to withstand the lateral forces, and relax the stresses upon the hull, I'll draw your building plans for you. And I'll charge you a fair price." His voice sobered. "Even though I am certain the scuppers of this barge will never be awash with even a single drop of seawater, I won't put my name to an unseaworthy design. Show me how to make it work."

There had to be a way. The Gardener would not have given him an impossible task! He took the drawings from Master Jerl-eze and stood. "Thank you for your candor. I'll be back with the answer to the problem."

Jerl-eze stood and took his hand. "I'll be curious to see the solution. Good day, Master Noah."

Lamech followed Kerche into an eatery where two long wooden tables ran down the middle, each seating six or seven folk bent over their food. The long room was hazed with cabweed smoke that stung his nose and eyes. No one paid them any attention.

Kerche skirted along the plastered wall to a passageway into a kitchen, then up an open flight of wooden stairs. On the third floor, they entered an interior hallway lit only by a row of pale blue, energized moonglasses mounted in frames upon the low ceiling.

Arched doorways with heavy timber doors pierced each side of the hall in regular intervals. Over the last three hundred-plus years, Lamech had been to hundreds of meetings with the dwindling number of Kinsmen in Far Port. He couldn't remember ever having met in the same place more than a few times, and this stark lair in the heart of Far Port was a new one to him.

Kerche ambled down the hallway in his rolling, boatman's gait and knocked on one of the doors, distinguishable from all the other doors only by the faded lime-green painted alcove.

"Who is it?" came a cautious voice from the other side.

"Good news. The Neph games went splendidly."

"What was the score?"

Kerche winked at Lamech. "Nephs zero, Sten-gordons six."

Lamech chuckled. There was a moment's delay, and then the sound of bolts opening. A man he knew well pulled open the door. He was a portly fellow with rosy cheeks and a thatch of straw-colored hair atop an egg-shaped skull. His blue eyes were bright but wary. When he saw Lamech, his face widened. "Master Lamech. Good to see you. And you, too, Kerche."

"Morning Peace, Master Fosh'ek."

"Honor my house." Fosh'ek stepped aside to admit them, then glanced cautiously up and down the hallway before shutting the door and throwing four iron bolts into their latches.

About twenty men and women bumped shoulders in the small space. Some sat on chairs, others on the floor or the edge of a bed. Many simply stood. The single window was open to let in the air while a young man in the corner heaved up and down upon a dingy red cord attached to a ponderous, grundy-feather fan mounted to the ceiling. The large iridescent feathers swishing slowly back and forth offered barely enough of a breeze to keep the air from stagnating.

Lamech shook hands with old friends and was introduced to new members of the Creator's Kinsmen. Although their numbers were shrinking, new Kinsmen came along every now and again. He struggled to connect these new faces with their names and lock them into his memory. In the background, Fosh'ek began to pass about cups of tea, cold water, or sweetened biddleberry juice. His wife, Margah, a short, heavy woman with dark hair and dusky skin that glistened in the heat of the crowded room, set out trays of stuffed mushrooms and roasted keelit rinds.

"We've been anxiously awaiting your arrival, Master Lamech," one man said.

"It's been a grisly wait," another added.

"We couldn't all arrive at once, Jeg'lg." The woman who spoke was named Leteah, her voice faintly scolding as she smiled at Lamech. The scented fan above her stirred the fragrance of bayolet blooms into the air.

"What, dear? You didn't want a parade through the kitchen?" Jeg'lg grinned, snatching a cup of water off Fosh'ek's tray.

"How long will you be staying?" Mistress Omamah asked.

"Only a few days." He worked his way toward the window.

"How is Noah? It's odd having the one of you without the other." Fosh'ek handed him a glass of chilled biddleberry juice.

Lamech nodded, at the moment too entangled in the bustle to dwell on how much he missed traveling and preaching with his son. His other children were content to work the 'gia farm, or take jobs in nearby New Eden. It was only Noah who had Lamech's same passion to reach lost souls with the Creator's message of redemption by way of the coming Strong Man prophesied in the stars....

But the Gardener had given Noah a new commission. Although he missed him dearly, he was honored that the Creator intended to work His will through his family.

Kerche brought the meeting to order. Folks settled down and the murmuring dropped to only a low, persistent undercurrent. Fosh'ek scraped a tall wooden stool across the floor and motioned Lamech to it, then squeezed himself beside his wife on a yellow wedge of couch exposed by the shuffling and compressing of three other people already occupying it.

Lamech perched himself on the stool, grinned at their attentive faces, and opened the meeting in a prayer.

"Looking around I see old friends, and hopefully new ones." He carefully caught the eyes of those newcomers who had introduced themselves to him. "As most of you know, I'm only in Far Port a day or two, so it's good to see you all again. I know there are many Kinsmen who could not be here on such short notice, and I do appreciate all of you who have come, even though we're sort of packed together like piddyquads in a green thumberbum."

They chuckled, their hand-fans busily stirring up a breeze he could feel from where he sat.

He introduced himself for those new to him, then opened the book he and Sor-dak had written together so many years ago concerning the Creator's message in the stars. He struck an easy rapport with his audience as he brought them through each star gathering in the story, from the Virgin clear through to the ruling Lion. Years of practice had schooled him in the skill of reading his listener's interest, and knowing intuitively when it was time to move on.

Most of them had heard the message many times, but for the newcomers, he spent time laying out the Creator's plan for mankind, and the Redeemer to come, the Strong Man shown in the Gathering of Taleh, and other star gatherings.

"The meaning of the names of the stars in each gathering actually tells the story the Creator has laid out for all to see. The stars are really only the markers. He has not left His people without a witness," he concluded, having lost track of the time, but not of the people's rapt attention.

A young woman asked, "You say you see these stories in the form of pictures in the stars, but when I look up in the sky at night, I don't see the pictures you describe, Master Lamech. Why?" She was one of the new believers. He noted how she squeezed the hand of a man next to her who glanced over with a reassuring smile.

"This is a common dilemma, Mistress Mar'al." He was relieved to have recalled her name. "There really isn't a picture as we think of it. Oh, sometimes you can imagine an image, like Oarion's sword belt, but then again you could form a double fist of pictures of your choosing, if you wish."

A low murmur told him some of them didn't want such an easy answer.

"Mainly, the Gatherings are named for parts of the story. Like I said earlier, Gatherings are composed of many stars, some more than a hundred, but what we are concerned about are the brightest few stars in each." If they wanted the deeper details, so be it.

"Let's take Oarion, for example—one of the Strong Man's many depictions. It is part of the Gathering of the Judge. The brightest star is in his right shoulder … err, that is, where we might imagine a right shoulder would be." He smiled. "The name of the star is Bet-el-euz, which means 'The coming Branch.' The next brightest star is Ri-go, 'The foot that crushes.' And the third is Bel-at-ix, 'Quickly coming.'"

Mistress Mar'al blinked, a vacant stare in her eyes. He smiled, used to that look from those unschooled in prophesies. They were confusing, which was why the Creator had carefully explained them to Father Adam, and to Seth, and to all of His chosen spokesmen since the beginning. It was Grandfather Enoch who gave the message to him before being snatched away by the Creator, never to taste the bitter sting of death.

"But what does it mean?" she pressed.

"Well, there are several other stars that add color to the story, but briefly, it means that the Strong Man, who is the Creator, will come again, and when He does, it will happen swiftly, and He will crush His enemy under His foot, that old serpent from the Garden."

She sat back, contemplating what he had said.

Another man spoke up. "I've heard that the Gathering of Thaumin really represents twin gods who will come from the stars."

Lamech nodded. "I've heard that too, but it's incorrect. Instead of twin gods, it represents the two natures of the coming Redeemer—part God and part man." It hadn't taken long for the Deceiver to begin perverting the message. He drew in a long breath to control the zeal burning in his chest. "What you have is a deliberate perversion of truth. That false interpretation has come out of Nod City, so you know who has spoken it. The Lodath! And we all know who the Lodath speaks for."

An agreeable murmur rippled through the crowd this time as heads nodded.

"You must be wary, my friends. The Oracle is a master of deception. Which is why I call him the Deceiver, but we Kinsmen know the rebel by his real name—Lucifer. The very serpent who led Mother Eve and Father Adam into sin, and has brought condemnation down upon all of us. The Deceiver is the last one who would want the truth of the coming Redeemer proclaimed." Their eyes told him they were listening. "Be prepared to face much opposition from him. Already he twists the pure meaning of what I bring to you."

Kerche raised a hand. "Master Lamech. Some people have been telling us that if the stars are read correctly, they can tell us about the future."

"The future?" This was new. "If by the future you mean the future plans of our Creator, then yes." Had he understood

Kerche's question? He thought he had made the prophesies clear, but the Kleiman's puzzled look said something else.

"That, of course." Kerche leaned forward. "But there is more. It is being said that each one of us is born under a Gathering's sign, and thereafter are marked by that sign's dominion. And by observing our own Gathering, and how all the other Gatherings influence it, we can know our own future."

"It is said? Who says this?"

Several people had leaned their heads together, quietly murmuring among themselves. One of them spoke up. "The notion is becoming quite popular in Nod City, Master Lamech. Seers have arisen to help people look at their futures. They even use the book you and Master Sor-dak wrote to construct the star charts that tell the future."

The muscles in his neck tightened. Nod City! Why should he be surprised? "I fear the Deceiver is at his old ways again, my friends." He kept the anger from his voice. "It has always been his way to take truth and twist it just enough to confuse and mislead the unwary."

"This is what is being taught." Mistress Omamah came forward and handed him a small, old-fashioned scroll. In spite of its intentional quaintness, obviously contrived to give it the appearance of an ancient work, the scroll was printed on modern paper.

He unrolled it enough to read the title: *The Twelve Houses of the Creator and Your Future.* "Might I keep this awhile and study it?"

"You may have it, Master Lamech. They're all over Far Port."

"Are they?" *And it is only now coming to my attention?* He rolled it up and rapped it upon his open palm, arranging his thoughts. "I will study what is written in this document. If it contains what you claim, I can tell you now it's a lie, fashioned by the Father of Lies."

"Why would he bother?" Fosh'ek asked.

"To pervert the truth of the Creator's message of redemption. I already told you the Creator has promised He will never leave us without a witness, and the witness for our day is written in the stars where every eye can see it. The Deceiver knows this and will do everything in his power to prevent the truth from being understood."

"That's certain," Margah huffed. "He's already banning your book."

Omamah said, "It's forbidden reading in Nod City, except by the seers. And even here in Far Port, we must be careful."

"And that's why we're meeting in this stuffy room," Jeg'lg groused, shaking his head. "It's no longer safe to be known as one of the Creator's Kinsmen."

"My friends, we live in danger every day. Our faith is being challenged in many ways. We are forced to endure lies all around us. The Oracle's lie—that people can grow and change into something more than the Creator has made them—has turned their hearts away from Him. They believe they can become as gods, and that man has changed over time and will continue to change. A second lie equally as perverse is that the Nephs are the very flowers of this new and improved race of man."

His voice hardened. "The Deceiver pollutes our bloodlines, and if permitted to continue, there will not be a single full-blooded human left. Lucifer can read the story in the stars as well as we, perhaps even better. He understands that the Creator's plan requires a human—a virgin—through whom will be born the Strong Man to redeem us." Anger crackled in his words in spite of his effort to control it.

He took in a breath. "And now we have these new freedoms called 'Oracle Liberties.'" He shook his head. "They've turned a once peaceful people into roving bands of renegades. Do not be amazed at all you are seeing. We have allowed the Deceiver into our lives, and now we must reap the consequences."

"But how do we fight this foe, Master Lamech?"

"We can't, Master So-wah. We must never forget that this is not our fight, but the Creator's." A stab of guilt made him grimace. How often had he himself forgotten that? "One day the Master of All Creation will disarm His enemy. Until then, only by remaining true to Him, and by believing that He will send his Strong Man to redeem us, can we hope to find peace—if not in this life, then in the life hereafter."

5

On the Way to Atlan

*I*n a room converted from a storage area to a place to carry out the task of following the Gardener's will, Noah sat rigid on the high stool, staring at the drawing spread out upon the board before him—his best efforts, hardly the quality of a skilled draftsman. The Gardener had called it an ark. Jerl-eze had called it a barge. At the moment, he called it one gigantic headache. A heavy despair forced his head down. With elbows propped on the slanted drawing table, he buried his eyes in his palms in an effort to ease the dull, throbbing ache behind them.

I'm to build it, yet it is impossible to build! Creator, what am I to do? You say three hundred spans long. Jerl-eze says it will snap in two like a brittle twig. You say take every kind of animal on your green earth, yet my friends scoff that you've placed me here on an island! You say it will pour down water from the heavens, they say no one has ever seen such a thing. You say judgment, they say I'm crazy. You say faith. They ask for proof. Oy, what a headache I have. What am I to do?

"Father!"

Wend's angry bark startled his head up. He winced at the stab of pain. His eldest son stood in the doorway, eyes narrowed, mouth cramped in a frown, fingers curled into fists at his side. He stalked into the room.

"What is it, Wend?"

"Japheth says you just pulled twelve men from the vineyard to work on your absurd boat! The vineyards are going back to the Wild Lands! I just rode out to inspect them, and the weeds are taking over the rows and trees are sprouting in them. The ditches are in need work, and the strands have broken in more places than I can count."

"I know, I know." He didn't want to deal with Wend's anger right now. His head did not need it. "They require tending. I know."

"How can they be properly tended when you've taken most of the workers away from me?"

"You know why I had to do that, Wend."

Wend anchored his fists on his hips, his bright green eyes glaring. "So that you can funnel more of our money into that thing!" His hand flung toward the drawings. "Meanwhile, the vineyards deteriorate, the harvest has become poor, our vintner complains that he can no longer produce the quality wine our land is prized for."

"All that you say is true—"

"Yet you spend every waking moment on that project."

"It's important, Wend."

"More so than our future? Where will we be in another fifty years if we let them go now?"

"Will it matter?"

Wend rolled his eyes. "Father. Do you know what people are saying behind your back?"

The increasing stress of their conversation gripped at his chest and the throbbing ache became like needles boring into his skull. "And I ask again, does it matter?"

"It does to me, Father. It may not to you, or Japheth, Shem, or Ham, but it matters to me. I am the eldest! Someone has to care."

Noah kneaded a palm into his temple. "So it is back to that again." He stood up from the stool and leaned against the desk, staring out the window at the silvery keelit trees and green and scarlet shrubbery. His eye momentarily followed a flock of parrots filling the azure canvas of heaven. "Wend, you know what the future holds for us. How can something like this be so important to you?"

"Everything has continued as it has from the beginning, Father. Nothing is going to change."

He looked back at his son, the fist inside his chest tightening. "That is the philosophy of this world talking. You can choose to listen to the Oracle, or to the Creator."

"Listen to the Creator?" A sneer thickened his voice. "It seems you're the only one who hears His voice, who sees Him."

"Your grandmother saw Him, and your grandfather," he reminded Wend patiently. "And so have many others."

Wend shook his head and a lock of thick black hair fell across his eyes. He swept it aside. "Those are stories you tell children; but I'm not a child anymore. My Coming-of-Age Rite was years ago, or have you forgotten?"

"No, I haven't forgotten." He massaged his forehead. "So what do you want of me?"

"For one thing, I want my workers back. And then you can tell my brothers they are needed here. There is work to be done."

"Your brothers have taken this commission seriously. I only wish you had too."

"They aren't the firstborn."

"The firstborn? Is that all you care about?"

"Everything I do, I do for you and mother, and my brothers and sisters, and the children we will someday have."

"Maybe that's the problem. Everything you do should be for the Creator."

"I'm working for our future, Father."

"As I am, Wend." His voice softened. "We see the future differently for now, but one day you will understand all I am doing here."

"Or maybe one day you will understand. I'll hire my own people." Wend turned and strode out the door.

"We'll bring the vines with us, Wend. We can grow a new vineyard," he called after him, and stared at the empty doorway. How could he get through to him? Had the world sunk its hooks so deeply into Wend? If so, it was up to him to yank them out. He halted that line of thinking. No, not up to him, but up to the Creator.

Turning back to the drawings, he buried his face in his hands again. "Creator, please let Wend understand."

"What was that all about?" Naamah's quiet voice asked a few moments later. Her hand touched his shoulder. When he lifted his face, her wide, worried eyes hovered close to his.

"He thinks I'm letting the vineyard go to ruin."

"The vineyard is not important anymore, is it?"

"It is to Wend. I suppose I should go talk to him."

"He's not here. He stormed out of the house without even a fair journey, mounted his gerup, and rode off."

"Naamah, what am I to do? He doesn't grasp the importance of what we are doing."

"He will, Noah. When the time comes, he will be on the ark with the rest of us."

"But the other—"

"The boys are all different. You know that. Japheth is shrewd, Shem is thoughtful, Ham is clever. And Wend ... well, Wend is just practical."

"What's that supposed to mean?" Noah's brow furrowed.

"It means he see things differently than you."

"He's ensnared by this world."

"No more than anyone else." A smile softened her face. "You always have demanded more from Wend than the others."

"He is the eldest son—as he's quick to remind me."

"And he is doing what the eldest son does. Taking care of business—the vineyard." Her smile would not relent.

"Wend's only taking care of his inheritance!" He frowned. "And maybe I ought to also." He gave her hand a squeeze and kissed her cheek.

"Where are you going?" she asked when he started for the door.

"To check on the fields. He's right. I have neglected them for that." He inclined his head at the drawing and the rat's nest of papers piled around the desk's edges. "I'll return some of the workers to help keep the weeds from devouring the rows."

Naamah nodded. "Yes, perhaps you should. Until the day comes when—" she hesitated. Even after so many years, he knew she had trouble accepting what was to come upon them and the world. "We still have to eat and live, and that project drains every extra gleck we have."

He looked back at the board. "Perhaps I should speak with High Councilor Rhone again." He left, relieved to have an excuse momentarily to put aside the problems of breaking barges and trying to save island-isolated animals.

"Where are you going?" Mitah came down the hallway as he headed for the front door.

"To find your brother."

"Can I come with you?"

"Not now. Stay here with your mother." He strode to the cyclart out front. *I still have time to reach the boy.* Of the Creator's 120 years' warning, only fifteen remained, but he still had time.

He shook his head as he drove off, catching a glimpse of his eldest daughter watching him from the doorway.

What was it she had asked?

❧

Lamech, Kerche, and Slo came into Nod City aboard the TT. Its single gleaming rail ran parallel to the Oracle's Worship Center with the magnificent Temple looming in its very center. The complex had sprawled over the years, devouring the once mighty forest to the north and much of what was now called Old Nod City. The prison where Lamech had spent so many years was now well within the Worship Center's towering walls.

The rail soared sharply up over the approaching buildings. He had a spectacular view of the enormous face staring heaven-ward—the Oracle's Image. It brought back memories of the time he, Noah, and Thore had crashed their wing-sailer into it.

At night the sculpture was illuminated. On those nights when a full moon stood just so, the Oracle's face appeared to reflect upon its surface. He reckoned that was the very effect the Oracle had wanted, and why he'd constructed a mirror image of the Worship Center on the moon.

As the Temple receded behind him, he turned his thoughts to grimmer matters. Rumors had it that recently the sacrifices within its magnificent walls had taken on a much darker form. Human sacrifices. Kinsmen sacrifices. He recalled the size of the altar and easily imagined hundreds of people losing their lives to the Oracle. His jaw locked down tight. And he'd had a part in building the thing!

Nod Station smelled of too many bodies—Neph bodies.

"They know we're different," Kerche said as they hurried briskly through the crowd to make their connection.

Lamech shifted his traveling bag into his other hand and glanced at a Neph festival hall where two of the giant men stood just inside the doorway, embracing. "Can opposing spirits exist side by side and not know of one another's presence? Nephs are in touch with the Oracle's realm, perhaps even more closely than we Kinsmen are to the Creator's."

"This world is the Oracle's realm." Slo's voice held disgust as she scrambled to keep in step. Kerche was double-stepping too. Lamech slowed his pace.

Back five hundred years ago he had sensed the evil in Nod City. That was what had gotten him cast into prison ... that and his big mouth. He'd been impetuous and on fire for the Creator back then. He made a wry smile. He was still on fire, only now a lot older and perhaps just a little wiser. His smile faltered. And perhaps now he understood the futility of preaching the Creator's message of redemption to a sin-infested world. Wrath would come to these people, he was certain. He doubted even his grandfather, the mighty Enoch himself, could have turned this Neph tide with his words of judgment.

The scroll in his traveling bag was a good example. He hadn't had time to read it yet, but had scanned enough to know that the Oracle, in his clever way, must have decided that since he couldn't stop the spread of the message in the stars, he would pervert it—just enough—to deceive man.

How effortlessly man permitted himself to be led astray. Look how readily Mother Eve had fallen to his lies.

They made their connection, and at the third of the fourth quartering the TT departed Nod City. From his pendant-carriage he watched rooftops rush past. Once out of the city the TT dipped down, skimming a mere ten spans above a busy roadway where cyclarts hurried to and from the city—workers and shoppers making the quick journey from outlying villages.

Eventually the TT veered away from the road and slipped back into the forest where large enclaves of the original wilderness still stood. But they could hardly be called the Wild Lands anymore. Once gatherers and wildlanders like Rhone had wandered this country in search of spider silk and spices. His spirit took on weight.

As night came, Kerche and Slo nestled down upon each other's shoulders in the seat across from him. He ached to hold Mishah in his arms. Soon he would be back home with her, but first he had to see their son and his family. She'd be anxious for news about the grandchildren.

He napped on and off as they rushed on through the night, pausing briefly at small switching stations along the way to take on or let off passengers, or to switch out spent magnetic packs for freshly charged ones. Dawn arrived about the same time the TT's magnetic drive whined down and the line of pendant-carriages glided to a stop at Wen's Slip Station.

The sky brightened to a crimson glow that hung too low over the city.

"Look at that lovely sunrise!" Kerche drew in a deep breath and with exaggerated theatrics gagged and coughed it out.

Lamech laughed.

Slo rolled her eyes.

The bite of sulfur and 'gia fumes stung his nose. Beneath the heavy, gray ceiling, he caught a glint of dark water in the distance, mostly obscured by the thick clouds rising from a triple fist of soaring chimneys.

They gathered their bags and trudged down the TT station's steps onto a busy street where cyclarts muscled for right of way and people on foot dodged their bullying. Kerche flagged down a hire-cyclart to take them to the ferry landing.

The ferry pushed off at four of the third quartering, leaving an oil-slick wake of floating trash and sewage in the brownish-yellow water as it headed out of port. A few leagues out of Wen's Slip Harbor the air began to clear. Finally sunlight broke the haze and streamed through the clear blue depths where the blue-green leaves of seavine shimmered beneath the ferry's lumbering hull, and steel gray dolphins and silvery orange talgons raced and leaped. Leviathan still haunted its depths, but few saw him nowadays. Well-armed ore barges had reduced the number of his attacks, and he now only preyed on the lone boat that might wander too far from shore.

Lamech took a deep breath, clearing Wen's Slip from his lungs. Kerche and Slo stood at the railing, watching talgons breaking the surface and doing double and triple rolls before slicing gracefully beneath the waves.

The balmy temperature and the freshening breeze eased the strain in his neck. The journey, especially through Nod City, had twisted knots into his muscles. He rolled his shoulders. He was getting too old for all this traveling. Too old to be separated from Mishah for months on end. Too old to fight the swelling tide of evil rising in the world. In his heart, he was ready for it all to end.

Toward dusk two jagged spires of stone came into sight.

Kerche pointed. "The Pillars of Herc."

Lamech set aside the scroll and frowned. Tomorrow they would sail through that gap, into the Great Sea.

"What's the matter, Lamech?" Slo asked.

"I remember when they were called something different." It seemed everywhere a man traveled he came upon some reminder of Nod City, the Lodath, or the Oracle.

Kerche nodded. "The Pillars of the Sun. That's what they had once been called. But when the Lodath's armies conquered this part of the Known World, they renamed many landmarks. The Pillars of Herc is what most folk call them now."

Lamech found his place in the scroll, but it was getting too dark to read.

"What do you think of that?" Kerche jutted his small chin at the scroll.

"Rubbish, half-truths, and downright lies."

"The people find it compelling."

"Unfortunately." He retrieved his red-ribbon bookmark from the varnished gopher-wood deck, set it in place, and rolled up *The Twelve Houses of the Creator and Your Future*, setting it on the desk.

6

A Toy Boat

*L*amech spent a restless night on a narrow cot in Marin-ee, and the next morning he, Kerche, and Slo boarded a fast passenger boat for Atlan. In an hour they had passed though the Pillars of the Sun—he refused to think of them by that other name—poised on opposite horizons, their jagged dark spires piercing the sky.

Standing near the bow, the wind ruffled his hair and cooled his skin. The sun in a clear sky warmed his face, and their swift speed left any lingering 'gia odor in its wake so that the sea air remained unspoiled by the cycler's exhaust. In a little while they passed over the shallow Atlan Ridge, in places the boat's keel skimming a mere hand's breadth above the white gravel bottom. Lamech leaned way forward to watch the schools of glimmer fish skitter out of the way like a million fragmented pieces of moon-glass of all different colors.

Atlan's Rim-wall grew slowly from a distant smudge on the horizon into a formidable ebony barrier. When the soaring black cliffs finally loomed tall and imposing before the boat, Kerche moved up alongside him. "This is my favorite moment." His view fixed upon a jut of land.

Lamech's eyes held that point as they rounded it and the statues came into view.

Hand in hand, arms arching over Hodin's Passage, Atla beckoned a welcome to them while Hodin, his mighty sword thrust point down into the bedrock at his foot in the traditional Makir watch position, stood guard over the main entrance into the island's interior. Even in this day of wonder and advancements, the statues never ceased to thrill him. Over a thousand years old, carved from a vein of pure white stone in the Rim-wall, they still showed the wondrous skill of their Atlanian artisans.

Once inside Hodin's Passage, walls of black rock, streaked in red and white, soared upward on either side of the boat. Here the once-endless sky was but a narrow azure slit through the Rim-wall. Soon the Rim-wall fell behind them and fertile farmland and orchards blossomed along the wide canal bustling with traffic. Atlan's famed landmark harbor came into view a little while later, and shortly the boat eased into its berth in the first of three concentric anchorages.

Lamech caught a ride with Kerche's waiting family, who were only too happy to drop him off at Noah's vineyard before heading to Kerche's ancestral home in Deepvale.

He would soon be seeing Noah and Naamah, and that eased his pining for Mishah—at least a little—as he sat, elbows tucked into his stomach, traveling bag crushed beneath his legs. The vehicle had been built with Kleimen dimensions in mind, and "big folk," as the Kleimen called people like him, just had to make do with stooped shoulders and bent necks.

Beyond Atla Fair, country roads quickly replaced crowded city streets, and the cyclart sped up. Slo, crushed beside him on the seat, said, "Excited?"

He nodded.

Her cheeks dimpled.

Kerche, riding on the upper level with his father-in-law behind the steering sticks, peered down through the long rectangular opening in the wicker roof. "Won't be long."

Lamech drew in a shallow breath, thankful Noah lived only a little way out of town.

They let him off on the road at the wide gate with the arched entryway and waved fair journey as the cyclart chugged away. The big overhead placard read simply: VINEYARD.

Lamech turned his steps up the driveway. The hardy purple and yellow verbiscus, soft underfoot, was rutted where cyclarts and harvesters had passed. Rows of grapes stretched out on either side of it, the pathways between them showing signs of some neglect. Weeds had begun reaching out for the vines, and here and there a wire was down, or a section of vines that had not been pruned crawled down into the furrows.

"Grandpa!"

He wheeled about and grinned. Mounted on a miniature gerup, Sheflah, Noah's youngest daughter, came racing up from the main road. She reined the red and yellow beast to a halt and leaped off. He grabbed for the reins with one hand while giving her a big hug with the other. She was dark-complexioned, like her brother Ham, with wide brown eyes and a gorgeous smile.

"I didn't know you were coming to visit." She untwined her arms from around his neck. "Where's Grandma?"

"Grandma Mishah stayed home this time. How's my little button?"

"I'm not a little button anymore." She turned in a circle so that her full skirt whirled wide and folded about her legs when she came to an abrupt halt. She had filled out and was nearly as tall as Mishah.

"I'd say not. When did you grow up?"

"I don't know. It just happened." Sheflah giggled and took his hand. The three of them started for the house, the gerup balking to nibble at a sarberry bramble growing up alongside the drive. "Do Mother and Father know you are coming?"

"Your father asked me to come when I had a chance. But I'm sure they aren't expecting me today. You know how uncertain my comings and goings are."

Sheflah grinned and teeter-tottered her hand in the air. "Far Port today, Havil tomorrow. Wand-ee last week, the Faroe's land beyond the Straits of Tamor next."

He laughed. "Your grandmother's been complaining again in her letters, I see."

Sheflah laughed with him. "It's just a saying."

"Hmm? Is it now?"

"It's been two years since you were here last."

Around a bend in the drive, the house came into view. "Has it been that long?"

She nodded. "Last time Grandma Mishah was here, I'd just turned twelve."

Naamah stepped from the door and shaded her eyes toward them. A smile widened out as he drew close and she met him in the drive. "Father. It's wonderful to see you again." She pressed her cheek to his. "You must be exhausted. Did you walk all the way from Atla Fair?"

"Hitched a ride with Kerche's father-in-law."

"Kerche and Slo are in Atlan?"

"We traveled together from Far Port."

"I should like visiting with them." She took his arm and led him into the house.

"Perhaps you'll have a chance."

The house was clean but cluttered. Books sat in precarious stacks on tables and chairs, and a profusion of potted plants filled every window. Naamah's sewing basket overflowed with material....

"Noah! Noah, come and see what Sheflah dragged home."

He heard movement in another room. "Tell Sheflah we don't need the animals yet." His son wandered out holding some papers. "Father!" Noah gave him a hearty embrace. "Why didn't you send word? I'd have come and picked you up from Atla Fair."

"Keli gave him a ride," Naamah said.

Kids began wandering in at the commotion. In a few minutes most of the family had gathered around. Shem pummeled him with questions about his travels, while the two middle girls, Leteah and Orah, asked about their cousins back in Morg'Seth, and of Grandma Cerah and Mishah, and Grandpa Kenoch.

Japheth and Wend were out in the vineyard, and Ham in the barn, tinkering with a model lifting crane they would need for the project. Good thing, or the attention would have overwhelmed him.

Mitah, Noah's oldest daughter, draped her arms around him from behind and kissed his cheek. "Where have you come from this time, Grandfather?"

"All over." He slid an amused glance at Sheflah. "Far Port today. Havil tomorrow. Wand-ee last week, the Faroe's land beyond the Straits next."

They all laughed.

"Did you come though Nod City?" Mitah asked, slipping around in front of him, her blue eyes big and eager for news of the world beyond Atlan.

"Unfortunately, yes."

"What's it like?"

He sighed. "You would get weary of it after one day."

Orah sat on the floor and spread her dress over her knees. "I want to travel across the Known World like you do, Grandpa."

"The Known World ... and beyond." He smiled and wanted to tell her how lonely it could be.

Mitah cut him off before he could elaborate. "It's so boring here. Mother and Father won't let us go anywhere."

"That's not true," Naamah said.

Mitah rolled her eyes. "The world beyond Atlan is evil."

Noah scowled at her mocking tone.

Lamech gave his son a patient smile. He'd heard the same complaints many times from his own children—even Noah when he'd been young. It was natural to want to push beyond the limits.

Mitah's eyelids narrowed slightly. "If it's all going to go away, like father says, I want to see some of it."

"I don't want it to go away," Sheflah said.

"Me neither!" Leteah's red lips pushed into a pout, her hands belligerently upon her hips.

Shem shrugged. "It will be exciting. Think of the adventure!"

"Boys!" Orah huffed.

"But it will be exciting," Lamech said. "Imagine the opportunity to begin the world afresh. All this evil we see spreading across the land will be swept away. But all of you, and your husbands and wives, will have a chance to do it all over again, and this time get it right."

"Will you be with us, Grandpa?" Sheflah asked.

"I don't know, button. I will if I can."

Mitah stood back and exhaled loudly. "Grandpa, you don't really believe the Creator will ruin the world? What of all the people who will die?" She cast an angry look at her father, then back. "And what if it never happens? Wend thinks it won't. Everyone calls us a family of dreamers." Her eyes glistened. "Who will ever want the daughter of a dreamer for a wife?" She turned abruptly and left the room.

❦

Dinner had been strained, the conversation stilted. The children all wanted to hear about their grandfather's travels, but they seemed leery of broaching the subject within earshot of Noah and Naamah.

Later that evening, when Noah and Lamech were away from the family in the room he'd converted for the purpose of working on the ark, Noah shook his head. "Children."

Lamech stood by the dark window, watching the flickering antics of the dancing lights in the northern sky. A faint breeze pushed the heat of the day from the room, filling it with the sweet odor of rush buttons, and the strong perfume of the sky lilies Naamah had planted in the garden.

Noah studied his father's back, how it stooped with age, how his hair, silver in the lamp's glow, had thinned. "Sometimes it tears my heart out the way my children so easily believe what others tell them, yet they take so lightly what I, their father who has nothing but their best interest at heart, have to say. To them I'm the villain, the dreamer, the one who hears voices and foretells doom." He shook his head. "The family embarrassment."

"They don't think that." Lamech turned from the window. "It's just their ages. Mitah is only thirty-two." He smiled. "Still twenty years from her Coming of Age. She has much growing up to do—they all do."

"Maybe. But Wend is old enough. He should know better." He leaned an elbow on the large table strewn with sheets of papers filled with drawings, figures … sweat and tears.

Lamech stepped away from the window. "So it's Wend who stirs discontent among the others?"

"Not all of them. Japheth is his own man. He's enthusiastic about the commission. He enjoys the business of making it all come together. Shem, he's so intent on knowing the Creator's words, he thinks of little else. He understands how all this had been foretold all the way from Father Adam. And Ham—" Noah smiled. "The boy's a mechanical and mathematical genius!" He winked. "He must have gotten that from you. This endeavor is just the tonic Ham's creative mind needs." He waved his hand at the sheath of papers piled about. "Most of

these are his plans—hoists, derricks, overhead trolleys for moving the animals' food. A thousand ideas, and the freedom to
explore each one of them, thanks to Rhone's generosity.

"But Wend …" A stab of concern clenched his gut. "Wend
has tied his future to the vineyard, and resents me for what I do—
or don't do. Mitah is only interested in experiencing the world
around her. Leteah and Orah, too."

"And you think that's unusual?"

"They think I'm cruel for trying to protect them." He looked
into his father's eyes and his voice thickened. "It hurts. Right
here." He tapped his chest.

"I've raised sixteen children, Noah. I know. In having them,
you agree to live with your heart outside your body for the rest of
your life."

Noah signed and wiped his eyes. It was healing to talk about
this, but his family's problems were not why he'd urged his father
to visit soon. "Enough of this." Turning back to the table, he
paged through several sheets of sketches, finding the one he
wanted. "I've run into a problem. Even Ham is stymied."

"You think I can help?"

"You spent so much time with Sor-dak, I was hoping some of
his brilliance had rubbed off on you." He grinned.

Lamech laughed and leaned over for a look, slowly scanning
the long sheet. His finger tapped the tiny figure of a behemoth,
drawn against the ark for scale.

"Hard to imagine something so large." He studied the line
drawings. "It reminds me of something," he mused, leaning a bit
closer. "And your problem?" He made it sound like building the
ark was on the same level as constructing a rowboat.

"My problem is it won't work."

"It has to work, Noah. Isn't this exactly what the Gardener
told you to build? Didn't He give you the measurements and
specify the materials?"

"He did all that. But it still won't work. I've contacted the top boat designers in Atlan. Each one said the same thing. 'It will snap like a sugar stick the first big wave it rides over.'"

"Then go to more designers. There must be several in Marin-ee."

"Father, this is Atlan. The sea has been her life for more than a thousand years. If I can't find the expertise here, how can I hope to find it on the mainland?"

Lamech frowned and glanced back at the sketch. "Have you taken it to the Creator?"

"Daily."

"And?"

"And the only thing that enters my thoughts is to ask you."

"I know nothing about boats. Ask me to design a geared platen to rotate a temple, and I could do it."

"This isn't the Oracle's Temple, and it isn't supposed to rotate." He filled his lungs, then slowly released the air. "I don't know what to do. I'm sorry you came all this way for nothing."

"For nothing! I get to see you and Naamah, and the grand-children, and you say that's for nothing? That's worth a trip clear to the pole station in the congregation of the north."

Noah didn't feel much like smiling, but couldn't help himself. "At least you can spend a few days with us before going back to Morg'Seth. We can visit the family altar, and I can show you the site where we will begin building, once it's cleared and leveled. In fact, Oormik, the timber merchant, is coming tomorrow to look over the land."

"I'd like that, Noah."

He stood. "I'll worry about all this later. Surely the Gardener wouldn't have given me a task impossible to complete. I know Naamah is anxious to hear more about Uncle Kenoch and Aunt Cerah. She gets to see her parents even less than I get to see mine." He started for the door, and stopped. Lamech hadn't moved.

"What is it?"

"I just remembered what struck me when looking at your sketches."

Noah cocked his head. "What?"

"The toy boat. The Gardener gave it to you on your birthday, while you were still in the Garden. You were only six or seven, but you had it with you when we left. You used to play with it when we moved here to Atlan."

He searched his memory, and images of that day came back to him now. He'd been splashing in the lake near the cottage where he had lived with his mother and great-grandmother. The Gardener had arrived unexpectedly, as He almost always did, as if appearing out of nowhere. He'd had the boat with Him— Noah's birthday gift. He remembered how the Gardener had walked into the lake, and how the water had parted before Him exposing a pathway of dry white sand.

"I recall now." He stared at the drawings on the table. The ark was identical to the toy boat the Gardener had given him. "He knew even back then. He gave me a perfect model of the ark. How could I be so blind?"

"You were a child. And children are easily blinded to the truth, Noah."

That stung, realizing what his father meant.

"Where is it?"

"I'm not sure. I haven't seen it in such a long time."

"But you still have it, don't you?"

He tugged thoughtfully at his beard. "I'm sure I must. I wouldn't get rid of it—I'd never do that. It was a gift from the Gardener, after all."

Lamech's eyes widened, and his excitement seemed to erase years from his creased face. "We must find it!"

❧

After rummaging through all the usual places in the house, Noah grabbed a light and dived out into the night to the dark shed behind the house. Naamah followed him and held the lamp for him as he worked the latch and pulled the heavy door open.

"You'll never find it in all this." She lifted the lamp high, directing its beam into the packed building.

"I put some old boxes in here. One of them might hold it."

She rose on her toes and stretched her neck to look over the clutter. "We should have cleaned this place out years ago. It's a fire waiting to happen."

He took the lamp from her, set it on a high barrel, and began clearing a pathway to the back wall, dragging aside crates and boxes, old rotting oars he'd fashioned years ago, kegs of nails, jars of screws, tubs of dried pitch, and rolls of sailcloth—left over from an attempt to build his own boat a long time ago. He grinned at the recollection. It had been a tiny thing for cruising the canals of Atlan, but he had failed miserably at it. Now look at what he was going to build!

Slowly he carved a gully through three hundred years of clutter, pausing now and again upon discovering an old box of pulleys he thought he'd lost, or an ancient proj-lance that might be worth a few hundred glecks to a collector.

"You're sure it's in here?" Naamah relayed a box of ancient letters to a growing pile outside, pausing long enough to peer inside. "I remember these."

He looked over his shoulder. The lamplight drew her features in sharp contrast as she riffled through the mementos. "What are they?"

"Letters from my mother and father."

"Oh. Here." He passed her another paperboard box that nearly disintegrated at his touch. "Just set it somewhere."

"Can't this wait until daylight?"

"She's right," Lamech said.

Noah hadn't heard his father come up and turned to see his tall silhouette in the doorway. "I'm almost there." He had reached an old shelf built along the far wall, and began opening dingy wooden boxes. "Move the light closer, Naamah."

She crowded behind him, directing the soft glow of the energized moonglass at the shelf, coughing at the dust he was raising.

"I know it's in here somewhere. I remember now putting it with some other things in a box and tucking them away in here. I'm sure of it."

He dragged over a musty wooden box and unlatched its lid, lifting it open. "Aha."

They backed out of the furrow he'd carved through the clutter. In the moonlight outside the shed, he sat on the ground and set the box upon his knees. "Sit down. I'll show you."

Naamah and Lamech settled at his side and peered into the pale moonlit box. He carefully removed a little black book; its covers still pliable, its pages not showing any hint at yellowing, even though the book was almost five hundred years old.

"What is it?" She stared at him wonderingly.

"The Gardener gave this to me when I was a child."

Her voice took on a quiet mix of awe and wonderment. "In the Cradleland?"

He nodded, opening it. "See? He instructed me to study all the animals in the Garden and to write down their habits, their diets, how much food they required. I didn't understand why at the time." He looked at the book, turning it toward the lamp to better see the childish scrawl: a primitive rendering of his present-day handwriting. "I never completed the task."

"Maybe the girls would like to work on it?" Lamech suggested. "It might make them feel more a part of the commission."

"Good idea."

Naamah leaned closer. "You've already written a lot in it."

"But it's still not complete!" He put the book into her hand and lifted the long toy boat from the box. "He gave me this, too."

"The ark," she said.

He nodded, turning it over and remembering the hole.

She moved the lamp a bit to see it better. "Why is there a hole in the bottom."

"I don't know. The Gardener told me it was part of a puzzle ... and that my father could help me solve it." He looked at Lamech.

Lamech took it from Noah and peered at the hole, tilting the toy this way and that. "I could help?"

"That's what He said." Noah turned to Naamah. "This is what the ark will look like when completed. And inside it we'll be carried through the Creator's flood." He had always thought of it merely as a toy, but now it represented their only hope of survival.

Lamech handed it back to him. "Curious. Who would have thought to build a boat with a hole in the bottom?"

"It must mean something important." Noah sighted along the length of the ark, studying it with a purpose in mind.

"Perhaps your boatbuilder can tell you."

Noah stared at his father over the port side gunwale. "I'll take this into Atla Fair tomorrow!" He placed the boat in Naamah's hands. "Our sanctuary from the Creator's wrath, Naamah."

She said nothing as she peered at the toy ark.

He looked up at the moon, nearly full in the velvet black sky. At one time it had been a flawless jewel—the pearl of heaven it had been called. Now its face was disfigured and ugly. The Oracle's five-pointed star covered a full one-quarter of its visible surface; his face sculpted into its surface in a manner that precisely duplicated the Oracle's Image in the Temple complex in Nod City.

Normally, Noah would not have gazed upon the flawed pearl, imagining it a shaking fist mocking his Creator. But tonight he grinned at it—for the first time in the more than two hundred years since that single, awful night when the Oracle's emissaries raised the grotesque monument. The moon's disfigurement stood boldly in the starry sky for all the Oracle's worshippers to gaze at and to be reminded of him, but the Creator would someday defeat even this affront.

He turned his smile to his wife.

Still staring at the toy barge, Naamah leaned her head against his chest, and he put an arm around her shoulders. If she could hear his heart beating, she'd have detected it suddenly racing.

7

The Earth Trembles

*E*arly the next day as Noah prepared to rush off to Atla Fair, Lamech politely declined his invitation to tag along. "I've been traveling so much, I think I'd rather stay close to home for a while." He had enjoyed having most of the kids gathered around the breakfast table, and really wanted to visit with his grandchildren.

"Japheth, I was supposed to meet Master Oormik at the site today, but I must see the boatbuilder at once. Would you take care of our business with him?"

Japheth shrugged, mopping up the last of the orofin and oats with a piece of thick bread. "I'd told Wend I'd help him work the rows in the east field, but I can see to Oormik instead if you wish. Wend will understand."

Lamech noted the worried look that came to Noah's face, but Noah said simply, "You know what we've talked about. Don't let that shifty dealer off the hook until he agrees to our terms."

"I won't. Grandpa can come with us." Japheth cast a hopeful glance at him. "You want to see where we are planning to build it, don't you?"

This was a tempting invitation. The site was not very far off, and the trip would fulfill part of his desire. He could always catch up with the girls later.

Noah nodded. "That would be nice. You wanted to see the family altar, after all. It's right there next to the cottage where we will be building the ark."

"Who all will be coming?" Lamech wanted to spend time with all his grandchildren.

"I am," Shem said.

"Me too," Ham piped in, smiling at the four pretty faces around the table.

"If they wish."

Mitah said, "Papa, can I go with you to Atla Fair?" Her eyes were bright and hopeful.

Lamech would have taken her with him in a heartbeat, but Mitah apparently had no interest in seeing the future resting place of the ark.

"No, not today," Noah said.

Her face fell.

"I'll be with Master Jerl-eze all day and that won't be any fun for you. Stay here with your sisters."

Mitah's eyes hazed. She stared a moment at her breakfast plate, then took it into the kitchen and didn't return.

Lamech felt a frown touch his lips. His son was so wrapped up in this boat. Didn't he see how he was neglecting his children? But he held his tongue.

❧

Master Oormik's eyes shifted as he peered at the stands of timber climbing up the steep valley wall and growing thick in the deep-soiled floor along the river. Lamech noted the way his lips pursed in a show of disinterest, while his eyes glinted with the sparkle of money.

"There're some potentially valuable trees here." Oormik

made it sound as though it had been a generous gesture on his part. "But for the most part, it is all new growth."

They paused at the edge of a long clearing, and Oormik peered at the forest perched along the hillside. Lamech caught Japheth's eye. Japheth corralled his smile and merely nodded.

"It was logged out about a hundred years ago." Japheth peered at the timber merchant. "You ought to recall. It was your company that did the cutting."

Lamech grinned. His grandson had seen Oormik's hungry look too.

"Was it?" Oormik remained aloof.

The three of them resumed walking down the valley, following a shelf of higher ground on the east side. Lamech kept silent, observing, marveling at Japheth's shrewd maneuvering. His presence seemed to make Oormik edgy. That would give Japheth a stronger hand. The river had dropped away to his left, its burbling muffled through the intervening stand of trees and brambles.

They paused at the shore of a large swamp that crawled back into a deep side valley. The shallow green water was carpeted with floating, tiny-leafed malikwings. Here and there soared giant cyper trees, their knobby roots poking up like old-men's knees through the mats of malikwings, their fanciful trunks soaring upward as if mounted upon thin sails of bark. Even up high, the trees were not what he would call round.

Lamech pulled his view back down to earth. The timber merchant stared out across the swamp.

Japheth said, "Now that you have seen some of the land, what do you think?"

Oormik pursed his lips. "Hard wood, soft wood, cedar, gopher, cyper," he said, gesturing. "You have a nice mix. Better wood up the valley than down here, or on the steeps." He glanced back at the cypers. "I don't think I'd be interested in the swamp trees. Not much call for exotic woods in our area, except from a few furniture makers." He stared at them for a long moment.

Lamech turned at a distant splash. On a far bank, a behemoth entered the swamp, crashing through thickets of rushes until deeper water rose to its knees and then its shoulders. Its small head swung left then right atop a towering neck, then plunged beneath the greenish water where it remained a long time before rising up, sheeting water off its glistening blue-gray hide, a great mass of vegetation hanging from its grinding teeth.

Oormik looked back at him. "I'd be interested in harvesting the timber."

Interested? Lamech grinned. The timber merchant was practically salivating.

"Good." Japheth's voice remained neutral, not giving away a thing.

Oormik glanced at the thick timber beyond the swamp, then turned and stared a moment longer at the cypers before they started back up the valley. He pointed to the steep slope as they walked. "Getting up there and bringing out timber will be difficult."

"I suspect so."

The timber merchant was trying to fatten out the liability side of the ledger now. Japheth just let the man talk.

"Roads to cut and level. Dangerous work on land like that, you know."

"You might build a sluice," Japheth suggested. "Lots of water up there."

"Possibility." By his tone you'd think it wasn't such a good idea.

Lamech's knees ached from the long hike as they arrived back at the little cottage his son had built near their family altar.

Oormik said, "Give me awhile to work up the numbers," and strolled back to his cyclart.

Shem and Ham emerged from the cabin.

"Well?" Ham asked as he approached, hands shoved in his pockets. Shem had a book in one hand—one of the old books Lamech's grandfather, Enoch, had written. He'd closed it on a finger to mark his place.

Lowering his voice, Japheth adjusted it to mimic Oormik. "You have a nice mix of timber."

Shem laughed, glancing at the timber merchant. "I'm so pleased to know that."

"But I'm not interested in the cypers down in the swamp." Japheth laughed. "Except that he couldn't keep his greedy eyes off of them."

"That's not what I meant." Ham screwed his thick lips together, his wide nose flaring in impatience. "What's he willing to pay for it?"

Japheth inclined his head at the cyclart. "He's working up an estimate."

"He's going to pick our pockets." Ham's dark skin made the sweat upon his forehead glisten in the sunlight.

"You were expecting maybe honesty from the area's most notorious gleck pincher?" Japheth waved a hand toward the valley wall. "Valley's too steep. Roads need to be built." He lowered his voice dramatically. "Very dangerous."

Lamech chuckled and Shem laughed.

Ham scowled. "I could design a crane on tracks to move those logs, Grandfather. It's not that steep."

Lamech put a hand on his grandson's shoulder. "Ah, but you're a mechanical genius. I'd expect no less. Master Oormik, on the other hand, is a scoundrel."

Shem said, "You forget, little brother, we're not in this to make money. Just to get the timber we need. Besides, if he cheats us, it's the Creator he will have to answer to."

Ham rolled his eyes.

Japheth crossed his arms. "He's not going to cheat us."

Ham rallied at Japheth's bravado and his face brightened. "Not when Japheth the Sly is making the deals!"

Shem laughed.

Ham rubbed his hands together. "Soon as we have the land cleared, we'll stake out a piece of ground and begin leveling it."

"While Oormik is busy figuring out how he's going to cheat us, what do we do? Just stand around here waiting?" Shem hitched up an inquiring eyebrow.

Japheth grinned. "Hopsmack!" He pulled a sopfer from behind his back and tossed the little beanbag into the air. "You wanna play, Grandpa?"

Lamech laughed. "I'm afraid I'd be no competition."

Ham grinned and leaped into action, catching the bag on the edge of his boot as it came down. Japheth jockeyed for position and kicked it away from his younger brother, sending it straight up over his head.

Shem handed the book to Lamech and joined the action, jostling for position with his brothers.

Lamech sat in the shade of a silver keelit tree and sat upon a stump, enjoying the sound of their laughter, the fresh air, a chance to temporarily put aside the burdens of life. If only Mishah was here to enjoy this with him.

When the timber merchant strode back from his cyclart a little while later, Shem and Ham made themselves scarce. Japheth invited Oormik into the cottage. Lamech stood surreptitiously outside a window where he could glimpse what transpired inside.

Oormik cleared his throat as a perfunctory gesture before beginning the negotiations. "I assume you have the authority to speak for your father, Master Japheth?"

"I do."

Oormik indicated the thin leather portfolio he carried. "I'd rather Master Noah was here to hear what I have to say."

"He would have liked to have been here, but he's occupied with other business, I'm afraid."

Had Oormik developed a conscience and now balked at cheating a young man? Lamech grinned. More than likely, he feared a village judge might overturn the deal if it was discovered he had negotiated with the son instead of the property's owner.

"I have my father's seal, Master Oormik. You can pledge with confidence."

Oormik set the portfolio upon the table and took his time unbuckling the straps. "I've assessed the marketable timber on your father's land." He opened the flap, withdrew a single sheet of paper, and turned it over at his elbow, then he drew out a slightly thicker sheaf and overturned it next to the first. "You have some nice timber, but," the frown was a good touch, "much of it is new growth. You were right. We did log this valley, about a hundred years ago." He smiled. "I failed to make the connection because Master Noah did not hold possession of the land at that time."

"He acquired it afterward, at a good price because it had been harvested."

"Shrewd." Oormik turned over the sheaf and studied it a long moment. "This is the estimated inventory." The timber merchant handed it to him. "Look it over. You will see each kind listed, my estimate of volume, and my offer." A smile slipped smoothly along his thin lips. "The value of the cedars and whipplewood, you will note, has been adjusted to take into account the steep terrain upon which they grow."

"I see that." Japheth skimmed the list. "And the oak, maple, and gopher as well, it would seem."

From his vantage point, Lamech watched Oormik's eyes harden slightly.

"What's this? You've listed the cyper as … nuisance clearing?" He glanced up. "I didn't think you were interested in our cyper."

"Cyper is of little value," Oormik replied curtly.

"Here on Atlan," Japheth added, completing what Lamech suspected was the timber merchant's unspoken thought.

Oormik's smile was brief and icy. "Transportation costs to the mainland would be prohibitive."

"Of course."

"Since my workers would already be on the land, I thought I'd clear the swamp as a service to your father."

"That's very considerate." He handed the paper back to Oormik. "Your inventory looks in order, but your offer is low."

Oormik's scowl hovered between anger and surprise. "Then you won't sell?"

"I didn't say that." He leaned forward and held the older man's gaze. "Here is the deal, Master Oormik."

The timber merchant's glower darkened.

"I want the land timbered out. I want the valley floor cleaned of toppings and trimmings. The stumps pulled, the ground leveled."

Oormik began to protest.

"Hear me out, if you please. I want one-third of the all the gopher wood that you remove milled into timbers and boards. And a quarter of the cedar. I will supply the dimensions. I want the wood delivered back here within an agreed-upon time."

Oormik began shoving the papers into his portfolio. "You have a lot to learn about business, young man."

"Perhaps. But then, can any one of us claim to know every-thing? Please sit down and hear my terms."

Lamech chuckled softly. Japheth was a natural. No wonder Noah had trusted him to this.

"I'm a busy man. I've already wasted time, and time is money."

"And you will be well paid for the time." Japheth indicated the chair.

Oormik hesitated.

"Please."

Grudgingly he returned to his seat.

"The cyper will make some beautiful furniture, won't it? You know as well as I how it is valued for its oils."

The timber merchant's tight jaw clicked to one side.

"It rarely grows on the mainland. Craftsmen in Nod City will pay fifty times your offer for good, straight boards, won't they? You've already noticed how tall and perfect that stand of trees is. Transportation costs will be a fraction of what you will net from their sale."

Oormik's smoky glare remained sparkrock hard. "There is a mainland market for the timber," he admitted.

"It's yours."

Oormik's eyes widened a fraction. "What do you mean?"

"I mean your cost for that stand of cyper has just been reduced to harvesting and shipping."

Curiosity cut through some of the smoke, yet suspicion edged his voice. "Trading that timber for the gopher and cedar milled to your specifications and delivered back here is no bargain, young man."

"You forget, the cleanup afterward, Master Oormik."

"There has to be more in it for me than that."

Japheth nodded. "That's why I'm throwing in all the oak, maple, saubor, whipplewood, ebony, two-thirds of the gopher, and three-quarters of the cedar."

Oormik stared at him.

Japheth withdrew a sheet of paper from an inside pocket. "It's all in here." He smiled. "I'm sure you will be pleased with the terms."

Oormik's eyebrows rose slowly as he studied the offer. Once he managed to crank his jaw back in place, he signed the deal, and Japheth affixed his father's seal to it.

As soon as Oormik left, Shem's head poked up above the windowsill.

"Wish I could have seen his expression!"

Japheth laughed. "It said this was the best deal he's ever made."

Ham came through the door, scowling. He shoved his fingers through tight black curls that fought against the copper band wrestling them together at his neck. "Do you realize how much timber you just gave away?"

He shrugged. "What does it matter? In less than fifteen years all this will be gone anyway. In the meantime, we'll have more lumber than we will ever need and, once Oormik is done with the cleanup, we'll have a cleared and leveled spot to begin constructing the ark!"

Lamech stepped through the door and leaned against the jamb. "Maybe you should have told him."

Japheth's face slackened.

"I agree," Shem said.

"Maybe I should have, Grandfather, but the sting of hearing mocking laughter again makes overtures like that difficult. Oormik wouldn't have believed me if I had. No one does."

Ham grabbed an orofin from the fruit bowl and began peeling it. "Not even Wend believes it's coming."

Lamech's chest tightened at the reminder. "Your brother is just worried about the vineyard. He'll come around … in time."

"And if he doesn't?" Shem's dark, concerned eyes searched his own.

"He will." What else could he say? To think of losing Wend to the Creator's coming wrath was too painful.

Ham slumped into a chair and tilted it precariously back. Taking a bite from his orofin, he spoke as he chewed. "If he doesn't, we'll tie him up and carry him onboard, kicking and screaming."

Without warning the cottage began to shake, the floor trembling beneath Lamech's feet. Overhead, the roof timbers creaked, spilling dust and plaster chips. Wide-eyed, Ham lurched to his feet as the chair smacked the floor. Shem grabbed for the window jamb. Japheth braced himself against a wall.

Lamech's view riveted upon the rafters overhead, grinding in their sockets. "Outside! Quick!"

Japheth and Ham lurched for the doorway. Shem dropped out the window behind the cottage. They staggered away from the building. Shem came around it and they clutched each other for support until the rumbling stopped.

"It's happened again." Shem stared at the dust wafting from the doorway.

Japheth shook his head. "The earth moves like it's angry."

The cottage had managed to remain standing, but wide cracks in the plastered walls spider-webbed up its front. "They're coming more frequently," Lamech said.

The air above them swarmed with thousands of frightened birds, their vibrant plumage painting the sky, their vast numbers casting a dark shadow over the land. The screeching and roaring of terrified animals filled the forest. Tree limbs snapped and the earth boomed as beasts scattered in panic just beyond their sight.

Ham gulped, staring at him. "What does it portend, Grandfather?"

Lamech shook his head. "Don't know."

Ham gave a shiver and wrapped his arms around himself. "I don't like it."

8

Adam's Book

*N*oah was amazed at the progress only four years had wrought. Oormik, holding up his end of the bargain, had leveled a vast stretch of land within the valley near the vineyard. With the arrival of the lumber, Noah and his son had laid a keel and raised up sides to a point where, now, from the cottage window that served as construction headquarters, he could no longer peer over their tops. Ham had gone wild building a rolling derrick with a crane, similar to what he'd seen in Atlan's boatyards, but much more massive.

Noah's view skimmed the detailed plans stretched out on the long table: sheets upon sheets of careful measurements, precise lines, tallied material lists, stress charts ... and on each page, Master Jerl-eze's imprimatur! The plans themselves had cost a small fortune, but worth every shaved gleck of it to see the surprise on Master Jerl-eze's face when he set the toy ark upon the boatbuilder's desk and said, "I want to build this."

Still doubtful, Master Jerl-eze had promised to examine the model. Six weeks later he sent a letter declaring to everyone's amazement that the hole was precisely what the structure needed to relieve hull stress. Not only that, but the rising and falling water within the interior tube that kept it from flooding the vessel would act as a gigantic piston, pumping in fresh air and expelling animal odors through the raised row of windows.

The growing edifice on the edge of his vineyard looked more like a warehouse than a barge, only built more solidly than any architect would have ever deemed economically feasible.

Economically feasible? "Oy, the hole in my savings! If not for High Councilor Rhone's loose purse strings, I would have had to sell the vineyard long ago. Still might have to." Noah frowned. "Wend would have a fit!"

He smiled with satisfaction at the plans, then at the sheets of paper rolled up and set aside, those sections already completed. The keel and hull framing had taken less than three years. Fair progress for an undertaking of such proportions. The work had progressed steadily, with hardly a bump in the road, considering all that could go wrong. But with only eleven years remaining, the pressure to move ahead was growing. "Hardly a bump." That made him nervous.

He glanced back out the window. Japheth and Desmorah were coming up the pathway that cut through mountains of building material. With her hand clasped within his, Desmorah looked radiant, and his son … he must have gazed into a bright light too long. Noah smiled. Love. At a time like this. He shook his head and smiled, recalling the day he'd first set eyes on Naamah. The girl's deep-green pools reminded him of his great-grandmother, Amolikah.

An unexpected longing opened in his heart; a deep pit that grew wider by the moment as old memories surfaced. The last time he'd seen Amolikah …

※

She'd looked so peaceful, a smile upon her ancient face, her clasped fingers holding a single yellow bayolet bloom … almost as if she were merely asleep ... except for her skin, so cold and unyielding beneath his gentle touch. He remembered the sting that pricked his eyes, even though more than a hundred years had passed....

"She's gone to her rest, son." His father's strong grasp folded about his shoulder as they stood over the stone box in Uncle Kenoch's gathering room. "She's at peace in Adam's Bosom."

"I know." But Amolikah's parting had cut deeply into his heart. "I feel as though I've missed so many years. If I could have only been closer to home for some of them." He glanced around the room at the family gathered together. Most of them lived right there, in the Lee-lands of Morg'Seth: aunts, uncles, cousins ... brothers and sisters—some he'd met only for the first time upon his arrival from Atlan. They had all known Amolikah's love, her wisdom, her laugh, and those sparkling green eyes.... A pang of jealousy colored his grief. He nudged it aside, reminding himself that he'd had Amolikah's love and attention almost exclusively for the first seven years of his life. The memories of those years spent in the Cradleland seemed incredible now, and he sometimes wondered if he had ever lived them at all.

In the beginning it had been just Amolikah, his mother, and, of course, the Gardener, living in perfect peace in a wondrous land that was no more. Most people nowadays denied the Cradleland ever existed. Noah scowled. But it had. He'd been there. He swallowed down a lump and turned away from the casket.

He and Lamech made their way from the crowded room. Outside, his mother stood beneath a canopy where family members crowded together. Grandfather Methuselah sat in a white wooden chair with wide arms, his walking stick clutched between his knees, his great white mane catching a beam of sunlight that managed to slant under the canopy. Uncle Kenoch, perched upon one arm of the chair, was laughing at something Grandfather Methuselah had just said.

Noah noted a bit more graying in his uncle's hair—that and the deepening lines in his face were the only indications of advancing years. Uncle Kenoch's boyish laugh was more telling than his appearance.

He watched his mother rest an arm over her brother's shoulder and whisper something in her brother's ear. Uncle Kenoch cocked a head to hear better. Aunt Cerah clucked her tongue and tossed her head back, absently pushing her fingers through the mass of her full red hair.

The mood was not somber, not like some funerals he had attended where the old faith had been lost. Though there was sadness, there were few tears. Amolikah would have wanted it that way. She had lived a good, long life, and now she was resting in Adam's Bosom. Her homegoing was a time for celebration as well as grief.

The smaller children scampered and squealed, happy in their games, some unaware of the reason for this family reunion. To them, it was an unexpected party. Here and there adults gathered in small knots, speaking of things that did not concern him. Others sat in the pavilion down by the little lake, watching youngsters splash in the clear, warm water, or diving off the side of the rowboat.

He sighed. These were Amolikah's family and friends, yet most of them were strangers to him. He might as well have been flung in with those hardy pioneers who'd recently begun settling the land beyond the Straits of Tamor, for all that he knew these people. Of all the family members, he resided furthest from the green, fertile Lee-land hills nestled beneath the looming green peak of Mount Hope. It had taken him three days by fast boat to reach Morg'Seth.

Spying him, his mother waved him over. Vaul, who'd been

waiting in the shade of a tall oak, fell in at his heel. Thore's long shadow stretched before Noah as he came up alongside, his dark, deep-set eyes casting wary glances all round. "We shouldn't delay here for very long, Noah." Thore stood a full head and a half taller than he, and with such broad shoulders and sharp nose and cheeks, there could be little doubt to those who knew such things that he was a Hodinite. That he also was a Makir Warrior of the Old Order might have been less obvious.

"I need to spend more time, Thore. I haven't seen my mother in almost a year, my uncles and aunts in over eight years, and my grandfather in almost twenty." He did, fortunately, see his father more regularly, often accompanying Lamech on trips to speak of the Creator whenever the duties of his vineyard allowed him to.

Thore studied the road that cut through the farm and met the main road some distance outside of the village of New Eden, where Grandfather Seth had finally settled with his wives and children at the end of his southward migration from the ancient land of Eden. "You don't even know most of these people." His soft, deep voice spoke guardedly.

"They're family," Lamech said. "They know each other. I doubt a stranger could move among them without raising eyebrows."

Thore shrugged beneath his long black cloak, trimmed in gray and red—the colors of Atlan. "Perhaps I worry too much."

Noah smiled. They'd known each other a long time, and he knew that Thore rarely looked at life with such intensity, unless he was trying to protect him … so unlike his father in that way. "It's your job to worry." He shot his friend a wide grin. "And mine to keep you from enjoying yourself too much."

Thore gave a quiet, rumbling laugh. "All right, I'll ease up … a little." Just the same, Thore's hand remained out of sight beneath the cloak.

His mother enveloped him in a hug, and Uncle Kenoch rose

from his seat and put a strong hand on his shoulder. "We're so pleased you were able to come, Noah."

"But I worry you've put yourself in danger." Aunt Cerah's misgivings showed in the creases that wrinkled her forehead and deepened from the corners of her eyes.

The family knew his past, and why he had lived out his life in Atlan, so far from the fertile green farmlands of Morg'Seth. "We're all watching out for him," his mother said easily, but she was worried too. Her gracefully aging face reminded Noah of Grandma Amolikah's, all those years ago.

"And Thore is watching over me ... as usual."

His mother gave Thore a quick hug. "We thank the Creator every day for you." She looked the Makir up and down, and her face brightened. "Have I ever told you how much you remind me of your father?"

"Only every time we meet, Mistress Mishah."

They laughed. Noah turned back to his father. "I heard about Sor-dak's passing. I'm sorry."

Lamech drew in a small breath. "Like your grandmother, he rests in Adam's Bosom. But I do miss him. He was a good friend."

"It seems everywhere I travel, I see the book. What's exciting is that people are taking it seriously." Growing up, Noah had known Sor-dak so well he almost thought of him as another grandfather. The brilliant stargazer had once been the chief architect of the Oracle's Temple; his father's overseer while Lamech was locked in the Lodath's Temple Prison. It was during this time that Lamech taught Sor-dak The Way, written in the stars. Because of Lamech, Sor-dak came to know the One True Creator. Noah smiled to himself thinking it would be impossible for anyone to be around his father very long without hearing about the Creator ... and The Way. On the other hand, Lamech had learned much about engineering from the wise old man.

"The Lodath has banned its reading in Nod City, you know?"

Lamech crossed his arms and grinned as though there was some great, hidden humor in that.

Sor-dak and Lamech had spent years crafting *The Prophesy in the Stars,* a thick volume that explained the Creator's message to mankind. They'd begun the work immediately after Sor-dak left the Oracle's Temple Project, and while Noah's mother and father still lived in Atlan. The two men had finished writing it here in the Lee-lands of Morg'Seth.

"That's wonderful. Now curious minds will want to know why he fears it so much as to have issued such an edict. Everybody will have a copy under their bedcovers."

His father smiled, but his tone was cautious. "The Creator turns obstacles into advantages. Yet we must always be wary of the Deceiver's wiles."

"Perhaps," but Noah had a hard time seeing how the Oracle could twist the clear story of Redemption written in the stars.

A little while later Aunt Cerah drew Noah quietly aside. "Speaking of books … we need to talk."

They walked down to the lake where the children were squealing and splashing. He bent down for a flat stone and skipped it across the water. "Six times! That has to be my record."

Aunt Cerah grinned, fingered through several stones for just the right one, heaved back, and sent it skimming across the surface. Four … five … Noah held his breath … six … plop. They laughed, then began to stroll slowly down a wooded path along the shore.

"You know the Book I'm talking about?" The way she emphasized the word left little doubt.

"The one the Mother entrusted to you."

She took his arm. "Noah, we all know of Enoch's prophesy."

"The Cleaving of the World?" He nodded.

She looked over her shoulder at the house where Grandfather Methuselah was leaning forward on his walking stick, discussing something with Noah's father.

"He's getting so old." She smirked. "Every time he sneezes, the family takes a collective gasp."

Noah smiled. "I know. I keep telling myself it won't be long."

"And when he falls asleep with his fathers ..." Her voice trailed off.

Tiny needles pricked his spine. "The Cleaving of the World ... and in a flood, all that we know will cease to exist. That's what the Creator told Grandfather Enoch."

Her blue eyes kindled. "This world will cease, but the Book must continue. I have it hidden safely away, Noah. Someday, someday soon, you must take it."

"Me?"

"You're special somehow. We all know that, even though the Creator hasn't revealed to us how."

He wasn't sure he wanted that responsibility, or even if it was necessary.

Her voice lowered. "Methuselah had a dream. He's mentioned it only to me and Uncle Enoch, and your mother and father."

"What was the dream about?"

"The Creator came to him, and told him man's days have been numbered. The beginning of the end is upon us, Noah."

A tightness took hold of his breathing. "Did the Creator say how long?"

"One hundred and twenty years." Her grasp cinched upon his arm. "Whatever the Creator has planned, we know you hold a special place in it. If the Book is to survive the Cleaving, it surely will be because of you."

The conversation disturbed him. He made no commitments, and she didn't press for any.

It was afterward, when they had circled the lake and were once again among family, that Noah first took special notice of his cousin Naamah, although he had known her all his life. Their gazes touched briefly and his heart melted like hot 'gia ... then she looked at Aunt Cerah.

"There you are, Mother." Naamah had Amolikah's green eyes, and Aunt Cerah's stunning red hair ... and now, even though those green eyes were a little older and a little wiser, Noah found he could still lose himself in them.

❧

He let the memory fade as Japheth and Desmorah came into the shack.

"Fair morning, Father."

"Fair morning."

Desmorah gave him a hug. "You're working early. We missed you at breakfast." She was a great-granddaughter of Methuselah, Noah's choice for Japheth, next in line for marriage. By all appearances, he had chosen well. The betrothal year had begun, plans for the wedding were well under way, and Naamah and the girls were bursting with new excitement. The ark, and all that it represented, had been slowly wearing away at them, and the diversion of an up-and-coming wedding was something they all needed.

Nevertheless, Noah would be thankful once the wedding was over. Japheth had moved in with Wend and his wife and kids while Desmorah took over his room in the family home. The growing tension between Japheth and Wend was becoming plain, and the distractions of setting up a second household, even a temporary one as theirs must be, had diverted Japheth's attention from his work on the ark.

"I've forgotten breakfast—again. But now that you remind me ..."

"I'll bring you something." She smiled with her mouth, her eyes, and her spirit, and hurried to fetch him something to eat.

Noah raised his eyes to Japheth. "She's a good woman."

Japheth laughed. "Why, because she thinks of your stomach all the time?"

He patted his belly, which had expanded in a dignified manner over the years as the result of too much good food and, sometimes, too much good wine. "That woman has her priorities lined up in proper order."

"Sebe says she's playing up to you and mother."

"Your sister-in-law listens to Wend too much."

Japheth frowned.

Noah gave a wry smile. "It will be better once you and Desmorah are in your own place."

"No doubt Wend and Sebe will be happy to see me out of their lives."

He waved a hand. "I'm at fault for that, Japheth. You know how it is between us." His spirits sagged. The vineyard was Wend's passion, as it had once been his, and they argued so often over it that nowadays Wend just naturally took the opposite side no matter what the discussion. And since Japheth, Shem, and Ham had embraced the commission as Noah had, they, too, naturally fell on the opposite side of every disagreement with Wend.

"Wend will come around once the time gets closer."

"I hope so." Wend had been the burden of his heart for years, but the two of them seemed to drift farther apart the harder he tried to pull them together.

They stood in silence, Noah staring out the window at the thing that had driven a wedge into his family. Even the girls seemed to resent him personally for it, as though it were his idea. As if he had requested the Creator to send the coming judgment!

"I just spoke with Jab-ek," Japheth said.

Noah pulled his thoughts back onto business. "Yes? Has he arranged for the pitch?"

"He has. He says he'll be ready to deliver it as soon as we're ready to receive it. But he wants to know why we need so much."

He extended his arm toward the window. "Master Jab-ek has seen this, and still he asks?"

Japheth leaned against the doorjamb. "He thinks it's a waste to pitch a boat inside as well as outside. He didn't come right out and say it, but I know he thinks you're off your head."

"Everyone thinks that. I'm building a boat where there is no water and no chance of moving it to water. What do you expect people to think?" He blew out a long breath. "It doesn't matter what they think."

"Maybe not, Father; but if you're cracked enough in the head to build a boat out of reach of water, maybe you are cracked enough to forget to pay him, or not be able to pay him. Jab-ek said he isn't risking his business on us. He wants payment up front."

"I've never let a bill go unpaid! Let people think me crazy, but dishonest …?"

"He says he'll have thousands of glecks tied up in new equipment and the extra workers he has to hire to prepare it, and the storerooms built to hold it for us until we are ready."

"He'll get paid!" But now was not a good time. Noah had tied up all his resources in hardware and in the extra men to handle the timber arriving daily from the mills.

Japheth raised his eyebrows. "Do we have the money?"

Noah scratched the back of his neck. Although he disliked doing it, he knew he must. "I'll go speak with High Councilor Rhone again—this afternoon."

9

Rhone's Help

The knock on his door was a welcome interruption this time. Rhone drew in a deep breath to freshen his lungs and whispered a brief close to his prayer. Usually he would have been annoyed by an intrusion into his prayer time, but his heart was heavy, and he was getting no answer. He stood stiffly and turned, gently rubbing his knees. They seemed to suffer most these days. He drew himself up tall. "Enter."

Enin slipped in and closed the door behind him. "I apologize for interrupting you, High Councilor. Master Noah is here to see you. I would have detained him with the others seeking audience, but I know your interest in this … err … endeavor of his."

Rhone smiled. "An endeavor it is. Show Noah in." His door was never shut to the man who indirectly was responsible for all that he was today, for all that Atlan had become over the last five hundred years. While almost two hundred years older than Noah, he considered their age the same, and often declared they had both been "born" on the same day. More accurately, Noah had been born and he had been reborn.

Enin nodded, slipped back out the door, and a moment later opened it wide, announcing the visitor.

"May your servant find favor in your eyes." Noah bowed briefly, then smiled, Vaul sitting obediently at his side.

"Your presence gladdens my heart." He grasped Noah affectionately by the shoulders. "Does your canic go everywhere with you?"

Noah gave a short laugh. "Nearly everywhere."

"What brings you here?" He was relieved to momentarily put aside the burden of his prayers.

"I need to speak to you about ..." Noah hesitated, looking uncomfortable. "It's about finances."

"What about finances?" He took Noah by the arm and led him toward an archway that opened to the outside, onto his private promenade. "Mind if we walk as we talk? I've got some kinks to work out." They strolled out upon the rooftop gardens and stood a moment on the parapet that surrounded the top of the Hall of Justice. This area was off-limits to all but Rhone and his family, and a few select guests. He loved the sweeping view of the harbor.

Noah inhaled the sea-scented air. Nearby rose the great red stone wall that enclosed all of Hodin's Keep's official buildings. His eyes traveled beyond it to the sparkling water of Haven Port, the smallest and innermost of Atlan's three concentric harbors. The sky was clear and filled with green divers that shrilled at each other, and gulls squawking and wheeling overhead. Some perched below on pilings, along guy wires and atop the tall masts of pleasure boats. Palm trees gently waved their brilliant fronds in the sharp sunlight.

"As you know, I've made good progress. Since contracting with the Oormik Mills, the lumber has been arriving almost daily."

Rhone nodded. They had discussed this a few years earlier. "And transportation?"

Noah approached the parapet cautiously and gripped the edge of the low wall. "It's all been arranged. Oormik Mills delivers the milled wood to the site. But the extra men to move it, they come at a price."

"Everything comes with a price, Noah. I should guess there is enough timber to build a small town." He leaned against the wall too, a full head taller than the mildly rotund, dark-haired man beside him. He rolled his shoulders to loosen stiff muscles. Below, a fast boat of Atla's shore guard left a long, frothy wake as it headed out of port. "But why build it on your landlocked property with all the shipbuilding facilities on Atlan? How will you ever manage—" He stopped himself, and then smiled abruptly.

Noah sighed. "The water will come to me."

He pushed away from the parapet. "I keep forgetting."

"I sometimes forget too. Naamah and I discussed this very thing. I could build close to the water, but there'd be nothing unusual in that. What sort of witness would that be?" They resumed walking. "The oddity of building the Creator's ark inland raises many questions, and when it does, I explain His plan." Noah looked up at him. "When they open the door, I walk in. Hopefully some hearts will be changed before … " He gave a wan smile. "We haven't much time left."

A frown pulled at Rhone's mouth. He recalled his prayer of a few moments before. It reopened the wound in his heart that he had tried so long to ignore.

"What's wrong, Rhone?" Concern narrowed Noah's brown eyes.

"Nothing." He fixed a smile. "You mentioned finances. Of course you know I'll help."

"I know. And I am beholden to you. This was something I'd hoped to do myself—as much as I could. I have my four sons and four daughters, and friends like you." His expression looked painfully earnest. "But the commission was given to me."

"Not you alone." He peered down into Noah's serious brown eyes. This man carried such a burden every day of his life! He admired Noah's dedication. For having been born of Sethite parents from the Lee-lands of Morg'Seth, Noah had none of the self-righteous arrogance he had once ascribed to all

Lee-landers. "Remember, I received a commission too. Now, tell me about finances."

Noah cleared his throat and watched a green diver swooping for insects, catching them on the wing. "The pitch provider is demanding payment in advance. He claims he has many expenses, which is true. But in truth, he thinks I'm a little off plum and suspects he might never get paid."

"I'll back your needs."

Noah gave a quick smile. "I know. I had considered selling the vineyard. But Wend would never forgive me."

"Wend's the firstborn."

"As he's quick to remind me."

"Your vines produce some of the finest grapes in the land." He laughed. "How would Atlan ever cope if you were to sell?"

❧

They turned a corner just as a small wing-sailer flashed in the sunlight, its small cycler buzzing ambitiously, pushing it along. Rhone paused to watch it bank low over the harbor then rise and turn toward the Rim-wall. "You ever fly one of those things?"

Noah's shoulders gave a slight tremble. "Once. And never again."

Rhone watched the blue and yellow wing shrink in the distance. "Ah, yes. Thore told me all about your adventure in Nod City. When I was young, it was skybarges. Big, slow-moving things, pulled along by teams of giant condors."

He drew in a sigh and dredged up a memory from the far past. While riding in a skybarge, he and Bar'ack had been attacked by mansnatchers. So long ago … it was hard to imagine that it was only one lifetime. How the years did seem to pile up—he rotated a stiff shoulder—especially when a man got old.

Bar'ack is a tool in the Oracle's hand. I don't know what can be done, Ker'ack, but if there is any way I can help him, I will. This I promise you.

The memory came unexpectedly.

"There is something wrong, isn't there?" Noah was staring at him again.

He grimaced. "Nothing anything can be done about." Bar'ack was his burden to bear, for he was to blame for what had happened to the young man all those many years ago.

He led Noah to a nearby table beneath a circle of shade from a wide sun umbrella of red and gold silk, embroidered about the edges in intricate Kleiman patterns. A gift to Leenah from Zei, a granddaughter of Ela. Kleiman silk was in high demand, and they produced it almost exclusively now that moonglass was rarely used. With the slow deterioration of the magnetic veil, moonglass had become, at best, a curiosity, sold only in specialty shops. Those who still used it—at least the unenergized variety—were usually hopeless romantics clinging to a bygone day. He motioned Noah to a chair and sat across from him. The canic stretched his long body upon the cool paving stones beneath the table.

"Keep the vineyard. The resources of Atlan are yours for the asking. You only have a few years left."

"The vineyards need constant attention to produce the choicest grapes. My sons and I are so busy building the Creator's ark, how can we tend the vines as they should be? To prune? To water in the proper season, and to hold back water?"

"Then give it all to Wend and let him take on the burden. The land will keep you and your family well fed during these remaining years. Wend will be happy and Atlan supplied with some of the finest wines available."

Noah grinned and nodded. "I knew you had an ulterior motive! Perhaps you are right, Rhone."

After Noah left, Rhone stared at the well-worn prayer bench. Less than eleven years left.

Feeling suddenly very old, he tried to force thoughts of Bar'ack from his mind, as he slowly left the room.

10

Nephilim in Atlan

*B*ar'ack forced himself into a shallow, hypnotic stupor, filling his mind with other thoughts as best he could to mask the voices inside his head. Sometimes a vision worked better, and sometimes simply the cadence of a single sound repeating over and over again guided his thoughts. Today he focused on the Rahabian Crystal atop the Temple, beginning to give off a pinkish light in the predawn glow spreading across the sky to the east of the Temple. He struggled to hold onto the vision in spite of the voices. Sometimes, if he concentrated, he could almost force himself into oblivion....

The high twitter of the leolpipes broke his concentration and his eyes snapped around. The row of dignitaries poised along the Grand Temple Way, most taller than he, turned and fixed their view upon the Triumphal Arch. Its gilded surface beamed in the lights that were directed onto it from the Temple. Riveted by the sound of the pipes, the voices inside his brain went silent.

Bar'ack shuddered a sigh of relief.

The distinguished guests, of which he was one, were mostly Nephs, or nephlings. Bar'ack was one of the few true-blood humans among them. He sensed their disapproval and didn't care.

Worshippers pressed around the Arch, held back only by a golden chain and a row of armed green-cloaks. Murmurs of, "Oracle" and "here he comes" rose among the excited crowds. Bar'ack couldn't stir up much excitement. Yet, it was because of the presence of the Oracle that the voices inside his head went still, and for that he truly relished this moment.

The procession of Separated Guards, resplendent in dress greens, the color of ivy and malikwings, appeared, the spotlights setting their bronze helmets afire. Again the leolpipes whistled the Oracle's impending appearance, and the crowd went wild with cheers.

There upon a pallet of gold, borne aloft on golden poles set firmly upon Neph shoulders, and seated on the golden Mercy Throne, rode the Oracle. Dressed in a gown of the purest white bisnek skin, the god from the stars fairly shone in the spotlights while his worshippers cast palm fronds before him, paving the Grand Temple Way in green.

The Appearing Ceremony—the Oracle's annual dawn march through the Arch of the Unveiling—was the high point of the year. It was four hundred and eight years ago, upon the completion of his Temple, that the Oracle's dawn arrival had caught the hearts and minds of the people of the Known World. Who could forget his radiant appearance in the midst of the Arch, upon a beam of light from the stars? The Appearing Ceremony was a time of celebration and gift giving. Bar'ack scoffed at the thought. He'd forgotten the last time he'd received a gift. Reprimands were more plentiful.

The Oracle rode past as though oblivious to the cheers. Behind the golden throne marched more Neph guards, and behind them came the sacrifice—several hundred of them— more than he had anticipated. This year the Oracle had forcefully moved to squelch the unrest fomented by the Creator's Kinsmen.

From out of the rare silence inside his head a thought emerged. A vague image of his parents took shape. They would have been believers—Kinsmen, they'd be called today, if still alive. He scowled. And they very well could have been numbered among these sacrifices. The thought pricked his heart. Remorse filled him with a weightiness he'd not known before....

And then the voices in his head resumed chattering with excitement, and the remorse was swept aside. In the growing light, he watched Kinsmen pass by on the Grand Temple Way, eight abreast and fifty in a row, dressed in simple brown robes. Connected one to the other by bronze collars and five spans of bronze chain, they stumbled along, pulled ahead by a green-and-scarlet-bedecked three-point. They dared not trip or they'd be trampled. Their eyes shifted warily, wide with fright. The crowd hissed as the sacrifice moved toward the Temple.

Kinsmen. Troublemakers is what they are, the voices inside his head chortled.

It's about time the Oracle showed his authority in this matter. Hepha chuckled.

Stamping out the pestilence is the only cure for their constant bigoted, narrow-minded carping, Per agreed.

No longer will the Temple Altar flow with the sacred blood of swine and ravens. A snarl pulled at Bar'ack's lips. These unrepentant humans made for a more entertaining offering. Something unfamiliar poked at his heart, and he winced without understanding why.

The feeling vaporized when the faithful all around him roared their approval as the sacrifice marched up the broad Temple steps and through the towering bronze doors, which stood wide this day ... the only day of the year they were opened.

As the last of the sacrifice entered the Temple behind the Oracle's entourage, the throngs of worshippers filed in to take seats in the gallery, to celebrate the day the Oracle arrived on earth—his Triumphal Appearing.

Bar'ack followed the dignitaries into the Temple by way of a tunnel into the lower regions. He and the others were ushered into overlooks, deeply carpeted rooms where polished wooden furniture, constructed mainly to Neph proportions, faced floor-to-ceiling glass windows. Once everyone was settled in, the door clicked shut and with a small jolt, the room began its slow climb. Before him, the worshipper's gallery came into view. As the overlook hummed higher up the Temple's wall, the worshippers fell away and the Grand Altar came into view. Its brilliant marble floor was incised with the golden unspeakable symbols, and in the center, partly obscured now by the sacrifice, the immense five-pointed star.

Around him, Nephs chuckled and snatched flagons of ale and roasted grundy legs dripping with hot fat off a passing tray in the hands of a servant. The air inside the overlook thickened, the rank odor of Neph pricking his nose. After all these years as captain of the breeding dens, he still had not gotten used to it.

Ignoring the food, he snatched a flagon of ale off a passing tray and guzzled it down. The voices pounded inside his skull again. As usual, Per and Hepha had begun to argue about something or other. The overlook thudded gently to a stop and he seized a second drink off the tray, hoping the alcohol would deaden their voices.

Far below, on a raised platform before the altar, the Oracle's bearers lowered the Mercy Throne and backed away, bent low at their waists. The Oracle stepped off and was promptly escorted to the elevated Honor Seat. The moment he mounted the place of honor, the crowd hushed.

As the Temple fell silent, a cadre of priests appeared upon the altar, leading a lone victim, a young woman this time. She moved sluggishly as though drugged, her shoulders stooped, her head bowed. The priests stood her before a table of gold, removed her robe, and laid her upon the table.

The offering prayer rose from the throats of a double fist of priests, and as they chanted, a golden knife passed from hand to hand, finally coming to the fist of the High Priest, Caelf, a Neph of renown in Nod City.

Bar'ack grew impatient and wished they would just get on with the sacrifice. He looked around for the servant, growled for her attention, and flagged her over.

On the altar below, the knife rose and poised over the woman's heart. Some of the Nephs around him had begun to chuckle. A few pointed and hooted. Inside his head, Per, Hepha, and Pose grew intent upon the scene. Bar'ack eyed the approaching tray.

The Nephs in the room went silent as tangible excitement filled the overlook.

He snatched up the flagon and threw back his head for a long drink. When he lowered the cup from his lips and looked back, the sacrifice was over. The High Priest had begun to collect her blood into the golden chalices, passing them to his assistants who now spread out among the bound Kinsmen huddled upon the altar. They sprinkled the sacrifice with the purifying blood while the Kinsmen recoiled and tried to hide their heads beneath their arms.

Bar'ack squirmed in the chair. He wanted it over so that he could return to his duties in the breeding dens. His eye caught the beams of light slowly rising up the opposite wall, marking the assent of the new sun. It wouldn't be long now.

The priests completed their baptism of blood, formed up in a line, and marched off the altar, leaving only the woman's mutilated body on the table, and the Kinsmen upon the altar platform. A hush as heavy as a morning mist settled over the Temple.

As he watched the ceremony unfold, a vision of his mother and father standing among the Kinsmen swam before his eyes. He shook the apparition from his head, leaving himself cold and aching. The voices that usually filled his head were easier to take than this abrupt unfamiliar pain in his heart. Then the building gave a gentle lurch, and somewhere far beneath its stony roots, giant engines hummed to life and immense wheels began to whir quietly. With a quick breath, he shook off the pain of the vision.

Down on the platform, walls swung inward and around, bringing mirrors into alignment—each more than a hundred spans and a quarter that wide.

Some of the Kinsmen tried to flee. Neph guards armed with projers herded them back into a group. Wails of fright reached up to the overlook where Bar'ack watched from.

As the mirrors folded into place behind the sacrifice, other mirrors rose from the altar's floor in front of them until the altar had been enclosed by the Offering Chamber. From his high point, Bar'ack had a very narrow view of the sacrifice writhing within the now mirrored chamber. He could hear their cries and see them trying to claw their way up the sleek surfaces. He grinned at their pleas, their laments for mercy.

He squirmed in his chair and took a long drink. The alcohol had begun to mute the voices.

Out of the ceiling, a crystal lens the size of the altar floor lowered, sealing them inside the Offering Chamber, muffling the sounds of terror. Clenching his fists, he watched the beams of light climbing the far wall.

"Soon." A chesty voice beside him rumbled with laughter. The Neph's fingers probed inside his giant mouth, found a piece of grundy meat, and yanked it free. The Neph looked over at him and grinned.

In spite of his dismal mood, anticipation quickened his heartbeat.

The sun broke free of the horizon and the marker gauge climbing the wall flared. A beam of brilliant light shot down through the ceiling from the Rahabian capstone atop the Temple, filling the Temple. He shaded his eyes against its blaze as the sun crept to its calculated angle. The glare sharpened and narrowed; energy concentrating upon the crystal ceiling of the mirrored Offering Chamber.

The stench of sizzling flesh filled the Temple. Below, the Oracle swayed slightly upon his Honor Seat.

A bolt of light shot from a slit in the chamber, filled the Homing Portal in the Temple's wall with a dazzling brilliance, and beamed into the heavens.

"As he came, so will we follow," the worshippers intoned, repeating the phrase, their voices rising in a frenzy.

The fiery light streamed hotly for several minutes until the sun finally crept off the capstone's exacting facets. The light dimmed. Bar'ack lowered his hand from above his eyes as the crystal ceiling slowly lifted away and the mirrored walls retracted. The crowds ceased their chanting.

A fine powdery ash was all that remained upon the altar.

The voices had begun murmuring inside his head again, but the numbing of the alcohol made them bearable at least … so why did his heart feel heavy?

Servants helped the Oracle off the Honor Seat. He moved like a man engorged; lethargic, satiated. Drunk on the blood of the Kinsmen. Sort of like Bar'ack was now, on the Oracle's wine. He grinned at the comparison.

Reaching to steady himself, the Oracle mounted the golden Mercy Throne. Once properly seated, his Throne Bearers carried the god from the stars out of the Temple.

With a lurch, the overlook began to lower back to its resting place beneath the grand gallery where already worshippers were filing out of the Temple.

※

Days after the Appearing Ceremony, alone in his chamber, brooding over a past he could not change, Lucifer stiffened at the subtle ripple that moved between the two worlds. His head came around, and a moment later the air shimmered with white heat as a rift opened.

Ekalon stepped through it.

"High Prince Lucifer." Ekalon lowered his head, but only slightly; a show of submission, grudgingly given out of duty.

It was only his power that kept these lesser ones under control. He understood that, and he would let it pass for now. At the moment Ekalon served his purposes adequately. "The reason for this intrusion?"

Ekalon cradled the well-worn battle staff in his arm. "I have learned a few things about Noah, Master. I knew you would want to hear them."

His attention sharpened. "What have you learned?"

"He and his family are building a boat. They call it an ark."

"An ark? Tell me more."

"The Tyrant of Old has commissioned him to this task. Noah speaks often of this matter to the Tyrant in his prayers. He is troubled by what it portends." Ekalon paused as though carefully choosing his next words. "And I think we ought to be also, Master."

"I know the prophecies," he said, irritated.

"Then you know He intends destruction upon this world."

"This has been told by the Tyrant's speakers. But exactly when … that has always been the question. It is difficult to get close to His chosen speakers. Their Guardians are many."

"But you are more powerful, Master."

He sensed a question in Ekalon's tone that irritated him further.

"The Tyrant set limits. I am forced to use you and others—my eyes and ears on this miserable stone—to ferret out what He is planning."

"I suspect His wrath is coming upon this world very soon," Ekalon said.

Lucifer stared out the long crystalline window at the Temple complex gathering shadows in the late sunlight. What could he do to stop it? Nothing. The Tyrant's speakers had been warning of coming wrath for years. Perhaps they would all be wiped out in the coming destruction? He smiled at that. If only the problem was so simply solved. A frown pushed the smile aside. The Tyrant never made it easy. Noah was the key. Noah had always been the key.

He turned back to Ekalon. "I want Noah dead."

Ekalon said, "On Atlan he will be difficult to reach. He is well protected. His Guardians are powerful."

"I won't tolerate excuses. Just do it."

Ekalon nodded. "Yes, Master."

❧

Noah's eyes opened heavily. A chill wind rattling the bolted shutters had drawn him up out of a deep sleep. The air all around him buzzed with a static electricity. He blinked away the grogginess and shivered with the gooseflesh rising upon his naked arms and chest. As awareness grew, his view shifted around the dark bedroom and halted at the window. Past the fluttering curtains, beyond the narrow slats of the shutters, a faint pea-green light pulsated its way into the bedroom.

He swung his legs off the bed and listened to the wind. From the next room Vaul's low, rumbling growl alerted him.

"What is it?" Naamah asked thickly, rolling to her back.

"I don't know." He went to the window and opened the shutters. Streamers of green light encircled the house. *What's going on?* He stared dumbfounded a moment, the wind moaning softly around the eaves of the thatch roof, buffeting the dark trees beyond the house whose leaves glowed faintly now in the green whirlpool of light.

He drew back inside, rubbing his arms, and hurriedly closed and barred the shutters. He looked at Naamah, now sitting up.

"Noah?" She peered at him in the soft green light.

"Stay here." He reached for the light, but Vaul's warning growl from the next room stayed his hand and he rushed out the door. In the gathering room, the canic was crouched before the open window, his ears plastered flat against his head, lips curled back, long, fighting teeth tinted the color of pea soup from the wisps of light scudding past.

Noah went to the door, the big canic instantly at his side. Outside, the normally balmy air was as cold as the bottom of an ice vault. The wind moaned deep and low. The distant rows of grapevines beyond his house seemed unaffected by the chilling green. The pond's still surface reflected only the milky moonlight. Whatever it was, it only hovered around his house. He shivered, and started outside, but Vaul moved in front of him and plunged into the darkness, barking.

"Vaul! Come back here!"

Naamah hurried up beside him, bunching her robe closed in one hand. "What does it mean?"

"I don't know, but I intend to find out." She grabbed his arm. "No. Let Vaul take care of it."

He hesitated.

"You're trembling," she whispered.

His breathing was coming fast and shallow, his muscles tingling from the electricity humming in the air. He drew her near. "Can it be?" His chest contracted.

"What, Noah? What is it?"

"They've found us."

Naamah stared up at him. "They?"

He shot her a worried glance. "The Deceiver. His servants."

Vaul's strident yaps merged with the moaning wind. A towering shadow lunged. Noah heard a groan and saw something like massive arms swing out. The barking stopped. At once the wind died and the green luminescence faded, leaving moon- and starlight. Silence enveloped him. Without thinking, he glanced up at the three-quarter moon, then instantly away at the sight of the Oracle's mark. It only added to the oppressive atmosphere.

Orah and Sheflah came from their bedroom, his future daughter-in-law, Desmorah, with them.

He drew in a shuddering breath. "Whatever it was, it's gone."

Naamah stared out the door into the still night. "Vaul?"

"I need to look for him." The canic had been so much a part of his life for so many years, he refused to think the worst.

She held him back. "Let's wait a moment."

"Vaul!" he called. "Vaul, come boy!"

She swallowed. "What's out there, Noah?"

He shook his head. "Not sure. I only saw shadows, but from the size of them, I'd guess there were Nephs prowling about."

"Nephs?" Her eyes rounded. "Here, in Atlan?"

A moment later Vaul trotted into the house, his brown eyes shifting around, his dark muzzle red with fresh blood.

In the distance a light flashed, mostly hidden behind an intervening copse of trees; a pale reddish orange ball, like washed-out sunshine through a globule of morning mist, rose above the distant treetops, then shot skyward and was gone.

The static electricity disappeared and Noah released his breath. "A star jumper."

"The Oracle?" Naamah's fingernails dug into his arm.

He nodded and backed her from the door and shut it, then went through the house, locking doors, bolting shutters, turning up the lights.

No one slept the rest of the night.

The next morning he surveyed his property. In Naamah's vegetable garden he spied several giant footprints. One had smashed through a watermelon.

Nephilim.

Stooping, Noah peered at a dark stain splattered across the

wide green leaves. He gave a wry smile and glanced at Vaul. "You got a good piece of him." He covered the footprint and stain so Naamah would not have to see it, and stared a moment at the shattered green rind mashed into the fleshy red pulp, trying to gauge the feelings building up inside him. He'd known something like this would happen. The Gardener had warned him.

"After all these years, it finally begins."

11

Temple Sacrifices

In an antechamber off the great hall that for over a thousand years had held the judgment seat known as The Heart of Justice, High Councilor Rhone listened to the report. His thoughts slid back five hundred years, to a time when he had been a young man and the Nephs—the Earth-Born as they had been called back then— had first appeared among men.

He peered out a nearby window, hardly noting the lovely harbor beyond it. Instead his mind's eye conjured the giants—Herc, Pose, Hepha, Per, and Plut.

The Nephs were different now. In the beginning they had been crude, misshapen beings with broad, bony heads, huge jaws, double rows of twisted teeth, and six fingers on each hand. Today they were more refined, as though a sculptor had taken a roughed-out work and chiseled away the flaws and polished the uneven contours. Except for their size, and the extra fingers, they were totally human-like. An updated version, as a marketeer might glibly proclaim while pitching his products to the unwary. Some might even call them beautiful. Most of the Known World had fallen for their deception.

The muscles banding his chest slowly constricted. He had struggled to keep the Nephs' influences from infecting Atlan with their deadly disease. Just the same, Neph blood had trickled across the Rim-wall and in through the waterways in spite of his best efforts.

"That's all I know, High Councilor."

Noah's voice pulled his thoughts back to the present.

"Naamah is frightened. Not so much for herself, but the family. Vaul took a hunk of flesh from one of them before they fled in one of the Oracle's star jumpers."

"A single canic drove them off?" He had fought the Nephs back in the days when he was young and strong; when he was the Pyir of the Makir. A canic seemed an unworthy opponent for these creatures of renown. "What do you feed that canic?"

Noah smiled. "It was luck—or the Creator's protection."

He took in a breath to loosen the bands. "Mistress Naamah has a right to be worried. This incident bodes no good for you or us. There'll be foul weather ahead if we don't end it now." Rhone glanced to his personal warder who stood nearby. "Enin, send word to Pyir Chrone to come at once."

"Yes, High Councilor." Warder Enin gave a curt bow and departed.

Rhone turned back to his friend. "Perhaps you should be accompanied by a Makir from now on."

Noah's lips cut a frown. "Here on Atlan? Do you think that necessary?"

"If these are Nephilim, you won't be able to protect yourself." He glanced at Vaul. "Nephs are fierce warriors. Your canic was lucky last night. Let's not press that luck any further. I'll tell Thore he must guard you here in Atlan as well. He will move into your home."

Noah's mouth took a wry set. "If you think it's really necessary...."

"The Gardener Himself charged me with your safety, Noah. Yes, I think it is necessary."

"All right. I will ready one of the cottages for Thore."

Rhone took him by the shoulders and smiled to ease his friend's worry. He had known Noah far too long not to see through his brave face. "I'll send Thore by the vineyard in the morning."

"Naamah will feel better with him around." Noah gave an anemic smile. "I better get back to her. Thank you, High Councilor."

He started for the door, nearly running into Leenah on the way out. "Noah!" She hugged him. "Where are you running off to?"

"Home."

"How is Naamah?"

"She's busy with the preparations."

Leenah smiled. "It will be a lovely wedding. Japheth and Desmorah will give you lots of fine grandchildren."

He grinned mischievously. "Let's hope so. Mankind's survival will depend on it."

Leenah's face tightened and her eyes grew ever so slightly sad. "Tell Naamah I will come to visit her soon."

"I will. She'd like that." Noah left.

Leenah watched after him a moment, then turned and considered Rhone. "When I see that look in my husband's eyes, I have to ask myself what is wrong with the world."

Long golden hair lay in a thick braid down her back, shining in the windowed sunlight, streaked with the silver currency of years—like his. Glints of cerulean blazed at him through eyelids narrowed by concern. He remembered seeing that same blue fire for the first time in the Lodath's palace as she single-handedly faced down a double fist of guards with nothing more than the jagged edge of a broken bottle. "You're too perceptive for your own good." He drew in a breath and let it out slowly, relishing the way her light perfume blended with the smell of the sea from the harbors beyond the walls of Hodin's Keep.

Just then Chrone strode in, his dark-gray cloak folded over his arm, his hand grasping a sheathed sword. He seemed surprised at finding them both there. "Mother ... Father. Enin said you wanted to see me. I passed Noah in the hall. He was in a hurry to be somewhere."

"Back at his wife's side. He and Mistress Naamah's home was attacked last night."

Leenah's eyes widened. "No!"

"They are all right," Rhone went on quickly.

"Attacked? By whom?" she asked.

"Not whom. What."

She stared.

Rhone said to his son, "Noah thinks it was Nephs. By what he described, it sounds as if there was a spirit presence with them too."

"Nephs?" Leenah's breath hissed and her expression turned momentarily to stone.

Pyir Chrone said, "They are not likely to have remained in Atlan, Father."

He nodded. "I suspect they fled back to the mainland. Noah said he saw what looked like one of the Oracle's star jumpers. I want you to check it out. Assemble a kal-ee-hon and see if you can't track them down."

"And if I find them?"

"You know how I want it handled. Make sure you burn the corpses afterward."

He nodded, then turned to his mother. "You don't look well."

She laid a hand upon her son's big arm. "I'm all right. I ought to go to Naamah right away."

Chrone smiled. "I should think Mistress Naamah would appreciate the company." He glanced back at his father. "I'll take care of this."

"Tell Thore to stop by my chamber after he completes his exercises."

Chrone nodded again, spinning smartly on his heel and striding out the door. After his son left, he took Leenah into his arms, mesmerized by the blue depths of her eyes, clear as a mountain lake. "Noah knew it would come. The Gardener told him it would."

"We all knew, Rhone. We should be thankful for the years of peace we've enjoyed in the land."

"If this is the beginning of Enoch's prophesy, those peaceful years are about to end."

Leenah wrapped her arms around his waist and pressed her head into his chest. "If they are to end, at least I've been able to spend them with you, Rhone."

He bowed his cheek onto her hair. "And I with you, High Counciloress." He kissed her.

⚜

Poised in the shaft of pure white light streaming down from the crystal ceiling overhead, Lucifer was enveloped in its hot white glare in a blinding brilliance that set his naked arms and chest aglow; his belly and thighs gleamed in the focused sunlight. Passing down all around him, the dazzling brilliance from the Rahabian Crystal coursed on through the lenses beneath his feet, through the glass floor, and onto the altar below where a few days earlier it had consumed the sacrifice that had made him giddy with their blood.

Closing his eyes, Lucifer saw himself one with the light … his glory. He was the light enveloping the offerings that had been placed upon the altar. It used to be sheaths of grain, the bundles of fruits and vegetables, a thousand small paper figurines of dead friends and relatives. But now it was the blood of Kinsmen, consumed by his light, disintegrated in a flash brighter than the sun. As the silvered mirrors rotated around the altar and concentrated the vapors of his worshipper's offerings, Lucifer basked in their pleasant odors—in his moment of glory—before the mirrors beamed his light through the Homing Portal in the Temple wall toward the Home Star.

The softly whirring mechanicals that kept his Temple properly aligned thrummed distantly. The suntracer mechanism had been beyond the engineering capabilities of man at the time of the Temple's construction; however, a little dream here and a quiet whisper there had solved the problem. Humans were so quick to accept his ideas. So easy to manipulate. Tempting them had become tedious.

It had been different in the beginning-time, when man was new and the Tyrant of Old walked with him. Back then temptation had required cunning. He laughed. Now all he had to do was show mankind some savory new trinket, a hint of sweet forbidden knowledge, and they lined up like children for candy.

He smiled as the radiance of his glory filled the Temple's upper chamber. This was how it had once been. He studied the way his skin shone ... and he remembered. A slight frown tilted his lips. It wasn't as wondrous as it once was. Anger boiled unexpectedly. It was unjust of the Tyrant to have taken this away from him. "I was beautiful! I will be clothed in glory again, and this time, it will be from within me. No more will I reflect the glory of another!"

The brilliance dimmed and the crystal slowly darkened as the sun crept higher in the sky, no longer striking the facets just right. With the light fading, gloom rushed back and leadened his soul. He stepped off the raised platform onto the glass floor, still beautiful in his nakedness, but now utterly empty inside. What was this hollowness? Was it really the Shekinah Glory he longed for, or was it love that he missed? Whatever the true need was, the more time that passed, the more the hunger grew.

"No!" The anger roared back. "I am sufficient within myself. I need no other."

He sensed Ekalon coming. Swiftly, he dressed, then peered into the silver wall, turning this way, then that. "I am still beautiful." He swelled his chest. "Someday I will ascend into heaven again. I will exalt my throne above the Tyrant's stars. I will be like the Tyrant of Old!"

The air shimmered, and parted. For an instant Lucifer had a glimpse of the Pit, then Ekalon stepped through the thin veil that separated the world of men from that of the Malik and stood before him upon the chamber's floor, which stretched away into the vast distance like a sea of glass. A breath of sulfurous fumes wafted in from the other side as the rift sealed and vanished. He recoiled at the grim reminder.

"You sent for me, Master?" Ekalon briefly bowed before the powerful cherub.

"You're here, aren't you?" He had little patience with the obvious. "Report."

Eyes wide and unblinking, Ekalon set the end of his battle staff upon the glass floor with a soft clack and gripped it with both hands. "The human is not easy to get at. Too much protection." Ekalon frowned.

"What went wrong?"

"Noah is accompanied by a Guardian and an ophannin. The Tyrant has put a strong hedge around that one. He reminds me of Enoch."

"Enoch?" Lucifer shot a withering scowl at the warrior. "Never speak that name in my presence!" The chill of despair deepened within his chest. He tried to sweep aside the thought of the human dwelling in the Tyrant's love-glow, but the ache remained. Noah walked with The Tyrant as Enoch had. The thought came unbidden, and he forced it aside.

Ekalon remained stoic. "From what Noah preaches, less than ten years is left as these creatures reckon time. But do we believe it? Or is this a ploy?"

Do we? Lucifer pursed his lips, considering. "I've learned that the Three do not use ploys or other deceptive ways. If The Tyrant has set a time, then we have to believe it is so. That is His weakness—His predictability. We need to find a way to Noah."

"The island is under Rhone's rule, and Rhone has been

marked for the Tyrant's service, Master. I cannot touch him. His Guardian remains near him always."

"Excuses!" Anger swelled, and he drew in an impatient breath. "Why is Rhone so unlike all those other believers I can reach? I've brought a claim on him to the Throne room, but the Tyrant refuses to open the man to me." He forced his anger aside, not wanting Ekalon to see the cracks forming in his veneer of self-control. "But I no longer grovel at the Tyrant's feet." He drew a thin smile across his face. "Rhone is unimportant now. It is Noah who must be stopped. We cannot allow him to complete the ark."

"The Guardian and the ophannin are with him always."

"You think only in terms of strength. There are other ways to reach a man. What is it Noah thinks about?"

Ekalon shrugged. "The commission. Atlan. His family. His wife."

"Wife?" He brightened. "Hum."

"I wouldn't count on finding anything there, Master. Their love is strong, and her Guardian never leaves her side."

Lucifer frowned. "There is always some chink in a man's life; some weakness that hasn't been explored. I want you to find that flaw. Search out what worries him. What intrigues him. What angers him." He curled a fist, blue lightning sparking from his clenched fingers. "Find it, Ekalon, then bring it here to me. I must distract Noah, and we haven't much time left."

"I will find the chink, Master."

"Soon," Lucifer shot back.

"In that case, I could use the help of one of Prince Abaddon's Seekers."

"Chose whichever one you want."

Ekalon bowed and stepped backward into the smoldering rift. As the rift wavered into nothingness, Lucifer summoned the Lodath of the Oracle to come at once.

❦

His long blue robes flowing, Herc, the Lodath of the Oracle, strode across the crystal sea and halted before him, going at once to one knee and bowing his head. The tall golden collar caught the sunlight and blazed about the huge head.

"You summoned me, my Lord?"

"Rise." At least in Herc there was none of the resistance to his authority he had clearly sensed in Ekalon. Here was a servant who understood his place. And although the office of Lodath was no longer a necessity now that Lucifer had taken up residence in his Temple, in his world, the Lodath was still useful. A god sometimes required an advocate to the people. Even the Tyrant of Old raised up advocates.

The giant stood. So unlike his predecessor, Herc was eager to serve. Sol-Ra-Luce had been a conniver who, like Ekalon, seemed to resist him. Sol-Ra-Luce had failed him and paid the price. Herc, however, had served him well for five hundred years. But then, Herc wasn't human.

"The time will soon come to off-world my children to Oric."

Herc nodded. "The sanctuary is not yet completed."

"What is the delay?"

"The Bleak Season lasts most of the Orician year. Temperatures become too frigid for even the children to tolerate. Jumpers freeze up, their power reactors drain unless kept running. That is impractical." His deep rumbling voice filled the expanse of the chamber.

"I want the pace picked up, Herc. I want to begin off-worlding as soon as possible."

"I will increase the workers."

"We need an overseer who will drive them, yet keep them … entertained. One who understands the needs of my children."

Herc smiled. "The commander of the breeding dens, perhaps? He is skilled in tending your children. He knows what they like, and he is easily controlled."

Lucifer smiled. "Your brothers have made him a useful tool, even for a human. Very well. Send Captain Major Bar'ack to Oric with orders that he is to see that the work on the sanctuary is completed within five years."

Herc nodded. "Yes, my Lord."

He dismissed the Lodath with a wave of a hand and the giant left.

Would the Tyrant really go through with it? Anger surged back. He would! "He'll destroy all I've worked to create. He has withdrawn His love from me and has placed it all on these weak, fallen creatures whose lives are but a breath of wind across this miserable stone. Yet He would destroy them all to get at me."

He strode to the clear crystal window that encircled the Temple's four sloping walls, and stared out at the ceremonial complex, coming awake in the blazing light of a new day. "My world!" His voice boomed in the empty chamber. "I won it according to Your rules, and I won't give it back!"

He held his hands in the sunlight streaming through the long crystal window. The glow of his glory would have once filled this room. Gone now. He puffed out his chest. He was still more beautiful than the others who had cast off their shackles and followed him. And the humans thought him a god.

"They are my people!" He glowered at the brilliant ceiling and shook a fist at heaven. "I won't give them back."

It infuriated him that even in his world, he still had to grovel at the Tyrant's throne for permission to rule as he saw fit. All that would change once his plan was complete.

He strode to his throne and sat, looking out over the sea of glass, pondering the situation. Now he knew where to point his efforts. He'd watched these fleshly creatures for over a millennium, closing in on his target as each clue became more clear, finally narrowing it down to one.

Noah! The tool the Tyrant would use.

In some way, not yet clear, the Tyrant was planning a new beginning. "All I have to do is get to Noah, to the blood from which his humanness springs, and I will have won!" Planting Malik seed in the generations of man would ensure there'd be no true human left to birth the Kinsman Redeemer, and the prophesy would fail. "I win by default."

Some of the heaviness lifted from his shoulders. He was well on his way to that goal. His servants had already mingled their blood with human blood. Soon there would not be one human left untainted. His brows plunged in a scowl. Less than ten years remained. Not a moment to lose! He needed to protect his Earth-Born ... just in case something went wrong.

12

Prince of the Pit

Once unbound by the realm of man, Ekalon drifted down into the Pit where the powerful seraph, Abaddon, oversaw the Seekers—pernicious sprites who haunted men's souls with memories from their former lives. The Seeker's sharp eyes missed nothing, and they delighted in parading lost souls to the very edge of the Pit and forcing them to peer across the Gulf, at Adam's Bosom, at what they had missed.

He continued downward; vaporous clouds of sulfur thickened, swirling about him. Controlling his revulsion, Ekalon descended into that place where not even the tormented damned were held. He cringed as a thought entered his head. If Lord Lucifer were to lose this battle with the Tyrant of Old, this gloomy place would become his prison, along with many others of his kind, forever. He shuddered and once again regretted having chosen to follow Lord Lucifer, but it was too late to go back. His fate had been set at the Tyrant's judgment.

He put aside the bitter feelings. His future—his survival—depended upon Lord Lucifer winning this eternal struggle.

"What brings a Messenger-warrior to my abode?" Abaddon's voice boomed from out of the depths. It held an edge of derision, and a moment later the Prince of the Abyss rose up from the Pit, trailing spiraling yellowish tendrils of sulfurous gas, his sharp features half in shadows, half reflecting a reddish glow from the molten rock.

The two circled in the midst of the vapors and heat rising up from tongues of blue flame below. Ekalon kept a tight grip on the battle staff and met the Ruler of the Pit's challenging stare. "I've come from the Master." He maintained eye contact. Prince Abaddon respected power, and in this realm, he was the Principal Malik who answered directly to Lord Lucifer himself.

"What errand of the Master's brings you here?" Abaddon's savage mien didn't relent, but uncertainty had crept into the ruler's voice.

"I've been given a task, and I need a Seeker to assist me, Prince Abaddon."

The ruler of the Pit looked interested. "What service can a Seeker do you?"

"I'm probing for a chink in the soul of a human who has the Tyrant's protection." Ekalon would have grinned, if such an expression wasn't so extremely difficult anymore. There had been a time....

"What wounds do you intend to prod?"

"I haven't decided. Pride seems inappropriate. Although the Tyrant honors him, he never flaunts it."

"His baser side, then? Repressed sexual fantasies?"

Ekalon considered the suggestion as they slowly circled above the Pit. "I've been watching the human for a long time, and have not seen this in him either."

"Greed then!" Abaddon said it as if it were the universal pitfall of all humans, and again Ekalon shook his head.

"He has access to the wealth of a nation. He has all he could possibly want."

"Fool! Those are precisely the ones who are most susceptible! Greed comes in many denominations. Wealth is only one.

Consider power and prestige!" Abaddon snarled. Snarls were easy, and Ekalon gave him one back in return.

"I don't think so. He's the destined heir to the world of humans if he isn't stopped."

Abaddon frowned, his eyes narrowing in a thoughtful scowl. "You say he has the Tyrant's protection?"

Ekalon nodded. "And a powerful Kinsman named Rhone." He recalled the time he had tried to mark Rhone for his Master's service, back when Rhone had taken his Master's pledge pendant. But Sari'el had interfered.

"I know where his wound lies." Abaddon actually managed a grin of sorts; the reddish light played along his thick lips.

"How can you?" Ekalon settled his battle staff in the crook of his arm.

"Because they all suffer from it."

"From what?" He was impatient to be away from here, and Abaddon's theatrics were only dragging it out.

"Past sins. They just can't let go of them." The words hissed through his still-grinning lips.

"Past sins? Hum." Maybe the Terror of the Underworld had a point. Quickly, Ekalon refined the idea. "Guilt. That just might be the chink I'm looking for."

"Org!" Abaddon's summons rumbled upwards to where the Seekers were busily tormenting lost souls, and a streak of black shot downward.

The many-eyed Seeker drew up and hovered between them, the row of small eyes peering at Abaddon and Ekalon. "I am here."

Abaddon redonned the truculent mantle he'd worn when Ekalon first arrived and snarled at the sprite. "You will accompany this warrior. He has need of your special talents."

Org nodded without comment, but his face seemed to brighten a bit at the prospect. Ekalon couldn't fault the little sprite for wanting away from the dark chasm too.

"Send the Seeker back when you're done with him." His lips curled and blood-colored light glinted along his long fangs. Abaddon sank sullenly back into the stinging vapors, and Ekalon wasted no time in leaving.

Once away from the fearsome abyss, he gave a great sigh of relief. With Org tagging along, he passed from the world of torment and almost immediately stood in the presence of Noah's Guardian.

"You don't know when to quit, do you?" Pher'el leveled his gold and ivory staff in warning.

Dressed in black trousers, tall boots, and a pale blue jerkin, Pher'el was a force to be reckoned with—all the Tyrant's Guardians were. Ekalon had tangled with the Guardians before … and each time he had ended up trapped beneath golden nets.

"What's that you have brought with you? A Seeker?" The Guardian shook his head, his mouth taking a twist of disgust.

Lord Lucifer had said this didn't have to be a contest of strength. What was needed was deception, and of that, Ekalon was the master. "Have the rules changed?" He spat the words out in his most menacing tone.

"The Elect One doesn't change the rules." Pher'el lowered the battle staff and smiled.

How he hated it when Pher'el smiled like that. Try as he might, he could never return the gesture. A faint, struggling grin maybe. A sneer certainly. But the pure joy of a smile was forever beyond his reach. That ability had curiously vanished when he'd crossed the line Lord Lucifer had scratched across the crystal sea of the Tyrant's throne room. He had made his choice and had willingly removed the Tyrant's name from his own. At that instant the contest between Lord Lucifer and the Tyrant had been set into motion. It was understood that the victor would eventually rule over all the Stones of Fire, and all the humans who inhabited them.

"The rules are still the same, Ekalon. You cannot touch Master Noah. He's been marked for Elohim."

Ekalon flinched at the mention of the Tyrant's name, while Org let out a soft moan and shot back a goodly distance from Pher'el.

"You may still tempt him in ways that are common for man."

Ekalon snarled at Pher'el's loathsome smile. "Out of my way, shackled one!"

Pher'el stepped aside and swept an arm toward the human striding across the red paving stones of Hodin's Keep, leaving the Sanctuary of Justice, his footsteps directed at the massive, ornate bronze gate that opened onto Atla Fair View.

Pher'el's confidence was a constant irritation! Ekalon looked around for Org, his scowl darkening at discovering the little Seeker a few spans away, still trembling. "Get over here!"

The sprite shot to his side, warily eyeing Pher'el.

"He isn't going to hurt you, and you'd better get used to hearing the Tyrant's name. Guardians like to bandy it about to annoy us." He cast Pher'el a burning glare, then pointed his dark battle staff at the human. "Find the darts that make him bleed."

The Seeker focused several of his eyes at Ekalon, and a couple more at Pher'el, who eased into an obnoxiously relaxed stance. With a look of caution, tempered by sudden glee, Org glided down toward the man about to exit the gates.

Captain Major Bar'ack's feet slammed the stone floor with angry steps, the sound of them echoing along the long hallway that cut through the upper floor of the Government House.

He's taken too many liberties with us, the voice inside his head growled. *We won't let him get away with this one!* the other groused. Per and Hepha were enraged … again. And shouting … again. Those two never shut up! It was enough to drive a man mad. Bar'ack tried to tune out the jumble of words.

The guards who stood before the Lodath's chamber saw him coming and hastily threw the lever that opened the doors, then leaped aside. The Captain Major of the Oracle's Neph army, and overseer of Neph breeding dens, slammed the sluggish doors apart and stormed through them.

The chamber, as always, appeared larger inside than one might imagine from the size of the building. Its walls were draped in exquisite tapestries and its tall windows overlooked the distant Temple complex. The soaring ceiling held a series of octagonal crystal lenses, each gathering outside light and filling the room with it. There had once been moonglass among the crystals, to add light after the sun went down, but it had long ago been replaced with modern fixtures.

Bar'ack had been in this room so many times before, he hardly noticed now the plaques of pulsating stones lining the walls; their rhythm synchronized to the crystal cap atop the Oracle's Temple. Some claimed the stones matched the god's own heartbeat. Bar'ack had never been interested enough to investigate whether or not it was true. And right now he was too angry to think about much of anything except the Neph sitting across the chamber, wearing a smug smile, resplendent in his dark-blue cloak and tall golden collar.

From his throne atop the raised dais, Herc's dark eyes, set deep in his broad forehead, watched Bar'ack stride across the polished floor. Bar'ack made no attempt to hide the anger in his lowered shoulders and bunched knuckles, or his scowl.

"What brings you to my chambers, Captain Major?" The Lodath grinned, mock innocence rumbling up from his chest as if from the bottom of a deep tunnel.

To most men, the Lodath of the Oracle was an intimidating being: Neph-Born and a full head taller than even the tallest Hodinite, Herc had once been a powerful warrior, before something happened to change him. But that "something" had taken place in the Oracle's realm, beyond the sight of man. And if Hepha, Pose, or Per understood any of it, they weren't telling Bar'ack—though they badgered incessantly inside his head about everything else!

Herc had been instrumental in King Irad's assassination, and then with the assassinations of Irad's heir apparents, Mahujael and Thusael. In only a few years after wresting the role of Lodath from its former holder, Sol-Ra-Luce, Herc had become the second most powerful being in the Known World, taking orders only from the Oracle himself.

Half human and half Malik, the giant that now sat before him was considered by most inhabitants of Nod City—and the Known World—to be a god. But Bar'ack had known Herc in the early years, when he'd been nothing but an arrogant, undisciplined bully. Not much had changed in the five hundred years since, except that the Neph had become more skillful at hiding it.

Bar'ack was one of the few humans left who had direct access to the Lodath, and one of an even rarer breed of men who did not fear the giant. Although the aging Neph was still more powerful than any human, Bar'ack's prowess was even greater. His body was home to the spirits of three Nephs—three invading spirits who neither aged nor weakened over time. He grimaced. Nor did they ever shut up!

Stopping before the Lodath, he crossed his arms in front of his chest with a belligerence that would put other men's necks on the block. They were alone, except for Herc's courtier hovering quietly in the shadows. Bar'ack dispensed with formalities. He had stopped bowing to any man—or god—years ago. Only the Oracle himself received a token of respect, and only because in the Oracle's presence, the spirits inside him cringed, and their voices went silent.

"Why have you taken the garrison from us! And the breeding dens?"

Herc extended a long finger, its polished blue nail pointing at Bar'ack's heart. "I should answer to you now?" He laughed. "Your insolence never ceases to amaze me, Captain Major Bar'ack."

He speared the Lodath with a fiery scowl. "Why, Herc? Why this disgrace?"

"Herc, is it? What happened to Your Eminence? My Lodath?"

"Have our garrisons not grown strong throughout the Known World? Is there any army that can challenge our warriors? Have not the breeding dens brought in the strongest, loveliest human females for the Oracle's emissaries and ruling Nephs? Are not the Nephs growing in numbers as the Oracle commanded; spreading into every corner of the Known World, and beyond? Has no square span of this miserable little stone not been touched by the Neph seed?"

Herc leaned back into the thick cushions of the throne perched upon a raised dais that came almost to Bar'ack's knees. "All that you say is true."

"Then we want to know why!" The voices burst from his throat; Per, Hepha, and Pose, demanding together.

"I don't have to defend my commands to you," Herc snarled. "And I don't have to put up with this insubordination! One word from me and a double fist of guards will be upon you in a moment to teach you the meaning of proper respect for the Lodath of the Oracle."

A trio of voices laughed from Bar'ack's throat. "If you think you can summon them before we wrench your spirit from that body, then try it, Herc." Bar'ack felt his hand move toward the fistproj at his side.

"Your threat is empty," Herc said with a dismissive wave of one hand, but Bar'ack noted how the other hand moved slowly toward a slit nearly hidden in the side of the throne. "Besides, you'll lose that pleasant home of yours, too, I promise."

"We can always find another," Hepha said. "As you will have to do."

Herc leaned forward. "If I do have to find one, you can be sure it won't be the son of a lowly Webweaver. I like power too much."

Bar'ack gave a sudden shout of rage and pain, and his chest burned as if it had been ripped open from gut to gullet. From inside him, the three spirits burst free of their abode and stood before Herc: emaciated, feeble, stick-figure wisps of black smoke.

With a groan, Bar'ack collapsed, convulsing on the floor and coiling into a ball; his joints all wrenched out of place, the mighty strength that masked the mounting years was gone. He lay there like an old man—older than his five-hundred-sixty years.

Wavering like the fragile ghost of a snuffed candle, Pose shook a gnarled finger at Herc. "We've served you well. This disgrace will not be tolerated."

"Disgrace?" Herc laughed.

Hardly able to catch his breath, Bar'ack rolled to his side and stared up from the floor as the Lodath looked the three disembodied spirits up and down with contempt. "You stand before me naked, and you worry about disgrace?" He laughed again.

Pose flickered in and out of view, as if unable to cling fully to the realm of man. "Look close at us, Herc, and consider well your next action. Today you are clothed in flesh, but someday you, too, will stand naked before Lord Lucifer as we have. You can't hurt us any more than we already have been hurt." Pose glanced down at Bar'ack. "That thing on the floor is nothing but a shell where a broken spirit cowers. Look at us well, Herc. You, me, Hepha, Per; we are of mixed blood. We are all destined to wander in search of tents of flesh to dwell in. It is the fate of all Neph-Born."

"So enjoy the flesh while it is still yours!" Per's smoky form faded in and out, threatening to dissipate altogether. Bar'ack forced his eyes to focus on the vaporous being.

"Enjoy it? I intend to." Herc cast a sultry glance at the young man waiting in the background.

Bar'ack struggled to get an arm under him and weakly pushed himself up, his back against a stone pillar. Every muscle ached, but thankfully the voices in his head had been extinguished. While the spirits argued with Herc, he relished the silence. How many years had it been since he could even hear his own thoughts? He'd forgotten.

He drew in a tight breath. His brain, unhooked from the disembodied parasites, cleared slightly, as it had in the Temple. Through the mist of repressed memories, a face swam toward him, murky with time. Sarsee? And beside her, hands roughened by working the weaving machines, stood Ker'ack. "Father? Mother?" he breathed.

The quarreling spirits ceased their rampaging and looked at him.

He tried to hold onto the memory as it faded back into the mists of yesterday, blurring in the prickly stinging of his eyes.

"Mother, Father," he moaned, vaguely recalling another face as well. "Master Rhone?" He began to weep.

Per drifted over and glared down at him, his twisted form swaying like a withered leaf. "Memories can be worse than the voices, you miserable tent. Heh?"

The spirits laughed and turned back to Herc. "See what you have to look forward to, what we all have to face once we shed the human flesh?"

"Don't lecture me, Per. I know full well what awaits me, and I intend to put it off as long as I can. Not only for me, but for all Neph-Born. That is why Lord Lucifer has ordered your removal."

The three frail spirits stopped swaying.

"Removal?" Hepha collapsed in slow motion to his knees, and sat upon the floor, his vaporous form spreading out. "What have we done to anger Lord Lucifer?"

"I thought the Master was pleased with our service." Per backed away from Bar'ack.

"He is," the Lodath replied grudgingly.

"Then why this disgrace?" Hepha pleaded weakly.

Through his tears, Bar'ack saw Herc's slow smile widen and his deep eyes glint in the light of the crystal ceiling. "When is a promotion a disgrace?"

"Promotion?" They looked at each other.

"I doubt any of you are deserving of it."

Bar'ack shut his eyes and had a glimpse of a roaring campfire with people sitting around it, singing songs, offering praises to the Creator. He couldn't remember the details, or when the memory had been placed into his brain.

... the serpent's head will rise no more, rise no more, rise no more ...

Past the lyrical refrain, he heard the Lodath say, "... need of your skills on Oric. The Oracle believes his Neph children are in grave danger. We must ready a safe haven for them. Plans are already being made, but progress is too slow. Lord Lucifer wants a taskmaster to see that the Sanctuary is completed in time." Herc paused, then with a sneer in his voice added, "We don't want to disenspirit any more Nephs than we must, do we? Now back to your home!"

Bar'ack heaved in a sudden gasp. His joints tightened and his chest swelled with renewed strength. The words of the old song vanished, and his eyes snapped open. In a leap, he was back on his feet and standing before the Lodath.

"There is a transport being readied for you as we speak. You will transfer your garrison duties to Tareh, and the breeding dens to Maglish. You will be off-worlded to Oric as soon as the sorphim are ready."

Memories evaporating, Bar'ack gave a low growl. "Oric? What's on that miserable stone?"

"Not much. Yet. I expect you to change all of that. Eventually the Oracle intends to house ten million Nephs on that miserable stone. So make it feel like home. They'll need housing, food," he paused, smiling, "and entertainment. Your previous duties in the breeding dens will have well equipped you to handle that, Captain Major Bar'ack."

The voices inside him said, "We will be ready to leave when the Oracle needs us."

The Lodath of the Oracle dismissed Bar'ack with a wave of one hand, and with the other summoned his courtier: a handsome young male Neph who had stood discretely in the corner the whole time. The man stopped behind Herc and began gently kneading the giant's shoulders. Herc leaned back, a smile growing across his face.

As Bar'ack strode toward the doors opening slowly before him, he knew there was something he had forgotten, something important, he was sure. He tried dredging the depths of his memories for it, but the voices inside his head returned, those taunting, quarrelsome voices again! He ground his teeth and bunched his fists, digging fingernails into his palms as he left the chamber.

13

The Ark

Streamers strewn from the scaffolding overarching the ark fluttered in the breeze as if they, too, wanted to dance to the gay music that filled the valley. Once the lumber and barrels and crates had been rearranged, the third deck made a stunning stage for the wedding party. More than two hundred people gathered in one corner, clapping and stomping their feet in beat to the traditional Jelim being performed upon a sprawling section of unfinished decking.

Noah's grin widened as he watched the dancers. Japheth and his brothers, and a double fist of other men, young and old, friends and relations, stomped and whirled to the sounds of drums and pipes. A long, shimmering red ribbon, woven from the finest Kleiman silk, fluttered as it was passed among them, swept along, and finally in a clever arrangement of passes, completely engulfed Japheth who staggered and tumbled backward and was caught in a web of arms and laid upon the floor.

The crowd applauded while Desmorah, dressed in an exquisitely embroidered wedding dress, bedecked with bright blue and white flowers, went to her husband and unwrapped the red ribbon. Once it was unbound, she slid the wide ribbon over her shoulders and draped the long ends over his and kissed him.

Again the roar of revelry rose up between the soaring walls of the ark. The completion of the Jelim was a signal, and men and women swarmed in. The musicians changed tunes, the music picked up, and the dancers whirled around the newlyweds, still symbolically bound by the red ribbon.

Noah glanced about for Naamah. He wanted to whirl her around the dance floor too. Ah, but she was chatting with Leenah and Aunt Cerah over by the long table draped in garlands of flowers and overflowing with platters of food.

He smiled. "Later." Then he eyed the row of barrels brought up from his cellars. Frowning at his empty cup, he started off. The deck seemed to pitch underfoot. He caught himself and giggled softly. "Whoa. We aren't afloat yet."

The music stopped in midtune. Noah turned back. The guests had gone rigid, some clinging to each other. The deck shook again, and this time Noah knew it had nothing to do with the four or five flagons of wine he'd consumed since the party had begun.

Then everything went still, except for the squalls of birds darkening the sky. After a moment a few nervous laughs led to a few more, and slowly the music resumed, hesitantly at first. Soon the party was in full swing again.

"I don't like this." Rhone's deep voice turned him around. The tall ruler of Atlan wore a splendid gray robe, trimmed in dark red. Upon his chest was a small crest of the House of Khore, and about his waist a leather belt and a long Makir sword. High Councilor Rhone wore it only ceremonially. His days as Pyir of the Makir were long past.

"They keep coming—more and more frequently." Although Noah could not see over the walls that soared upward, waiting for the roof to finish them off, he nodded in the direction of the cottage that had served as construction headquarters all these years. "Our work shack has become unsafe. So many shakings have loosened the roof beams."

Rhone looked grave. "Some of the buildings in Atla Fair have developed cracks. Hodin's Keep is showing the strains. The Deep Chambers beneath the Keep have flooded to the third level."

He raised his eyebrows at Rhone. "I hope you removed the prisoners first."

Rhone laughed, but his eyes remained worried. "Since the days of Zorin, the Deep Chambers haven't had many guests."

Zorin. Noah had heard tales of the tyrant, Rhone's twin brother, but he'd been too young to know anything of the matter firsthand. Still, the name sent a cold shiver up his back. He glanced at the cup in Rhone's hand. "You like the vintage?"

"Excellent, as usual."

They started toward the casks. "We can thank Wend for this. If it was up to me, we'd be churning out vinegar."

"Wend manages the vineyard well. That's as it should be. You have other things to see to, Noah. More important things."

He frowned at being reminded and looked around at the hundreds of guests who swarmed the ark's unfinished deck. He sighed. "Sometimes I think this might be a curse." He filled their cups and stared at the bright red wine in his glass. "Without friends like them and like you, Rhone, how will life have meaning?"

"It will only be for a season. Soon your children will have children, and their children will have children, and in a hundred years, your life will overflow with friends."

But in what sort of world? What waited on the other side? It didn't seem so simple to him. "You accept what is to befall mankind so easily."

Rhone smiled. "You forget, I've already died once at the hands of Nephs. How much worse can this time around be?"

"This time there will be no Gardener to resurrect you, Rhone."

"This time I won't need it. Nor will I desire it."

His acceptance of the inevitable was to be admired. Perhaps it was the Makir in him—the Katrahs and Kimahs that had honed his mind and body. "And you are right, of course. We are told that Adam's Bosom is a glorious place. Just the same, I'll miss you, old friend."

Rhone saluted him with his cup. "Only for a season."

Noah watched the lines of dancing people, friends and family huddled in amiable conversation. Laughter and music vibrated along the heavy timber decking. Young boys bravely climbed crates to peer over the ark's towering walls at the ground far below, while little girls whirled their skirts out wide and danced to a music all their own.

"Your relatives have traveled long and far to come to this celebration. You should be savoring their company, not burdening your soul with the future, my friend."

"Again, you're right, Rhone."

Thore was encircled with female company near the big door in the ark's side, half his attention upon them, the other half watching everything else.

Wend and Sebe seemed to be enjoying themselves. He was encouraged by that. A rift had grown between him and these two dear children, and the vineyard sat right in the middle of it.

Shem was enduring the attentions of a pretty, twelve-year-old cousin from Morg'Seth named Kitah, who had developed an obvious crush on him. Noah smiled. Shem had caught Kitah's eye the day she arrived from the Lee-lands with Noah's mother and father, Grandfather Methuselah, and several aunts, uncles, and other cousins.

Methuselah sat in a circle with five men and two women in earnest conversation.

Noah's daughters seemed to be enjoying the wedding most of all. Each had a young man by the arm—Sheflah had two. Their turns to untie the red ribbon would come soon enough. The

Creator's timetable was rushing the inevitable. Only seven years left. He must be about the business of finding husbands for them.

He didn't immediately spot Mitah. He'd seen her earlier on the dance floor with Aaros, a young ship's captain from Atla Fair. As he looked for her among the crowd, he spied Ham in the midst of six men, including his father-in-law, Uncle Kenoch, coming toward him and Rhone.

"Father. High Councilor." Ham bowed respectfully in Rhone's direction and introduced his following. All but Uncle Kenoch were eager to meet the famous ruler of Atlan. Uncle Kenoch and Rhone had known each other since before Noah's birth.

Merc'ik, a thin, white-haired fellow maybe a hundred years younger than the patriarch, Methuselah, said he remembered Amolikah telling of their adventure in the Garden.

Barchor, a bit younger than Noah and thicker even around the middle, scoffed, "Legends tend to expand to fit the ears listening."

Kenoch and Rhone exchanged glances. Rhone merely nodded, a small smile upon his lips, a sparkle in his eyes. Not everyone believed the story of their flight to Eden, and it was apparent Rhone cared little if they didn't. Uncle Kenoch, too, knew the truth, but didn't challenge Cousin Barchor.

Since they were near the casks, Eleoc, Merc'ik, Krinok, and Uncle Kenoch grabbed up flagons and filled them. Orelin wasn't partaking of the fruit of the vine. Barchor, already clutching a silver cup, topped his off and took a long drink. "This is quite a building, Noah." His view traveled down the long length of it. "Your boy was telling us about it."

"Ham's cleverness shows all throughout this," Noah replied.

"He inherited that from his Grandmother Cerah." Uncle Kenoch sent a wink Ham's way.

"Must have cost a fortune to build." Barchor didn't try to hide his disapproval.

"Not to mention a fortune in time," Eleoc noted.

"Very impressive." Orelin lifted his view up the soaring sides of the ark that poked at the clear pinkish-blue sky. "But what do you hope to do with such a thing?"

Sometimes Noah got tired of repeating himself. They all knew what he and his father and Grandfather Methuselah had been preaching for the last 114 years. Some believed while others refused. He had long ago given up on leading the gerups to the trough and trying to force them to drink. Patience. He smiled. "I can always rent it out as a barn."

They laughed.

Barchor rolled his eyes. "Noah, anyone ever tell you you're a shaved gleck light of a full roll?" He said it with a laugh, and not unfriendly, but it stung just the same.

"Many times." Noah forced a smile and took a quick gulp of wine. *Let them think what they want.*

Ham said, "I was going to give them the tour, but thought you should be the one to do it."

"Quite impressive," Orelin repeated as though unable to come up with any better descriptor.

"What is that? A chimney?" Barchor pointed to the square shaft that rose up from the floor as tall as the sides that stabbed at the bright blue sky.

"I'll show you." He started along the deck with his entourage in tow. Rhone came along too. Rhone had not seen the ark since the hull had been completed, nearly half a year earlier. He noted Thore becoming alert, and Rhone's subtle nod to his son, and grinned. It was either father or son. Between the two of them, he was never alone. Thore nodded back and returned his gaze upon the ladies.

The hot sun shone down on piles of lumber and crates of bolts and nails, wooden pegs, and barrels of pitch. All along the way, corrals, partially built, stood as rows of fencing. As the music and the sounds of dancing diminished in the distance, the chimney shaft Barchor had pointed out grew wider and taller.

"A room, Noah?" Uncle Kenoch asked.

"Not a room. But it is roomlike. You might call it a pump," he said. "Or you might call it an engine. I call it a marvel of engineering. It's designed to ease the pressures on the keel to prevent it from snapping in two. The idea isn't mine, or Ham's. It was given to us by the Creator."

"Bah!" Cousin Barchor glanced at the others for support, but they seemed not so quick to jump to conclusions.

Noah ignored him. "Once we understood the principle involved, Ham took the design and turned it into a marvelous piece of machinery." He saw the smile upon his son's face. Turning, he went on speaking, walking backwards. "What's more, there is hardly a moving part in the whole machine."

"You can't have a machine with no moving parts," Barchor said emphatically.

"Can't you?" He rotated back around on his heal and nearly lost his balance. The crimson fluid in his flagon sloshed dangerously near the rim. *Getting a little unsteady, aren't we?* He grinned and tried to recall how much wine he'd consumed, but his brain had become a bit foggy.

"Come, come." He waved them on and started up a flight of stairs that spiraled two walls of Barchor's "chimney." In a way, it was a chimney, but no fire would ever blaze in its base. They ascended the stairs until they reached the lip and everyone peered down into it. Thirty spans below, the timbers that held the ark off the ground looked like pier pilings. Bare ground lay only two spans below the bottom of the vessel—just enough height for men to work beneath the hull if need be.

"It's just a hole," Merc'ik declared, as if that wasn't apparent to each man there.

"Exactly." Noah grabbed the edge and peered over.

Barchor scratched his head. "You're building a boat with a hole in the bottom?"

"Where's the machine?" Orelin demanded.

"You're looking at it."

Barchor stared at him and a small grin lifted the corner of his mouth. "Now I'm certain you're a shaved gleck light."

Ham said, "Basic physics says a hull will displace just so much water. A craft this size, fully loaded, will sink to half its height in the water. If you will notice, this hole is framed up solid from the bottom to the top where we're standing. No water can actually enter the vessel. When the roof is finally in place, this opening will pierce it, partially covered by a section of raised windows fifteen spans wide—a skylight—that will run the length of the vessel, opened along its sides."

They peered down the shadowy shaft. Twenty spans to a side, it covered a large amount of deck real estate. "I call it the Deep Pool." Noah laughed. "Once afloat, it will become very deep indeed!"

"So where's the machine?" Orelin's eyes narrowed with impatience.

Noah said, "This is it."

They scowled as though played for fools. He didn't want to give that idea a moment to take root. "You see, my friends," he went on quickly, "as the ark rides the waves, the water inside this shaft will rise and fall."

"Well that's pretty obvious." Barchor glared at him.

Noah noted Rhone growing impatient with the man's arrogance. He wasn't exactly sure upon which limb of the family tree Barchor sat, but he was certain it must have been a goodly distance from the main trunk.

"But what isn't obvious—all the things you don't see, Cousin Barchor—is the ductwork; the vents and diverting flaps. As the water rises up the tube, it acts like a huge cycler piston, expelling foul air from the lower decks, and replacing it with fresh air from the upper deck through a series of ducts and vents. As the water—the 'piston'—falls, it will draw fresh air into the upper decks, mainly where we will be living." He winked at Ham.

Ham grinned. "It is a giant pump to keep the air clean and circulating."

The cleverness seemed lost upon them, though Uncle Kenoch looked impressed and patted Ham on the shoulder a couple times. Noah sighed and led the party back down the steps and away from the Deep Pool, over to a hatchway in the deck. Rhone tagged behind; the ruler of Atlan plainly had no need to stand on center stage. But then, that was Rhone. That was the Makir in him. Always quietly observing, never the center of attention.

Noah shot a long look back at Thore, still standing near the door as though it was a pleasant place to be. Few would suspect his true motive. Makir or not, Thore had become the center of attention, at least for a certain gathering of females. And he seemed to be enjoying it. Noah finished the last of the wine in his goblet and his grin twisted into a frown. He should have stashed an extra cask along the way. He set the cup upon a railing and guided the troupe down a long, wide stairway into the ark's shadowy depths.

"This is amazing." Orelin halted at the foot of the steps and peered into the vast distance, lost in the gloom. "You built this all by yourself, Noah?" His voice bounced about the cavern and lost itself in its depths.

"My sons and I did much of the work." He glanced about at the hundreds of wooden posts and beams, each one sturdily braced and cross-braced. Regularly spaced openings in the low ceiling above their heads spilled shafts of sunlight alive with shimmering motes. A long rectangle of light brightened a section of decking spans behind them. "But we hired out most of the main framing." He gave a short laugh. "It would have taken two hundred years if we'd done the work ourselves."

"How did you afford it?" Barchor's derision was replaced with awe.

It was only after someone got down into the guts of the ark and Master Jerl-eze's complicated construction became apparent, that the magnitude of the project could be appreciated. He cast a secret glance at Rhone. "I had some help." His view sharpened upon Barchor. "Some people actually believe the rantings of this old fool."

In the dim light, he thought the man's cheeks had reddened.

The others silently stared, eyes wide, and not a few jaws slack. "Come, let me show you." He started off, his step a bit uncertain, but then he wasn't the only one. The vineyard had supplied more than enough wine to keep everyone slightly off balance. "This second deck will be the storage area. But it will also house those animals that do not require too much light. I suspect many will end up sleeping a lot, hopefully reducing the maintenance problem."

"Storage for what?" Merc'ik asked.

"Food … mostly. For the animals and for us, even though we'll grow large gardens up above along the skylight."

Ham said, "I've designed a walkway, and beds for the soil. We can raise fresh vegetables, and start seedlings for replanting once we touch ground."

Barchor huffed. "All very impressive, Noah, but how can you seriously believe all this nonsense about a flood, and water falling from the sky?"

Some of his guests chuckled. Rhone, as was his habit, narrowly studied this small slice of humanity.

Noah grinned. "If it doesn't happen, I've built myself a very expensive barn." He could have lectured them more, but what was the point if people still refused to accept what admittedly was a preposterous notion—one that even he, in times of frustration and despair, had misgivings over?

Krinok, who up until now had remained silent, said, "See here, Noah, if you and your family and all the animals of Atlan pack yourself into this boat, and the skies do open up and water should fall from them, and the world is flooded, what will become of us Kinsmen?"

He wanted to tell him all would be spared, but he knew that wasn't to be. He shook his head. "I don't know the answer. We must trust in the Creator for the solution to that."

"Bah. Easy for you to say," Barchor groused. "You'll be snug in your big boat."

Noah raised his eyebrows. "I thought it was all nonsense."

Barchor's eyes grew stormy and he took another drink of wine.

Rhone cleared his throat and pointed at the distant piece of machinery sitting in the shadows. "What is that, Noah?"

He appreciated the High Councilor's timely diversion. "That is a cycler and whirl-mag. So we can have a small amount of magnetic flow. For the energized moonglass, and other conveniences."

"All the comforts of home," Eleoc quipped.

Feeling the tension, he wished he had another flagon of wine to numb the sting of their derision.

"And what is below this deck?" Orelin stomped a foot a couple times upon the heavy planking.

"Nothing really. Come, we can take a look." He led them down a second staircase, holding tight to the railing and watching his step. Very little light filtered down from above. What did reach this lowest level came mostly through the still-unfinished vent-work that Ham had designed.

Merc'ik sniffed the air, turning in a slow circle. "What is that smell?" His voice had lowered a bit, as if the darkness demanded a whispered tone.

"Pitch." Noah matched his volume, his voice losing itself in a vast cavern.

"The inside?" Barchor gave a short laugh. "You pitch the

outside of a boat, Noah, not the inside. Here's a lot of glecks wasted."

Did Cousin Barchor work in a counting room? "Master Jerl-eze said the same thing, Cousin Barchor. But it is what the Creator specified."

Barchor huffed. "Gopher wood and pitch. One thing is certain, this barn will be standing long after we and our children and their children are gone."

Noah blinked a couple times. Barchor didn't realize how true that statement was.

"The ceiling is so low." Orelin reached up and almost touched the timber truss.

"No need for much height down here, Cousin Orelin. This bottom deck will mainly hold stones for ballast, and the manure the animals produce. You can't see it from here, but there are chutes all along the ceiling."

"Whew." Barchor flagged the air in front of his nose. "There is going to be some deep girt down here." He laughed. "The smell will drive you out into your falling water in a week."

"You forget Ham's ventilation system. And also we'll be composting much of it using earthworms. This will solve the—"

Rhone took Noah's arm and put a finger to his lips. He cocked his head, listening. The far-off sounds of music wafted down through the decks, but that was all; yet Rhone had heard something else. The Makir honing was still sharp.

"Someone is down here," he whispered.

Noah stiffened. "No one is supposed to be." He glanced into the deeper gloom. "Which way?"

Rhone pointed, and they quietly moved out, the darkness waxing and waning as weak shafts of daylight found their way through vents and open stairwells. They had not gone far when Rhone stopped and indicated a room that would eventually house the earthworm farm.

Noah heard the telling sounds ... they all did ... and his heart squeezed.

Rhone gave him a sympathetic look.

"Let me go." Noah quietly climbed the three steps to the opening and stepped inside.

Mitah gave a startled cry and grabbed for her clothes. The young man with her scrambled back and stared. Noah recognized him as Aaros.

Overwhelmed with a deep disappointment, he could only whisper, "Leave here at once."

14

Pher'el

His black robe fluttering, Org hovered slowly about Noah's head, keeping his distance, but still testing his limits from time to time. The sprite's myriad eyes hardly missed anything, and Pher'el had been extra vigilant since the little Seeker's arrival.

All the while, Ekalon remained silently aloof, floating a little above them where he could quietly observe. It was unlike the surly warrior to restrain himself so. Lucifer's minion had hardly stirred from his place since the Seeker had showed up, and that made Pher'el uneasy. How long would these two remain? Thankfully unrestrained by temporal limitations, he did not overly concern himself with things like time—except when the Creator's plan was in lockstep with human suntracers, as it was now.

Time was running out. Pher'el knew it, and surely the Deceiver knew it as well.

Pher'el's main job consisted of keeping tormenting spirits at bay, and fighting off the pernicious imps whose task it was to swarm about humans and whisper discouraging words. Although his was a never-ending task, Noah's faith kept him strong; Noah's frequent and heartfelt prayers filled him with spiritual nourishment. Yet, recently Pher'el had detected a growing weariness in Noah's soul, and unfortunately, Org had picked up on it too.

As if testing some theory or another, the little sprite cast out barbs when he thought Pher'el wasn't watching. A few of the heart-wounding darts even managed to reach Noah's ear.

Now, as Noah's daughter stood before him in disgrace, Pher'el soaked in Noah's sadness and disappointment.

Org had felt it as well and the imp suddenly shot away from him and whispered something to Ekalon as several of his eyes cast sly glances back at Noah. The Messenger-warrior lifted an intrigued eyebrow as he looked at Noah. Then Ekalon shook himself from his repose. He cast a gloating look at Pher'el; and at the other Guardians there, his gloat seeming to swell as he stared a moment longer at Sari'el who stood close to Rhone.

Without a word, Ekalon and Org passed through the structure of the ark and disappeared.

Pher'el exchanged glances with his companion Guardians, and saw the same look of concern on each of them. A new evil stirred the continuum of eternity. A cold shiver tickled his neck.

"Those two have brewed up something," Sari'el, Rhone's protector, said.

The Guardians standing watch over each of their wards nodded.

Pher'el tightened his grip upon the gold and ivory battle staff and moved closer as Mitah and Aaros, heads bent low in embarrassment, left the deep bowels of the ark.

What mischief were the emissaries of Lucifer up to now?

He would have to be especially vigilant.

❦

Standing before the massive crystalline windows where the morning sun streamed in, filling the Temple's chamber, Lucifer, bathed in the light, was vaguely annoyed as he stared down at the

Seeker huddled at Ekalon's side. He sneered at the creature then shifted his view to Ekalon. "Have you been successful in your mission?"

Ekalon nodded. "I have discovered where the human, Noah, is weakest."

The presence of the ugly Seeker disturbed him. "Why have you brought that creature with you?"

"He assisted me."

"Do you have further need of him?"

Ekalon shook his head. "None."

"Then away from here! Back to the Pit where Prince Abaddon awaits your return!"

With a mewing whimper, Org tumbled through a rift that had suddenly opened, wailing as he plunged into the sulfurous depths of Abaddon's kingdom. Lucifer gave a thin smile of satisfaction at having the annoyance removed from his presence. The rift sealed itself with a final wisp of smoke and a dying spark. He returned his glare to Ekalon. "Tell me what you have learned."

"The human bears a burden of guilt. It's a growing weight, and he will not let go of it and thinks he can only be rid of it by virtue of his own efforts."

Lucifer laughed. "That is such a human quality. They all believe that, by their own good works, they will somehow pay for their transgressions." His fingers clenched. "But the Tyrant of Old is not so merciful. He expects them to grovel on their knees for forgiveness. I am not so harsh with my subjects."

"It is true, Master," Ekalon said in a flat voice. "Your ways are easier."

"I try." He sensed Ekalon's hesitance and ignored it. Ekalon had made his decision, as had the rest of them. He smiled and spread his arms, letting the sunlight envelop his skin, imagining how it had been in the beginning—how it would be again. Taking on the form of a human endeared him to his worshippers, but he would shed the illusion of this tent without a second thought once it no longer served his purpose.

"Tell me of the human's sin. Was it unfaithfulness? Has he stolen something of great value? Has Noah lusted?" A rush of excitement warmed his neck as he looked back at the Messenger-warrior.

"No, Master. None of these things."

The twinge of disappointment was only momentary. "What is it that lingers in his heart?"

Ekalon's expression didn't change much; a slight twitch of his lips, but Lucifer noted that Ekalon had found humor in whatever wound it was that Noah was nursing. "He has regret over the way-ward ways of his children. A daughter's lust for the flesh has brought disgrace, a son's attachment to this world's riches has brought disappointment."

"He blames himself."

"Yes."

"Good." Lucifer instantly conjured up a number of ploys he might throw against Noah. "I can use this information to lure him from his task. Distracted, he might be prevented from completing it in time."

"Just the same, the Tyrant of Old has placed a hedge around this human. I can't get close to him with his Guardian protecting him. And you … err … you know the restrictions placed upon …" he swallowed hard, "… you." Ekalon's watchful eyes grew wary.

"Do you think I've forgotten!"

Ekalon recoiled. "No, of course not, Master."

"I will not grovel at the Tyrant's throne. This is my world! I rule as it pleases me." A surge of pride burned inside his chest as a sly grin crept across his face. "There are many who will do my bidding. All I need do is lure Noah out of Atlan and keep him from returning. Once away from the protection he enjoys in Atlan, my army will grind all memory of him from off this miserable stone, and with him goes his seed, and with his seed, the Tyrant's plans crumble." Lucifer opened his palm and puffed across it, imagining Noah's powdery dust whirling and sparkling in the sunlight, dissipating into nothingness. "I triumph, and the Tyrant loses. Crush my head, will you?"

He focused on Ekalon. "Guilt is a weapon even the Tyrant can't defeat if Noah refuses to let go of it. Encourage these notions of his, Ekalon. Give them deep soil to take root, and I'll raise up a bitter fruit that will poison him."

※

Naamah had taken Mitah under her wing to comfort her daughter in spite of her own distress at Noah's report. The connection between mother and daughter was something he would never comprehend, and he envied Naamah for it. He glanced at his friends, finding a measure of comfort in Rhone's understanding face. No one had said anything, and he tried not to put words to what might have been their thoughts.

No matter what might be said for Cousin Barchor's cynical opinion of the ark, his eyes were the most understanding of all. Perhaps he had dealt with something similar? Noah knew he had eight—or was it nine?—daughters.

Barchor put a consoling hand upon his shoulder, shook his head, and simply said, "Children," and melted into the crowd along with the others, who also hadn't known what to say. Only Rhone and Uncle Kenoch remained.

He sighed. "The tour was less than spectacular."

Rhone opened his mouth to speak when a commotion grabbed their attention. Noah narrowed his view down the long, unfinished deck at Ham, Shem, and Wend, their strident tones grating in his ears. The argument had caught the attention of their guests.

Wend flung his arm in the air and pointed more or less in the direction of the vineyard. Shem's back went rigid and he wagged an angry finger at him. Noah noted the growing exasperation on Ham's face as he uncrossed his arms and planted his fists stubbornly upon his hips.

Noah slapped a hand to his forehead. "What now? Those boys can't go five minutes without something coming up." He rushed to stomp out whatever fire had just sparked to life. Thore watched them from the ark's door, but this was obviously a family matter, and he kept his post among his female admirers.

"Boys, boys, what is going on here?" Shem and Wend were near to blows when Noah stepped between them.

Wend backed off and shoved his fingers through his dark brown hair. "Nothing. Nothing at all." He turned to leave, ran into Rhone's chest, looked up into the tall Makir's aged face, and backed off.

"High Councilor Rhone." Wend gulped. "I'm sorry."

Rhone nodded. "War should be waged among enemies, not brothers, Master Wend."

Noah said, "What's it about this time, Wend? Shem?"

The boys went mum.

He stared at Ham whose arms were still crossed. "Will you tell me?"

Ham's lips tightened, and in frustration he grabbed and pulled at his tight black curls. "The usual, Father. Wend was complaining how we never help around the vineyard, and Shem ..." Ham gave a lopsided grin. "Well, Shem's like you and Grandfather. He began preaching to him."

Wend's eyes burned with fury. "I'm running the business by myself, hiring workers, paying them out of my share, while my brothers spend their days working on this thing!" He drove a heel into the deck. "I don't need to be warned what the Creator thinks of me." He scowled at Shem. "As if he has an ear to the Almighty's throne room." His glare narrowed at Noah. "And you're no better than they are, Father."

Wend strode toward the big doorway in the ark's side and stomped past Thore without a glance. His footsteps pounded all the way down the long ramp to the ground.

Noah deflated as he watched Sebe follow her husband off the ark. His guests tried not to appear obvious in their curiosity, but who could not be? He frowned. Japheth and Desmorah stood among the guests, looking concerned.

Rhone took Noah's arm and started him back. "Passion burns within that one."

"But for what, Rhone? For something he cannot keep?"

"Wend doesn't see it that way."

"Have I raised him so differently from the others? And Mitah? What goes on inside their heads?"

"Youth rarely grasps the importance of the future, Noah. It stretches too far out ahead of them to be of concern, unlike the here and now."

"The future is not so far off anymore." The encounter had emptied him, had dulled his heart for what should have been a day of festive celebration. As he started back to join his guests, Japheth and Desmorah met him.

"What was that about, Father?" His son Japheth's pale-green eyes shifted searchingly, his voice thickened by worry.

Desmorah took her husband's arm, her deep-blue eyes fixed upon Noah, her skin fair and bright and lively in the sunlight and blue sky. The fragrance of skylilies wafted from her flower-strewn wedding dress.

Noah shook his head. "You know how Wend feels about all this." He looked at the great walls, the living quarters still under construction, the rows of pens, feeding troughs, and chutes. So much work had gone into it, but if he lost his children over this, was it really worth it? How could the Creator demand so much from him?

"Should I go talk with him?" Japheth offered.

"No, not now, Japheth. Give his blood time to cool."

"Maybe he'll come back."

"Maybe," but Noah didn't think so. He felt old and tired, and as he stood there, only remotely aware of the joyful music, he imagined a small voice accusing him of failing his family, of putting too much faith in the Creator's words.

He shook his head, but the accusing voice inside refused to budge.

15

Mementos

*T*his is it. This is where we'll call home for however long the Creator sees fit to keep us here. What do you think?" Noah glanced around the room: stark and hollow, a few crates here and there, a partially open roof. A watertight port hatch to an outside window stood open to let the daylight stream in. "Still needs a few finishing touches of course, but all in all, not bad." He nodded with approval.

"A few finishing touches?" Naamah sighed a tired breath. "It needs finishing, Noah."

He grinned. She saw this work from a different perspective than he. To his eyes, the ark was shaping up nicely in spite of his earlier fears that such a daunting project would never see completion.

With the sheaf of papers clutched to her chest, Naamah looked at crates he'd set about as pretend furniture, then out the window. She gave another sigh, crossed the room, and placed the papers on one of the crates. "It will do, I suppose."

She hadn't even tried to muster enthusiasm for the quarters. Her sadness pulled at his heart. "It will only be for a little while."

She sat on a corner of a wooden box. "That's not it."

He understood the huge burden in her heart. He carried the same millstone. "We'll just have to convince them," he said.

Her green eyes glistened in the sunlight. She patted them with a handkerchief from her pocket. "It's not only the children. It's ... it's everyone. All our friends, our families. Leenah and Rhone, our parents. Sometimes I think my heart is being ripped from my chest."

Like the Oracle's sacrifices, he thought with morbid humor. Only with Naamah and him, the heart kept on beating. He sat beside her, pulling her to his chest, feeling her tremble quietly as she wept.

He should have been there for the children more often. Could he have found more room in his life for Mitah? If he had, would she still be with them, instead of in Atla Fair with Aaros? She'd left three years ago. How time raced by. The day of reckoning was on the horizon ... and his family was in shambles.

Leteah's move to Marin-ee had been an awakening too. Why did he think he could keep them all under his roof until the day arrived? There she was, rubbing shoulders with Nephs and nephlings, and he didn't even know how to find her. And Orah— her speedy wedding and unexpected relocation to Sea Side on the far eastern edge of Atlan with the father of her child had hit him like a falling tree. He shook his head. Orah was definitely following in Mitah's shoes.

What had he done so wrong? How was he ever going to gather the flock back under his and Naamah's wings when the time came?

Naamah sniffed and wiped her eyes, then stared at her hands in her lap. "I'm beginning to put together a library."

He nodded, his thoughts still mired in the tangled lives of his children.

"We will need reference books. I don't want our grandchildren growing up with no connection to their roots."

"I hadn't thought of that."

"We will need vast amounts of knowledge to rebuild." She stood and went to the crate that served as a desk. Organization was Naamah's strong point, and she used it as a balm for her pain. "I've begun making lists."

He smiled. List-making now. Could there be a surer sign that his dear wife was caught in the throes of his commission?

"Once I have this inventory complete, we can begin acquiring the necessary items. You know, Noah, I've been thinking." She turned from the crate, some papers in her hand, her eyes still red, but dry now. "We won't have a healer on"—her voice cracked a little—"on the other side."

So many details. Good thing she was here to help him. Neither he nor Desmorah nor Sebe had the skills. "We need to get one of you trained."

Naamah nodded. "I want to learn. Maybe all three of us should learn."

"We'll hire a tutor."

"Yes. And we should acquire as many scrolls and books on the healing arts as we can find."

"Good." His brain grabbed that problem, thankful to let go of his children for a while. "My mother might know of someone. I'll ask her on my trip to Morg'Seth next month."

She stepped to the window and peered through it. Beyond her shoulder in the distance he watched three behemoths drifting slowly toward the lake. From this angle high up on the third deck, only their small heads atop long, slender necks were visible.

"I'm going with you this time, Noah."

"No. Such a journey is too dangerous. Especially with the Oracle's Terror spreading across the land. I'll only be there long enough to get the Book from Aunt Cerah."

Naamah turned. "She may be your Aunt Cerah, Noah, but

she is my mother. It may be the last time I will ever see her, or my father."

Her eyes gathered moisture again, and his resolve weakened like warm wax. "You know what the Oracle does with the Kinsmen, when he can catch one."

"I know."

"If something should go wrong—"

"My mind is made up. I'm going with you."

Vaul, stretched out on the floor in the sunlight streaming through the window, raised his massive head off his paws and stared at the doorway. A few moments later Desmorah's footsteps tapped to a stop outside it. Naamah looked up and Noah turned.

Desmorah peered over the lip of a wooden box in her arms. "Dishes. I've been saving them for my own home. Where are we putting the long-term items?"

"Middle deck. I'll show you." He glanced at his wife. "We'll both show you." He took Naamah's hand. She gave a wan smile and set the papers aside as they left. Her heart ached as his own did for all that was to come upon this world—upon their lives.

The echo of their footsteps in the vast chamber of the ark's upper deck mixed with the pounding and sawing coming from various directions. Overhead, Shem and Ham hammered nails into the last section of roofing trusses still exposed to the sky. The skylights had been completed and filled the deck with a soft, muted light. Most of this deck contained pens and cages. He'd built their living quarters amid ships, central to where most of their work would take place. Ten compartments in all, five on each side of the Deep Pool—one for each one of his children, and for his and Naamah's parents. These last two were a hopeful gesture, with no confirmation from the Creator that it would be honored.

With Vaul trotting a few paces ahead of them, they started

down one of the several ramps to the middle deck below. Noah took the box from Desmorah. She sighed, gripped the railing, and gave Naamah a womanly look. "Well, it's not going to be this month."

Naamah simply took Desmorah's arm and held her close. The subject had already been talked to death.

Noah grimaced. Desmorah and Japheth had been married five years and still no children. There had to be a good reason the Creator had closed Desmorah's womb. It couldn't be a permanent situation, not if His promises were to remain unbroken. But try telling that to a young, healthy woman who longed to hold and suckle her own child, whose eyes held such longing whenever Sebe and her children came to visit. And Mitah, with two children and another on the way.

They stepped out onto the middle deck. Gaping holes in the ceiling let in plenty of light to see by, yet not enough to raise food crops. All their growing would have to take place above. He had begun to think like a planter again, and it felt good.

They penetrated deeper and deeper into the vessel, past the food storage lockers that someday would be bursting with grain, hay, vegetables, and dried fruits. Finally, near one end of the ark, they reached the bins. Some were already filled. The vast majority, however, still awaited the precious cargoes that would help build a new world on the other side of the flood.

After Desmorah found a secure place to put her dishes, they started back through the long, dim, cavernous ark to another ramp and climbed up into the sunlight again.

✲

Rhone enjoyed how the evening light rode upon the water in the wake of a boat, how the setting sun lit up the distant Rimwall. With the approach of night, the harbor below seemed to come alive with the thousand twinkling lights that lined winding shoreside walkways, marked the apexes of towering mainmasts, located outstretched anchor chains, brightened cabins, and delineated stern decks. He inhaled the fragrance of sleepyeves growing on the rooftop garden, their pink leaves fading into the shadows even as the moonglass walkway seemed to wake up and come to life.

It was times like this that made him look back over his life and see how all the twists and turns had led him to his place. And it was times like this that made him marvel at the Creator's provisions. He had once tried to run away from his duties, but the Creator had led him back here to Atlan, back to Hodin's Keep, which was his rightful place. And in the process, He had given him Leenah, and had put an end to his wanderings.

Rhone smiled, and couldn't be sad, in spite of what he knew was coming upon the world. His only regret was that so many would perish. Might he have prevented it, had he been a stronger warrior? He shook his head. To do so would have meant he'd have had to take on the Known World and overthrow the Oracle. An impossible task, even for a nation as strong and rich as Atlan.

He returned to their private chamber and heard Leenah back in the bedroom rummaging through something. He went to investigate.

She had pulled out a dusty chalsoma-stone box from the back of a closet—one he had not seen for many years.

Leenah smiled up at him as she brushed the dust from the pure white stone and worked the four gold catches. "I've been thinking about this for quite a while." She easily lifted the light chalsoma lid and set the cover aside.

He lowered himself to the floor, cross-legged, at her side and looked into the box at the collection of mementos.

Leenah lifted out the smooth, round golden globule of pure moonglass. "Remember this?"

How could he forget? The Kleiman had given it to her when she'd stumbled into their village, after the delirium of a mansnatcher's poison had driven her from the fortress Imo-suk on the coast of Marin-ee. Upon it she had scratched a message to him. The words were faint, nearly unnoticeable in the daylight. It was only in the dark, when the stone glowed, that he eventually discovered them.

A pang, perceived or real, seemed to stab at her. "Moonglass will never glow again, at least not naturally. Those days are gone, Rhone."

He nodded. There were ways to make moonglass light up, but they required the inventiveness of man now that the natural magnetic veil had weakened so. He recalled first becoming aware of the weakening veil in the tunnels beneath the wall of Chevel-ee, fleeing the Earth-Born.

She set the stone aside and lifted out the heavy dagger with a sten-gordon talon for a handle. "You took this off of one of the Lodath's green-cloaks?"

The memory hitched up the corner of his mouth. The guard had not been expecting him and Klesc ... the next instant he was sprawled out on the floor, unconscious. "Why do you keep it?"

"I think of it as a trophy." She smiled at him. "It reminds me of when we first met."

"In other words I was your catch?" He bent over and kissed her, his lips lingering upon hers, his heart filling.

She turned back to the box. From it came the woodsman cape. "Another special gift from the Kleiman, Ela. It protected me more than once, and it aided in Lady Darha's escape from her Rim-wall prison." Moisture gathered in Leenah's eyes. She had grown to love his mother, he knew, almost as much as she loved him. "I sorely miss her, even though I know Lady Darha is now at rest in Adam's Bosom."

She set the cloak with the dagger and moonglass, and lifted

out the heavy black puzzle box, exquisitely made. Only in Atlan could such a box have been fashioned. The finest craftsmen had constructed it at his bidding. Made from the blackest stone mined from the heart of Atlan's Rim-wall, the seam where the lid touched the box was practically indistinguishable. The box had been an expensive and frivolous novelty, but it had intrigued Leenah, so he knew it had been worth the expense.

"What was the occasion? Our three hundredth anniversary?"

"Three hundred and fifty." She turned it toward the light coming from the moonglass panel upon her desk. Shaped like a lo-tiss melon, the puzzle box was heavily encrusted with gold and silver. There were three broad golden bands about its middle, each representing one of Atlan's three concentric harbors.

Her eyebrows knit together as she tried the combination. He watched her turn the lid to the left, then rotate each of the three gold bands—the Merchant's band first, the Haven band next, and finally the Kinsman band. She tried the lid and frowned.

He laughed. "Forgot the combination already?"

A scowl told him she would search her memory ... later. For now she set the puzzle box aside. "The correct order will come to me eventually." Her voice refused to harbor doubt.

She caught her breath now as she reached in for the last item. The old manuscript crackled as she carefully lifted out the thick sheaf of papers and placed it upon her lap. She just looked at it at first.

His eyes followed the flowing script of faded ink.

The Cradleland Chronicles.

She flexed her fingers as though they remembered the feelings of writer's cramp. The project had taken her years to compile. The interviews with Mishah and Lamech, correspondences with Amolikah, and of course, sifting through Rhone's memories, had taken most of fifty years.

Her finger traced the line of ink penned over four hundred

years earlier, and he wondered why she had thought it important to record all that information. He had never pried deeply
into the matter, but at the time it had seemed very important
to her.

Carefully, she turned to the last page. "It's all here, from the
people who had lived the adventure: the flight to Eden, the battle for Atlan ... but the story is still not finished."

"And you intend to?"

She nodded, opening the thick book by chance to the place
that spoke of Bar'ack.

Rhone's throat constricted. Bar'ack and his father, Ker'ack,
had convinced him to teach Bar'ack to be a Webmaster, even
though the young man did not have the gift. Eventually the bod-
iless spirits of Per, Hepha, and Pose had invaded his body.
Afterward, Bar'ack turned to the Oracle, eventually becoming an
officer in his and the Lodath's service.

All this happened so long ago! He swallowed hard. Why did
it still hurt so?

A shadow darkened the window, and a whoosh of wind
shoved the hanging curtains inward. From beyond them came a
crunch, like a miner's pick chopping into stone. They set the box
aside and went out onto the balcony where Gur was ruffling his
wings, folding them tightly down his scarlet body. The dragon
shifted its weight on the stone wall, its shiny black talons clenching tightly as its long neck lowered and its great head leveled with
Leenah's.

She stroked his cool, pebbly muzzle. "What have you been
up to?"

The sweet, syrupy tang of bdell-m was upon his breath.
Rhone smiled. "You haven't given the Rim-wall growers reason to
come complaining to me, have you?" The dragon was old—they
all were old. Time had passed them by and each of them knew it.
Leenah spoke with Gur in the way sensitives communicated, as

Rhone used to with javian spiders. But there were few javians left, and it had been years since he had reached out and touched another mind.

He left the two of them there, returned to the bedroom, and retrieved the old manuscript from the floor. It was still incomplete, she had said. He placed it carefully upon Leenah's desk. How would the end be penned?

16

Oric

The night always concerned Noah now.

Each evening before retiring he went around the house locking doors and barring shutters, even though there had been no spiritual attacks since the first. Sometimes he almost wished there would have been. It might have diverted his growing concerns over his children. Nowadays his thoughts seemed to linger ever more often upon them, especially the girls who were beyond his reach and influence. A smile touched his lips. All but Sheflah.

Sometimes, lying in bed with Naamah breathing quietly at his side, asleep, his stomach would burn with worry; hot flames blazed below his sternum and climbed into his throat.

The self-accusations whispering in his head were worse in the midsecond quartering, when the night was quiet except for crickets and frogs, the oster's wake-up crow still hours off. Maybe he should go to them—take time off from the ark and rebuild the relationships that had crumbled so quickly. Could he afford the time? They had made good progress. The rooms and pens were nearly complete, and only the roof remained unfinished, and then the ark would be enclosed. But there was still much to be done. Plumbing. Running wires for the magnetic flow. Pitching and painting, and stocking ... and the animals? Oy. He hadn't figured out that problem yet. Many of the animals that lived on the mainland also lived on Atlan. But then again, many more did not. How was he to collect them all?

Faith, Noah. Have faith and trust the Creator to see to it. But the self-talk didn't help, and the worries mounted, and sleep would be a long time coming this night.

He turned his thoughts to the journey he and Naamah would begin in the morning. Sheflah would be with them—he still had her under his roof, and he wasn't going to make the same mistakes he had in the past. Though having her along would increase his worry over their safety, at least Sheflah would know she was an important part of his life. And how much danger would they really be in?

He had convinced High Councilor Rhone that they must make the journey, that having the Book delivered to Atlan was not an option. But there was more to the trip than just retrieving it—there was the family he and Naamah wanted to see again, maybe for the last time.

"All right, Noah," Rhone had relented at his stubbornness, "but I insist you be accompanied by two Makir."

Noah had agreed to that. Thore of course would be with them, and a young statre named Immac, whom Noah had met several times.

The trip would be good for his family. There was a renewed excitement in the house that Noah had begun to miss. Japheth, Ham, and Shem would remain behind to continue the work. Wend, of course, had the vineyard to manage, and the harvest was already in full swing.

His racing thoughts suddenly broke off at the deep rumble, distant at first, growing louder. Noah bolted up. This one was stronger than in the past. The house had begun to shake.

Naamah woke with a start, disoriented. Noah grabbed her hand and pulled her out of the bedroom.

His family! He shoved Naamah toward the door. "Outside." Then he dived down the hallway to his daughter's room, the floor rocking beneath his feet, the ground groaning, dust grinding from the seams between the stones. Sheflah was sitting up on her bed when he burst through the door. He pulled her to her feet. "Outside, quickly!"

Shem and Ham staggered from their rooms, bracing against the walls. He waved them toward the door.

Thore burst through the door, taking inventory with a quick glance. He helped Sheflah, and Noah took up the rear, Vaul at his side.

They hurried away from the structure. This violent shaking made all the previous ones seem inconsequential. Impossible to remain on their feet, the family huddled together upon the ground as the trees waved in the black sky and bolts of electricity glowed like fireballs in the heavens.

"Everyone out of the house?" Thore demanded.

Noah nodded.

Gradually the shaking ceased, but the fireballs persisted.

The sky had filled with dark shapes of startled birds and dragons. In the distance, orangish glows located those buildings that had been set ablaze.

Thore stared at the heavenly displays. "What is it?"

"Magnetic fire … from the sheering rock."

Thore looked at him. "This time the shaking has done much damage."

Noah only nodded. His heart was pounding, and he wondered how far the shaking had been felt. Were Mitah and his grandchildren safe in Atla Fair? Leteah and his grandson in Sea Side near the Eastern Passage? And what of Orah in Marin-ee?

Wend came jogging up the road from his house on the far

side of the vineyard. "You're all safe!" There was relief in his
voice.

"Sebe and the children?" Naamah asked.

"We made it out of the house before it fell in on itself."

"Thank the Creator for His protection." Noah could put
aside that worry. He wouldn't know about the other children for
perhaps days, or weeks, and prayed for their safety.

※

Soon word of the destruction spread across Atlan, and for
days afterward, the ground trembled as if in the throes of
birthing contractions. Reports came in that the shaking had actually moved the island. It had cleaved the Rim-wall in two places,
one being very near the Kleiman village of Deepvale, and had
raised the seabed. The most startling result was that the Atlan
Ridge now stood high and dry three spans above sea level and
more than a league across; a massive curving stretch of land that
had once been shallow sea floor now reached from Atlan clear to
the mainland. Atlan was no longer an island, but a peninsula.
The water level in Hodin's Passage had fallen more than eight
spans as a result of the upheaval, and the Golden Hills Passage
was now a mere span and a half deep, too shallow for the sea
traffic it had once carried.

With great relief, Noah began to get word from his daughters. Mitah and Leteah were unharmed, and a letter arrived
from Orah telling of the destruction in Marin-ee. The ancient
ruins of Imo-suk had slid into the sea, as well as many expensive
seaside homes. The shaking had been felt as far away as Nod
City. Had the Settled Lands of Hope been spared any damage?
He worried about his family there. Although the news from
around much of the eastern part of the Known World was dire,
Noah praised the Creator that his family near and far had been
protected.

The ark, too, came through unscathed, its massive under-pinning holding it securely in place, its stout construction a testimony to Master Jerl-eze's excellent truss design. Curiously, the stacks of lumber, barrels of pitch, and keg of nails were in perfect order, as though the shaking had not affected them.

Of course! The Creator would have assured His ark had been protected. How could he have doubted? Was his faith wavering now, when the end was so close? This shaking could only have been a foretaste of what must happen to the world once the fountains of the deep were broken up. He shuddered to think what that event would be like.

They delayed their trip two weeks to clean and repair the house, and help their neighbors put their places back together. But soon the time came to set off on their journey to Morg'Seth. With Thore and Immac accompanying them, he, Naamah, and Sheflah boarded a coast-bound boat in Kinsmen Harbor, which still had enough depth to handle such crafts, and sailed into Hodin's Passage.

Within Hodin's Passage, the entry ports and inspection lanes, now useless, rose up out of the water. Noah craned his neck back as the boat chugged past their stony legs, hewed from living stone. The passage's sheer black stone walls wore a rimelike coating, like a wide, pale-gray sword belt, from the level of the water upward eight spans. A small example of what powerful changes the earth-shaking had wrought. The more impressive image of that power yet lay beyond the Rim-wall, in the Great Sea.

Their boat sped out of the passage's mouth, past a small fleet of boats and crews of divers busily pulling ropes into the water and fastening them around Atla's arm, which had broken off the monument and now partially blocked sea travel into the island. Peninsula, not island. Noah winced. It would take a long time to fix that idea in his head. Could the immense statues ever be repaired? A frown tugged at his lips. Likely, not in the short five years left.

Leaving Atlan in their wake, they rounded the point and headed out into open sea. Where water had once stretched to the horizon, now a mass of land rose like a behemoth's spine, bending away toward Marin-ee. The Atlan Ridge exposed.

In the two short weeks since the shaking, land animals had already begun crossing the newly exposed land, browsing on the mats of drying seavine that filled the air with a pungent stench. Looking back along the ridge, Noah spotted the place in the soaring Rim-wall where the shaking had split it wide open, as though with a powerful blow from a gigantic Makir sword.

He glanced at his two Makir protectors standing silently at the stern, watching their homeland shrink in the distance. Seeing the changes from the sea shed a new light on the destruction they had previously witnessed only on land. He wondered what differences the Makir were noting. Possibly how the island—the peninsula—had now become vulnerable to a mainland attack. Perhaps Thore was thinking the old Rim-wall watchtowers should be rebuilt and fortified. Maybe a fort established at the rubble foot of the new breeches would offer a first line of defense.

Noah watched a small flock of goats on the new shore, picking through wilting seavine. Thousands of birds soared in or took off, wheeling against the bright sky, feasting on the sweet seavine fruit, or scavenging the withering carcasses of a million dead fish. A perpetual black haze hovered low across the land, and he was thankful to be far enough out to sea so as not to attract any of those billions of tiny black flies.

The boat followed the new spine of land for hours, until the Pillars of the Sun—like his father, he refused to think of them in their present name—rose like two slender daggers in the distance.

Late in the fourth quartering the boat docked in Marin-ee. He helped Naamah down the gangplank and hoped to find Orah waiting for them. He had written her of their arrival, but as he anxiously scanned the faces, his daughter was not among the busy seaside crowds.

"Maybe she didn't get the letter?" Naamah's grip tightened upon his arm.

Sheflah looked disappointed too.

"Can we wait a little longer?" Naamah's eyes pleaded with him.

Noah ached to see Orah again, to assure himself that she was all right. "Maybe. If we had more time ..."

Thore's view shifted warily about the crowds. "Not now. Our connections are too tight."

"Perhaps on our way back?" she asked.

Thore looked at her. "Perhaps, Mistress Naamah."

Immac scanned the harbor, his hand discretely out of sight beneath his cloak. "Our connection to Wen's Slip leaves within the hour, Master Noah. We should be making for the ferry."

He tried to put his disappointment aside as he grabbed up his traveling bag from the stone wharf, which contained mostly his wife's and daughter's clothing.

The trip to Wen's Slip took all night. The rising sun wore a sickly pallor as the heavy-laden ferry pushed under gray, swirling clouds of smoke from the many refinery chimneys, nearing its destination. Sulphur stung his eyes, its smell an assault on the sea air. Ore barges and 'gia tankers made up most of the traffic in the sea lane. Nearing the harbor, the water darkened to a brownish gray, streaked with the oily red and green of 'gia. Cans and boxes, and floating mats of reeds and dead birds, bobbed past the scarred hull.

Sheflah scrunched her lips as though she'd bitten into something sour.

He put an arm around his daughter's shoulder. "Not a pleasant place."

She looked up at him with brown, worried eyes. "Is all the Known World like this, Father?"

Such innocence. He was glad for that, but had his daughters been overprotected? If he had loosened the strings somewhat, had allowed them to see what the world was like beyond the pleasant borders of Atlan, would their lives be different today?

"Not all of it. Some is still unsoiled, as the Creator first made it. But not much of that is left."

"Is … is Nod City like Wen's Slip?"

"You mean the smell and the smoke? No, not at all. All this, it's because of the Tubal-Cain Company, its iron and bronze works. But Nod City has its own problems."

"And what about Morg'Seth?"

Sheltered on Atlan where the air was clean, the city streets wide and pretty, the countryside neatly divided into villages and farms and vineyards, she had no idea what life beyond the protection of the Rim-wall and High Councilor Rhone's beneficent rule was like. How it must have stunned Orah when she moved to the mainland. He subdued a pang of regret. Marin-ee was nothing quite as shocking as Wen's Slip.

"Morg'Seth is a lovely place, Sheflah. Small country villages and wide-open farmland. Some farms, like your grandfather's 'gia farm, extend for leagues."

The ferry docked and the party made their way through the city to the TT Swift's station and boarded a pendant carriage for the Settled Lands of Hope. Their first stop on this leg of the journey would be Quinal-ee, in the land of Morg'Jalek, where Noah was to meet briefly with some of the Kinsmen. And then from there by cyclart to the Lee-lands of Morg'Seth where they would stay at his father's farm, and he would retrieve the Book from Aunt Cerah for safekeeping.

❦

Bar'ack squeezed his head in both hands, fingernails gouging his skull, thumbs pressing into his ears.

Per and Hepha were disagreeing on some finer point of the Oracle's power ... or was it judgment? He didn't know, didn't care!

Covering his ears was no help. It only amplified the voices in his brain. Recently, the bickering had gotten worse, and his tolerance for such things was becoming less and less the older he got.

"Shut up!"

The voices went silent for half a breath, then an explosion of laughter cackled inside his skull. He paced his quarters, stomping from the bed, across the small sitting area to his food pantry and table and back again. Only one remedy ever silenced the voices. He yanked open a cupboard door, and grabbed down the jug of grog. Ripping out the stopper, he tossed his head back and spilled a single mouthful of the stinging liquid down his throat. He shook the jug and glared at the lone drop forming on its rim, then flung the jug to the floor sending shattered splinters of pottery skittering across the red baked tiles.

Shrugging into a heavy coat, he flung open his door and went out into the long corridor, heading for the stairs to the cold Oric surface. As he approached them, the tall windows at the end of the corridor opened onto a bleak view. Beyond them lay the stark red plain that covered most of Oric, a part of it filled with the imposing sculpture of the Oracle's face: a gigantic monument of stone that dominated the center of the complex. From this close it appeared only as an oddly shaped mountain, but from a jumper approaching Oric, one could clearly see the image of the Oracle's face staring up through the cold pink sky. The sculpture, a duplicate of the one on Earth and another on the moon, was only partially finished. Work on it would have to wait for the fleeting warm months to return. There never seemed to be enough time.

Bar'ack pounded down the steps and pushed open the outer doors. A fist of icy air momentarily stunned him. He staggered, and almost immediately his lungs burned from the thin, frigid

Orician atmosphere. He never could get used to the bleak season. Hunkering his neck deep into the thick fur collar, he started across the compound, trudging doggedly through the still, icy air toward the activity hall.

The sun sat low in the pale pink sky, a distant, weak glow. So far out, it grudgingly lent little warmth in the summer season— barely enough to thaw ice for a few months and permit the short, scrubby Orician growth to transform the red landscape to a velvety green. It gave practically no warmth at all in the bleak season when the vast, shallow seas froze nearly solid and the land grew a rim of pink ice over raw red soil.

In the cold, thin light, Rahab, the fifth stone out from the sun, stood just above the horizon like a drop of curdled milk upon the rim of a rusty bucket.

He looked away, grabbed his head and shook it, trying to rattle the voices as he aimed his feet for the recreation facility. His breath crystallized in clouds of steam before his eyes. To his right, off in the distance, rose a line of six low pyramid-shaped temples. As on Earth, and on the moon, this complex had been laid out in the image of an immense five-pointed star.

To his left were the new housing units, which were quickly replacing the original excavated quarters. When he first arrived on Oric, the hastily bored burrows had been all there was of the Oracle's off-world sanctuary. It had been quicker and more efficient to tunnel into the native rock than to build on the surface. Once hewed out, the sleeping quarters had been equipped with crude heaters that drew on the subsurface furnace of this cold, nearly barren stone. Inefficient as the heaters were, the Nephs didn't seem to mind. They required less warmth than humans did. The women, however, couldn't take the cold well, but Nephs cared little about broodbloods. In the early days, Bar'ack had lost almost as many of them to sickness as he did to the Nephs' peculiar relish for lusty entertainment.

But gradually, living conditions on Oric improved. Over the last few years almost six hundred Earth-Born had been transported to Oric, and new arrivals never stopped coming, except in the dead of winter. He glanced at the fleet of jumpers, frozen to their landing pads, encased in a crust of ice. At least they weren't pink like almost everything else in sight. He growled and tried to mask the uproar inside his head with thoughts of his own—a difficult task even when the voices would permit it.

He burst through the outer door of the Neph facility just in time to hear a woman's scream, and the throaty guffawing of three or four Nephs echo down the corridor from a doorway. Bar'ack grinned. The voices in his brain chuckled. It was warmer in here, but then he was still wrapped in his heavy coat.

The recreation room held fifty or sixty Nephs, shouting and laughing, drinking and fighting. A few eyed him suspiciously as he went behind the bar and snatched a jug of biddleberry grog. They didn't like authority any more than he.

Everywhere Bar'ack looked, one Neph after another was having his way with the broodbloods, using them, then casting them aside. No pretense of privacy here.

He shook his head, frowning. At this rate, they'd use them all up! There would be precious few left by spring. It was always like that. He gave a low growl at the problems he knew that would make for him. What could he do to keep these halflings occupied once the women were used up? A wry smile snarled his lips. They'd do what they always did—turn on each other. Most did anyway. It was the rare few who didn't want to be used like broodbloods.

He vacantly gazed at two Nephs who violently heaved the arms of a limp broodblood back and forth—a brutal tug of war that clearly had nothing to do anymore with the lifeless body. He mused: The trouble was, when they used each other, jealousy became rampant. Every day there would be at least two or three stabbings or shootings. The Oracle didn't like losing Nephs that way.

A woman screamed. He turned to see her running from a gathering of Nephs, blood streaming down her neck and spreading into a wet slew across her shoulders. From a crowd, a Neph leaped to his feet and went after her. He caught up with the woman in a few long strides, grabbed a hunk of her long hair, and wrenched her back. His backhand snapped her head violently around. Bar'ack winced at the sharp crack of bone. The woman shuddered and slumped to the cold stone floor.

The Neph stared a moment at the body, his rage draining from him. Then he picked up the corpse and casually tossed it across the room. A chorus of chuckles arose as he strode back to his friends.

Bar'ack shook his head. They'd be all used up by spring. Not one in a thousand broodbloods survived much more than two or three seasons. He tucked the jug under his coat and buttoned it up again. Fortunately there would be a steady supply of them— that is, when the jumpers thawed and flew again.

He was surprised to realize that Per and Hepha had ceased their argument. In that brief, lucid instant when the voices inside his head were silent, he glanced back at the broodblood's body. An unaccustomed twinge, a squeezing sadness in the middle of his chest, pressed the air from his lungs.

Then the voices began to argue again.

He turned his back to the unbridled violence, half-wishing he could exercise more control over these creatures. But the Oracle's Liberties strictly forbade him from taking a heavy hand. In this place, so far from the home stone, there were no rules, no discipline. His only job was to keep these halfling children of the Oracle happy and well entertained, and to keep the construction of the sanctuary moving ahead.

And so far he had managed to do the job well.

They had too much free time on their hands. That was the way things were here on Oric. When the warmth returned, they'd expend their energies enlarging the complex for more halflings, and finish the work on the temples, and of course, the Oracle's Image. But for now, it was drinking and broodbloods....

Striding out of the hall and back into the frigid Orician bleak season, Bar'ack was more anxious than usual for spring to arrive.

17

Ambush

*T*hore stirred Noah from his nap as the TreeTop Swift pulled into Quinal-ee station at the fourth of the third quartering.

They were the only five passengers who disembarked, and they stood upon the shadowy, stone-paved landing as the TT pulled quietly away, its low magnetic hum fading in the distance, carrying the pendant carriages off into the night with it.

"They didn't even pause to switch out magnetic packs." Thore watched the pendant carriages fading into the night.

Vaul's ears turned forward, and his lips peeled back, showing his fighting teeth.

"Great planning," Noah mumbled softly, staring down the long street with hardly a light showing anywhere. The moon was a mere sliver, its bright, narrow curve like the edge of a rusty-tailed oster's egg peeking out of a nest of stars. He liked it that way.

"The planning was fine." Thore turned and peered back along the single overhead rail disappearing in the dark toward the Illackin Mountains. "It was TreeTop's connections that ran us afoul. You can blame our delay on the breakdown at the border of Morg'Jalek."

That had been quite unusual. The TT didn't usually allow mag-packs to run dry.

"I don't like this." Immac stared into the dark village. "Where are all the lights? It's too dark." He sniffed the air. "Smoke."

Noah sniffed it too.

"There's been a fire recently." By Thore's tone of voice, Noah could almost feel the Makir's hairs rising on his neck.

He hefted his bag. "Where is Chief Gate Warden Monik? He was supposed to meet us." They started off in the dark down the street, Vaul trotting a few spans ahead. Thore, wary as always, stuck close to him. Immac lagged a little behind and off to the left. The two Makir communicated in a way Noah didn't understand, except that it had to do with the binding, which was forged through the practice of the Katrahs and Kimahs, and the shared blood of their ancestor, Hodin, the fourteenth son of Adam.

"Where does Master Monik live?" Naamah asked.

"I don't know." He held his wife's arm close to his side, with Sheflah latched onto his other arm.

Thore stopped and looked at him. "You don't know?"

He shook his head. "He was supposed to meet us, remember? He probably waited after we didn't arrive on schedule, then left."

Thore exhaled. "You'd think he'd come back for us."

"Maybe we ought to ask someone?" Naamah peered down one of the streets where a few lights outlined the dark shapes of buildings.

"We might try in there." Thore pointed to a dimly lit festival hall a little distance away where the sounds of laughter spilled out onto the street. "On second thought, I'll ask. You stay here with Immac and your canic."

Immac said quietly, "Something's wrong here."

Thore nodded as he loosened his fistproj in its holster.

Vaul's low warning growl raised prickles on Noah's flesh. The canic seemed aware of something they had missed. "Maybe we ought to just pass that place by, Thore. When Vaul lays his ears back like that ..." He left the rest of the warning unspoken.

"Let me check it out." Thore gave Statre Immac a glance that communicated more than Noah could catch. Adjusting his cloak to conceal the fistproj, his right hand falling out of sight beneath it, he started for the festival hall.

An uneasy tightness clamped Noah's chest. He drew in a breath to ease it and hustled his wife and daughter off the street, up against a dark stone building.

Although Thore wasn't dressed in the colors of Atlan, there was no hiding his Hodinite heritage, or his Makir bearing. In some places these days, that was the same as asking for a fight. The Oracle had spread poisonous rumors about Atlan. It was becoming more and more difficult for Thore to travel as freely as he once had.

"Why hadn't I remembered to get a location before taking off on this trip?" Noah said. Just too many things to fill his brain these days. "The teacup overflows." He sighed, repeating Naamah's excuse whenever she forgot something.

She smiled at him.

Sheflah whispered, "The air stinks."

Immac said, "The fire must have been a big one. Come daylight we're likely to see a large portion of Quinal-ee has been razed."

"It's not the smoke. It's something else." Sheflah's usual vivacious optimism was overshadowed by her clear concern. Her view remained fixed upon Thore.

Naamah took Noah's hand, entwining their fingers.

Vaul's attention remained riveted on Thore. Vaul was unlike any canic Noah had ever owned. His unswerving loyalty was typical, but his uncanny understanding made him seem more human than canic.

Noah's skin crawled. Why so few lights? He sniffed the air.

And where had all the people gone? Vaul growled softly again.

Down the street, Thore paused at the open doorway, looked back at them, then stepped inside. Noah's fingers tightened in Naamah's hand. There was really no reason to expect the worst— except for Vaul's wariness. The fire must have driven most folks to find new lodging. His stomach sank. *This whole business is getting to me.* He took a couple more deep breaths to settle his nerves, then sat upon the edge of the raised wooden sidewalk to wait.

I'm doing the Creator's business, so why do I fear so? It wasn't for himself, but for his family. Now he wished he had insisted Naamah stay in Atlan. And Sheflah, too.

About the only encouraging thought he could muster was that in a few days he would be in Morg'Seth. A small smile puckered the corner of his mouth. That was the whole point of this trip. To see family, and to retrieve the Book.

It had been at Jepheth's wedding, five years ago, that he'd last seen his mother and father, his brothers, sisters, cousins, nieces, uncles, grandfathers. He sighed. Had it really been that long ago?

He looked at the canic. Vaul appeared to have calcified with his nose still pointed at the festival-house door, his ears flattened. He had seen Vaul stand like that for hours when something had snagged his attention.

Immac took a couple of steps down the street and paused as if listening. Noah couldn't hear anything, but that meant nothing. He couldn't compare his senses to those of a Makir Warrior.

All at once Thore emerged from the festival hall. Walking stiffly, quickly, he glanced hurriedly over his shoulder.

Noah recognized that rigid look on the Makir's face. Trouble!

Thore grabbed his arm and started him down the street, Naamah and Sheflah clinging to him and hurrying along. Immac drew out his fistproj and covered their rear.

"What happened?" Noah asked. He saw the tautness in the Makir's face as he kept glancing back.

"That's a Neph den."

"Nephs? Here? In Morg'Jalek?"

"I didn't believe it either. The place is filled with them. It reeked of cabweed, and there was at least a fist of broodbloods there too."

Naamah gave a quiet gasp.

"Broodbloods?" Noah's breath went to ice in his lungs.

Thore's eyes seized him in a narrowed view. "You know how they look, sort of vacant, as if something crawled inside them and killed the person they used to be?"

He nodded, confused. Nephs here? He'd seen broodbloods in his travels, especially the few times he and his father had gone to Nod City. He'd observed them on rare occasions emerging from the Oracle's breeding dens, a dead-eye look on their faces, their spirits gone, their wombs burgeoning with Malik seed, their futures inexorably set in stone. Some went voluntarily into the dens. He could never understand that, considering the awful price a woman paid to bear a Neph. Others were taken against their will. The chill in his lungs radiated out into his body, and he shivered thinking about his own daughters. He glanced at Sheflah, trotting along at his side.

Thore's grip tightened on his arm. "We need to get out of town."

Naamah cast them both a worried look.

From behind, Immac's gentle but firm urging kept them moving.

Thore said, "They knew who I was. As if they were expecting me ... us, Noah. The Oracle must have placed his emissaries in here. You aren't safe."

"Emissaries!" Noah moved as though his body had detached from his feet, his thoughts slogging through a fog of confusion. "How could he know?"

"Who understands the Oracle's powers? When I stepped into that place, the evil was thick enough to suffocate me."

"The delay in the schedule at the border? Our arriving here late at night?"

"Very little is beyond his control anymore."

Vaul spun suddenly and glared into a shadowy alleyway between two buildings, eyes glinting greenish-orange. Thore stepped in front of Noah and drew his heavy fistproj from its holster.

Immac stared down the street, back the way they had come.

Drawing a second fistproj from a holster at the small of his back, Thore shoved the weapon into Noah's hand. "Use it if you have to."

Noah gathered Naamah and Sheflah behind him. The air grew heavy, each breath an effort. From the alley, a shadow moved. A Neph stepped out of it into the thin starlight, but drew up at the menacing sound of Vaul's growl. He stared at the canic. Behind him a second, and then a third Neph cleared the alley and spread out.

Noah shifted to keep them in sight as his heart hammered in his chest, Naamah's fingers gripping his shirt, Sheflah's rapid breathing hissing near his ear. More Nephs came from the festival hall. Immac turned to face them.

He squeezed the fistproj, and his finger curled around the trigger like Thore had taught him. The air grew cold and streamers of green light flickered in the darkness, swirling in a slow whirlpool about them.

"Maliks!" *Like the time they had invaded his home!*

The giants rushed them. Vaul leaped and sank his teeth into an arm. The giant tried to shake him off, but the canic clung tight. A fistproj cracked. Vaul lurched and went to the ground.

Thore ducked and fired. The Neph staggered. Another raised his weapon.

Immac's fistproj banged three times.

Thore's sword leaped from its scabbard to his other hand,

moving faster than an eye could follow. There was a thud, and a giant who was about to fire gave out a moan of pain. The fistproj and the hand that had held it fell to the ground.

Noah saw a Neph lunge from the shadows. Noah's fistproj barked and the projlet tore through the giant's side, hardly slowing him down. Noah threw his arms up to protect Naamah, catching sight of a flash of steel from the corner of his eye. The sword whistled past his head, followed by a groan of pain.

Thore grabbed his arm and he, Naamah, and Sheflah went flying after the Makir down the dark, deserted street. Thore sheathed his sword as he ran. "More coming!"

The night erupted with projfire. Noah's heart raced as he tried to keep himself between the danger and his family.

Thore was holding back so as not to leave them behind. Clutching his bag to his chest, his heart pounding, Noah glanced back as nine or ten Nephs came scrambling up behind them. His ears began to ring from an electric charge filling the air.

The Nephs slowed as they neared their fallen brothers, then with a shout of rage, plunged after them, fistprojs cracking and projlets whizzing past his ears.

The charged air snapped all around them, driving needles into his skin. Was this fear or something else? His racing brain didn't have time to figure it out. His skin tingled all over and his hair seemed to be dancing off his scalp! Did the others feel it too? The traveling bag slowed him and he was about to cast his bag aside when the surrounding air exploded with static electricity.

A soft whirring emerged from the blackness up ahead, a dazzling row of pink lights glared all at once, momentarily blinding him. He shielded his eyes, stumbling to a halt.

A voice shouting from somewhere urged, "This way! This way!"

Past the glare, he spied a woman leaning out of an oval of blackness, waving them in.

Thore broke stride, glanced at the woman, then back at the Nephs.

A dark mass raced past him and leaped into the opening. Vaul was alive! Trusting the canic's good sense, Noah shoved Naamah and Sheflah ahead and dived into the oval hole.

As he tumbled through the hatch, a woman yanked him to his feet. Stunned, he stared at her a moment, then at Thore and Immac, who were left to face the Nephs alone. The woman leaned back out the doorway and waved them on, becoming more and more animated, shouting for them to hurry up.

"Thore! Immac!" Noah yelled. "Get in here!"

With a glance at the Nephs, the two Makir sprang through the opening. Noah grabbed Immac's arm, the woman taking Thore's. The big men tumbled inside an instant before the door hissed shut.

Thore turned about, brandishing his sword. The woman sprang back from the deadly point. Thore glanced at Noah. "What other crazy stunts have you in mind?" His eyes darted about.

There wasn't much Noah could see of his murky surroundings. He gulped, his breathing ragged, his heart slamming his ribs as he looked around. "It's all right … I think. Vaul is here." They were in some kind of room, but he couldn't make out any details; his eyes still flared with the lights from a moment before. A low hum filled the air, and the room gave a shudder. The humming grew louder, changing in pitch, and they lurched sideways. His stomach plunged as everything seemed to rise heavenwards.

"Vaul?" Thore sounded doubtful. "I saw him go down."

The woman stared at the sword. "You can lower your weapon. You are in no danger from us."

"I'll determine that!" Thore shot a glanced at Noah. "You all right?"

"Yes."

"Immac?"

The Makir nodded, his fistproj leveled at the woman as he held tight to a metal rod.

Thore glanced at the canic. Vaul leaped up a short flight of metal steps and sat upon a darkened platform of some kind. "I saw him hit by a proj."

"He appears unharmed," Noah said between breaths.

Vaul cocked his head at Thore.

Noah looked into Naamah's wide eyes. "Are you all right?"

She nodded.

"Sheflah?" His eyes were adjusting to the soft glow within whatever it was they were in. His daughter's face was the color of alabaster, but other than that, she seemed unharmed.

The room canted steeply and he grabbed for a metal rung.

The short, stoutly built woman looked at Thore. "Are you Noah?" She was young. Early hundreds. Dressed in sturdy, shiverthorn trousers and a light, pale blue shirt beneath a leather vest with bronze hoops for attaching things. Right now, one of the hoops was clipped to a safety strap from an overhead bar that ran along the length of whatever it was they had leaped into. In the pale glow, Noah noted that the woman's eyes were dark, and her complexion a shade or two fairer than his son Ham. Her black hair, cut short, barely covered the tops of her ears.

Thore narrowed his eyes at her. "Who wants to know?"

"My name is Majiah." She pointed to another hatchway. "And that's Zinorah."

A woman's face appeared briefly around the edge of the hatch, then disappeared again. Noah barely had time to notice her features, except for her distinctly square jawline. Her golden-brown hair was cut close to the scalp, like Majiah's.

Majiah looked at the point of Thore's sword. "I know how confusing all this is, but we mean you no harm. You must believe that."

"Confusing? That's putting it mildly." He considered a moment. "I'm Thore. That's Noah."

Majiah's view shifted.

Noah figured he must appear a rumpled, frightened man. And he was. "This is my wife, Naamah, and my daughter Sheflah. What happened to your village?" His grip tightened on the metal rung as the room shifted sharply. The warm texture was like no other metal he was aware of—almost like the hard flesh of some creature.

"Six days ago a Neph swarm invaded Quinal-ee. There were forty or fifty of them. Mostly men, some women, some children."

"They took over the town?" He gulped a couple times to swallow the phlegm building in his mouth.

She folded her arms across her chest. "They murdered most of the council, ran the others off—those lucky enough to escape. Many of our people were captured and marched off to Nod City. Afterward they set fire to the village, making sure they left enough standing to house and entertain themselves."

"I saw some of their entertainment," Thore said wryly.

"We expected it would happen eventually." Her voice became low and somber. "We even prepared for it … only … some of us didn't move fast enough. We have a camp in the mountains." She frowned. "The mountains are filling with refugees as the Oracle systematically takes over the Settled Lands of Hope."

"So we've heard," Immac growled from the shadows where his fistproj remained in his hand.

Noah nodded, suddenly worried about his family still living in Morg'Seth, just south of here. "I was hoping I could talk to the people before trouble came."

Majiah frowned. "So were we." She went introspectively silent for a moment, then drew in a breath. "We knew you'd eventually show up in Quinal-ee. We also know the Oracle hates you—your message—and that he'll stop at nothing to get his hands on you. When we heard of the TT's delay, we waited, cloaked."

"It seems the Creator smiles on us ... again," Thore said.

Noah helped Naamah to the metal stairs, which had the same living-warmth. She sat, gripping a handrail as the room shifted and swerved. Most of the room was in shadows. A span and a half above him was the open floor where Vaul sat. Beyond that was the open hatchway where, presumably, Zinorah was performing some vital functions. "What is this ... this place?" The faint hum of an engine of some sort rumbled lowly through the room, but with none of the charged electricity that had frizzled his hair and tingled his skin earlier.

Majiah glanced about the small compartment, its nooks and crannies obscured by the dim lighting. "They call it a star jumper."

"A jumper." Thore whistled softly and took another look at the craft. "I've seen these. The Oracle brought them from the stars." He thumped the metal bulkhead behind him with a fist, then his view narrowed suspiciously. "How did you come into possession of it?"

Majiah uncrossed her arms. "Call it a spoil of war, Master Thore. You can put aside your mistrust ... and your sword. You, too, Master Immac. If we were in alliance with the Oracle, I'd have left you to those Nephs." She slipped her arms through a harness. "Hold tight, we'll be earthing in a few moments. Unfortunately, we had to exorcise the gathering spirit. Keeping it aboard would have been"—she hesitated, searching for the proper word—"unwise. And anyway, the jumper hauls more without it."

Noah sat on the step, squeezing Sheflah between him and Naamah, and grabbed tight to the railing.

Thore sheathed his sword and braced himself. Immac holstered his weapon and gripped his handhold.

Humming quietly, the jumper swooped to one side and Noah's stomach lifted into his throat. Then with a rise in the pitch of the magnetic purring, the craft leveled out. Next came the sound of a mechanical whir and clank of some device. The craft settled smoothly as a feather to the ground, letting out a soft sigh as it came to rest.

Thore put a hand to his stomach.

"You get used to it after awhile." Majiah unattached herself from the safety harness and opened the door. Fresh air spilled into the jumper, helping some with Noah's nausea. Vaul jumped out first. Thore stepped down cautiously, drawing his sword again.

Noah helped Naamah to her feet. She still breathed heavily, and as yet had not spoken. Her round face turned toward his. He gave her a false smile of confidence. "It'll be all right now." *How can I know that for sure?*

Majiah marched down the three metal steps and glanced at the long, archaic weapon in Thore's hand. "We're safe here."

The Makir stared at a distant line of lights wending its way down a craggy ridge whose sawtooth rim snarled its fighting fangs against a night sky bright with starlight. "I'll determine that."

Majiah put a hand to his and gently lowered the sword. "I said, we're safe."

Vaul appeared unconcerned as Noah climbed out, clutching his bag. They'd earthed in a dark bowl beneath rocky peaks rising all around them … except to the north where a swath of unobstructed night sky stood above the treetops.

"A welcoming party." Immac moved up alongside Thore, watching the approaching line of lights.

"My father, and others," Majiah said.

Noah handed Thore the fistproj he still carried. "I hope I won't be needing this anymore." He smiled, his skin still tingling from the close call back in Quinal-ee, his hands clammy. "Looks like I'll get a chance to speak today after all."

Thore slid his sword out of sight beneath his cloak and tucked the fistproj into the holster at his back. "So long as the Oracle doesn't find us. That jumper isn't exactly inconspicuous. Come daylight ..." He turned and his jaw dropped. Zinorah was just stepping out of a black oval hole in thin air. She came down the steps, which appeared attached to nothing. She pointed something at the jumper and the steps slid into the door. The door clicked shut, vanishing too.

"Phase-shifted ... cloaked," Majiah said at his startled look.

Immac said, "I didn't know they could do that."

"Some can, some can't," she replied matter-of-factly. "It's some sort of interdimensional shift."

Thore worked his jaw shut as Zinorah strode silently past him, heading for the approaching lights. As she faded into the night, Thore turned to Majiah. "Doesn't speak much, does she?"

Majiah's face softened in the moonlight. "No. Not anymore."

Noah caught Thore's eyes and raised his eyebrows at the deep sadness he heard in her voice.

She started after Zinorah.

Thore shrugged.

Naamah adjusted her small traveling bag on her shoulder and took Noah's hand. They followed Majiah through the deep shadows of the mountain valley where the jumper had landed, toward the welcoming party.

The uneven ground rose sharply beneath Noah's feet. Ahead, the line of lights broke apart and scattered about either side of the path. There were about fifteen people waiting for them, mostly men.

One of the men came forward, a bandaged arm in a sling, and gave Majiah a hug. In the flickering light of the torch that he held high overhead, Noah saw he was an older man, not awfully tall, but well muscled beneath his tight, sleeveless shirt.

"We pulled them out of there with Nephs on their heels." Majiah introduced them. "This is my father, Monik, Chief Gate Keeper of Quinal-ee."

"Honor our homes, humble as they may be." Monik bowed briefly, and glanced at Noah. "And accept my apology for the less-than-hospitable greeting you received in Quinal-ee." Although he wore a stern face, he managed a thin smile in spite. "Needless to say, the town is temporarily under new management."

Noah returned the greeting. Monik's optimism was admirable, but no town invaded by Nephs ever went back to what it was before. "Mistress Majiah said some of your people didn't make it safely out of town. I'm sorry."

The gate warden's faint smile disappeared. "We live in perilous times. And the times will only get worse so long as the Oracle remains in control." His eyes, reflecting the light of the torches, grew intense. "And if what you say is true, Master Noah, there is little on the horizon for encouragement."

The last thing he wanted to instill in the hearts of his listeners was the notion of no hope left. Rather, the only true hope in these troubled times lay in turning to the Creator. He wanted to encourage them to shun the Oracle's evil influences rumbling across the Known World like a pendant-coach express. "You've heard my message?"

"The land is abuzz with your words, and those of your father, and grandfather. The Oracle calls them the wild ravings of a madman."

"Yet he tries to silence his wild ravings," Thore noted. "Makes one wonder why."

"To restore sanity to the world." Monik frowned. "Or so he claims."

"And many believe him," a second man said. He was taller than the Chief Gate Warden, and older, a thin man with white hair, a prominent chin at the end of a strong jaw, and deep furrows down his cheeks that gathered shadows in their depths. He'd been standing near the Chief Gate Keeper, and now he came a step closer. "But we know the Oracle is a liar and a wicked being. We welcome your message, Master Noah, even if it means our own destruction."

"This is Master Joset," Monik said.

Noah bowed toward the older man. Where Monik had a sense of humor, albeit at the moment properly held in check, Joset's soul seemed to harbor only a deep bitterness; in his scowling countenance, Noah sensed dark resentment. He tried to read beyond the painful anger in the man's face, and when he did so, he discovered something familiar in the shape of the man's eyes, and the stark, bony line of his jaw, but he couldn't place him. Maybe it was only the poor light.

"I bring a message of encouragement, even though it is wrapped in the bitter cloak, Master Joset. The Creator gave man a hundred and twenty years to repent."

"From the looks of it, man is not doing a very good job," Monik said wryly.

"You're correct." Noah drew in a breath and forced a smile. "I am looking forward to explaining it to you."

"Well, come, come," Monik said, taking Noah's arm. "This is a poor place for holding such discussions. We may not have all the comforts of Quinal-ee to offer you, but I can give you, your family, and friends a safe place to rest. The food is excellent, in spite of our primitive circumstances."

The party started back along the narrow trail, some of the torchbearers lighting the way in front, others closing in behind. Most of the men were armed. Monik had said they were safe and Majiah had insisted that no one was likely to find the jumper, but by all appearances, no one was taking chances.

Vaul stayed close to his side.

18

Majiah

*I*t appeared an old cut, its sides rough and square. It was a good-sized opening, as if it had at one time accommodated large equipment. From the outside, little showed to reveal its location; no stray light leaked from the gap. Noah followed Thore into the man-made breech and took a sharp right-hand turn. The walls lit up before him, glowing softly with a mismatch of moonglass; pale orange and green, some faintly pink, some vibrant red, a yellow panel, a gaudy purple one—probably scavenged from the ceiling of a smoky festival hall.

"Energized moonglass." He glanced at Naamah whose hand pressed reassuringly about his arm. "Surprising to find them so far from a magnetic grid."

"Where do you get the power?" Thore asked.

"Earth heat," Chief Gate Warden Monik said, guiding them deeper into the passage. "We bored down into an underground reservoir and plumbed the hot, high-pressure water through a small whirl-mag. It provides enough Directed-Magnetism to power the moonglasses and cook our food. At first we used D-M to hollow out living quarters from these ancient mines. We had hoped the pool of water we tapped would have supplied all our needs, but it came up salty, undrinkable."

Majiah said, "When we channeled the outflow into a stream, it killed off most of the fish and creepers, and the beasts of the field avoid drinking from it." She looked over her shoulder at Thore. "Curious, but a few of the fish have survived. The Creator must have built into them ability to adapt to higher salt content."

Thore's view traveled over the tunnel's high ceiling and then to her. "How long have you been planning this escape, Mistress Majiah?"

"Since the Oracle began moving against the Settled Lands. We all knew it was only a matter of time before Quinal-ee was taken. Once nearby towns began to fall to his Neph army, we started moving fresh stores of food, clothes, medicines, and weapons into these old mines. We had a plan, Master Thore." Her eyes narrowed. "But we didn't expect this surprise attack. When it came, too many people hesitated. They were taken."

"What does the Oracle do with the captives?" Noah's view lingered a moment on an ancient ale advertisement sign not made of energized moonglass, but of the original stone from back in the days when the magnetic veil had been powerful enough to ignite moonglass all on its own. The antique sign barely showed at all.

"Some are forced to abandon the Creator and worship the Oracle. Those who accept are reeducated. Those who refuse …" Her voice trailed off, then continued more softly. "We never hear of them again. They enter the Temple and never come out again."

"The sacrifices," Noah said, glancing at Sheflah's face, innocent and wide-eyed.

Monik's eyes flicked momentarily to Joset, walking at the head of the party. He lowered his voice. "Some of the women find themselves in the Oracle's breeding dens." Noah barely heard his whisper above the echo of the scraping feet in the wide passageway. "That's why women cut their hair short." Monik looked at Majiah.

"We do what we have to," Majiah said stoically.

Noah looked around. Immac as usual was watching their rear flank, the Makir's eyes in constant motion as though mapping the place inside his head, as was his habit. Thore, too, appeared to miss nothing.

Sheflah's hand went back to her own long tresses. "I've heard that the Oracle's emissaries find long hair appealing."

Majiah gave a little shiver. "It's true. No one knows why."

Noah's thoughts ran aground on his own daughters again, and he couldn't seem to free them.

The tunnel opened up into a larger room with tunnels leading off in four directions. "Majiah, who dug these mines?" Thore asked.

"You might say the Oracle dug them for us. Ironic, don't you think?"

He shrugged. "How so?" They turned down one of the branching tunnels.

"Back five hundred years ago, when the Temple Project began, the Lodath set up two quarries. One in the Hawk Mountains, where he got the good, hard stone for his buildings, and a second one here, in the Illackin Mountains, for the chalcedony and marble to finish it off. The finest stone lay in the heart of the mountain, and it was cheaper to bore a tunnel than to remove the overburden."

"How did he transport the stone?" Noah asked. "We're far off any roads, aren't we?"

"Yes," she said, "but we're not that far from the Hiddekel River—sometimes called the Idakla this far south. Transportation was easily arranged. There's an old canal nearby. The Lodath had it dug to move the quarried stone."

"A canal? I didn't know of it."

"It silted in years ago, Master Noah. It's now mostly cropland, with a few small lakes scattered along the old waterway."

The tunnel ended at a large, poorly lit room that still showed the uneven cuts left over from its quarry days. About a hundred

people occupied it, cooking, carrying crates, erecting shiverthorn privacy cubicles. The hum of a whirl-mag drifted over the
sounds of activity, and a cool, steady breeze stirred the hair
above Noah's ears.

Thore gave the place a careful study. "You'd all be in a bad
way if the Oracle's army were to bottle you in here."

Noah recalled a story Lady Leenah sometimes told of the old
days when Thore's evil Uncle Zorin once moved against the
Kleimen, trapping them in their mines and sending his canics in
to ravage the harmless folk.

The men who'd accompanied them began to disperse to various points in the cavern now. It occurred to Noah that he hadn't
seen Zinorah since she had left the cloaked jumper.

"I'll talk with you later." Majiah gave Monik a hug. She said
fair journey to them and left.

Monik watched her for a moment, then looked at Thore.
"Our position here has its problems. We've a work quort right
now extending an escape passage to the outside. To our advantage, so far the Neph armies haven't taken to pursuing those who
flee. It appears as if securing the towns is the Oracle's main concern." He drew in a breath and let it out. "That's likely to change
as well." A frown settled on his lips. "Hungry?"

"Is your wife here?" Naamah asked as they walked.

Monik shook his head. "My wife passed on to Adam's Bosom
several years ago."

"I'm sorry." Naamah's grip tightened upon Noah's arm.

They walked along low walls, dodged tables, and circumnavi-
gated stacks of food and clothing. The place vaguely reminded
Noah of the hedge-maze in Atla Park. Was this how the ark would
feel someday, crammed with animals and the necessities of survival and starting over again? His traveling bag was growing
heavy, and he was relieved when they arrived at a dining area
made up of mismatched chairs and tables.

The food cooking on large mag stoves smelled wonderful. Noah tried to recall his last meal. It had been over a full two quarterings ago, and he was famished, and his poor wife and daughter had never uttered a word of complaint.

❦

The following morning over breakfast, Thore watched the Chief Gate Warden wend his way through the cluttered maze deep inside the Illackin Mountains. A fresh bandage dressed Monik's wound. He was the center of attention wherever he was. People constantly came to him with questions or reports. "He moves like a man with a purpose," Thore said. He glanced at Noah who was closing the traveling bag containing, among other things, his books and charts, and looked across the ancient mine.

"Keeping up morale while trying to rebuild here underground is purpose enough." Noah paused, then gave him a quizzical grin. "In some respects, we both have a similar mission. I'm becoming all too familiar with the logistics of organizing people, matériel, and time." He sighed and began buckling the bag shut. "It's something that doesn't come naturally to me. Fortunately, I have sons to help." He glanced at Naamah across from him. "And a wife and daughters. Did you know Sheflah has taken on the task of completing an inventory of animals and their nutritional needs?"

Thore nodded toward her and saw her blush faintly and smile.

"Japheth," Noah went on, "has a gift for bringing men and equipment together in a timely, orderly fashion, and making sure they complete their tasks on schedule. Ham is ingenious, and Shem is willing to do anything for me."

"And Wend?" He knew of Noah's growing disappointment toward his eldest son.

"I'd hoped Wend would ramrod the project, but he's more interested in the vineyard." He sipped his tea.

"It is his inheritance." Naamah brought the tin cup to her

lips, pinching the hot handle between two fingers, watching him over the rim.

Noah scowled, setting his cup down. "The boy—well, man, now—should realize the importance of what we're doing. The vineyard will be gone in only a few short years."

Thore winced. *And so will everything else.* "They are all different, aren't they?" He spoke from observation, not experience. He'd never married. He sometimes wondered if the emptiness he felt didn't draw him closer to Noah and his family. "Particularly your youngest ones."

"Different?" Noah gave a short laugh. "Shem and Ham are two of the most contentious boys I've ever known. It's hard to believe they're brothers."

Thore glanced past his shoulder. "Here comes Monik."

Noah turned, watching Monik and Immac stride along an old quarry cut between standing slabs of rough chalcedony that had never had their roots severed.

"They just need some more growing up is all," Noah said, his thoughts still stuck on his sons.

"Morning peace. Sleep well?"

"Morning peace," they replied. Thore said, "Some of the best accommodations we've had in days, Master Monik."

Monik smiled. "Good." He turned to Noah. "I've assembled the people who have shown an interest in what you have to say." His smile wavered a bit. "There are a few who have no interest. I'm not forcing anyone to attend, even though I could."

"My message doesn't appeal to everyone, Chief Gate Warden, but it's for those who have an ear to listen that I'm here."

Thore glanced at Immac. "The tunnel secure?"

"I just came from there. All quiet outside, and Master Monik keeps the opening well guarded.

"Good." After the trouble in Quinal-ee last night, he wasn't taking any chances with Noah's safety.

They followed Monik down to an area cleared of clutter and filling with people, some settling on the cushions strewn across the floor, others dragging forward some of the many wooden folding chairs that had been assembled. A huge block of stone served as his speaking platform.

Vaul halted at the foot of the stone as if he knew the stage was not the place for him. Thore shook his head. That canic was something else. He couldn't quite figure out the connection between Vaul and Noah, unless Noah was a sensitive to canics. His own mother was a sensitive to dragons, and his father to spiders, but he would never know what it was like to communicate with animals. He'd not inherited the gift. Few people had it these days. In the beginning times, Adam and Eve had been given the gift by the Creator, but it had quickly faded away with succeeding generations.

As Naamah and Sheflah took seats below the makeshift podium, Thore scanned the growing crowd, with an eye for possible danger. This place was relatively safe, but his lifelong task of keeping an eye on Noah had conditioned him to judge all circumstances, no matter how innocent they appeared. His Makir training had honed that ability. He'd excelled under his father's coaching, and he might have eventually become Pyir, if he hadn't committed himself as Noah's guardian at his father's request. Instead, when Pyir Klesc had become too old to hold the title, the honor had passed to his younger brother, Chrone. Thore's lips gave a twitch. What he was doing was important. The prestige of being Pyir, like the gift, simply had not been meant for him.

Immac stopped at his side. "I'll be watching the tunnel."

Thore nodded.

Immac drifted off in the direction of the main tunnel.

Thore studied the crowd filling the place and settling down. Zinorah among them, and beside her was the stoic man he'd met last night, Joset.

His muscles tensed when someone came quietly up behind him, and his hand crept instinctively toward the hilt of his sword.

"You've heard Master Noah's talk before?" The sound of Majiah's voice released the tension. He turned. She wore a green dress with yellow embroidery around the cuffs and hem. Her short hair, brushed back in a wave, looked … practical. She appeared taller than she had the previous night aboard the jumper. Maybe it had been the pants and vest with all its rings and buckles? Maybe the darkness? Even so, Majiah was still a compact woman, unlike the long-limbed Hodinite beauties he had loved and lost. Her olive skin shone beneath the artificial lighting as if she had treated it with oil, and her brown eyes were wide and intelligent. In spite of the transformation, her mouth held that same stern frown he remembered from the previous night.

Thore flashed a smile, hoping to surprise one out of her. It didn't work. "It has been awhile since I've heard it, but I can still probably repeat it word for word. Why do you ask?"

"Because of the way you watch our people, instead of him."

"The Oracle would love to get his hands on Master Noah."

She considered him, her jaw clicking to one side. "You're a Makir, aren't you? Both you and Master Immac."

"Us?"

She barked a short, sarcastic laugh. "Who else wears swords under their cloaks these days?"

He laughed. "Yes. We're Makir."

"And your job is to protect Master Noah."

"You're observant."

"One has to be these days." She drew in a sharp breath. "Do you believe what he teaches? That the Creator is going to destroy this world if mankind doesn't turn from the evil that has ensnared it?"

Her jump in topics caught him off guard. "Yes. Do you?"

She crossed her arms with that same determination he'd noted in the jumper. "I don't know. I don't want to believe it." Her snort defied the present appearance of femininity. "I don't want to die, Master Thore. I just want things back the way they were."

"We are all destined to die. It's the curse Adam brought on us." He heard Noah's opening prayer in the background and tuned it out, concentrating on her scorching eyes. "Things can never be as they once were."

Her frown deepened. "He says a flood is coming to destroy everything."

"The flood was preached long ago by his great-grandfather, Enoch. After Enoch, Noah's grandfather proclaimed the message throughout all these lands until he became too old and frail to travel much. Noah's father, Lamech, has taken the same warning to the ends of the Known World." He watched her eyes narrow. "It's not a new message, but it has now become very timely."

"I hear he's building a boat for himself and his family to escape."

"He is?" Noah had tried to keep that activity quiet, but it was impossible to hide such a monstrous boat from curious and scornful eyes.

Her dark eyebrows hitched together. "Seems rather selfish, don't you think?"

Behind him, Noah opened his message in the usual place: the heavens and the stars. Thore gave the room a quick glance. Vaul was hunkered near the stage and there seemed little threat here. "Maybe we ought to go somewhere else to talk."

Majiah inclined her head toward one of the exits, and he followed her out of the meeting room.

❧

The communal dining room where he and Noah had earlier taken their breakfast was nearly deserted. Thore and Majiah shared the room with only a trio of men, bent over their cups in earnest conversation, in a far corner.

Majiah had fixed cups of tea for him and herself, and as she took her first careful sip, he said, "Noah isn't building it for just himself. He has been commissioned to preserve all life that walks, flies, or crawls on the earth, Majiah."

"How many people could he take. A hundred? A thousand? What difference would it make?"

Thore noted the anger that brewed just beneath the surface. He shrugged. "I don't understand the Creator's purpose. And neither does he—not completely. It's not so much what he is doing that matters. It's that he's doing the Creator's will that's important. As I am."

"And you're prepared to die for His will?"

"I don't want to die. But a Makir is always prepared to die. The Katrahs and Kimahs teach us how to face death. And yes, I am prepared to die for His will."

She stared at him. "How can you be so certain what Noah preaches is the Creator's will?"

He had been there at the commissioning. He'd spoken with the Creator. But that had been something special ... and private. "I've had previous experience. And why else would the Oracle be bent on stopping him?"

She opened her mouth to protest, then shut it. "There is logic in that," she said softly.

"You have the means of escaping the coming destruction sitting outside this mine, if you wanted to do so."

She looked confused, then her eyes widened with understanding. "The jumper?" She scowled. "But where would I go? Where could anybody go?"

"Oric?"

Her eyes shot open and the tendons down her neck went rigid. The reaction fascinated him. "I hear the Oracle is building some kind of fortress up there." He pointed at the rocky ceiling.

Her startled face went pale. "Never." Her voice trembled, and horror gathered in her eyes.

He hadn't expected the offhanded remark to affect her so. In retrospect, he should have guessed it would have. "Sorry. It was a bad joke." It was time to change subjects. "How did you manage to get that jumper?"

She took a long breath, her lips settling again into their perpetual frown. In control and self-sufficient again. At least that was the face she showed him. She studied her folded hands a moment and then said, "Zinorah figured it out." Her voice dropped as though she were peering into an open casket. "She'd ... watched it being done."

"To do so would mean she had to have been among the Nephs, and the Oracle's emissaries. Otherwise, how—?" He stopped. Majiah's eyes had begun to glisten, the strong facade showing another crack. "Tell me what happened." He put a hand upon hers. She didn't protest the gesture.

"Zinorah was a br ... a broodblood."

The muscles across his chest cinched tight. "I'm sorry." His words sounded hollow. What did a person say to something like that? But that brought up a big question, one he knew of no delicate way to ask. "Was it ... forced?" He braced for a strong reaction.

Instead, she simply shook her head. "Zinorah was taken. Like so many women these days. She had such beautiful long hair, and that caught the attention of one of those ... those creatures that have infected our world." She stared into his eyes. "There's no stopping them. They're renegades. They take whom they want."

He could see it was painful for her to speak of it. "You don't have to say any more, Majiah."

She sniffed and blinked a couple times, her eyes no longer shining. "Zinorah is my cousin."

"I suspected a family connection."

"We've always been close." Her voice was strong again. "I was crushed when it happened. Confused. I cried out to the Creator to save her ... but Zinorah conceived and had a child." Majiah looked at her hand, momentarily mesmerized by it as she slowly moved one finger at a time, counting five, then she held up one more from her other hand.

Six fingers. He understood. "She gave birth to a Neph. Then what?"

"You know what that does to a woman, don't you?"

He nodded. "If she survives the ordeal, a human can only birth one Neph."

Majiah studied her fingers, then balled them into fists and set her hands back onto the table with obvious restraint.

"They keep mother and child together for the first two years."

He nodded again. "Until the child is weaned."

"Afterward, mother and child are separated. A few, those who become broodbloods voluntarily, have some part in raising the boy." She gave a bitter laugh. "Some even have what resembles a family, if you can call cohabiting with a star-creature a family."

Although it was plainly happening all around him, the mechanics of it confounded him. "I don't understand how this can happen. Humans and Maliks are two different beings. How is interbreeding possible?"

"Nobody understands fully—no son of Adam, that is. Zinorah told me they have ways of manipulating the life forces. At first they weren't very successful at it. All they got were all sterile males. The star-beings worked on the problem for generations in a remote fortress in the Olphus Mountains, away from prying eyes. They didn't want to spring their creations on the world too soon, horrifying us into rejecting them. They finally solved the sterility problem, but they still only produced males. All this was in the days before the Oracle's Temple was built and he took up residence there."

He nodded. "My father encountered the first of them."

"In the beginning the Nephs were deformed monsters. Most didn't survive. But the emissaries learned from their mistakes. Now they do such a good job, you can hardly tell a Neph from a human, except for their size … and their hands." She flexed her fingers again. "As the product improved, more and more woman began to see opportunity in birthing a Neph in spite of the cost; their road to wealth and prestige. After all, the Oracle places Nephs in positions of power: governors, gate wardens, judges, advisers, the military. Surely they would be healers, too, if they weren't all male-born."

"But Zinorah wasn't one of the volunteers." Thore sipped his tea.

"No. Zinorah was a forced broodblood. They are treated differently. After her child"—Majiah gave a slight shudder—"was taken from her, Zinorah was … was sent to Oric."

Thore winced. Had he any idea, he would have never mentioned the place—even jokingly.

"Apparently the Nephs need lots of entertainment, isolated as they are. And Nephs aren't what you'd call gentle or loving beings." She rubbed her arms as if chilled. "Most women don't survive their affections very long. That doesn't seem to pose a problem now that the Oracle has begun moving against the Kinsmen. He takes villages like Quinal-ee to assure his halfling children a steady stream of women—and men, too, depending on their leanings."

Thore's stomach knotted. "How did Zinorah survive it?"

"I don't know. She won't talk about what happened, not even to me. She was, however, a habitation to an invading spirit, and they lend a certain unnatural physical strength to a person. You know about them?"

"A little. When a Neph dies, his spirit is denied entry into the eternal realms. It's cursed to wander, seeking a body to inhabit." He had heard his father speak of such things.

She nodded. "It's how intractable broodbloods are controlled."

"That makes the puzzle even bigger. There is no escaping an invading spirit. No way to be shed of them. My father inquired about it once."

"That's not true, Master Thore." Her eyes brightened. "They can be cast out, but it isn't easy. It takes a man of great faith. A holy man."

"You have a man like that here?"

"Not here. In Morg'Seth."

He was intrigued. "So, how was it done?"

"First, we had to make sacrifices to the Creator, to cover our sins. Our worship had become stale and old, but the holy man had access to a book that had been penned by Adam himself. It explained the way the Creator had commanded Adam and his children to offer sacrifices. We'd forgotten about the clean and unclean animals. We'd forgotten much."

"I know of such things." He leaned closer.

"The holy man read the Book and understood the Creator's wishes. We built an altar of natural stone; no shaping tools were permitted to touch it. Then we gathered the clean animals and sacrificed them in the prescribed way. The sacrifices continued for twenty-one days. Curiously, during that time, Zinorah's child became ill. They brought Zinorah back from Oric, thinking her presence would help the child heal."

"That is a coincidence."

Majiah smiled the first real smile he'd seen her give. Her eyes widened, her eyebrows arched, and her cheeks lifted and dimpled in a way that made Thore's heart thump a little harder. "We thought so too, but the holy man said coincidence is not a ceremonially clean word."

He laughed.

She sobered again, but the memory of the smile stayed with him. "What happened next? Did the child get better?"

"No. She never made it to his side. But it was at the very time she was returning to Earth that the holy man lifted his voice to the Creator, and in the name of Elohim, ordered the invading spirit to flee from Zinorah."

"She was still in the jumper?"

Majiah nodded. "Distance is no deterrent to the Creator of all. As Zinorah tells it, she felt a burst of warmth fill her, and then the spirit fled from her, shrieking, pleading not to be cast out naked into the world. The jumper was carrying Nephs, too, but they were held in a gathering spirit when it happened. Apparently, casting it out weakened the gathering spirit some-how. Suddenly they were all free, Zinorah and the Nephs. Confusion gripped everyone."

Thore tried to imagine the scene, his blood heating with the thought of what a glorious battle could have been fought among such chaos.

"With the invading spirit no longer in control of her body, she suddenly found she had her wits again. Thinking fast, she moved into the pilot's chamber and told the sorp at the controls that there was panic among the Nephs. When he stepped out to see what was happening, she shut the airtight door and opened the outer door. Everyone was sucked out—all but the gathering spirit and the sorp. The spirits were somehow weakened by the event. Still, she fought them all the way back to Quinal-ee."

"Fought? How?"

"A battle of will and prayer, Master Thore. Once Zinorah earthed the jumper, the sorp fled. But a gathering spirit is bound to a jumper. The holy man offered sacrifices and implored the Creator to dislodge the gathering spirit. It was very difficult as they are almost a part of the craft. Still, it had to be done. The jumper would have been useless to us had we left the spirit intact."

"What is a gathering spirit?"

"That's not its name. That's just what we call it. I don't know what its real name is." Her eyebrows puckered as she considered his question. "You know how jumpers move in ways that defy natural laws?"

He nodded. He'd seen jumpers change direction with enough velocity to rip them apart and jelly the insides of any humans within them. Yet, they did it with no apparent damage.

"It's the gathering spirit that makes that possible. But that's not all it does. You see, Nephs, unlike their Malik fathers, have a human side to them. That makes them vulnerable."

"I heard that's why the Oracle is building his fortress on Oric and not Rahab. Oric has an atmosphere, water, and temperate climate ... at least three months out of the year."

"Exactly. Well, the spirit gathers Nephs and humans in its arms, so to speak, to protect them. That way the jumper can move swifter and turn sharper than a Neph body could normally withstand." Her lips hitched to one side. "I guess you might say it's the spiritual part of a jumper. The craft itself is material and functional on its own, but without being inhabited by a gathering spirit, its abilities are limited. On the other hand, with the gathering spirit gone, the Oracle has no way of tracking a jumper's whereabouts—at least he hasn't found ours."

"Fascinating." The military possibilities with a craft like that were endless. "This holy man, who was he?"

"Joset's grandfather, Zinorah's great-grandfather."

Zinorah was Joset's daughter! Suddenly the reason for the man's bitterness was obvious. "Majiah, what was the holy man's name?" Thore knew his father would want to know this.

"His name is Methuselah."

He stared at her.

"What's wrong?"

"Methuselah? The son of Enoch, of the line of Seth?"

"You know of him?"

He looked over his shoulder, although Noah was not in view from this place. "Your holy man is Noah's grandfather."

"Methuselah is also the father of Elokim, Joset's grandfather. Joset is my uncle."

They were both silenced a moment by the coincidence. Ruefully, Thore reminded himself that coincidence was not a ceremonially clean word.

"I wondered where you two went."

He turned to find Chief Gate Warden Monik peering down at them. He had been so occupied, he'd failed to detect the man's arrival. That could have been dangerous.

"You've missed Noah's lecture, Majiah. It was enlightening."

"It's over already?"

"Already? It's been almost a third of a quartering."

"Master Thore was asking about the jumpers. We had a good talk. Did you know Master Noah is the holy man's grandson?"

"Yes, I knew." He crossed his left arm over the one in a sling in that same deliberate manner he'd seen Majiah do a time or two, and looked at Thore. "Noah is looking for you. After what happened in Quinal-ee, he's anxious to be on his way to Morg'Seth."

"I suspect he would be. Most of his family still live in the Leelands." Thore stood. "Mistress Majiah, thank you for an enlightening and pleasant talk."

She nodded, no smile breaking through that tough exterior. Considering all that had happened, he couldn't fault her for her stoicism. Like Joset who had endured the horrors of a daughter taken by the Nephs and turned into a broodblood, these people were entitled to their solemnity.

❦

They had traveled but a short distance from the mountain shelter when Noah stopped and looked back. "They had so many questions ... perhaps I should have stayed an extra day or two?"

Thore shrugged. "We could have stayed."

"No, Noah." Naamah's eyes looked worried, as though he might change his mind. "We must reach our families."

Vaul trotted on a few paces, then turned and stared at them.

Thore shook his head. "Then again, maybe not. Vaul seems anxious for us to be on our way too."

Noah pursed his lips and looked at the rock cliff that hid the mouth of the cave, then he smiled at his wife. "We'll leave. Now that we're afoot, we haven't the luxury of tarrying."

Vaul started along the narrow path, down into a declivity.

Noah hefted his bag under his arm and Naamah and Sheflah shouldered their own light luggage.

"Perhaps we should find some transportation," Immac said as they started on their way.

Thore shook his head. "The main roads will be watched. Best if we keep to the backcountry." His eyes brightened. "If I could get my hands on a jumper we'd be in the Lee-lands like that." He snapped his fingers.

"Your hands wouldn't know what to do with a jumper," Noah replied.

"Zinorah could teach me. Did you know Zinorah and Majiah are cousins, and that Zinorah is your cousin, too?"

Noah shifted his heavy bundle, hugging it under his right arm. "She is?"

"Majiah told me. She said Zinorah's grandfather is Methuselah. That would make Majiah your cousin, somewhat removed."

"Thore, we're all related, if you search the tree closely enough."

"I suppose." He stared ahead at the shelving rock that narrowed the trail.

Noah sensed there was something else on Thore's mind. "What's troubling you?"

Thore looked at him, then took the bag from his arms. "Let me carry that for a while."

"If you wish." He didn't press the Makir for an answer. If Thore wanted to talk about what was burdening him, he would do it in his own good time.

"You know what happened to her, don't you?"

"To whom?"

"Zinorah."

Noah frowned, recalling Joset's grinding bitterness, and Zinorah's cool detachment, as if the essence of her being had been sucked out of her, leaving only a dry, empty husk. "She and her father spoke with me after my lecture."

"I can't imagine what they went through," Thore said.

"I try not to." Noah put a hand upon his daughter's shoulder and they all fell into an uncomfortable silence as they walked. In spite of his desire not to go there, Noah's thoughts insisted on traveling along the troubling road that Thore had started down. He formed an image of Zinorah's face, but it became vague and merged startlingly into Mitah's face. For a while he held onto the vision, remembering snippets of his eldest daughter's life, growing from a babe in Naamah's arms to the pretty young lady she was today—but separated from the family, like Orah and Leteah.

He must have been deeper into his thoughts than he realized. Thore took his arm and drew him to a stop.

"You haven't heard a word I've said, have you?"

He breathed a short prayer for his daughter's safety and looked around. They were standing upon the edge of a wider trail; the rocky declivity he remembered was now several hundred spans behind them and nearly out of sight. "I guess not."

Thore rolled his eyes. "I was saying, it might be wise if we cut this trip short and returned to Atlan."

"We can't do that," Naamah said firmly.

"I know you want to see your family in Morg'Seth, but consider the risks. The Lodath knows you are in the Settled Lands of Hope. He's sure to mount another attack to get at you."

Noah said, "It's not only the family, Thore. It's the Book."

Thore became silent.

Noah put a hand on his lifelong friend's arm. "I know how hard this must be on you—on everyone who hears my words. But I want you to know I do appreciate your company, Thore, and Immac's, and all the risks you've taken just to keep me out of trouble."

"And that, Master Noah, has turned into a full-time job."

He smiled.

Thore's lips twitched into a faint grin. "This morning Majiah asked me if I was afraid to die."

"And?"

"And I gave her the glib answer. 'I'm a Makir. I'm always prepared to die.'" He made a wry smile. "But the truth is," he hesitated, "some deaths do not bring honor."

Noah smiled, understanding. "It scares all of us, Thore."

A few paces behind them, Immac grunted.

19

The Pledge Pendant

*E*scaped!"

The air trembled with his fury while attendants in waiting cringed before his fiery bolts of anger. Freed from the confining human body, Lucifer glowed with the brightness of a star, and at the moment the star was a violent, angry red. Sheets of purple and blue lightning rippled from his arm as his fist rose to clench the air.

Ekalon drifted back a little farther. When the Master was in a rage, the more distance between them, the better. Far beneath them, the Temple and Nod City were specks upon the green curve of the Known World, bent from horizon to horizon. It was here in the air that the ruler of this stone called Earth held court, and it was here he meted out punishment.

Ekalon's grip tightened about his battle staff as Lucifer stalked back to his throne, red, swirling tendrils of light fading to orange, then yellow. He swept aside myriad attendants and plunged broodingly into the golden seat.

The heavens went silent a moment, then his finger stabbed out accusingly. "You had everyone in place, Ekalon. My children were there, your warriors. What went wrong?"

One would think the chill in these upper reaches would have cooled his fury. Ekalon set aside that thought. He'd spent so much time around humans that he was beginning to think in their woefully limited terms. A wry grin might be appropriate, but of course, that was too much like a smile—and both hinted at emotions that were stubbornly beyond his ability now.

"There was"—*how does one inform the ruler of the world about this?*—"some interference."

"The Tyrant's Guardians?"

"They were there in great numbers, as they always are, but this time it was different. Human interference."

"Human. Guardian. It's all the same. It's the Tyrant meddling in the affairs of my world." His eyes narrowed, his fingers impatiently drumming the arm of his throne.

Ekalon recognized the signs of some scheme or another forming. And just in time. He was about to inform Lord Lucifer of the jumper, too, but since his master's thoughts had apparently turned away from his rage and onto more constructive avenues, he hesitated bringing up anything that might reawaken the fury.

After a moment, Lucifer's eyes narrowed toward him. "Away from Atlan, Noah should be easy to reach."

"He is escorted by two Makir. And since we are forbidden to touch him, any attack will have to come from the Earth-Born. Just the same, Master, getting to him is not easy."

Lucifer's eyes darkened. "Then we need to separate him from his Makir, don't we?"

"Yes, Master. And I have already started moving on that. I have arranged for a diversion, and if it is successful, we very well may have a means of eliminating one, if not both, of the Makir."

Ekalon spoke with forced confidence, while inside he feared the plan too uncertain to work. In any event, he had to put forth a confident face or risk the Master's further wrath. He caught his breath, then released it as Lucifer's flames of rage appeared to lessen even further.

Lucifer leaned forward. "Tell me of this plan."

"Part of our difficulty is keeping informed of Noah's whereabouts. His Guardians are always interfering. Shielding, diverting your servants."

Lucifer's aura reddened. "The Tyrant keeps meddling where He has no right to."

"He apparently thinks He does." Ekalon stepped closer and cast a sly glance in the direction of Morg'Seth, lowering his voice. "But if there was some way to follow Noah closer, we could move on him in a moment of weakness, send in the Earth-Born, and do away with the Makir protectors."

"That still leaves Noah alive," Lucifer pointed out, "and since he is the Tyrant's darling, he will still be beyond our reach."

"Perhaps—but consider, Master. Noah is traveling with people who are important to him. And they do not enjoy the Tyrant's undivided attentions. You yourself have said we don't have to kill Noah. All we have to do is distract him."

Lucifer's countenance brightened. "True."

Ekalon wished he could have smiled. Now would have been an appropriate time for a small Sari'el kind of smirk. A little gloat over an idea well conceived and well received.

"Keep me informed, Ekalon. I'd do it myself except—" He broke off, catching himself, as if to have said more would have revealed some dark secret.

But Ekalon already knew why the Ruler of the Air was not seeing to the task personally. The Tyrant of Old had forbidden him to take any part in it. And nothing irked Lord Lucifer more than to have to abide by the Tyrant's demands.

Ekalon said, "I'll see that the plans are carried out properly." He was about to depart, but Lucifer's voice halted him.

"And these humans who came to Noah's aid. See to them, too. We've treated the Settled Lands of Hope far too gently. It's time to change that."

"Yes, my Lord." He bowed stiffly at the waist. Turning from Lord Lucifer, Ekalon stepped momentarily into eternity and emerged instantly upon the vera-logia fields of Noah's ancestral home in the Lee-lands of Morg'Seth.

❧

Several nights after leaving Monik's exiled villagers back in the abandoned mines, Noah and the others made camp in a little valley for the night. The dark peak of Mount Hope loomed far to the south. Mount Hope had been the landmark Noah had been looking for since leaving the Quinal-ee stronghold in the Illackin Mountains of Morg'Jalek. It backed up to the farm that his family operated. Their holdings included a vast, fertile track of land that was perfect for growing the tall, greasy vera-logia plant from which was pressed and distilled the oil that ran much of the Known World's cyclers.

Now with the peak in sight, he was almost home. "How are your feet holding out, Naamah?"

She groaned softly and sat upon a wide, flat ledge of rock, removing a shoe and kneading the ball of her foot. "If I'd known we were going to walk the last leg of the trip, I'd have packed different shoes."

"And you?" He glanced at his daughter.

Sheflah found room enough on the ledge, beside her mother. "I'm just tired ... and hungry."

"I am too." The anticipation of seeing their family again soon had energized Noah's appetite. Mount Hope was all that lay between him and them. Once across it, his feet, which also ached, would be treading the family's property. Even so, his parents' home was still another day's journey southwest.

Immac went about gathering firewood while Thore strode off into the scattered stands of trees at the valley's edge, as was his habit, to scout the area, coming back awhile later apparently satisfied that there was no danger.

They sat around the fire, roasting keelits and orofins, the sweet and tart aromas mixing with the cedar coals. Noah licked his lips in anticipation as Naamah expertly moved their dinner about the hot, flat rock embedded in the coals.

"Nearly a full moon tonight," Thore noted casually, leaning back on his elbows.

Noah refused to look up into the starry night sky. "If you say so."

Thore glanced over and grinned at him.

Vaul lifted his head off his paws and stared up into the blackness. Automatically, Noah's view moved in the same direction. Three dark shapes outlined in a faint pinkish glow passed before the moon, momentarily blocking out the Oracle's vandalism. The objects moved silently past it, and the Oracle's five-pointed symbol reappeared on the moon's once-perfectly smooth surface.

"Jumpers." Thore tilted his head back, watching the crafts. "Coming from the north. Moving toward Mount Hope."

Mount Hope? "Where can they be heading?" Noah's stomach knotted with an unnamed dread even as he spoke.

Thore didn't answer.

"They're flying far too low to be heading out of Earth's firmament. And there isn't anything south of Morg'Seth except the Great Sea ..." His throat squeezed. "Maybe one of the islands?" He barely managed to get the words past the tightness. "They might be going anyplace. Across the Great Sea, to the Outer Lands."

Thore glanced worriedly at him but remained silent, keeping his thoughts inside.

The jumpers quickly became faint reddish spots, merging with the stars, their winking lights fading against the night sky. Vaul watched the dark patch of heaven long after the crafts had become too faint for human eyes to see. Worry, like a lump of raw bread dough, settled in Noah's gut. Stiffly he turned back to the fire.

Naamah began carelessly pushing the food around the hot stone with her stick, her breathing quickening, her lips pressing hard together.

The food no longer tempted him. His appetite had disappeared as swiftly as the jumpers. He caught the exchanged looks between Thore and Immac.

Sheflah continued staring into the sky long after the jumpers disappeared. "They're heading out over the sea, to the Outer Lands. That must be it, Father." Her confident declaration sounded just a little forced.

He appreciated the gesture anyway.

※

All the next day their feet carried them ever southward, up the gentle foothills of Mount Hope and across its rugged spine ... the last obstacle standing between them and their family's farm. Noah tried not to ponder the meaning of the previous night's sightings. When at last they came over the pass and started down the other side, that lump from last night returned to his throat and refused to budge.

It wasn't until the southern foothills were conquered and the vast fields of vera-logia appeared in the distance like a green carpet across the gentle lands of Morg'Seth, that the weight of anxiety lifted from his shoulders.

They paused on a low ridge. Everything looked perfect. The dark green fields were ripe for harvest. To the east, harvesters crawled slowly through one of his father's fields—too far away to hear their chugging cyclers—cutting a wide swath. Conveyor belts from the harvesters carried the freshly cut vera-logia back to the wagons in tow.

"This brings back memories," Naamah declared, shading her eyes toward the endless green.

Vaul sat at his side and his big, dark head turned to the southwest.

"Well, isn't that a peaceful sight." Thore swept out an arm then planted his fists on his hips.

"All looks normal," Immac noted, his keen eyes making a more methodical sweep of the vista before them than Noah had, or even Thore.

Noah nodded. But it was Naamah who seemed most elated by the sight. She'd grown up here on this farm. He had only experienced it vicariously through his mother and father's stories, and firsthand on only a few occasions when he'd visited it over the years.

Like Naamah, Thore shaded his eyes toward the field. "What are all those roads for?"

"Roads?"

"Cutting through the fields every few thousand spans."

Noah followed Thore's pointing finger. "Those aren't roads, although 'gia farmers use them for that purpose sometimes. Those are firebreaks."

Naamah said, "Ripe 'gia is quite flammable. When the sap is running, like now during harvest season, one spark can set a whole field ablaze." She looked at Thore. "I'm anxious to see my family. Let's not stand here gawking."

"How long has it been, Mistress Naamah?"

She grinned and shifted the bag she carried to the other arm. "I haven't been back here in thirty years—give or take."

Noah scanned the green fields, imagining the pungent aroma of freshly cut vera-logia. His view halted on something far to the southwest. The vast green blanket of vera-logia gave way to an abrupt disconformity of duller green as the light from the setting sun struck the long, slender 'gia leaves at a different angle. He squinted against the low western light slanting across the land. "Something crushed the 'gia."

Thore peered out from beneath a flattened hand in the same direction. "Yes. Crushed it. But more than that. There's a pattern to it." He studied it further. "A tapering tail of circles coming off the end of five very large circles. All but the tail appears nested within a larger shape of some kind … a star …"

Noah's skin tingled and he shot a look at the Makir. "Is it a … a five-pointed star?"

"Yes, a five-pointed star." Thore's gaze lifted skyward, even though no moon was yet visible. "Maybe it's only coincidence."

Noah's thoughts lurched back to the jumpers of the night before and he gathered up his bag. "Let's go, Naamah." They started off, Vaul loping easily ahead. "Thore, you coming?" he called over his shoulder.

Thore took off in a run. "Wait here," he shouted as he passed them by and turned down the double-tracks of a utility road running through the vera-logia field.

Noah drew to a halt. Vaul trotted back to his side and sat. "Where is he going?" Noah stared at the edge of the field where Thore had disappeared.

Immac's hand had fallen out of sight beneath his cloak, his broad forehead furrowed in concentration as he scanned the fields.

"Is there any reason why we should wait? Where is the danger?" Noah exhaled an impatient breath, looking around.

"There might be danger, Master Noah. Thore will investigate."

Noah had to find out for himself that their families were all right. "I need to get to the village, Immac."

Vaul rose and started toward the double-track. The canic had a strange sense about these things. He obviously didn't sense danger now. Noah followed him.

"Master Noah!"

He ignored Immac's call. An instant later the Makir was at his side, and Naamah and Sheflah with him. Immac didn't look happy, but short of tackling him to the ground and sitting on him, it was fruitless to argue.

They entered the 'gia field by the same road Thore had taken. They walked for quite a while before Thore's voice reached them through the rows. "I'm over here."

How had he known, unless he had spotted them? Or had it been that peculiar Makir communication?

A few moments later Thore came jogging down the road. "I told you to stay put." He cast Immac an angry look.

"I could have tied him up, if I'd had a rope." The Makir crossed his big arms, and gave a small smile.

"I couldn't sit around waiting, Thore. I need to know that everyone is all right. Besides, Vaul didn't seem concerned."

Thore scowled. "When are you going to stop putting so much trust in a canic?"

"As soon as Vaul proves untrustworthy." Noah exhaled a breath. It wasn't Thore's fault. Thore's sworn task was to protect him, and that's just what he was doing—or thought he was doing. "Where did you get off to anyway?"

"Let me show you."

He didn't want to waste time running down a rabbit trail. He wanted to learn about his family's safety. "Will it take long?"

"Not too long." Thore led him back to a trail he'd stomped through the 'gia, and they threaded their way into the tall plants. As they moved deeper into the rows of crops, the biting smell of oily husks, moist black earth, and ripening pollen blanketed them. Noah swatted at the gnats buzzing in his ears and swirling before his eyes.

Vaul trotted ahead of them, his ears flattened against his head. "Vaul doesn't like this," Noah whispered.

Thore looked back at him. "There is no danger. I've already checked it out."

Abruptly, the 'gia ended and they stood in one of the curious circles. The crops had been crushed flat by something, their stalks all pressed to the ground in the same direction. Thick, golden, oily sap glistened in the sunlight, filling the air with the 'gia's astringent odor.

"These circles and lines were made not long ago." Thore went to his haunches and touched one of the bent stems, rubbing the oily secretions between his fingers. "Who could have done such a thing, and why?"

"Or how?" Naamah stepped into the middle of one of the smaller circles and turned.

Noah strode out into the center of the vast design, careful not to slip on the slick sap. From here the design showed little of the strange symmetry he'd noted from higher ground. "I don't know." He looked at Thore. "Those jumpers we saw last night?"

Thore stood and wiped his fingers on his trouser leg. "No sign of an earthing here. A jumper would have crushed the 'gia in every direction." He tilted his head back, shading his eyes. "Something like this could only really be appreciated from the air."

Sheflah followed his view. "A sign then? To someone passing overhead?"

"Could be, Mistress Sheflah."

Noah's uneasiness grew. Vaul pacing and sniffing the ground didn't help either. "The jumpers? It had to be. Someone made this sign in the 'gia to guide them."

Thore lowered his head and looked at him. "Perhaps."

Noah's hands had begun to sweat, his heart skipping against his ribs. "Why did you bring us here? This is only wasting time. We should be heading for the village."

"I brought you here to show you this." Thore pointed. They crossed the circles to the other side where a wide, trampled trail led off to the west. "Whoever did this came and left along this trail."

Noah stepped a few spans into the pathway, stopped, and looked back at Thore. "It leads away from the village."

"Exactly. North, more or less. Your parents' village is south, more or less. What's north of here?"

He had to think. The Lee-lands were not his home.

Naamah spoke before he had it figured out. "Nothing but the River Laine Crossing, about four leagues above New Eden. It's on the main road from Morg'Seth into Morg'Jalek. The one we would have traveled if we had taken a cyclart as we first planned, instead of fleeing Quinal-ee on foot."

"Interesting." Thore fell thoughtfully silent for a moment.

Immac said, "It may mean nothing. We still have no idea who stomped these designs into the 'gia."

"Or even if they were stomped." Thore peered at the flattened vegetation. "None of this looks man-made. It's too perfect, the stalks all lying in exactly the same direction."

Immac nodded. "I agree."

Thore said to Noah, "I wanted you to see it. Now, let's get you to the village." He turned back the way they had come, stopped, and bent for something caught among the stalks. Thore took the end of a leather thong and worked the object free.

Sunlight caught in a crystal pendant, its colors swirling deep within the crystal's heart.

Noah watched how the colors seemed to move. "A pledge pendant?"

"Looks like one." Thore laid it against his palm, shading it from the sunlight. "The colors are generated from within."

Noah grabbed his hand and pulled it away. "Don't touch it."

"It's warm." His fingers moved toward it again.

Noah restrained him. "You should get rid of it, Thore. A thing like that has no place in our lives."

"What harm can it do to hold onto it for a while?"

"What harm? Ask your father about pledge pendants. How

one worked its way into his soul, how it almost took him over and destroyed him."

"My father?"

"Has he not told you what happened to him?"

"He's told me nothing." Thore looked back at the finger-length crystal, flashing red to green, swirling with blues and yellows.

It was an easy thing to stare at, and it nearly mesmerized Noah. "My mother told me how a pledge pendant once took over your father's life, how its sway over him grew stronger and stronger until the day he realized he was no longer in control over his actions. That was when Rhone finally found the strength to throw it into the Border Sea."

"His encounter with Leviathan? Yes, he told me about that. But he never mentioned a pledge pendant."

"I might understand why. Rhone was Pyir of the Makir. He was a proud, mighty warrior back in those days. It's not strange that he wouldn't want to talk about something as small as that crystal taking control over him."

Thore looked back at it. "At least we know one thing. Whoever made these crop circles is in league with the Oracle."

"The Deceiver," Noah said.

Thore whirled the pendant by its thong, watching it shatter the sunlight upon its facets, casting blue, green, and red light across the broken stalks. "What should we do with it?"

"Throw it away."

"You're right." He heaved back, but stopped at the last moment. "No. I think we ought to keep it, to show to the Village Council. They'll want to know what's going on in their own fields and borders."

Noah felt the scowl wrinkle his forehead. "I think we should just get rid of it."

But Thore carefully wrapped it in a scrap of cloth from the pouch on his side, then dropped it into the pouch. "It will be all right. I understand how it works now. It seemed to come to life when I touched it. So long as I don't touch it, it can't influence us. It should be safe to carry bound up."

Thore understood less than he knew, and Noah gritted his teeth against his better judgment. "All right. But only until you can show it to the Village Council."

20

A Reunion in Morg'Seth

*N*ew Eden had changed much since he was last there. Once a humble little village, it now bustled with self-importance. It had grown fat around the middle with the gaudy baubles of the prize homes of the successful 'gia planters. The quaint little houses of old now rubbed shoulders with sparkling new palaces, which seemed much too large to Noah's more practical sensibilities. He was used to Rhone's lavish palace, but these weren't heads of state or dignitaries. These were planters who had found new money in the growing demand of 'gia throughout the Known World.

"I'd get lost living in something like that," he said to Naamah, pointing to one of the gleaming edifices on their way into town.

"I'd wear my hands and knees out trying to keep it clean it," she replied.

Sheflah's eyes were wide and in constant motion. "What grand parties I could throw for my friends."

They laughed and she looked embarrassed.

The road to his parents' farm used to be a long way beyond New Eden's limits, but now the little lane that led to the ancestral home appeared at the very edge of town. He was sure the road hadn't moved. In a few years the village would be sitting upon his mother and father's very threshold ... but then, he mused wryly, what difference would that make anyway? All the changes—all the hopes and aspirations! It weighed sadly on him that all he beheld would be swept away. All these people ... his family, his friends.... He cast a glance at Thore striding tall and quietly at his side, his keen gaze probing every corner, every side street, every shadowed alcove.

They had been friends for so long, he could hardly imagine a world without Thore in it—and High Councilor Rhone and Lady Leenah too. He loved them as though they were his own parents. He pondered the extra space on the ark, and the extra rooms. What would it take to build two more? Could he somehow take them with him? The Gardener had mentioned only his family, but weren't these people his family too? Could he somehow find a way to include his mother and father—his sisters and brothers too—and Thore, Rhone, and Leenah? There was plenty of room for all of them.

Noah prayed as they walked the lane to the farm, but the only answer he received was a heavier heart. The Gardener had been clear in His instructions, and it was wrong, he knew, to try to cajole Him with supplications into changing His mind.

❦

The muscles in his back seemed too taut, and his shoulders, with a mind of their own, had refused to square-up at his command. Even now as Rhone watched the harbor below—a sight that should have cheered him, a shadowy anxiety weighed heavily on him. The morning's feel had morphed from a small uneasiness to full-blown worry. He placed his hands upon the stone merlon and leaned over a crenel, watching the red-paved meeting floor below The Sanctuary of Justice where people took on the dimensions of ants.

A flicker of movement from the corner of his eye caught his

attention. The dragon banked into view, turning ponderously above the harbor. Gur flapped his immense leathery wings to gain a bit of height then glided toward the rooftop garden, ruby scales glinting streamers of sunlight. Rhone marveled at the old dragon's agility as he rotated wings to break his descent and reached with great curved talons. Gur came to rest upon the battlement, the spread of his feet spanning six merlons.

"Out for your morning constitutional?" He scratched the dragon hard between his scaly eye ridges, right where Gur enjoyed it most. He was rewarded with a soft, guttural purr that lasted all of a few moments before the beast discovered an irresistible itch. Rising up on one foot, Gur scratched violently beneath his left wing.

Rhone smiled as the dragon shook himself and settled back down. The weight in Rhone's heart eased for a bit, then slowly, inexorably, settled back in place. He sensed Leenah coming from their chambers and turned to catch her smile.

"You've been out here a long time, Rhone."

"Watching the harbor."

"The ruler of Atlan has the luxury to muse the morning away?"

"The ruler of Atlan can muse when he chooses. Such are the benefits of the High Councilor position."

Her mouth spread and her eyes caught the sunlight. She reached up and scratched Gur under the chin. The dragon stretched his neck and turned his head to get the full benefit.

She paused abruptly and looked at him. "Gur thinks you are unhappy."

He must have showed in his expression his surprise. "What do dragons know?"

Her smile faltered. "You are, aren't you?"

There was no use denying it. "How can he tell?"

"Animals just understand. You of all people should know that."

He turned back to the harbor where crews of workers were

busy repairing the damage the shaking had caused. New construction had quickly risen to accommodate the lowered water level. Her hand slid up his back to his shoulder.

"What is it?"

"I don't know. I thought at first it might be from dealing with all the suffering of late. The damage. The repairs to the Keep, as well as Atla Fair, but it goes deeper."

He tried to pin it down, but the feeling was just too elusive. The only thread he could catch was a fleeting image of his son. But even that was too nebulous for him to be sure. Still, when he thought of Thore, the weight grew slightly heavier, his mood faintly darker.

They heard the door to their chamber open and a moment later Solah appeared in the arched portal to the rooftop garden.

"Yes, Solah?" Leenah turned away from the battlement.

The handmaiden came out into the garden. "The kitchen sent this for you, Lady Leenah. Nic'im said you were expecting them." Mistress Solah held a small paper bag.

"What is it?" Rhone asked.

"Keelit seeds." Solah folded her hands in front of her. "Lady Leenah has been collecting them."

He slanted a curious eyes toward his wife. "Lady Leenah has been collecting keelit seeds?"

Leenah smiled at him then turned to Solah. "Thank you. You may go now."

Solah bowed curtly and went back to her chores.

"Keelit seeds, Leenah?"

"For Noah."

He draped his arm around her and walked her into the chamber. "What is Noah supposed to do with keelit seeds?"

"Plant them." She disengaged herself from his embrace and went to the chalsoma box upon the desk next to the manuscript she'd been working on when Gur's arrival had drawn her out to the garden.

He leaned against a marble pillar and folded his arms across his chest, watching her remove the puzzle box and work the three concentric rings in their proper sequence. The lid sprang open as the catch released. He bent a little and raised his eyebrows. "You've been collecting them for some time."

She carefully poured the dried seeds Nic'im had sent her in with the others. "Ela said the keelit is cousin to the Tree of Life. It gives long life and health. When Noah and his family begin a new world for the Creator, I want him to have all the health he can. Who knows what plants will survive the flood? The keelit may not. This way he can start anew."

He laughed. "I'm sure the Creator can see to Noah's health, and to keelit trees."

"Just the same, I will give him this before the time comes." She snapped the lid closed and placed the puzzle box in the chalsoma box. "And the manuscript. Naamah is collecting the important knowledge of our world to help them rebuild. This little history will live on as well."

"Then you better tell him the combination." He winked. "It took you a year to figure it out, and only after I dropped enough clues to lead a blind beggar to riches."

"I'll tell him." She wrapped her arms around his neck and kissed him. "Now, you tell me what's bothering you."

"I don't know."

She peered at him. "Truthfully?"

"Truthfully." He hesitated. "Except …"

"What?" Her blue eyes narrowed worriedly.

"Whatever it is, it has something to do with Thore."

"Thore?" She released her hold and stepped back. "Thore is thousands of leagues from here." She scowled. "Is this one of those Makir things?"

He shrugged. "I'm not sure."

"Don't worry me like this, Rhone."

"You asked."

"I wish I hadn't."

⁂

"Noah! Naamah!" Mishah stepped out the door of her house and greeted them on the house-path. She squeezed them in a group hug and kissed Noah's cheek, the pale purple crescent of lavender flowers in her graying hair brushing his nose. "You've put on weight."

"A little." He grinned. "It comes with the years."

She turned her smile on Sheflah. "And you have put on height and beauty. Come give your grandmother a hug."

Next she hugged Thore, her cheek barely reaching the big man's heart. Then she gave Immac a warm handshake.

"We were expecting you days ago."

"An unexpected delay, Mistress Mishah." Thore smiled. "We ended up walking from Morg'Jalek."

Concern sprang full bloom to her eyes. "Serious trouble?"

Noah nodded. "Quinal-ee has been invaded by the Nephs."

His mother's golden brown eyes grew large. "I hadn't heard."

"The Lodath and the Oracle are careful that news of their offensives doesn't spread too quickly," Immac said.

"But you're all right?" She felt Noah's arm as though checking for broken bones or torn muscles—the healer instinct coming out. He smiled at her predictable response.

"The Creator was looking out for us." He glanced down at the canic. "And so was Vaul."

His mother glanced worriedly around, her view skimming the small lake and then narrowing up the lane toward New Eden. She turned and peered across the land past the scattering of houses where family members lived. Her fingers tugged at his arm. "Come into the house." She sent Mel'corik, their Good Man, to inform Cerah and Kenoch of their arrival.

Lamech was hunched over a table, writing, and didn't look up until he heard Noah's voice. Then he sprang to his feet with a nimbleness that belied his 777 years. "Noah!" He engulfed him in a hug, and then stood back to look him up and down, his face stretching with a huge smile. "We were getting anxious. Fair journey?"

His mother spoke first. "They had trouble in Quinal-ee."

Lamech's face sobered. "What kind of trouble?"

"Nephs were waiting for us there," Noah said. "They've taken over the town. Burned most of it. Fortunately, most of the citizens escaped into the mountains. They got us out of town just in time."

"Most?"

Thore nodded. "Some didn't move fast enough. They were captured and taken to Nod City."

Lamech shook his head. "It's happening all throughout the Settled Lands of Hope." He frowned. "Fortunately, Morg'Jalek is a mountainous land. The people there have places to run to and hide. Here in Morg'Seth there will be no place to run except south, into the sea."

"Lamech, you don't think he will—"

"I fear that time cannot be far off, Mistress Naamah," Thore interrupted. "The Oracle is moving to crush all Kinsmen under his boot. He won't be satisfied until every last believer has been rounded up and either forced to renounce their faith or killed."

"You're right, Thore. But he's moving throughout all of the Known World, not just the Settled Lands of Hope." Lamech turned back to the table where he had been working and took up a copy of the Book he and Sor-dak had written so long ago. "It's because of this that the Oracle has begun to move with force."

"I don't see how your Book can be so much of a threat to him," Thore said.

"The truth is always a threat to the Deceiver." Lamech

dropped the Book back onto the table. "But the truth is out, so now he does what he can to change it."

Noah said, "It's not only the Creator's message to man in the stars, Father. Although your Book has touched many lives, it's the lateness of the hour that's the true reason the Deceiver has stepped up his attack on us. He knows his time is short."

Lamech straightened a bit and nodded. "My father is approaching the end of his days, and when he is gone, judgment will be reckoned upon this world. The Deceiver knows this too." Lamech's eyes narrowed at Noah. "You should be home in Atlan, making preparations."

Thore said, "Almost my very words to your stubborn son."

※

"The ark is nearly complete. You know why I had to come— why we had to come, Father."

Lamech smiled. "Yes, of course. The Book."

"And our families," Naamah said.

Mishah gave her another hug.

Noah said, "I'm hungry."

"I'm not surprised." Mishah herded both of them over to the table and then hurried into the kitchen, coming back a moment later with a fruit bowl in her arms. She divided several scarlet strawberries into quarters and passed the pieces about. She began shaving the tough skin off a ripe keelit.

"Always eat your keelits." Thore grinned. "Mother said that at every meal when I was growing up—still does. I don't often get to eat with the family anymore."

"Nor I with mine," Immac's deep voice said thoughtfully.

"Well, you two will eat with ours." Lamech tucked his napkin into his shirt and said to Noah, "Afterward, I'll go tell the family you're in for a visit. We'll have a reunion. Everyone is always asking about you."

Noah took a bite out of a shiny red strawberry wedge, dribbling juice down his chin. He wiped it with his napkin. "How are Uncle Kenoch and Aunt Cerah?" He glanced at his wife. "Naamah hasn't seen her parents since Japheth's wedding."

His mother smiled across the table at her. "Kenoch and Cerah should be here any moment now. They've been asking about you almost every day."

"I can hardly sit still." Naamah's big green eyes were full of anticipation.

Noah looked back to his father. "And Grandfather Methuselah's health?"

Lamech plucked a slice of keelit off the plate. "My father is slowing down, but he still gets around," he said, grinning. "And he still doesn't miss a chance to preach whenever he can. Kenoch has taken over the management of the farm; and Cerah, along with some of your cousins, watches over the younger children while everyone else tends to the fields."

"We're looking forward to seeing them all ... especially Aunt Cerah."

Lamech looked at him. "The Book awaits you."

The stiffened tone of his father's voice shattered the congenial moment and flashed a vivid reminder in Noah's thoughts of the dark reality rapidly closing in on all of them. He grimaced. "It's time I took charge of it, don't you think?"

Lamech considered him a long moment, slowly chewing the keelit. He nodded. "It's time."

Then Uncle Kenoch and Aunt Cerah came through the door, and the mood lightened.

❦

Cousins, nephews, sisters, brothers, uncles, and grandparents all descended upon him at once ... and a hundred questions pummeled him from all sides. Thore and Immac weren't immune either. The two Makir regaled them with ancient tales of mighty Makir Warriors of the past—from those misty days long ago when the warrior sect battled Atlan's enemies with swords and immeasurable skill. Nowadays the glamour had faded, although the Makir symbol, a sword bearing the patriarchal crest and name of the house from which the warrior hailed, remained a Makir's most prized possession. But practicality had superseded romanticism. A fistproj was by far a more effective and deadly weapon than the blade, especially in trained hands, and the Makir still prided themselves in their training. The Katrahs and Kimahs remained their daily ritual, just as prayer was to Noah.

A great burge melon stuffed with tubers and vegetables, mushrooms and nuts, seasoned with a quantity of puff pollen, was wrapped in honey-soaked grape leaves and nested among hot stones in the coals of a fire. Nearby bubbled a tub of elephant tusk rice. Kenoch had earlier tapped into a barrel of last year's vintage, spiced it, and filled a cauldron upon a bed of coals. While they waited for the food to cook, he passed around mugs of the mulled wine.

Noah relished the sweet, numbing drink. The vintage was not quite as aromatic as that which his vineyard produced, but delicious just the same. He looked around for Naamah and spied her with her mother. Aunt Cerah looked much the same as she had at Japheth's wedding. Thinking of the wedding made him wonder how the boys were managing. Were Ham and Shem keeping peace, or was Japheth constantly refereeing those two? He thought of Wend, too. His smile drooped a little and he revitalized it with a long drink of Uncle Kenoch's wine.

Before the dinner began, Lamech helped his father to the chair, gently lowering him upon the seat. Methuselah was a mere wisp of the man Noah remembered. Age had sapped his vitality, drained his muscles, and turned his skin to rice paper. His once black hair was now a crown of white about his head, his face long and bony, carved with the deep, dry rivulets of age. But his soft, watery brown eyes were still alert, his hearing keen, his eyesight sharp enough to spy Noah among the crowds of family members.

"Noah. Come. Sit by me." Methuselah motioned him over with a slender arm.

"I'd be honored, Grandfather."

Grandfather gave him a gap-toothed grinned as his arms struggled to encircle him, their touch featherlike.

"Are you well?" Noah asked.

The old man grinned and thumped his chest. "I'm marvelous— for having endured nine hundred sixty-three years."

"Here's to another nine hundred," a cousin exclaimed, and everyone around them seconded the hope.

Everyone but Noah. He held his tongue and merely smiled.

Methuselah prayed for the food, for the Creator's blessing and protection, and the feast began.

After eating a huge meal where the talk rambled and the wine flowed freely, Noah gathered his family around him to answer as best he could the many questions that burdened each of them. Methuselah sat by his side for a little while, riveted by Noah's answers, but fighting fatigue. The ancient patriarch finally succumbed to exhaustion and Lamech helped him to his room.

Noah had wanted some time alone with the old man, but that would have to wait. The others were crowding around him. Foremost, the question on everyone's heart was how the Creator would protect them from the coming judgment.

Kenoch, the prankish rogue he always was, kept Noah's mug filled with the spicy beverage, and Noah's head was skimming the peaks of reality, purposefully avoiding the deeper, weightier valleys. The wine dulled both his senses and the pain in his heart at seeing his family's worry.

The big-eyed children were the hardest to face. At times Noah's eyes dampened, knowing how few years were left to them.

He should stop drinking. Instead, he held out his mug and let his Uncle Kenoch refill it yet again, and soon his eyes were dry.

Vaul's dark, sleek bulk remained at his side, his midnight eyes staring at him. Through the buzzing alcohol haze, Noah imagined the canic scowling a reprimand. He grinned and glanced around for Thore.

The Makir had disappeared somewhere. Perhaps down by the lake? He tried to focus beyond the nearer sea of faces with little success. Immac had his own circle of ears, eager for more tales of the Makir. The crowd as large as the one he'd spoken to in the cave, but the difference was, here they were all near family members, and that made the biting pain go deeper, its sting just that much more venomous.

Stumbling a bit over his tongue, he tried to assure the children that the Creator had a way out for them, but in his heart, even he didn't believe it. There were scoffers hovering close too, Cousin Barchor among them. Some, he suspected, may have even had a trickle of Neph blood in their veins. After so many generations of Neph offspring intermarrying with man, the pollution had touched nearly every family. But so long as they didn't marry pure Nephs, no one complained too loudly. The initial stigma had softened over the years to mere clucking and head-wagging. No family was completely immune. If you looked closely enough into their genealogies, a Neph would turn up sooner or later, even if the heavy jaws, the towering stature, or the most telling feature of all, the six fingers, weren't apparent.

Some tainted families even boasted of their open-mindedness and rebuked the less tolerant who still clung to the old ways. Those folks of a more conservative leaning, in their own defense, had begun keeping exact genealogies to prove their purity—his own parents chief among the record keepers. Noah knew for certain the generations down through his mother and father, and his Uncle Kenoch and Aunt Cerah, were unpolluted. His wife,

Naamah, and consequently their sons and daughters, were therefore untainted, but the bloodlines that crisscrossed the tips of the family tree were definitely suspect, a few known to be muddied.

A hand took his shoulder. He turned and grinned at Aunt Cerah, her fiery red hair brilliant in the setting sunlight.

"When you're free here, we need to talk." She smiled, but her blue-gray eyes just barely held back a scowl—or so he imagined.

21

The Word's New Guardian

H ow much did you drink?" Aunt Cerah crossed her arms with a martial snap and glared at him. Just as sharply, she wheeled and aimed her narrowed eyes at her husband. "And you, too, Kenoch. Urging him on like that. What got into you?"

Uncle Kenoch gave a lopsided smile and spread his palms to the ceiling of their small welcoming room where Noah had managed to slump into one of the hanging chairs. His head was whirling, his stomach churning. He willed himself not to get sick and shoved a foot hard against the floor in an attempt to stop the room from spinning. He could see that Uncle Kenoch was nearly as drunk as he was.

"Cer, what harm did it do? We were celebrating Noah's visit...." Uncle Kenoch cast a pleading glance his way. "Isn't that right?"

Noah nodded, which was a mistake as his stomach lurched. "I'ms not shrunk, Aunt Cerahhh—"

She shook her head. "Kenoch." His name graveled from her throat on a note of exasperation.

"Noah seemed so weary, so depressed. I just wanted to help."

Her nostrils flared. "At your age, Kenoch. Will you never grow up? Sometimes you act as if you're still a boy of fifty, wanting to run off and slay mansnatchers or Nephs." She cast her glance between the two of them, then with fists bunched at her side, stomped off into the kitchen.

Across the room, Naamah sat in a chair, her eyes narrowed, her lips bent slightly in disappointment.

Uncle Kenoch winked at him. "How do you feel?"

"Serable." The raspy response emptied his lungs and he hauled in another breath and shut his eyes. The room spun faster. He lolled his head back, and his stomach began to gurgle with an urgency he could no longer control. Someone grabbed his arms and the next instant he was out in the cool night air ... and then he lost it.

Later, he didn't know how much later, Naamah put an arm around his shoulder and lifted him slightly from where he scrunched down in a corner, his knees into his chest. "Feeling better, Noah?"

"I want to die." He tried to moisten his lips with the thick, gritty slab of old leather that filled his mouth. A vice squeezed his head, and the stinging, foul residue of stale vomit burned his throat. "Water."

Naamah put a glass into his hands and helped him gently to get it to his mouth without a major mishap. He drank deeply, imagining his body a parched sponge, barely responding to the water. He lowered the glass to his lap, laid back his head, and shut his eyes to the glare of the room's lights. "What time is it?"

Aunt Cerah said, "Third of the second."

He lurched straight and recoiled at the spike of pain in his head. "The second quartering?"

She nodded, the corner of her lips lifting slightly, deepening the fine lines that radiated across her cheeks from her eyes.

"I'm so sorry, Aunt Cerah. The others must think I'm a disappointment."

She took the empty glass from him. "The others don't know. I simply told them you fell asleep in our welcoming room, that's all.

Your mother looked in on you before she and Lamech went home."

"And?"

"And they said they would see you in the morning."

"Where is Sheflah?"

Naamah said, "She's spending the night with her cousins, Efie and Depinah."

Good. He didn't want her to see him like this. "Never again." He held his head and shook it gingerly.

"I've heard that promise before from your Uncle Kenoch."

His feet bumped something warm. Vaul peered up at him from the floor. He looked around the otherwise empty room. "Where's Thore ... Immac?"

Aunt Cerah inclined her head at the door. "Thore said he prefers the night air for sleeping. Immac is wandering around someplace. They both are suspicious of everything."

"That's their job." He stared a moment at the apparently new lock that had been installed on the door, not recalling it being there the last time he had come visiting. The days were definitely changing, growing more dangerous. "Thore's worried."

"We all are, Noah." Aunt Cerah's eyes shifted briefly toward the door.

"Did he tell you ... the others?"

"Tell us?" She gave him a quizzical look.

"About the circles and lines in the crops? About the pledge pendant we found?"

Aunt Cerah shook her head. "He said nothing about it to me or Uncle Kenoch."

Noah glanced at Naamah who shook her head. "It's up to Thore to tell them."

"Maybe he's waiting for me to bring it up."

"Tell us what?"

"It seems the Oracle may have his eyes on Morg'Seth. We saw three of his jumpers the other day moving southward." He tried to work up some moisture in his mouth. "Near as we can figure, the thing in the crops was a signal to them. Could I get another drink of water?"

Aunt Cerah brought it to him, and he took a long swallow.

"We know our time is short, Noah. You need to return to Atlan. You have important things to finish up there."

He gave the glass back to her, and in spite of his discomfort, forced a smile and glanced at his wife. "Naamah has been after me to stay home for years."

"You should listen to my daughter. She has a good head." Aunt Cerah exchanged glances with Naamah, and set the glass on a nearby end table. "Your traveling puts you in danger—you and Thore ... and now us."

"You know why we had to come. This might be our last opportunity before—" He left unspoken what he and she already knew. The wine was leaving his brain, and with its ebb, the knowledge of what was coming to his family began to burden him again.

"Yes. The Book."

He nodded—and wished he hadn't.

Aunt Cerah pulled a chair around and sat facing him. "Noah, how much do you know about the Book?"

"A little. I know it is important." He was in no condition for clear thinking, but he forced his way past the throbbing in his head, trying to remember. There had been six of them who knew the story. Grandmother Amolikah had long since gone to her rest, and their Good Man, Kleg'l, had been laid in the family tomb not long afterward. That left four still alive who had firsthand knowledge of the meeting—well, five, if you counted Master Bar'ack: his mother, Mishah, High Councilor Rhone, Aunt Cerah, and Uncle Kenoch. No one knew very much about what happened to Bar'ack after the spirits of the dead Earth-Born took over his body—or even if he was still alive.

His mother had spoken little of the matter to him, except to stress the Book's importance, and how it had been entrusted to Aunt Cerah by none less than Mother Eve herself.

"Important is too tame a word, my dear nephew. Priceless comes closer, but hardly does justice." Her pale eyes kindled as she leaned forward, zeal burning within their deep bluish pools. "There is so much knowledge already lost to the people of today, and it's so sad. Sad to think that all which exists today began only a little over sixteen hundred years ago. It was less than five hundred years ago that some of the firstborn still walked with us. Yet what we are being told by the Lodath and the Oracle, how the Oracle planted in him the seed of humanity, and all that we are today has developed from that single act."

"Like the Nephs," Noah agreed. "From manhood to godhood in the span of a few generations. The next leap in man's change. My father told me he heard those very words spoken before the Oracle's Temple had been completed. It's all a lie, Aunt Cerah."

"Of course it's a lie, Noah. You and I know that, and the remnant of believers knows it. But the rest of the world has bought into the lie—the lie that leads unto death, the Messenger Gabriy'el called it before he took Mother Eve home."

She straightened and considered him. "The Book, as you know, was given to me the day Mother Eve went to Adam's Bosom. The Earth-Born—the Nephs, as we call them today— were razing her village, Chevel-ee, trying to reach Mishah, pregnant with you at the time. Rhone—Pyir Rhone back then—your Uncle Kenoch, Grandmother Amolikah, Kleg'l, and I all escaped beneath the village wall."

Most of this was familiar from the stories he had already heard. "High Councilor Rhone told me how the Earth-Born burst through the village's defenses and attempted to murder Mother Eve. But the earth shook and opened, and swallowed them up, and the mighty Messenger of the Creator, Gabriy'el, carried her home, to Adam's Bosom."

Aunt Cerah's eyes glazed at the memory. Noah took her hand, giving it a squeeze. "You were special to Mother Eve, weren't you, and she to you?"

"I was her ward. She took me in after my parents died, and I loved her as my very own mother, Noah." His aunt wiped her eyes and abruptly left the room. He glanced at Naamah who returned a small smile.

It seemed a long time before Cerah returned, carrying an angular bundle wrapped in an incredibly ancient oilskin pouch. Sitting again with a hand placed gently upon it, the tears were gone and that fiery zeal back. She stared at him past a hank of burning red hair that had come lose and fallen across her forehead.

"Noah, the Deceiver has wanted to get his hands on this Book since it was first penned by Father Adam."

"Surely he would only destroy it."

"That's exactly why he wishes it. This contains the true beginnings, Noah, the very truths the Deceiver fervently wishes to wipe from the memory of man." Wonderment filled her voice. "In here, in the Creator's own words, we are told how the worlds came into being, how life sprang from the Creator's breath, how He walked with our first parents in the Cradleland."

The Cradleland. Noah's thoughts leaped back over the dim and misty wisps of five hundred years, recalling memories of his earliest recollections of living in the Creator's Garden: the sounds of animal voices speaking in a language he understood; the whispering songs of towering silver-leafed trees; the bright sweet or sharp murky odors of flowers that conjured up colors and music as no flower had since.

"After the banishment," his aunt's tone leveled, taking on the harder edges of regret, "Father Adam chronicled life beyond the shining Cradleland walls, in a harsh and unyielding world—at odds with mankind who now faced it naked, stripped of the Creator's glorious light." Her fingers slowly stroked the oilskin covering. "In this Book is the true history of the world, not some fantasy of 'millions of years' and 'clawing upward.'"

"What stopped the Deceiver from finding it?"

"Prayer and provision. The Creator has ways of protecting His words. Mother Eve cared for it first, surrounded by the Creator's unseen Messenger-warriors. Then I, in this land blessed with the Creator's protection because of believers like Lamech and Kenoch, Methuselah, and Jared." A shadow darkened her face. "But now I can no longer keep it. The wrath coming upon the earth is too great. But the Book must survive, and you are the only one who can assure that, Noah."

She hesitated, then gently placed the Book into his hands. "As Mother Eve passed it on to me, I now pass it onto you, Noah. Guard it well." Her expression echoed her solemn words. "You can't afford another celebration like last night. Go home. Watch over it with your very life. Finish the Creator's ark and then bring the Book, our daughter, and grandchildren safely into the world that is to be afterward."

He took it from her, equally as hesitant. "I will, Aunt Cerah."

"Promise me."

His breath caught at the urgency he noted in her face. "I promise."

The Book pressing upon his knees was heavier than he first imagined. Carefully he parted the oilskin and withdrew the ancient tome. Its chestnut leather covers were stained and scuffed, the binding stiff. It groaned like an old man rising from a long sleep as he opened it, releasing the musty odor of a distant past. In the muted light of an energized moonglass, he stared at faded greenish-brown ink upon dried, tawny reed-paper. The script was tight and precise, written by a careful hand; a hand that had never been taught how to form letters, as a child is taught today; a hand created with writing already etched into its nerves and trained into its muscles.

He looked at Naamah. "Tomorrow we will return to Atlan."

Naamah took her mother's hand and nodded. Both women's eyes shone, understanding tomorrow would be their last time together, this side of Adam's Bosom.

It was way past bedtime. He decided to spend the night here in Aunt Cerah's house rather than returning to his parents' house down the lane.

22

Attack and Flight

The boom wrenched Noah from a fitful sleep, shaking the house and nearly flinging him off the bed in Aunt Cerah's side room. Naamah startled awake beside him. He grabbed at the bed frame to steady himself and sat up, his brain exploding with raw pain. He clutched his head as the throbbing sent hammer blows down his spine and drove needles of pain to the backs of his eyeballs.

Vaul nudged up against his leg as he struggled to his feet and hurried into his clothes. A low whine filled the room, and an instant later a second boom threw him to the floor. The east wall burst inward, and stone crumbled as it spewed across the floor toward him. Timbers cracked and crashed, tumbling a waterfall of shiny red roofing tiles with them. In an instant a fine, choking dust enveloped the gathering room.

He clawed up a broken timber, pulling himself to his feet. He grabbed Naamah from the bed. A third explosion slammed them back onto it and he banged his head against its carved-wood headboard. Coughing up the dust, he managed to get himself and Naamah to their feet again. She grabbed for her dress and shoes as he hauled her out of the room.

"What's happening, Noah?" Fear etched her face, as he knew his own also must be.

"I don't know!"

Outside the house came panicked shouts. Voices shouting to run for cover, others calling for loved ones, and yet others wailing from fright or pain.

He instinctively started for the door, concern for his daughter and mother and father foremost in his thoughts. Then he stopped.

"Aunt Cerah ... Kenoch!" His aunt and uncle hadn't emerged from their bedroom.

Dread showed in Naamah's eyes as they rushed down the hallway, fanning the stinging dust before their eyes. Pointed shards of rubble from the ceiling, cast across the floor, jabbed the bare soles of his feet, but he was hardly aware of the pain.

A timber fallen across the passage blocked the bedroom door. Roofing tiles strewn across the floor clattered beneath his feet, pricking the tender skin.

"Uncle Kenoch!" He put his shoulder to the door that sat askew in its frame. It wouldn't budge. The arching stone overhead had crushed down on it.

The house shook again. Noah reeled, his shoulder slamming into the stone wall. Pain bolted up his neck. He coughed the dust from his lungs and grabbed his arm to his chest. In the thickening air, he drew in a stinging breath.

"Mother! Father!" Naamah called, fighting the door.

"Naamah!" It was his Uncle Kenoch's voice.

"I'm here. I can't open the door."

"Your mother's hurt!"

Gritting back the pain, Noah tried to move the timber. It was useless. He shoved on the door. Nothing. "Vaul. Get help."

He put his weight to the door again, bracing against the timber. Vaul backed up and then leaped, throwing himself against the panel. The door burst inward half a span, and seized tight again. Outside, the air rocked with explosions. A faint, worrisome odor of smoke began to permeate the house. He hadn't time to think about it.

Vaul plunged through the gap while Noah surmounted the logjam of rubble and squeezed through after him, his shoulder aching in a vague way, as if only distantly attached to his body. He fought to keep panic at bay.

Naamah crawled through the gap after him.

The room was misty with rock dust. Through it, he saw that an outside wall had collapsed inward. Above him a jagged hole looked to the dawning sky. The air vibrated with a magnetic flow, the same electricity he'd felt in Quinal-ee when the Nephs had chased them and the jumper had phase-shifted and uncloaked.

Holding his breath while vainly batting the dust aside, he spied Uncle Kenoch at the bed, straining at a fallen timber. A corner of the bed had been crushed to the floor. With his heart racing, he glanced around for Aunt Cerah and nearly buckled at what he saw.

Vaul bounded to the bed and stood over his aunt's still body. Naamah rushed to her side. Noah ignored the pain in his shoulder— nothing compared now to the pain in his heart. Straining with his uncle against the beam, it suddenly lifted as if having no weight. They cast it aside.

Uncle Kenoch nearly fell upon his wife. "Cer! Cer! Can you hear me?"

Her eyes remained shut, her red hair spread out across the pillow, which glistened in a brighter, moist hue of crimson.

"Mother!" Naamah frantically rubbed her hand.

"Cerah?" Uncle Kenoch's eyes welled, tears choking his voice.

Noah wrung his hands, twining his fingers until they ached, helplessness crushing his insides. His panting breaths burned with each inhalation. Aunt Cerah was bleeding from the head and mouth. Her injuries were serious, really serious, and there wasn't a thing he could do to help. Her chest, where the timber had struck, bore an unnatural dent, several ribs clearly shattered. As it rose and fell with shallow, erratic breaths, he imagined slivers of bone grinding at her insides. He forced that image from his head.

"Noah!" Thore's husky bark came from the hallway.

He spun toward the door. "In here, Thore."

Thore folded his bulk through the narrow gap, his powerful muscles forcing the door wider.

"It's Aunt Cerah!" Overhead, a shadow darkened the room. He looked up through the hole in the ceiling as the silhouette of a jumper skimmed low. The air sizzled again.

Naamah was trying to rub life back into her mother's hand and arm to bring her around to consciousness.

"Do something, Thore, do something!" Naamah cried. She and Kenoch were losing control.

Thore examined her head wound then felt for a pulse. "She's in a bad way."

"A healer! We need to get a healer!" Uncle Kenoch's face had paled sickeningly. Maybe it only appeared so because of the thick dust in the air?

Thore looked over at Noah. "Jumpers have leveled everything. Nephs approaching from New Eden. We need to leave now."

"We can't leave Aunt Cerah, Thore."

"Bring the healer!" Uncle Kenoch's wild eyes, glazed with fear, chilled Noah's blood. "Mishah! Noah, get your mother. She can save Cerah!"

Concern for his parents resurfaced. He turned to Thore. "I've got to find Mother and bring her here." But he saw Thore's stubborn refusal even before the words had left his lips.

"I'm taking you out of here right now." His powerful hand clamped vicelike on Noah's arm.

The room shook again, the blast further off this time. More

ceiling tiles clattered down around them. Uncle Kenoch bent over Aunt Cerah, protecting her from the falling debris with his own body. Thore hauled Noah toward the door, but Aunt Cerah's low moan stopped him.

"Mother," Naamah cried.

"Cer." Uncle Kenoch hovered close to her face, gently stroking the blood-soaked hair from her eyes. "I'm here, Cer. I'll take care of you." His words choked. Tears streaked the powdery grime on his cheeks. "We'll get a healer ... we'll get Mishah. You know she's the best. Mishah will help you, Cer."

Noah tried to wrench his arm free. Thore reluctantly released it. He fell to his knees at his aunt's side and took her hand. She gave it a feeble squeeze. "I'll go find my mother and bring her here."

Her grip tightened in his. "Noah." Her blue eyes slid toward him. "The Book?"

He'd forgotten all about it. "It's safe." He hoped that was true. The last he'd seen of it, it had been sitting on the table next to the couch where they'd left it.

"Protect it," she breathed.

A high-pitched whistle shrieked low overhead. The house shook and rubble tumbled out of a black cloud of smoke above the gaping hole in the roof.

He tightened his grip in hers. "I'll protect it with my life."

Uncle Kenoch fell across her neck, sobbing. Naamah was sobbing too.

"Noah." Thore's voice was restrained but firm while Vaul paced toward the door. "Now."

Aunt Cerah's hand came up weakly and caressed Kenoch's neck. "Kenoch, my love. My task is over. The Book ... passed." She heaved in a ragged breath, her mouth twisting in pain. "I will wait for you on the other side." Her words ebbed.

An explosion jarred the roof, spilling tiles onto the floor.

"No, Cer. Don't go!" Kenoch's tears gushed.

Noah knew they had to leave with Thore, but he couldn't—not just yet.

Aunt Cerah's eyes fluttered open. "Naamah … Kenoch. I love you."

"Oh, Cer, I love you more than life," Kenoch sobbed.

Her fingers began to spasm, then fell from Kenoch's trembling neck as sobs of grief wracked him.

Noah gently drew Naamah to her feet. Thore took his arm, and Uncle Kenoch's in his other hand. "Cerah is with Mother Eve now." He hauled Uncle Kenoch to his feet.

"I can't leave her like this."

"You can't do her any good now, Kenoch. Cerah would want you to go, to save yourself." Thore wheeled around and drew his fistproj at the crunch of footsteps in the hallway.

"Noah … Kenoch …?" It was Lamech's voice.

"In here," Noah shouted.

A moment later his father stuck his head through the gap where the door sagged on one hinge. His view halted on Aunt Cerah, and he groaned softly as he came all the way into the room. "I'm so sorry, Kenoch." He took his brother-in-law into his arms.

His mother gave a startled cry at the doorway, scrambled through the opening, and rushed to Aunt Cerah, unshouldering her healer's bag as she grabbed Aunt Cerah's wrist, searching for a pulse. After a moment she gently laid the hand across Aunt Cerah's stilled chest. She turned; her eyes were wet. "Has this world gone mad?"

His father took her into his arms too and held them both a moment.

"If you'd only gotten here sooner, Mishah," Uncle Kenoch sobbed.

"There's nothing I could have done to save her, Kenoch."

"Out of here now!" Thore barked.

Noah glanced back at Aunt Cerah, then scrubbed his eyes

with a dust-caked sleeve and squeezed out the door, shattered rock stabbing his bare feet.

In the rubble-strewn hallway, Thore rushed them toward the door.

Lamech shouted, "The farm is destroyed, most of the homes, too."

A distant explosion rumbled in lowly from the north.

"The sky was filled with them," his father said. "They hit the farm first, then moved off toward New Eden. Nephs are advancing. We have to get away from here." He helped Mishah over a timber, and made for the front door, but it was blocked.

"Where's Immac?" Noah asked.

"He's all right." Thore shoved him toward a crack in the stone wall. Mishah and Lamech squeezed through to the outside first. Noah was about to go next when he remembered. "The Book!"

"Not now!" Thore grabbed for his arm and missed.

"I've got to find it!"

The gathering room was half buried under roofing beams. He began tossing the rubble aside.

Thore gave an exasperated growl and attacked the mess like a human earthmover, clearing a path to the little table. The Book, still in its oilskin wrapper, lay beneath a blanket of stone and dust. Noah grabbed it. Thore practically picked him up and thrust him through the hole in the wall. Outside, his father steadied him on his feet as he tumbled through.

※

The ragged edges of the broken wall tore at Thore's cloak as he squeezed through the crack. Noah, Naamah, Mishah, Lamech, Kenoch, and Vaul watched him emerge into the morning air, which was thick with drifting brown clouds of dirt that burned their eyes and filled their noses. At least they had sense enough to stay together.

"Sheflah?" Noah glanced around, hugging the Book. "We have to find her."

Everywhere Thore looked, there were piles of rubble where there had once been homes and outbuildings; even the barns had been leveled. At the detonation of the first missile, his brain switched into defense mode. It raced as he scanned the ruins, the warrior in him taking control. He sensed Immac nearby, but didn't immediately see him.

Across the road rows of barns were blazing. A dazed three-point staggered across a smoldering pasture. The bleating, bellowing, and trumpeting of injured or frightened animals mixed with the cries of terrified people fleeing past. Thick, acrid smoke blanketed the farm.

Dead children ... wailing parents ... bloodied bodies everywhere, some not moving, some staggering in shock.

Thore said, "Where was Sheflah?" Although Noah was his main concern, he knew he'd have a difficult time making him leave without his daughter.

"My sister-in-law's house," Naamah said, casting a frightened look up the lane. Just then the rumble of pounding feet emerged from a cloud of smoke, growing louder.

"Nephs!" Through the swirling dust clouds, they saw ranks of armed giants marching on the farm.

"My Sheflah!" Naamah cried at the sight.

Everything in Thore's being cried out for him to stand and fight—the Katrahs and Kimahs, the Makir oath he'd sworn to were hooks of responsibility he could not simply ignore. The warrior blood of Hodin burned like liquid fire in his veins, but he'd taken another oath and sworn his sword to the protection of Noah, and it bound him like no other.

"This way."

"No! We have to find Sheflah!" Noah dug in his heels.

Immac bounded around a corner. "We haven't a moment to

lose, Thore. The farm has fallen."

Noah pointed at the lane. "But my daughter is there."

"She is either dead, or a prisoner," Immac said with the cool detachment of a warrior who had seen death and destruction before.

Thore grabbed Noah's arm. "I'll come back for her."

Noah hesitated. Naamah, too, had taken root to the spot. Nephs were fanning out. Lamech said, "We'll all come back."

Thore pulled Noah toward the burning barn. They folded through the corral rails and hurried across the smoking pasture, past dazed and startled animals. The vera-logia in the distance, yet to be harvested, stood tall and green and beckoning. It would not have been his first choice, but with Neph troops closing in behind them, it was the only place to hide Noah and his family until he could put together a better plan.

Abruptly, Mistress Mishah stopped and dropped to her knees beside the body of a young girl sprawled in the grass, still dressed in her bed garments. "Kitah!"

Thore remembered the little girl—the one who had danced with Shem at the wedding party.

Mistress Mishah quickly examined her. Kitah moaned at her gentle touch.

Thore wheeled back. "We can't stop." He pulled her to her feet.

"She's hurt! I won't leave her." To fight her would consume more time then they had. Mistress Mishah was a healer; the urge to comfort the hurting was as strong in her as the fervor to stand and fight was in him.

Neph warriors had begun rounding up the people and herding them into a circle. "Take her with us." What else could he do? It tore at him to see all the pain, but he had to protect Noah above all else. *It's what I have sworn to do!*

She slung the healer's bag back onto her shoulder and Lamech gathered the child into his arms.

"They're taking our children, Lamech," she cried, watching the Nephs move from building to building.

"I'll come back for them, Mi. I promise."

Thore didn't know how Lamech intended to fulfill his promises to her or Noah, but now was not the time to broach the matter. As they hurried past the barn, Noah suddenly craned his neck, staring at something. Not breaking stride, he veered off, Vaul obediently at his heels.

"Noah!" Thore scanned for what might have arrested Noah's eye and pulled him off course, and spied an old man staggering from a plume of dust billowing from a small building whose roof leaned precariously toward the ground. Methuselah!

Anger boiled up. How could he be expected to protect Noah and the rest of them if they insisted upon stopping at every diversion? He shot a glance at Immac. "Get them into that field!" He bolted after Noah.

"What are you thinking, Noah?" he growled, drawing up alongside him as they reached the old man.

"We need to take Grandfather with us, Thore."

"And how about the rest of the family?" The sarcasm was unintended.

Noah glared at him, his lips compressing. "Yes! Let's take everyone!"

"I'm sorry."

"It's the prophesy, Thore. It's not time. We have to protect him, too."

Thore scowled. Was Methuselah his job too? *Couldn't the Creator see to the particulars of His prophesy?*

"Grandfather, come with me."

"Noah?" the ancient voice creaked, and Methuselah reached out, groping in Noah's direction. His eyes were tearing, the dust caking in their corners. "Is that you?"

Noah wiped his grandfather's eyes.

"What's happening?" The old man looked around, confused.

"Come. We must hurry." Noah put an arm about the old man's waist. "The Oracle has attacked Morg'Seth."

A Neph spied them and signaled to some others. Thore's jaw clenched as five giants headed their way. "Both of you get out of here! Hide in the field where the 'gia is tallest. I'll find you later."

Noah tried hurrying the old man, but his weak-kneed, tottering gait had only one speed. Putting the Book into Methuselah's arms, he swooped him up into his arms and dashed for his waiting family.

Thore shook his head. The essence of valor must have been coursing strong in Noah's blood judging by the ease with which he trotted off, bearing the burden of a full-grown man. Vaul went with them. Thore almost called out to the canic, but didn't. Vaul was loyal to Noah and no one else—more so than any canic he'd ever known. Thore frowned. More than the canic, he could have used the binding where two became three, but Immac was needed elsewhere. There was reassurance at least in sensing the Makir's life force nearby.

He drew in a breath, steeling his resolve and centering his thoughts upon the oncoming Nephs. He'd handle these five alone.

One of the Nephs raised a projer toward Noah and Methuselah.

Thore grabbed the fistproj from under his cloak and fired. The Neph bellowed and clutched his gut. Thore dived behind a bale of hay as projfire plucked at the ground all around him. He sprang to his feet and dashed into the building Methuselah had just staggered out of.

Choking dust burned his throat and nose. He spied a hole in the roof streaming morning sunlight down past hazy rubble that had once been ceiling and walls. Springing off the seat of a chair, he caught an exposed rafter, swung forward, drew his ankles up, then kicked down, impelling himself upward. With toes perched upon the rafter, he leaped for the edge of the roof, heaved himself up, locked his elbows, and rolled onto the roof. Loose tiles clattered away as he hunched low and sprinted to the far end of the roof. He halted a moment, listened, then dropped silently to the ground on the far side, settling upon his haunches.

Pressed against the cool stone wall, he heard the Nephs inside, cursing and casting furniture aside as they searched for him.

A tight grin lifted the corner of his mouth and he dashed for the green line of 'gia, moving swiftly, like a silent shadow over the ground.

Another burst of new projfire filled the air. The Nephs had begun to fire blindly into the 'gia field.

Thore winced as though one of the projlets had pierced his heart, and he groaned softly, as a great sadness filled him and he felt the binding break, the ebbing of a Makir's life....

23

Flight from Morg'Seth

The biting odor of 'gia hung thick in the air, its oily sap dripping like pale honey down the snapped stems. Thore cut across the trail that the fleeing Sethites had stomped through the 'gia, and caught up with them a few moments later.

"Praise the Creator, you're safe, Thore!" Noah's brown eyes dodged back and forth.

"Where's Immac?" Thore hoped he might have arrived in time.

"He was behind us." Noah peered down the trampled trail they'd left.

Thore started off in the direction, then stopped. He knew what he would find. It was too late to save his friend, and he still had Noah to protect.

"Dare we wait for him?" Naamah said.

"No." Thore drew in a long breath.

"What is it?" Noah had detected his sadness.

"Immac is gone."

"Gone?" And then the truth became clear to him.

Naamah touched his arm. "I'm sorry."

There was no time for sadness. He appraised each of them.

Methuselah, tottering on his own feet, would never be able keep up. Noah, Naamah, and Mishah would manage, but Kenoch was still dazed with grief. And Lamech, burdened by the girl in his arms, might have trouble keeping up. None of them was young anymore, and the Nephs would be in their prime. He glanced around for Vaul and spied the canic prowling the broken rows between them and the Nephs. "Let's move. Try to stay between the rows." Whatever tracking skills the Nephs possessed, it wouldn't take much to follow six fleeing people through a field of trampled 'gia.

"Where?" Mistress Mishah looked back at him.

"I don't know." His mind raced. He was out of his territory and moving blindly. Distantly now came the rustling crash of bodies moving through the 'gia behind them.

Kenoch drew himself from his grief long enough to say, "There's a toolshed east of here."

"I know the place," Lamech said.

Thore didn't like it. A shed was sure to have a road to it, and that would make it easy for the Nephs to find. He hustled them ahead, giving Methuselah a helping hand and keeping an eye on their back trail. Vaul had dropped from sight. Somehow, that canic understood what was going on. He shot a glance at Noah who was hurrying behind his mother, hugging that heavy Book. Was Noah a sensitive? He set the puzzle aside. "What sort of tools are in the shed?"

"Finishing-up tools." Kenoch was rallying some from the initial blow of losing Cerah.

"Finishing-up? What's that?" The sounds of pursuit grew louder.

"It's how we put the fields to rest after harvest," he said between heavy puffs. "You know. Stump grinders, rakers, fire-starters."

Lamech, in the lead, veered to the right, steering by some internal compass. The new tack sent them crashing across twenty or so rows of plants, snapping stems as they went. The evidence of their passage couldn't be helped, and would make tracking easier. The sounds behind them grew more distant.

They came upon a wide, graveled swath cutting across their path. Without breaking stride, Lamech dashed across it and into the stand of plants beyond.

Noah hobbled gingerly, his naked soles bloodied.

"Was that a firebreak?" Thore asked.

Kenoch nodded.

Methuselah was flagging. Thore swept the old man up into his arms, amazed at his lightness. No wonder Noah had been able to dash off with him as he had. "Sorry."

Methuselah's soft brown eyes smiled at him, although his creased face and the steep bend of his lips revealed only concern. "I'm too old to let the indignations that my failing tent causes me bother me very much, young man."

Thore grinned. Being well over five hundred years old himself, "young man" sounded good to him.

A piercing wail reached them through the thick growth. A fistproj cracked once ... twice, then three more cracks came almost simultaneously. Another bellow rose in the hot air, muffled by the dense foliage.

"It's Vaul," Noah said.

"They'll kill him," his mother said.

Noah caught her under her arm and got her moving again. "He's giving us time."

"There! Just ahead!" Lamech crashed through a final couple rows of 'gia and halted on a little dirt road that ended at a squat wooden shed with round barn windows and a wide sliding door. He staggered and caught himself, half-bent and breathing hard.

They'd entered a small, circular clearing. An old, rust-encrusted harvester sat alongside the building. Lamech put the child into Mishah's arms and heaved on the door. It's creaking wooden wheels rumbled lowly as it rolled open.

Thore surveyed the building, the road, and then the clear trail they had left through the 'gia. "Nephs will be on us in a few minutes." He went to the shed and cast about in the shadows. The contents were all meaningless—a collection of tools as foreign to him as the intricacies of the Katrahs and Kimahs would have been to any of them. Turning, he squinted at the smudge of smoke in the distance where the farm buildings had been turned to rubble. A little farther to the right, a second, more distant plume climbed in to the air. New Eden, ablaze. The hazy peak of Mount Hope rose to the north. "We have to reach those mountains."

"They'll never make it on foot, Thore." Noah stepped up beside him and lowered his voice. "They're all too old."

Old or not, that was their destination. Wheeling back to the shadowy maw of the shed, Thore rushed inside. "Kenoch!"

Kenoch gave a start and turned moist eyes toward him. "What?"

"What's inside here?"

"Err … well there's …"

Lamech said, "Mainly tools to grind the stumps of the harvested stalks, attachments to rake them into rows, and a fire can to set them burning."

"Fire can? Where?"

Lamech dug the riveted iron canister from a dark corner. Thore shook it. Liquid sloshed within. "'Gia?"

"Yes."

"How do I ignite it?"

"Sparkstone starter here. You have to pump it up first."

Thore spun the lever and drew it up. As he stroked pressure into the canister, he tilted his head toward the harvester. "Does it still run?"

"Yes, but it's not used for anything anymore except pulling the stump grinder between each harvest. In there." Lamech pointed at an implement sitting inside the shed.

"Get it started."

"What are you doing, Thore?" Noah asked.

"Buying us some time. Get aboard that thing and point it at Mount Hope."

Kenoch rallied again from his despair and handed Kitah up to Mishah who had already climbed aboard. It took Methuselah longer to climb into place upon the narrow iron frame. Thore anchored the pump lever and hefted the tank's strap over his shoulder, taking the bronze nozzle and triggering lever.

The ancient cycler coughed to life, belching a cloud of smoke as the tired old cycler shook itself awake, filling the air with the smell of unburned 'gia.

"Go. Now." Thore moved to the stand of 'gia, waving an arm for them to get moving. Slowly the machine groaned and began rolling forward, smashing a five-span-wide furrow through the 'gia field. Thore drew in a breath and glanced heavenward. *Father Creator, be with them ... and me.*

He plunged back into the 'gia, retracing their steps along the broken stems and foot-trampled ground. At the firebreak he paused and studied the swath of gravel running ruler-straight as far as he could see in both directions. Behind him, the harvester's growl began to fade. Ahead, in the next field beyond the break, came the muffled sounds of vegetation grinding beneath heavy footfalls.

Thore crossed the firebreak. The trail of broken stems oozed thick yellow 'gia. He stomped down a line of stems along the break, opened the nozzle, and pulled the trigger. A roar of fire gushed from the nozzle like the hot breath of a dragon. He aimed it at the seeping 'gia, which burst into flames; a breeze at his back fanned them inward.

He hurried down the line setting the 'gia blazing as he went. A commotion behind the wall of fire drew his head around in time to see a Neph burst from the flames, the 'gia sap that had clung to him flaring like a torch. Running blindly, the Neph plunged across the firebreak and into the stand of 'gia on the other side, heading in the direction of the shed.

Something leaped from the flames. Thore spun around as Vaul landed at his feet. "There you are." He was relieved to find the canic alive. "You were just running them in circles to give us time, weren't you?"

The canic's black eyes peered at the flames. A moment later two more Nephs sprang into view, frantically batting the fire from their clothes. They spied Thore and grabbed for their weapons. Thore turned the flamethrower on them and drew his fistproj. As the report of the shots died away, the two Nephs lay smoldering on the ground.

A shot rang out behind him. He dived to the ground and pulled the trigger. The Neph grabbed for his shoulder. Vaul leaped as three more emerged, his glistening fighting fangs taking the nearest one by the throat and tearing the scream from it.

A projlet zinged the fistproj from Thore's hand. He grabbed his sword as the Neph cycled a fresh round. The long Makir blade hissed from its sheath and in a blinding swipe took off the Neph's arm at the elbow.

The Neph went howling to his knees, grabbing the spurting stump.

Sword in hand, Thore's spirits soared. This was the true weapon of a Makir Warrior. This is what he had trained with all his life. A fistproj was effective, but a poor substitute for forged Makir steel! Fixing a grin on his lips, he moved in on the final Neph, his sword whirling in a hypnotic flow of glinting sunlight, holding the Neph's eyes until all at once it drove forward, piercing his leather armor and driving clear through his heart. Shock momentarily filled the half-man's face. Thore yanked the blade free as the Neph collapsed.

With a lunge he pierced the one groveling on the ground through the neck, then spun around, not seeing any more attackers. Fire roared along the break. It would slow any further pursuit for a while as it raced back toward the farm. His father had cautioned him to burn Neph bodies. He knew that was more symbolic than necessary. It had to do with the blood, with it polluting the earth.

He retrieved the fire can and set the bodies ablaze, then glanced at Vaul.

"Let's get out of here, boy!" He dived into the 'gia, Vaul at his heels. They hadn't gone but a few paces when the crackling of fire and the swelling of smoke rose up to bar their way. Thore turned and crashed off in another direction, snapping the ripe, oil-burgeoning stems as he fled before the advancing flames. His normally excellent sense of direction had become scrambled. With no idea which way he was heading, and rising smoke obscuring all but the haziest hint of the sun, he plunged on in yet another direction, hoping to come upon the little road.

He ran up against another wall of flames. He'd somehow turned in a complete circle. Coughing the searing smoke from his lungs, he reversed himself, only to find his way blocked. Again he turned, and again he only made a few steps before hot flame and gagging smoke stood before him. The inferno had become a roaring ring of death closing in on him.

The first hint of panic began to rise within him. He stifled it, centering his thoughts on the problem, drawing from the Katrahs and Kimahs for a level head. He held his breath now as flames licked nearer. Then Vaul rose up and pressed his forepaws upon his chest. With a bark, the canic leaped away and started into the flames. Somehow he had detected the only path through them that still remained open. Hunched forward, Thore followed the animal, the fire just far enough behind him not to ignite the 'gia that covered his clothes. And then they were free and standing on the little road. With heat growing ferociously behind him, he drew in a deep breath and took off in a jog after Vaul.

When they passed the shed, Vaul picked up speed, following the wide trail that the ancient harvester had plowed through the 'gia. Thore cast a glance over his shoulder at the 'gia field behind them where flames leaped skyward—a sheet of orange and billowing black smoke. Ahead, the muffled growling of the harvester's cycler grew louder. The path of crushed vegetation cut across another firebreak. At least they'd be protected from the spreading fire now.

Finally the rusty, lumbering machine came into sight.

※

Moving along a murky path, Lamech stepped out from under the overarching shroud of treetops at the forest's edge. Standing on a rocky overlook, he stared back at the bulk of Mount Hope above the silhouetted forest, looming darkly against a bright night sky. The three-quarter moon showed most of the Oracle's five-pointed star. He grimaced and bile rose in his throat, anger momentarily displacing the crushing grief. He wanted to shake a fist at the moon.

He looked away to the south, at the orange glow that hung in the sky like a lingering sunset. Only the sun had never set in that direction, and night was already several hours old. But Thore had not wanted to stop until they'd reached the safety of the forest, even if that meant the Makir had to carry Methuselah all the way.

He watched the glow pulsate slowly—the sickly beat of a dying heart. Although too far away to see it, he knew the family farm was part of that fading life. Memories of smoldering ruins and of Nephs corralling his relatives haunted his thoughts. Not knowing what happened to Sheflah was even worse. He squeezed his eyes shut and brushed at a tear that had seeped out and rolled down his cheek. Eight sons and six daughters had been there, and he didn't know if they lived or not. He remembered seeing Emiah and Ker'ee among the captives, but what of the others? Fortunately, not all his children had remained on the farm.

He prayed, but felt a small comfort. Maybe most had fled before the dragnet had closed about them, or had died fighting. Especially the girls. His heart shriveled at the thought of his daughters in Neph hands.

He drew in a ragged breath. The odor of burning 'gia tainted the air even this far away. The flames must have leaped several of the firebreaks. Fortunately the field they had chosen to flee through had not burned—at least not until well after the harvester had run out of 'gia and they had abandoned it and fled on foot.

He turned from the awful glow and peered at the stars that crowned Mount Hope. His heart was too heavy to take comfort in the Creator's promise written in the signs of heaven.

Someone took his arm. "What are we going to do, Father?"

"Noah." Lamech saw the tears in his son's eyes. "We lost much today." He tried not to let his own grief show, but his voice quavered anyway. He had never been very good at hiding his feelings. Mishah would be the first to agree with that. He'd spent his fair share of time behind prison walls because of his mouth, which he sometimes couldn't control. But right now, words eluded him. He swallowed to loosen the knot in his throat. "How are your feet?"

"Mother put a salve on them. We wrapped them in part of my shirt." Noah grimaced. "I should have thought to take my shoes."

"You had something more important to grab."

Noah shifted his view to the Book in the weak luminescence of Mishah's light where she tended to Kitah's burns. "Aunt Cerah made me promise I'd protect it with my life." He lifted a foot and frowned at it. "I guess that includes my feet, too." He glanced at the silhouette of Kenoch sitting just beyond the edge of trees, head hung, arms limp upon his knees. "His heart is breaking, like all of our hearts, only different."

Lamech recalled how they used to argue so. Kenoch had never taken life as seriously as he should have—at least in

Lamech's opinion—and now.... He looked back at Noah and knew his pain. "We'll come back for Sheflah."

Noah nodded, swallowed hard, and sleeved the tears from his eyes.

They went to Mishah.

"Lamech." She reached for his hand. Her eyes glistened in the faint glow of the magnetic light by which she worked.

He went to his haunches and stroked his little niece's long, tangled hair. She looked up at him, her lips caught in her teeth, her eyes round and frightened. "Aunt Mishah will make you better."

Mishah cast him an admonishing glance.

He winced. *Don't make promises you might not be able to keep.* He frowned. Speaking with his heart again, instead of with his head. He had only wanted to comfort the little girl.

Mishah's look held his eyes. "Our children?" she whispered.

He shook his head. "Maybe some escaped."

She began to cry silently, plainly holding back for Kitah's sake.

"We'll come back for them, Mi. But first we have to get you, Kitah, all of us someplace safe."

She was too distressed to see the obvious folly in that. He had thought about it so much, he'd almost convinced himself he could save his children. To think otherwise was impossible.

Thore came suddenly from his lookout post and shut off her work light. "We need to move deeper into the forest."

"What happened, Thore?" Would they never find a moment to rest?

"Jumpers." The Makir pointed to the canopy of dark leaves overhead.

Lamech tilted his head back as three faint pools of reddish light coasted silently past, hovered a moment, then slowly moved backward.

"Somehow, they know we're here." Thore helped Methuselah to his feet. "Can you make it a little farther?"

"Yes, yes, I'm fine. Just point me in the direction you want me to go, young man." The ancient patriarch swayed a little, leaning upon a makeshift cane Thore had fashioned from the branch of a saubor tree.

Methuselah looked all done in, but the determined set of his bony jaw told Lamech he'd push on even if it killed him.

Lamech took Kitah, careful for the burned skin glistening with the salve Mishah had applied. Vaul had vanished earlier, but was now among them. Noah roused Kenoch out of his catatonic state. His uncle startled at his touch.

"We have to move on."

Kenoch nodded and Noah helped him reluctantly to his feet.

As they started away, Thore went one way and Vaul veered off in another direction. Thore balked, then shook his head and let the canic lead.

24

Star Jumpers

*I*t was well into the second quartering when Thore brought the party to a halt at a dark grotto beneath a shelving overhang of rock. The trail had taken them well up the slope of Mount Hope where the trees were widely spaced and the terrain was steep. Below them lay a deep hollow, shadowy in the moonlight, a carpet of treetops stretching out at their feet. Tendrils of lambent creepers cast an eerie green glow down among the trees.

They'd been hounded by jumpers all night. For hours Thore had searched out a place to hide when Vaul stumbled upon this shallow cave. In the grotto beneath the overhang, Mistress Mishah opened her work light. Thore ducked and squeezed into the tight space. He eased Methuselah to the ground and leaned him against the rock wall. Mistress Mishah raked together a pile of leaves, and spread her cloak over them. Lamech put the child, who'd finally fallen asleep, onto the crude bed.

Noah remained outside. When Thore crouched out of the grotto, Noah was scanning the heavens. "Any sight of them?"

Noah pointed into the darkness. "I thought I saw a glow off in that direction, but I can't be sure whether it was a jumper or just a swarm of gauze moths."

"The hour's too late for gauze moths to be out." Thore studied the dark sky. To the north, dancing lights swirled green and gold in their nightly ballet. His father once told him the lights used to stream clear to the horizon, but with the breaking of the magnetic veil, the colors had drifted so far north that today the dance only filled a small portion of the sky.

Noah lowered himself to the ground outside the shallow cave, moaning softly as he stretched his legs out and leaned back against a rock.

"Why don't you go inside and get some rest, Noah?"

"No, thank you," he said emphatically.

Thore grinned. Tight places had always bothered Noah.

"What are we doing, Thore, taking an injured child and a nine-hundred-sixty-three-year-old man on a run through the mountains?"

Thore sat beside him. "Trying to save their lives, and yours."

Noah winced and stared into the darkness. "With Sheflah gone, I hardly care."

"Think how your grandfather must feel." He shifted his sword and leaned back.

They sat quietly for a long while, occupied by their own thoughts. Thore was thankful their flight hadn't taken them across the path of any Turnlings.

Noah drew in a breath. "She's gone. Dead, or worse." He began to weep quietly.

What could he say to that? Angrily, Thore burrowed his heel into the dirt and dug a shallow groove, wishing he had just the right words to say to encourage his friend. But he was not eloquent. He was a warrior, not a priest. "The Nephs'll take them to Nod City."

Noah sniffed and cleared his throat. "And stand them before the Lodath."

"Probably."

"And they will be forced to renounce the Creator, or …" He couldn't go on.

Thore's thoughts fashioned up an image of Zinorah: a woman shattered in body, her future cut out of her, her spirits left in ruin. Another long silence passed.

"Thore, we've got to do something," Noah said.

He shifted uncomfortably and stared at the stars. The dancing lights were fading, morning mist beginning to settle, dampening his clothes. "Not we, Noah. I'm getting you back to Atlan. Afterward ... well, we'll see. Maybe I can convince my father to let me form a Kal-ee-hon."

Noah glanced over, his eyes rounding. "Yes. A contingent of Makir could free Sheflah and the others. And those from Quinal-ee, and the other villages that have been overrun."

Thore decided to leave it like that and not to follow Noah's line to its logical end. An invasion of Nod City by Atlan would shatter the fragile peace his father had worked to maintain all these years. It would not only endanger Atlan, but Noah himself. His father took seriously the commission the Creator had given him regarding Noah's safety. And Thore took it seriously too. He doubted his father would ever permit anything so risky as a contingent of Makir, or even two or three warriors, moving stealthily through the night to descend upon the Deceiver's stronghold, even if they could rescue Sheflah. Thore rubbed at the moisture beading up on his hands, his sleeves, his trousers. "Dawn isn't far off."

Noah tilted his head toward the grotto. "They need to sleep longer. Especially Grandfather."

"We'll linger so long as it seems safe." He glanced around for Vaul. "Most canics would be curled up at your feet sound asleep, considering all we've been through the last few quarterings."

"He's out there somewhere." Noah plucked an alecup fern and squeezed a drink from its fat stem.

"It's almost as if he knows—understands."

Noah peered at him. "I think he does."

"How can he, unless you're a sensitive?"

Noah laughed quietly. "I'm no sensitive."

He tried to detect subterfuge, but Noah seemed sincere.

"The Creator has been withdrawing the gift since the Fall. Few possess it anymore, and those who do are all old." Noah winced. "Not that five hundred and ninety-something isn't a respectable age." He shook his head. "I'm not a sensitive. Vaul is just … special."

The night waned, lambent creepers dimming as the distant treetops grayed, emerging slowly from the darkness. Noah sank back into silence. Maybe he had drifted off to sleep.

The far edge of the forest flared, and a brilliant, verdant glow stretched out as the sun climbed above the horizon.

Still in the shadow of Mount Hope behind him, Thore watched a swath of colors race ahead of the rising sun as though unfurling a carpet of emerald and silver leaves. The bright orange-crested blooms of tree creepers added splotches of color, like forest ornaments cast out by the Creator's hand; the exalted liswyle trees, poking above all the others, slowly uncurled their glittering, corkscrew tops to the new day.

A flock of red and blue parrots took to the sky, moving as a single body, like a shoal of glimmer fish crossing the shallows of the Atlan Ridge. Thore's chest squeezed. The Ridge was no more, he reminded himself.

To his left a flop of scarlet dragons glinted like rubies in the sunlight as they winged out over the forest. The sunrise was like peering through a child's toy spectraview.

Noah straightened up, and looked at him. "The Creator has given us a new morning." His voice was heavy with grief.

All around him the air buzzed with whistling cicadas, squawking woodhoppers, drumming burrow cocks, and the fluty whoo-whoo of cuddle doves. Thore inhaled the sweet scent of dayspring flowers stretching their purple and white striated petals to the warming sunlight. "Thought you were asleep."

"Just thinking."

He frowned, listening to the forest humming with life. "Sometimes it's better not to."

"I don't have that luxury, Thore. None of us do."

Thore cocked his head, aware of a faint buzzing he didn't immediately recognize.

"Thore, if I hadn't come here, the farm wouldn't have been attacked and Sheflah would still be safe. Immac would still be alive, my family all right. It was me the Oracle was after."

"You don't know that for sure. He's moving against all the Settled Lands of Hope."

Noah went silent.

"How are your feet?"

Noah looked at the makeshift bandages. "They hurt."

Thore stood and stepped off a few paces to where the ground fell away to the valley below. Vaul trotted to his side and stared. Thore reached down to pet him, but the canic moved from beneath his hand. "You're a strange one. I haven't thanked you yet for getting me out of that fire."

Vaul tilted his head at him, then looked back at the valley, his ears cocking forward.

"You hear it too." He rotated an arm to loosen the tense muscles across his back.

Noah stood and brushed off the seat of his trousers, joining them, taking careful steps. "What is that noise?"

The air had begun to pulsate, and smelled mildly of launderer's whitening. A low humming separated from the forest sounds and settled into a quiet whirring.

Thore scanned the distant treetops below their high viewpoint. "I'm not sure." He'd heard that sound before.... His eyes narrowed into a scowl as the air began to compress and fill with static electricity. The space above the treetops had begun to ripple like the surface of a pond.

"Decloaking!"

An enormous triangular shape appeared out of a shimmering ripple of hot air and hung above the treetops.

Vaul leaped and drove Noah to the ground. Thore threw himself to one side. A sheet of fire erupted from the jumper's belly and a proj screamed overhead, exploding into a nearby tree.

As the ground rocked, Noah staggered to his feet and plunged into the grotto. A second proj exploded above the ledge and began a landslide of cascading rocks and debris over the grotto's entrance.

Thore slid into it on his belly right behind Noah and was slammed against the wall by the concussion of a third blast. The grotto was quickly filling up with rubble and he hoisted Methuselah into his arms. Noah hauled his mother, then Naamah, to their feet and grabbed the Book. Spilling rock had begun to pile up around their feet. Coughing out the gagging dust, Thore snagged Noah by the sleeve and shoved him through a billowing black cloud.

Smoke and dust hung heavy in the air, and under cover of it, they fled down the trail as a final proj hit its target and blew a fireball out of the low opening.

As the smoke cleared, Thore saw with relief that Lamech, too, had managed to escape the deathtrap, with Kitah in his arms. Kenoch helped Mishah and Noah helped Naamah. They scrambled down the mountain path, forging deeper into a narrow ravine.

Thore caught a glimpse of the jumper following in the distance, but the narrow trail between rising walls of rock kept it from getting too close. It fired again, ripping a flaming hole in the forest, but not able to get a clear shot, the missile went wide of its target. As they descended the mountainside, the ravine squeezed in about them like a closing fist, and the jumper fell farther behind until only a low, magnetic whirring could be heard, charging the air with an electricity that made Thore's skin prickle.

The whirring died away and eventually even the tingling faded.

Gasping for breath, Lamech staggered to a stop and grabbed for a jagged rock to steady himself. Thore brought the party to a halt and set Methuselah on his feet. Noah knelt by a stream and drank the cool water, then went to his father and took Kitah from him. "Drink."

Lamech went to the water's edge.

Kenoch leaned against a tree, staring at a patch of sky visible through a rocky overhang. Their flight had momentarily pulled Kenoch from his grief, and Thore hoped he wouldn't go right back to it. Mistress Naamah helped Mistress Mishah onto the ground, her back against a tree. Noah's mother moved the healer's bag from her shoulder to her lap. Vaul kept in motion, threading among them, his fur bristling, his head snapping left to right.

Thore drew in another breath. "We're okay for a while. That jumper can't get to us down here."

"They'll send Nephs to find us." Lamech dragged a sleeve across his mouth.

"Maybe." He surveyed their surroundings. Narrow, rocky walls hemmed them in on two sides. Towering trees hid them from view. A safe haven on one hand and a narrow, deadly trap on the other. Noah couldn't stay here very long. He jammed his fingers through his hair. "How could they have known where we were?"

He trudged up the trail a little way for a wider view of the sky, for the moment empty. Lamech was right. The Nephs would come. His first duty was to protect Noah, but he could not do it on the run. How could he best serve Noah and remain true to his oath? "Noah."

"Yes?"

"You and your family have to get moving again."

"Us? What about you?"

"I need to finish this job here and now."

"No." Mistress Naamah came to him. "We'll go together, Thore."

"I can't protect all of you, and Master Lamech is correct. They will mount an attack on foot now that they know where we are."

"You can't fight them alone, Thore!" Noah took his arm. "Together we are stronger."

"Can you find your way back to the mine, and Majiah's people?"

"I don't know."

Thore inclined his head toward Vaul. "He can. If he understands so much, make him understand this. You have to reach Majiah's people, and from there make your way back to Atlan. But you must leave now, before the Nephs come for you."

Kenoch stepped away from the tree, his hands curling into fists at his side. "Thore's right. You must flee before they come. You have to make it back to Atlan, Noah. You have the commission. I'll stay with Thore."

Mistress Mishah stood. "Kenoch. You can't fight this enemy. They're Nephs!"

He grinned. "Sis, don't you remember? I've already fought them once. At his father's side." He glanced at Thore, then back. "Rhone and I, we kept them occupied long enough for you and Grandmother to reach the Cradleland."

Her eyes glistened. "You were a young man. A boy. Look at you. You're old, like me. What chance would you have against the Nephs?"

"Those creatures killed Cerah. I'm staying, Mi. There's nothing you can do to stop me." He stared at Thore. "Nothing either of you can do."

Thore understood him perhaps better than any of them just then. Noah needed to flee, and Kenoch needed to stay behind and kill some Nephs. A smile spread his mouth. "You can stay."

Kenoch grinned. Was it the same grin he had worn that day when he and his father faced the Earth-Born all those hundreds of years earlier?

Mishah hugged him. "You'll come back to me. I know you will."

Kenoch nodded. "If it's in the Creator's will, Mi."

Lamech took his hand. "I won't say good-bye, not this time—not like we said it once, long ago." His eyes misted and he gave Kenoch a hug. Lamech helped his father to his tottering feet. Noah put the Book into his mother's arms and lifted Kitah.

Thore watched them disappear down the torturous trail, Noah hobbling on his sore feet. Thore's military mind had already analyzed the situation. They needed high ground and the advantage of surprise.

Kenoch's resolve of a few moments before began to turn to fear in his eyes.

He couldn't allow Kenoch to think about what was coming. "You need a weapon."

Kenoch gulped, glanced at the family receding down the trail, then at him. "What have you in mind?"

"Come with me." He recalled a ledge of higher ground that would give them a slight advantage. "So you fought Nephs once?" He had to keep his thoughts from dwelling on the inevitable outcome of their sacrifice.

"I did. Your father and I." His voice took on a slim note of confidence. Thore knew he'd done the right thing by letting him stay. Kenoch needed to do this … for Cerah … for Sheflah … for himself.

He put a hand on Kenoch's shoulder. "Well, my battle-hardened friend, let's do it again."

❦

Pain burrowed up Noah's ankle and set fire to his calf. He stumbled, nearly dropping Kitah. The child's extra weight only made it worse. Each step was like stomping on nails and razors. The hard spines of the suckle thorn, scattered everywhere, pricked the cloth bandages, and tipping his weight onto the edges of his feet no longer helped. Finally he could not endure the bite of one more twig or the gouge of one more sharp stone.

He stopped, swaying and dazed in a fog of torment, eyes tearing, his lips raw from gnawing them.

"Let me look at them again." His mother took his arm and guided him to a patch of soft green seal moss and helped him down. She lifted Kitah from his arms and passed the moaning child to his father. Her soft hands gently lifted his feet.

She opened her healer's bag, selected a copper tube, and twisted off the cap. The odor of lemon and camphor tinted the forest air. "I left so much behind. I should have stopped to think."

He took her words in the broader sense—home, family, peace, and security. Everything she'd grown comfortable with since leaving Atlan more than four hundred years earlier after he'd become a man and was on his own.

And he'd left his daughter. His eyes stung and he looked away as she worked more salve into the soles of his feet.

※

"It will only hurt a moment, darling."

It couldn't hurt any worse than a broken heart. Slowly the teeth of her medicines eased their jaws.

"That will begin to numb your feet. You shouldn't feel the pain for a while now."

Naamah ripped the hem of her dress and helped Mishah rewrap his feet in a tight cocoon of cottonhemp.

"I should have thought to grab a pair of shoes."

Mishah glanced at him with grief-filled eyes, her mouth tightening. "With so much happening, we were fortunate to have escaped at all, Noah."

But what had they left behind? He didn't want to think of that. The ache was too fresh, too raw. Worse than the cutting pain in his feet.

She secured the improvised stockings with the last of her binding tape. "Hope we have no need for this." She dropped the empty spool back into her healer's bag.

Noah looked up the narrow, snaking path they had come down. What of Thore and Uncle Kenoch? Had they found the Nephs? Or, had the jumper simply left? That was almost too much to hope for. Were they even still alive? He shivered at the thought, and prayed that any moment now they would come jogging into sight with word that the Nephs had gone away.

"Can you make it, Son?" Lamech stood over him, looking worried.

He stood with the aid of his father's hand and tested his new bootery. They made standing a little awkward, but the extra padding, along with his mother's salve, eased the pain considerably. "I'm much better."

"You steady your grandfather. I'll carry Kitah awhile." Lamech was exhausted, but was trying hard to be strong for all of them.

Could he do no less? "All right. For a while. Then we'll switch off."

The party got moving again with Vaul trotting in the lead. Noah looked over his shoulder. He frowned. Wishing rarely made hopes come true. He peered ahead. Forward was the direction he had to go. Everything behind was gone.

25

Against All Odds

*T*hore drew his sword and backed down the trail where a stand of young saplings reached lacy green leaves toward the filtered light high above. With a single swing, he severed two of them above the roots, trimmed the branches, shortened them to spear-length, then quickly chopped a long, sharp point into each of them.

"These will have to do."

Kenoch's face had taken on the pale hue of the rocky ledge upon which they'd found a safe nook among the jagged tors. "I don't suppose you have a plan in mind?"

Thore looked at him.

Kenoch gave a wry smile and his voice trembled with a panic barely under control. "You know, Makir strategy one hundred and fifty-six ... or something?"

The stab at humor was Kenoch's way of coping. Thore could hardly blame his fear. The jumper hovered five hundred spans off, just above the treetops. Its quiet, persistent whirring set up a resonance that buzzed in his teeth.

He unclenched them and pulled back behind the rock outcrop, out of sight of the dark craft. "No Makir strategy. I am open to suggestions, Master Kenoch." His hair had succumbed to the charged air, the loose strands not bound by the leather collar at the back of his neck slowly rising as though connected by invisible threads.

Kenoch shook his head. His throat bobbed with a loud gulp. "Why are they just hovering? Why don't they do something?"

He ran a hand along the wide, polished blade of his sword. "It won't be long." The sword may have been the proud symbol of the Makir, but right now he sorely missed the fistproj he had lost back in the 'gia field. He missed Immac, too. Another Makir at his side would have given them a huge advantage. With the Makir binding, one plus one equaled three.

Kenoch hefted the pair of spears. "What am I supposed to do with these?"

"Kill Nephs. Isn't that what you want to do?"

"Oh? I didn't know it was going to be so simple." He rolled his eyes. "Thore, this is 1650. We're not back in the days when your father and I fought the Earth-Born and all anyone carried were swords or primitive proj-lances. Good grief, they'll have projers!"

Kenoch had shared something with his father once long ago, something that had drawn them close together as only warriors can know. A connectedness that even a son could never know. And now he might never see his father again. The thought was dangerously distracting. An unexpected pang stabbed at his chest.

A sharp clack, like an iron hook unlatching, came from the direction of the jumper. It was followed a moment later by the metallic grinding of gears.

"What's that?" Kenoch's eyes rounded toward the hovering craft.

Thore pushed his head past the shoulder of the rock for a look. "Seems they must have heard you."

Kenoch's face blanched.

As the grinding drowned out the low whirring, the jumper began to drift closer. Thore shook his head. "We can run, but we can't hide." How were they tracking them?

Kenoch drew back. "Somehow they always know just where we are!"

The grinding ceased. Up close, the girdle of pale red light about the jumper's edge hinted at movement. By blinking fast, Thore could detect a sequential flashing. An oval panel in its belly had slid out of sight leaving an egg-shaped opening. Thick ropes, like umbilical cords, unfurled and dangled through the treetops.

"Not enough room to earth," he whispered.

After awhile, Kenoch said, "What are they waiting for?"

"You in a hurry?"

Kenoch looked at him. "I want to get back to the others."

He laughed at the unexpected smirk that spread on Kenoch's face. "The longer they delay, the more time Noah and the others will have to escape."

Kenoch drew a puzzled scowl across his face. "Which brings up the question."

"What question?"

Kenoch thought a moment. "Why that thing is bothering with us at all instead of following Noah? The Deceiver is after Noah, not us."

"Good question." Thore recalled the stories his mother had told him about how his father had first met the Lee-landers. The Deceiver was pursuing Noah while still in Mistress Mishah's womb. The meeting forever changed Rhone's life. He frowned. "Kenoch, tell me something."

"If I can." Kenoch sat back against the rock with his spears across his knees.

"What was my father like back then, when you were fleeing the Lodath's Guard?" He was surprised he'd asked it. Was it because now he might never know the answer, might never hear about a time long past ... an adventure his father rarely spoke about?

"That was a long time ago, Thore. High Councilor Rhone was a young warrior," he hesitated, "running away from ... from himself."

"That was a dark period in my father's life. He never spoke of it except to my mother. I know little about it."

Kenoch glanced nervously at the dark jumper hovering over the treetops. "I first met your father in Far Port, long after Mishah, Grandmother Amolikah, Lamech, and I had left the Lee-lands on Mishah's pilgrimage to the Mother. Lamech was imprisoned in Nod City and Mishah wanted to abandon the pilgrimage, but he had made her promise not to. Lamech knew, somehow, of the Creator's intentions."

"Master Lamech has always been in tune."

Kenoch nodded. "We hired Rhone's sword, not knowing he was a Makir. Only that he had once helped Mishah and Lamech in Nod City." Kenoch stared as though watching a scene unfold in his memory. His voice thickened. "Your father wasn't himself in the beginning."

Thore leaned forward with interest while a part of his awareness remained steadfastly focused on the jumper. So far, other than the hatch sliding open and the craft drifting a bit closer, nothing new had happened. Its steady drone remained constant, and the charged air still tingled about them.

"You see, your father had inadvertently entered into a pact with the Lodath, and that had permitted the Lodath to sink his fingers into him, controlling Rhone in subtle ways that didn't become apparent until much later."

"My father once spoke of this. He fought the influence, and he finally freed himself from it. I've heard this much only. The details remain a closely guarded secret."

"He was ashamed for having fallen for the Lodath's gift."

Thore nodded. "Go on." A slight change in the whirring drew some of his attention.

"Once Rhone realized what was happening, he struggled mightily to overcome it. But you must understand, the Oracle was the true power behind the Lodath, and the Oracle is none other than the Deceiver. His ways are evasive and powerful, and he draws many unwary souls into his clutches." Kenoch's fingers curled into a fist as he spoke. The fist loosened and dropped to the spears across his knees. "Your father finally rid himself of the Deceiver's hold on him. Afterward, he fought valiantly to bring my sister, Grandmother, Lamech, me, and," his voice faltered, "Cerah to the Cradleland where we would be safe."

Thore's throat constricted. "You were there. You saw what happened. Tell me, Kenoch, how my father ..." He hesitated. "How my father died."

"Like a true Makir Warrior. We were fighting the Earth-Born—the Nephs—your father and I. Bar'ack had already been taken over by the spirits of the dead Nephs, and he was there, fighting against us. We were trying to delay them long enough for the women to reach the portal into the Creator's Garden. Mother Eve had told us we'd be safe once inside it."

Thore nodded. "I know that part."

"We didn't know how we would be protected, but we believed her ... believed the Creator would watch over us some-how within the Cradleland's massive walls. Standing before the entrance to the Garden were two soaring golden statues with crossed swords, every bit as tall as the walls and the portal behind them. Once the women were safely inside, Rhone and I retreated after them. We were both wounded, and bone weary. As we fled before the Nephs and the Lodath's Guard with Captain Da-gore at its head, Rhone put himself between them and me." Kenoch grimaced. "He could have easily outdistanced me." He looked at the spears across his lap and lifted one of them. "Rhone was run through. It took three spears, each twice as thick around as this, thrown by the Earth-Born called Herc."

Thore flinched. "The one who sits as Lodath now?"

Kenoch nodded. "Rhone fell at the feet of the golden stat-ues." Awe filled his voice. "But before the Nephs could reach your father, the statues came to life, their swords flashing like sunlight, keeping the monsters at bay while the women pulled Rhone into the Garden." He stopped and drew in a breath. "Then so many things happened, they whirl in my brain. I was nearly unconscious from my wounds. Mishah was in labor and delivered Noah, and Rhone breathed his last and died ... and then the Gardener appeared."

Movement at the corner of his eye brought Thore's head around.

"What?" Kenoch started.

"It's time." Nephs, partly hidden by the deeper shadows inside the belly of the jumper, had begun to gather at the rim of the oval hatch. The first wave of warriors took to the dangling ropes and dropped like spiders on a tail of web toward the treetops, projers and proj launchers strapped to their backs. Their leather and bronze armor glinted in the sunlight, the green of their uniforms merging at once with the forest as they plunged out of sight.

In spite of overwhelming odds, the impending battle brought every nerve, every muscle to life. The essence of valor filled Thore's blood, burned in his cheeks, and sent a surge of strength down his arms and into his fists, the blood of Hodin awakening to what it was bred to do. Fight. "We won't have much time once the corn starts popping, Kenoch."

"What do you want me to do?"

Kenoch wasn't a warrior. He was a farmer, and he'd have to learn fast. "I'll distract them and draw them away from you. While I'm keeping them occupied, you single one out and attack without warning. If we're lucky their backs will be toward you and their attention focused on me. That will give you the advantage."

Kenoch swallowed hard and his fingers wrapped around one of the spears. His face was ashen, his breathing coming in unhealthy pants.

"Take a long breath and let it out slowly before you faint." He bent his view toward the spear. "Once you select your target, come in low, fast, and hard. Aim for a gap in his cuirass. Remember, you'll only get one shot at it, so make your aim true, and put all your strength behind the thrust. The thing to remember is, you only need to kill one of them and snatch up his weapon. You know how to use a projer, don't you?"

Kenoch nodded.

"Once you get his weapon, open fire on everything that moves." Thore grinned. "Except me." He glanced back as a second wave glinted in the sunlight toward the treetops. "They're well armed so we have to rely on surprise and speed. In a moment of confusion we can do a lot of damage."

"Damage maybe, but can we hope to win this fight?"

"Is this much different than it was five hundred years ago, at my father's side?"

He blew a ragged breath. "Like Mi said, I was a lot younger. And so was your father."

"Where there is life, there is hope. And don't forget, in this battle, we are on the right side."

"Then we ought to take this to the Creator."

Thore nodded. They could use all the help they could get.

Kenoch bowed his head and asked the Creator for protection and success.

When he finished, Thore dropped a hand on Kenoch's shoulder and was reminded by the narrowness of it that Sethites were not overly large people. Maybe that would work to Kenoch's advantage. Sethites made smaller targets than Hodinites. Even so, he wished it was Immac's shoulder he gripped. With a Makir, there was the touching of thoughts during battle that came through the disciplines of the Katrahs and Kimahs. With Kenoch, there could be no binding. Each of them would be fighting on his own.

The second wave of Nephs had disappeared beneath the treetops, and now the distant crunch of gathering soldiers and the

rustle of movement drifted over them. The usual forest chirps
and twitters went silent. The crashing of the Nephs' advance
sounded to Thore's ears as though a herd of sten-gordon was
drifting past. "They're coming."

"You sure?"

"Don't you hear?"

Kenoch cocked an ear, then shook his head.

"Trust me. They are on their way." Thore moved off a few
spans, hunched low, and turned back. Kenoch remained rigid as
a bronze statue. "Well?"

With a loud gulp that seemed hard to swallow down, Kenoch
rose and followed him down the steep side toward the shadowy
trail below. Thore quietly slipped his long Makir sword from its
sheath, then halted in a copse of denser vegetation on an outcrop
with a wide view of the trail. Kenoch crept up beside him.

"They will pass right there." Thore pointed, then shifted his
finger. "You wait for them there. The vines and trees will hide you.
I'll move down the trail fifty spans or so. Once they pass your station, I'll cause a distraction. As soon as they come after me, make
your move. Pick your target and dispatch him with a spear, or both
if need be, then grab his projer. I'll get hold of one of their projers
too, and if we are swift and decisive, we'll catch them in our cross-
fire. Then it's just a matter of who shoots fastest."

Kenoch nodded. His face, the color of gauze moth's wings,
was slowly pinkening up.

Thore rolled his eyes. "And for Dirgen's sake, breathe! I can't
afford to have you faint on me."

His command startled a sharp gasp from Kenoch.

"That's better."

Kenoch moved into position while Thore sprinted down the
trail and climbed a tree alongside it. With a swipe of his sword,
he severed a wrist-thick grapevine from its roots below and gave
the tree-bound length a testing tug. If he judged it right, he

would be swinging through the middle of them before they knew what was happening. He slipped his dagger from his boot top, hefted it lightly to check the balance, and tucked it into his belt where it would be close at hand.

The stomping of feet and snapping of vegetation grew steadily louder. He tried not to think of the terror Kenoch must be struggling with now. His own heartbeat had quickened and his breathing, in spite of his admonition to Kenoch, was too fast. Every nerve vibrated so that the magnetically charged air was barely noticeable anymore. He centered his thoughts, and out of long habit reached out to Kenoch as though Kenoch had been another Makir—had been Immac with whom he could bind. But his probing brain found nothing. No touching of minds. No surging strength. No increased awareness. No one plus one …

"So be it." He lifted his eyes. *Into Your hands I commit this battle, and for Your glory I fight Your enemies. Be with Kenoch. Strengthen his heart and resolve. If we fail here, see Noah safely back to Atlan where he can finish his commission under the protection of my father's strong arm.*

A giant appeared on the trail a hundred spans away, at the very limit of his visibility. He braced himself in the tree as a line of Nephs appeared behind the leader. His breath caught as the giants marched past the place where Kenoch lay hidden. Their armor did not glint in the dappled light, and their green clothes blended well with the vegetation crowding near the trail.

Thore wrapped a fist around the grapevine, the other tightening upon the hilt of his sword. He caught a glimpse of the etching in the blade just below the guard—the crest of the House of Khore, his grandfather. Twin dragons, tails entwined, grasped the sword of Hodin between them while their other hands, upturned, held the Flame of the Creator. It hadn't always been so. At one time the dragons lifted up the heart of Dirgen. His father had changed it after finally wresting Atlan from his evil brother, Zorin, and vowed the land would forever honor the Creator, so long as he ruled.

The Nephs came closer. Thore pushed the pleasant memory of his father from his thoughts and readied himself. As the giants marched below, he leaped from the tree, the grapevine swinging him in a smooth arc toward the other side of the trail. Sweeping through the middle of them, he struck out with his sword at the leader, severing the huge head from its shoulders.

Bedlam erupted. Projers fired and projlets zinged past his ear as the vine completed its swing. He dropped lightly to his feet, batted a projer aside, and ran his sword through a Neph's heart. He hadn't time to see if Kenoch was following orders.

Shots rang out. A Neph fell from a projlet launched by one of his own comrades. Thore somersaulted beneath a volley of proj-fire, sprang back to his feet, and dived again as Nephs swung their weapons, unable to get a clear shot.

Projlets pounded the ground where he'd stood a heartbeat before. Keeping in constant motion so there was nothing to aim at, Thore's sword sliced and jabbed this way and that, mostly ineffective against the Nephs' armor. He caught a glimpse of a Neph drawing a bead on him, and sent his dagger whistling through the air, burying itself in the giant's neck. He lunged for a fallen projer and as he tumbled, pulled the trigger, dropping two more Nephs. The ground around him shredded from exploding projlets.

A volley of rapid-fire shots rattled the air from down the trail. Kenoch!

The Nephs divided their effort. Thore clambered behind a tree and sprayed the trail. The air resounded with exploding projlets and filled with their smoke.

The remaining Nephs dived for cover. He had to pick his shots carefully now. A whoosh followed by a jaw-rattling explosion knocked Thore to the ground. One of the Nephs had unleashed a shoulder proj launcher. Thore shook his head, clearing it.

Kenoch seemed to be holding his own. Constant fire from his direction kept the Nephs pinned. No one was moving from cover. He checked the loads remaining in the projer. Almost out!

The firing slowed until only sporadic shots cracked from time to time. They were keeping their heads down, biding their time. Scattered across the forest floor were at least ten bodies—bodies that had given up their spirits, which now were destined to wander the earth in search of new homes. Thore gave a wry smile. In the long run, killing Nephs wasn't such a good thing after all.

He peeked around the tree and flinched back. A weapon cracked and a projlet blasted a chunk of bark just above his head. Pressing his back against the tree, he scanned the forest, sensing more than seeing movement out there. Someone was circling behind him. He had a vague impression of darkness creeping closer. If only there'd been another Makir here. Between them, the binding would have allowed his senses to probe deeper, move quicker. He exhaled sharply, whirled to his left, and fired at a rustling bush. A Neph lurched out, his weapon skittering across the ground, stopping a few spans from his hiding place.

Rolling back to his stomach, he spied the round tube of a proj launcher peeking out from behind a rock. Sighting down his projer, he waited. A small patch of flesh revealed itself among the brushy cover. He caught his breath and squeezed the trigger. As the crack of his projer died away, the Neph with the proj launcher slumped in the bush, a bloody hole between his eyes.

The battleground went silent. His heart drummed, his breath rasped harsh and quick in the sudden quiet. The darkness that had been steadily creeping into his consciousness seemed to dissipate a little.

Bent low to the ground, he slipped around the tree, swinging the projer to cover the area. But there was no movement, no sound except the blood whooshing in his ears. "Kenoch." He glanced down the trail, littered with giants. On the other side, more bodies lay crumpled in the rank forest vegetation. "Kenoch!" A rising dread clutched at his chest.

"I'm here, Thore."

An upswell of relief doused his growing alarm. Standing warily from behind a rock, Kenoch stared at all the bodies, then tottered from cover and reached for a tree to steady himself.

He went to Kenoch, pausing a moment to peer down at the sprawled Neph with the green-wood trunk of a gopher sapling protruding from his back. The essence of valor was still coursing through his blood, and his senses were on heightened alert. The air buzzed with energy.

Kenoch appeared uninjured, and now that the battle was past, his teeth had begun to chatter. His white-knuckled fingers had fused to the dark barrel of the Neph projer. "Is ... is it over?" he whispered, shock draining the color from his cheeks.

"For the moment."

"We're alive!"

The skin at the back of Thore's neck began to crawl. He glanced upward. The jumper was moving, a fresh contingent of warriors already assembling at the hatch. The humming electricity spread from his neck and sank deep into his chest. There'd be no surprise attack this time. No convenient ambush. The jumper knew exactly where they were, and it was coming to get them. He grabbed Kenoch's arm and hurled him down the trail. "Run!"

Startled, Kenoch stumbled a few steps the glanced back at the black shadow sliding nearly soundlessly over them, eclipsing the sun.

"Move!" Thore growled, his brain grasping for possibilities. The quiet whirring of the jumper ceased as it hovered to a stop at the treetops. The next rush of Nephs latched onto the ropes and began sliding to Earth, their projers blasting as they came.

The ground exploded around him. He tumbled over a dead Neph and grabbed the proj launcher from its fingers. Swinging toward the jumper's open belly-door, he pulled the trigger. The launcher punched his shoulder, and a proj raced for the jumper's vulnerable navel. Casting the launcher aside, he ran for cover.

An instant later the muffled detonation rocked the earth beneath. A ball of fire burst from the jumper's belly and slammed into the ground, scorching his back and singing his hair, momentarily engulfing him in a searing haze. Through the orange heat he saw the jumper tilt, wobble a moment, then slide into the treetops and crash with the earthshaking roar of a falling mountain.

The concussion slammed him to the ground. He grimaced at a stabbing pain in his leg, and then the explosion sucked the air from his lungs, and everything went black....

26

Fallen Warriors

Striding across the Grand Gallery that bisected the Sanctuary of Justice, Leenah at his side, Rhone suddenly bolted straight and stopped.

"What is it?" she asked.

He narrowed his view toward the distance. Although the wall of the Sanctuary intervened, he momentarily seemed to see past it. "Thore."

Eyes widening searchingly at him, Leenah's breath caught. "What about Thore?"

"He's in trouble."

"How can you know, Rhone?"

"The binding."

"Thore's in Morg'Seth. The binding doesn't reach that far."

"I'm Hodinite, and Thore is flesh of my flesh, blood of my blood."

"As he is mine, yet I feel nothing. And I'm Hodinite too—well, half Hodinite."

His eyes shifted toward her, noting the worry lines deepening in her face.

"But I'm Makir."

The trail took a steep incline. Noah bent into it, one arm around his failing grandfather, the other clutching a walking stick he'd picked up, daggers of pain stabbing into his feet. He didn't know how much longer he could press on. His hobbling gait had slowed to a crawl, and Grandfather was flagging badly, each breath coming harder and harder, like the chugging of a worn-out cycler about to sputter to a stop.

Naamah came up alongside Grandfather and put an arm about his waist. "Let me help, Noah."

He nodded.

Ahead, past the tight weave of tree branches, the sky became visible in wider and wider blue patches, and then all at once the trees parted and they came out onto a long, steeply rising ridge, arching toward the summit pass. Open ground lay before them, swathed in the green of dowry-lace fern abloom with yellow and red flowers. The deep-forest fragrance of damp earth, old leaves, and cinnamon and cedar trees gave way to a heady bouquet of sleepyeves and rush buttons, dragon eyes and skylilies. The nature of the path changed too, now that sunlight freely reached it. Yellow and purple verbiscus softened the hard ground, and Noah breathed a welcoming sigh when he saw it, but his feet had been too battered by now to appreciate the difference.

Lamech drew to a halt and braced his feet, swaying a bit. "Worlon Pass."

Like Methuselah, his father was exhausted. Noah would have carried both of them if he could. As it was, he could barely carry himself.

"We will soon cross over into Morg'Jalek." Grandfather's thin voice wavered, and he lifted a narrow arm and pointed at the ridge. "Over there."

Vaul continued up the path as if none of them had stopped. He turned back and stared, his ears in motion, catching sounds too faint for human hearing.

His mother said, "Can we rest awhile, Lamech? I should put more ala on Kitah's burns. I hope I have enough to last." Her mouth screwed up angrily. "Why didn't I think to bring my other bag?"

Noah exhaled a long, weary breath. "We must stop second-guessing ourselves, Mother. How can anyone have thought it would come to this?" He sat his grandfather on the ground amidst a pink cluster of sleepyeves.

Vaul returned to his side.

His mother sat among the ferns and dropped her healer's bag from her shoulder. "Maybe Kenoch and Thore will catch up with us here?"

His father gently transferred Kitah onto her lap. "Thore would be upset if he thought we were waiting for them."

"He says run and we run," Grandfather declared with a tremulous voice.

Naamah went to help Mishah with Kitah.

Noah turned and peered back into the shadowy depths of the forest from which they had just emerged. Maybe they would appear....

The distant boom rocked the peacefulness of the mountaintop glade. Every eye turned as a fireball rose high above the treetops.

Tormented feet forgotten, Noah sprinted up the path for a wider view of the pumpkin-shaped projectile. "The jumper!" The fireball expanded and darkened as if rotting from the inside out. It now looked more like a snake pit of inky serpents, coiling and folding onto themselves until nothing remained of the fireball but a dirty writhing mushroom cloud growing higher and denser.

The angry coil spiraled upward in the still, clear sky.

The sight pried open an abyss inside Noah, spilling the icy vapors of fear for Thore and Uncle Kenoch into his soul. He wasn't aware that his father had come up beside him until Lamech's hand fell lightly upon his shoulder. "Maybe they got away?" Noah asked. The hope had a dull ring. His ears had begun to buzz.

"If it's the Creator's will." His father's face remained turned toward the towering cloud that now hung nearly motionless, the vipers within it calming.

The buzzing grew louder. "We should wait here for them, or go back and meet them on the trail."

"That would do no good now. We need to move on. It's what Thore would have wanted."

Would have? Noah's eyes burned. He squeezed them shut as he wiped a tear with the heel of his hand. As the mushroom cloud began to dissipate, he knew no one could have survived being anywhere near that explosion. If they were, they were gone … truly gone … Uncle Kenoch and Thore. "Yes, we need to go on." He looked around for Vaul, but the canic was nowhere in sight. "Where's Vaul?"

His father cast about the mountaintop clearing. "He must have wandered off."

That was unusual. Noah shook his head to clear the buzzing. Instead it grew louder, changing in pitch. And the air had begun to vibrate with a familiar magnetic charge….

❦

At the moment of impact, Gorn'el braced his battle staff against the ground and bowed his back to the onrushing fireball. The white-hot heat slammed into his back and roared around and over him, incandescing his clothes in a blue haze that streamed across the edges of the bubble over the unconscious human before him. In an instant the inferno sucked away the air, ignited the forest, and vaporized the Nephs. The destruction rushed outward in an all-consuming circle of heat. Flying bits and pieces of the jumper, impelled at nearly the speed of sound, mowed wide swaths through cinder-sticks that had once been trees.

A hunk of metal the size of a sten-gordon crashed into his

back and careened skyward, dissolving into molten globules, fizzling and flashing into their elemental particles.

In the midst of it, Gorn'el became aware of a new presence. He looked over his shoulder into the glaring heart of the incandescence as the ophannin approached through the flames, bent against the onrushing heat, his golden battle staff clutched tightly. The roaring firestorm ignited his tunic and pale blue jerkin in an incandescent glow.

The ophannin stopped and peered at the fallen human encased in the protective bubble of the Creator's grace—a mere particle of the Creator's power. "Elohim has spared this one." Not a question, but definite curiosity.

Gorn'el nodded and inclined his head toward Mari'el, a little bit away. "And that one too." Mari'el caught his gaze and nodded, still bent low over Kenoch, his arms slightly opened, funneling the heat in a dazzling reddish flare.

"Elohim is good."

Gorn'el nodded. "Why have you come, Jas'el?"

The ophannin gave a small grin. "I have a certain interest in the fate of these two, if you recall."

He laughed and permitted the protective sphere to contract a little as the main force of the blast moved beyond them. "You always did have a talent for understatement."

The other's smile waned a bit. "And I thought you and Mari'el might need an extra battle staff."

Gorn'el stiffened, sensing their arrival even before the ophannin jutted his chin at something. His lips tightened as the six dark Watchers stepped through a sheet of wavering light and stalked toward them, battle staffs in hand. He shook his head. "They still think they have a claim on Thore."

"I suspected they might. Once they have ground to stand on, shaky as it might be, they don't give up."

Gorn'el cast a glance at his companion down the way,

hunched over Kenoch. But the Watchers ignored Mari'el and spread out to circle Thore.

The ophannin spoke quietly out the corner of his mouth. "I would have removed it from him, but you know how such things work, Gorn'el."

He nodded and stepped away from Thore, turning a slow circle to keep the closing Watchers in sight. "He who takes it must relinquish it himself. Another cannot do it. His father once faced the same test."

The Watchers halted and looked at the unconscious human. Gorn'el knew each of them. They'd fellowshipped together before the Rebellion, and he'd fought them ever since.

"Why has this human been spared?" Biror was a stout warrior in a gray tunic so dark it appeared almost black. His view lingered a moment on Thore, then lifted and considered Gorn'el with apparent curiosity.

"He's not yours. How many times do I have to tell you?"

Biror's eyes narrowed darkly. "My Master thinks otherwise. He's put in a claim."

"It's a false claim, and you know it … the Deceiver knows it. This human carries the righteousness of Elohim within him."

A quiet groan arose from the Watchers, lips snarling as though in pain. Anger burned in their eyes.

Gorn'el let a smile tug at his lips. "The righteousness of Elohim," he repeated deliberately, knowing how the Holy Name grated upon their ears, "imputed to him by his faith."

"He carries the mark," Slieor declared, shaking a threatening fist in spite of his slight build.

"Carrying it and accepting it are two different things. Now go away and leave us alone. I weary of your feeble attempts."

"Feeble?" Toromor, built bulkier than the others, stepped forward, his glistening battle staff tipping menacingly at them. "Would you care to see how feeble we are, Gorn'el?"

Jas'el whispered, "I thought it might come to this." The ophannin grew taut, ready to move at an instant's warning.

"I know how to deal with the Deceiver's minions." To these creatures, caution was weakness and a flourish of confidence was half the battle. So he laughed at them, even though the tension of looming battle had taken hold of his insides, for to show fear could be disastrous. He looked the big warrior up and down with open disdain. "Toromor, you forget I knew you before the name of El was stripped from your name."

The Watcher flinched at the reminder.

"You have broad shoulders, but you were a weak servant even then, and I can't imagine you improving much since making your choice."

If there was one thing he had learned over the eons of dealing with the Deceiver's Fallen Ones, it was that bravado was their preferred medium of exchange, and pride their weakness. Gorn'el knew how to broker both commodities.

Toromor bristled. "And you, Shackled One, are still bowing to the Tyrant of Old. How do you see yourself as any better than we, Gorn'el?"

He shrugged. "The Pit will never be my eternal prison. I see that as infinitely better." He held Toromor in a steady gaze while watching the others from the corner of his eye. They'd begun to close in on him.

Toromor shifted his view to Jas'el. "An ophannin. You come running to help Gorn'el when he gets out of his league?"

"Me?" Jas'el chuckled. "I'll step in should he need me." He cast a scornful look at the Watchers. "But so far I can't see where he'll require my help." He gave a dramatic yawn and glanced at Gorn'el. "You're right, these creatures are wearisome."

"Creatures?" Biror leaped forward and craned his head around and up at him as if inspecting a lowly insect. "Your arrogance turns my stomach! Our flesh is the same as yours."

"Don't insult me." Jas'el stabbed Biror away from him with the end of his battle staff. "You're nearly mortal."

Scarlet rage burned up Biror's neck.

Slieor stepped in front of Biror and pointed his staff at Gorn'el, but spoke to the ophannin. "Gorn'el called us wearisome?"

Jas'el shrugged. "He or someone did. It's difficult to recall, so many say the same thing about you."

Gorn'el grinned. Jas'el understood how to play the pride card too. The air had cooled as it rushed in to fill the vacuum created by the exploding jumper, and he permitted the bubble to dissipate.

Biror lunged forward, seeing his opportunity. "Stand back so I can mark this one for my master!" The anger in his voice strangled his words.

Mari'el advanced from behind, so far unobserved by the Watchers. He'd been sizing up the situation and now placed himself where he might instantly fling a bolt from his battle staff across their backs.

Gorn'el's fingers resonated from the mounting energy within his battle staff. "I'll say it one more time. You have no claim to this one."

Biror glanced at his friends who were obviously weighing the risks of pressing the issue, of attacking a Guardian and an ophannin, regardless of their superior numbers.

In the distance came the keening of the disembodied spirits of dead Nephs; the ground seemed to be sucking them down to the Pit. The mournful sound filled Gorn'el with a cold desperation. They'd soon be standing before their master. He grimaced and tried to ignore their wailing, waiting for Biror's next move.

In a remote part of his consciousness, Gorn'el was thankful he was not human, in spite of the glorious future many would someday enjoy. At least he'd never have to deal with those Neph spirits seeking an inroad to inhabit his body. He was content in the role the Creator had given him. He'd watch over his charges and do the Creator's will. Such was the highest calling for Malik.

"Come mark him, Biror, if you think you can." Gorn'el firmed his grip and his stance, then cast a look at the other Watchers. "It seems your friends are having second thoughts. Is one human worth the risk?"

Biror's view shifted between his partners and Gorn'el. "Well?" he hissed.

Toromor looked uncomfortable, eyeing Gorn'el's battle staff. "Since this claim is still in dispute, we can wait a little longer until the master has clear title to him."

The other's nodded.

Biror growled, his lips curling in rage, but he backed away.

Another thing Gorn'el knew about Watchers was that they were cowards deep down inside, unless backed up with overwhelming numbers. Six against three wasn't overwhelming enough, he decided, watching the Fallen Ones slink away from him and disappear in a sheet of garish light.

The ophannin lowered his battle staff and gave a tight laugh. "You do have your work cut out for you, Gorn'el."

He nodded, setting the end of his staff on the ground.

Jas'el tilted his head as if hearing a command, then looked at Gorn'el and Mari'el. "I need to return to my charge."

"Trouble?"

"Maybe … maybe not. I'll know soon enough." The ophannin turned and a waterfall of golden light snatched him away.

❦

The air snapped with static discharge as the whirring Noah had mistaken for a ringing in his ears grew louder, vibrating deep inside his chest, electrifying the nerves in his clenched teeth. He stared at his father who felt it too. "A jumper. They've found us!"

Lamech, at first too stunned to move, rushed to where

Mishah and Naamah sat among the green ferns, grabbed Kitah, and hauled the women to their feet.

The way the magnetic field had the air humming, Noah knew the jumper had to be close, very close. Maybe hovering right overhead! He helped Grandfather Methuselah to his feet. Wrapping an arm around the ancient patriarch's narrow waist, he glanced around. Where had Vaul gone, and why now? "Vaul!"

His father scrambled up the path, glaring back over his shoulder at him. "Quickly, Noah!"

There was no place to run, no place to hide atop this wide, treeless mountain pass. Noah took off after them. Grandfather seemed dazed by the buzzing atmosphere. "Let's hurry," Noah urged, but there was no way the old man could keep up, and he wouldn't consider leaving Grandfather Methuselah behind.

The popping air made his hair dance to the unseen energy, his skin prickling like a pincushion. A dark shadow materialized before him—indistinct at first, but it quickly took on shape and mass. Noah's breath seized in his lungs. His mother and father veered away as giant earthing pods extended, smashing vegetation beneath the jumper's great weight.

Lamech cast about, his escape blocked by the immense craft. The band of red lights racing around its middle threw crimson flashes out across the glade. Noah's heart hammered in his chest. He braced himself as he stared into the proj ports in the lower hull, which looked darkly back at him like round, dark eyes. A metallic clack sounded and a small oval port in the jumper's side began to slide back.

Before it had completely opened, Majiah stuck her head out. "Quick! Before they get a fix on us!"

Noah gave a gasp of relief and rushed to the craft, grabbing his father's arm. "It's all right."

Lamech resisted but Noah pulled him along. "Majiah? What are you doing here?"

"No time now." She scanned the sky and helped Grandfather Methuselah, then his mother, up the steps. Noah turned at a sound behind him. Vaul bounded through the tall ferns, leaping past them into the ship. Noah took Kitah from Lamech, handed her up to Naamah, then hurried his father into the jumper and scrambled in after him. The hatch slid shut. The jumper seemed to slide sideways a bit, then shot upward.

The sudden acceleration forced them back toward the hatch. Majiah helped them onto the floor where the gathering spirit had once held Nephs safely in place. There were six other people from the mine who Noah recognized, strapped in harnesses against the main bulkhead. As Noah and the others grabbed for handholds to brace themselves, Majiah's view slid across them, widening with concern. "Where's Thore?"

The grief of the loss of his friend squeezed in his chest.

She read it in his face. Her view leaped to the closed hatch. "That explosion?"

"Thore stayed behind to give us time to escape."

She gave him a wide look. "You know for sure?"

"How could anyone have survived it? Even a Makir Warrior is mortal."

From the other side of the open pressure door to the cockpit, Zinorah said, "Our decloaking gave them a reference point. Strap our passengers in and tell them to hold tight. The ride is likely to get rough."

She directed them against the bulkhead with the others and helped them buckle the straps over their shoulders and around their chests. "We can hide from them while cloaked, but when we phase-shifted to pick you up, they got a read on us."

Noah wedged the Book between a strap and his lap and grabbed Naamah's hand. She looked scared. He probably did too. The padding against his back was thin and obviously a makeshift arrangement.

"Sorry about the accommodations," Majiah said. "Jumpers are designed to protect their passengers with the help of a gathering spirit. Without one"—her mouth hitched sideways apologetically—"the padding and belts will just have to do."

All at once the jumper lurched to one side. Majiah grabbed for a bar encircling the wall.

Noah snugged up his belts and checked that Naamah's harness was tight. "How'd you know where to find us?"

She opened her mouth to speak. Just then Zinorah called for her from the cockpit. Majiah glanced to the control room then back at them. "Got to go." She pulled herself along the handholds, up the inclining deck and into the cockpit.

Lamech turned to him. "Where do you know her from?"

His weight increased against the meager padding as the jumper accelerated. "Refugees from Quinal-ee."

"And all this?" His father indicated the dim interior. A ring of milky illumination—pale intensity of old-fashioned moonglass circling about the domed roof—was the only source of light.

"Spoils of war. Taken from the Oracle en route from Oric to Earth. Zinorah, the woman in control, had been a broodblood."

"Zinorah?" Methuselah's hoary eyebrows lifted questioningly. "The woman with the Neph spirit?"

"The very same one, Grandfather. The woman from whom you drove the invading spirit."

His white head nodded. "Not I." He pointed a finger at the ceiling. "The Creator. I only prayed for her." He thumped the metal floor beneath them. "And He released the gathering spirit from this thing too."

The jumper swooped. Noah's stomach pressed back against his spine. His hand tightened around the leather strap and his lips peeled back with the nearly instant acceleration. Talk ceased as everyone became intent on simply bracing themselves. Naamah's hand gripped his hand tighter. His father clutched Kitah, fighting

to better secure her. The little girl whimpered as he carefully
threaded her burned arms through his safety straps.

The engine's muffled scream raced beyond human hearing.
Noah looked for Vaul. The canic was huddled against one of the
curving walls where he seemed to have found anchorage enough
to keep from being flung about the lurching craft.

The jumper moved in ways that seemed to defy the laws of the
Creator, changing directions in a moment, plunging suddenly, or
careening over on its side. The force of its movement for the most
part kept Noah pressed hard against the meager padding. He
thought he heard an explosion, and the ride got bumpy for a
moment. Were they being shot at? How could they be if they were
cloaked? But he understood so little about jumpers that the
thought was only a fleeting one. A second explosion sent the
jumper cartwheeling.

Zinorah recovered from the reeling plunge and pushed the
jumper's nose straight down. His stomach caught in his throat,
then slammed back to his spine when the jumper reversed direction and shot straight up. The jumper shuddered once, twice,
then dived again for the basement as the sound of distant explosions penetrated the metal hull.

And then they were flung hard against the straps, and the
jumper stopped in an instant and hung there, vibrating lowly, the
familiar idling whir returning. He gulped, his stomach in a state
of turmoil. Naamah's face had drained of color, her green eyes
wide, her white-knuckled fingers wrapped in the straps.
Surprisingly, Grandfather had managed to remain calm all
through the maneuvers. Noah looked around. Each of them
seemed in mild shock. His mother was panting, her hair scattered
about her face, her healer's bag clutched tight against her stomach. His father kept a firm grasp on Kitah, looking as though he
expected to be swept heavenward at any instant. The others from
Quinal-ee began to ask if everyone was all right.

Majiah bent through the low door and glanced at her passengers. "We're safe for the time being. We'll wait here until they lose interest and leave the area."

Noah worked his buckles and slid his arms from the straps. "Was that shooting I heard?"

She nodded, her mouth locked down in its usual frown.

"How did they find us? We were cloaked."

"We were near enough for their gathering spirit to sense us— actually, the residue of the gathering spirit that Master Methuselah exorcised awhile back."

His grandfather nodded sagely, as if he understood.

Noah wished he did. "But now they can't?" His back ached and he stood to stretch.

"We had to put enough distance between us for the lingering influence to fade. They're still up there, looking." She jabbed at the ceiling. "They'll get bored after a time and move off." She turned to the control chamber's hatch, but looked back at them again. "I wouldn't unstrap just yet."

27

On the Run

As the roaring in his ears subsided and yellow splotches swirled wildly against his eyelids, Thore imagined a heavy hand slowly lifting from his back. His lungs gathered in a much-needed breath, and then another. The heat that nearly fried his skin, like the pounding surf in his ears, lessened by degrees, and with its ebb, a knifing pain began to methodically excise flesh and muscle from his leg, vaguely in an area below his knee.

He remembered seeing the jumper crash through the trees, feeling the earth leap beneath his feet, and then that terrible shattering of rock and wailing of metal, a noise so terrible no amount of imagining could have conjured it up. He remembered a shock wave of searing fire that had slammed him into the ground and ... and then what?

His brain still reeled from the blow.

Gritting his teeth against the growing fire in his leg, he moved an arm. Wrenching muscles shot fiery needles into his neck. He tried to feel for exactly where the knife was working its deviltry.

There was a warm wetness below his knees, and something hard ... His fingers pressed against a sharp edge and a wallop of pain kicked the breath out of him. He squeezed his eyes tight as the wave washed over him. It had hit him too suddenly. His ingrained training hadn't been prepared for it. Taking a breath, he willed the pain back to a tolerable level and at the same time opened his eyes.

Blackness stood about him everywhere. Not the blackness of night, but the dingy grime of a fireplace after the flames had been extinguished. Swirling wisps of smoke circled upward from the charred ground like dirty tendrils of morning mist. Where trees once stood, now only charred spikes remained, snapped like twigs, all bent precisely in the same direction. Within their gutted trunks, reddish orange embers sketched flickering lines.

He stared at his hands. His skin, now merely warm, appeared unburned. He'd survived! He wanted to laugh if it wasn't that his body hurt so much. Then he remembered the Nephs and looked around. Nothing but smoldering trees. Even the rocky rise to his right had been stripped of its vegetation and charred black by the fireball. The Nephs were gone ... but he was still here?

Kenoch!

Scanning the charred landscape, his view stopped upon the shape of a man fifty spans ahead of him on what had once been the forest trail. Gritting against the pain, he pushed himself up, grabbed his sword, and stared at it. From its hilt to nearly its tip, the blade was unmarked. But the final hand's length of steel was gone, the end jagged like a badly healed scar. All he could think of was that some peculiarity of the terrain had caused the fireball to leap over him and spare him—and most of his sword.

He turned his attention to his leg, carefully pulling up his pant leg. Where the broken bone had ripped through the skin, blood flowed freely. He'd had enough training as a soldier to know that such a wound could be fatal in short order. He had to stem the bleeding before he checked on Kenoch. Rifling through the bag he carried on his side, he found cord and quickly bound it around his leg. He twisted the tourniquet cord until it dug deep into his skin. The flow slowed. He carried a powder that would help coagulate the blood, but he'd get to that later. He had to see about Kenoch.

He groped along the charred ground, one hand pulling him along, the other keeping the tourniquet tight. Every movement sent renewed surges of pain up his leg.

Kenoch was stirring by the time he reached him, shaking his head, looking dazed. "Thore?" His eyes moved slowly about the destruction, his mouth dropping. "What ... what happened?"

With a groan, Thore came to a halt, panting, the pain too intense, fighting against his will to keep it in abeyance. "The jumper's power core. It must have ruptured when it crashed."

Kenoch swallowed hard and looked at him. "The Nephs?"

"Vaporized."

Kenoch's fixed stare widened.

"I know. Incredible. We must have been in some sort of storm-eye. I've seen it happen at sea." He looked around, the hairs at his neck tingling. "But never on land ..."

"Thore, you're bleeding."

"Bone broke."

"That looks bad." Kenoch leaned closer to examine the wound. "Got to stop the bleeding. What you've got there isn't working well." He cut the leather shoulder strap off his bag and bound it tight around Thore's leg just above the knee. "Need a stick or something to cinch it down." He glanced about, but there was nothing usable around.

A tingling at Thore's neck had slowly begun to work its way down over his shoulders and across his chest. Was he going into shock? He knew he wasn't—not yet at least. There was something else going on.... Thore used the knife handle on the leather strap, gave it a twist, and held it. His leg had began to numb. "We've got to find cover."

Kenoch's head snapped up; his eyes narrowed at the bright

sky showing through where the dirty cloud was breaking up. He slapped a hand to his neck, and felt his arm. "They're coming back!" Kenoch stood, still shaky on his feet, and helped Thore up onto his good leg.

Thore leaned his weight onto Kenoch's shoulder and the smaller man threw an arm around his waist. They started off in a clumsy hobbling gait, the magnetically charged air running electric fingers down his spine.

Kenoch was breathing heavy already. "Maybe they've come back to look for survivors?"

"I hope that's all." But he didn't believe Nephs had an altruistic nerve anywhere in their bodies. They weren't looking for survivors. They were looking for him and Kenoch. They knew. Somehow, they knew!

Three triangular shapes darkened the sky. He cast about for somewhere to hide as they struggled for the distant line of still-standing trees. What remained of the forest offered little cover. Hobbling lock-stepped with Kenoch, the distant edge of the standing forest seemed a long way off indeed.

The crafts hovered to a stop above the crash site, blocking the hazy sunlight; the whirring of their mag drives resonated in the air.

"Faster," Kenoch hissed between clenched teeth.

Each jarring step pulsed hammer blows of searing pain through him. He focused his thoughts, drawing upon the Katrahs and Kimahs to overcome the physical pounding. The exercises should have helped him cope, but they were of little help now. The Katrahs and Kimahs were elements of the binding, and without another Makir to bind with, he had to do it all on his own.

Plunging headlong through the shattered forest, he noted the blackened spikes begin to stand a little taller, their charred limbs a little fuller. Thore concentrated on keeping the band around his leg tight and staying in step with Kenoch. His head was swimming, his vision blurring. A false step would bring them both down. Kenoch's heavy breathing filled his ears. He was only vaguely aware that now some of the trees had remnants of bark clinging to the leeward sides. As that fact made its way into his consciousness, his strength renewed. The pain had begun to numb. He was better able to cope.

"They still behind us?" he gasped, afraid to take his eye off the ground for even an instant to look.

He felt Kenoch nod. "Just ... sitting ... up there. Haven't moved."

A scattering of green appeared among the monotonous land-scape. They were going to make it into cover. His brain shifted into a more pragmatic mode. Once into cover, they'd tend to his leg. Lay low a few days. Then he and Kenoch would make their way back to Atlan.

If the jumpers were here, they wouldn't be following Noah. That was good. But why had they remained? Didn't they know Noah had escaped? It was a puzzle that could wait. Right now he had more immediate problems to deal with.

※

"We'll rest here awhile," Kenoch said. "I don't hear them or feel them. They must still be sitting out there."

Thore was more than ready to stop. Kenoch lowered him carefully to the ground. His leg exploded with renewed pain.

"Sorry, Thore."

He nodded, words taking too much effort. They'd made it into the standing forest beyond the circle of destruction. Here, at least, beneath towering trees that closed out the sky, they'd be safe.

"What can I do?" Kenoch asked.

Thore shook his head again, swallowed, and drew in a ragged breath. "Need to set it."

"I can't do that. This is bad, Thore. You need a healer."

He took another couple of breaths. "Know of one nearby?"

"My sister."

"She's far from here." At least he sincerely hoped she and Noah, and the others, were far away.

"Oh, Thore! All right. How? The bone is through the skin."

"Let me think." He knew how to set minor breaks, but this was different. He replaced the knife with a stick and used the knife to cut away the material around the wound. He shivered. Chilling. Not a good sign. The bleeding had slowed, seeping through thickly coagulated blood. Angry red skin spread down into the top of his boot and up toward his knee. Kenoch was right. This would require a healer's skill and her medicines. He'd already lost a lot of blood. Cutting on it now could be fatal. He shivered again and laid his head back.

"First, you need to pull it—to draw the bone back inside." He gulped and licked his lips. "I've powder to help with bleeding. Bind it tight, then go for help."

"I won't leave you."

He glared at him, his voice hardening. "Then you'll watch me die."

"This isn't fatal, Thore."

"It can be, if we don't stop the bleeding, and if poison lodges in my blood—" His shoulders convulsed. He waited until the icy wave passed. "I … I think I'm going into shock." He controlled his breathing, trying to keep his head clear, and felt inside his pouch. He put a container in Kenoch's hand. "Use this to stop the bleeding. I … I might not be conscious afterward to give it to you."

Kenoch shoved the tin box into a pocket. "You need to get warm. I can build a fire."

"No. Attract jumpers."

"All right. What do I do first?"

"Straighten leg. Pull firmly." He braced himself, centering his thoughts.

Kenoch took the leg by the ankle, then stopped and looked up at the treetops. "Feel that?"

All he felt was a deep cold working its way through his body.

"The air, Thore. It's tingling again!"

A shadow moved slowly over them, and the magnetic pulses began to penetrate the curtain of pain that enveloped him. "They've found us."

Kenoch gave him a panicky look. "How?"

"You have to get away from here."

Kenoch stared at him, then at the darkening treetops. "We'll both go." Struggling against Thore's vastly greater bulk, Kenoch managed to get him to his feet again. The effort sent renewed pain coursing up Thore's leg and pounding into his head. He tried to focus as they struggled deeper into the forest. Unseen branches reached out to stab at him and slap his face. The ground seemed to roll beneath his feet. Drawing on reserves he didn't know he had, his vision cleared a little.

They stumbled onward, patches of sky whirling into view then whirling out, the ground rising up then receding. His ears buzzed with a noise he couldn't distinguish from the closing jumpers or the effect of too much pain and too little blood.

Kenoch was yanking him down to the ground. Branches snapped and poked—rough rock scraped alongside his head. Then the light muted, the odor of moist, rotting leaves becoming stronger. "Where are we?" He tried to focus against the dimness of the place, tried to sit up. Kenoch put a hand atop his head an instant before it came up against a ledge of rock.

"A cave." Kenoch, breathless, scrambled over him, silhouetted against the brighter light beyond what looked like a narrow slit.

The charged air hummed and made the rocks sing out. Moonglass, Thore mused in a detached way, would be glaring! "They'll find us," he groaned. His leg had become twisted beneath him.

"How?" Kenoch pulled back. "You're bleeding again, Thore. Got to stop it or it won't matter if they find us—you."

"Powder," he hissed through grinding teeth.

Kenoch fumbled for it. "What is this?"

"Belar'mik root. Blood thickens at its touch." He exhaled and drew in a steeling breath so he could concentrate on battling the pain.

Kenoch pried open the lid of the tin and poured a goodly amount around the protruding bone. "It's working, Thore. The blood's congealing."

He nodded, swallowing as he concentrated on driving the pain down to a tolerable level. "There're some birch-bark pills … in a bag … in my pouch."

Kenoch dug through the pouch. "Got it." He worked the thongs open.

The whirring outside the cave grew louder. He took a handful of the pills from Kenoch and tossed them into his mouth, swallowing them down at once. "You need to get out of here, Kenoch."

He nodded and began throwing items back into Thore's pouch. Then he stopped and stared at something. "Thore. What's this?" He drew out the pledge pendant.

"Found it. In your 'gia field."

Kenoch stared at him. "You know what it is?"

"I was going to tell the Village Council. Never had a chance."

"Thore, your father had one just like it, and it almost took him over."

He shook his head. "Haven't touched it."

"That doesn't matter. The Oracle can track you through this!" Kenoch stared at the faintly glowing crystal. "This is how they know."

"Get rid of it." The pain made it too hard to think. He didn't want to be bothered with this right now.

Kenoch started to toss it away, but stopped. "No. I can't do it for you. You have to be the one who gets rid of it. Otherwise its influence won't be broken."

"Just toss it away, Kenoch."

Kenoch grabbed his hand and hung the thong over his fingers. "All you have to do is throw it away. Like your father did. But you've got to do it yourself."

The crystal's warm glow brightened, and with it came an easing of his pain. Thore heaved back, and hesitated. His breathing settled a little and his vision sharpened, his brain clearing. "Can't I hold onto it? Just a little while longer?"

"Thore! Once a pledge pendant like that almost got us all killed! You can't keep it! It will do the same now. We'll never escape the jumpers if you don't get rid of it."

"But it's taking the pain away."

"That's only an illusion, Thore. Another of the Deceiver's lies."

"Illusion or not, it helps."

"Throw it away!" The light outside dimmed. Kenoch stared at the cave's entrance. "They're moving into position."

Thore wanted to get rid of the pledge pendant, but something stayed his hand.

"Thore!"

He made a fist around the thong. He had to do it ... but he couldn't.

"We'll be incinerated any moment, Thore! We have to leave now." Kenoch scrambled out of the cave and turned back to him. "I'm going. Come with me. I'll help you."

He stared at the warm glow that seemed to pulse relief throughout him. To call to him. Had it called to his father, too ... and finally controlled him? "No." He was a follower of the Creator. He had power over the Deceiver that his father had not had. "I won't let you take me over." He threw it into the back of the cave.

It lay in the shadows, its glow brightening for an instant, then slowly faded away....

Then Kenoch was dragging him from the cave. He grappled his way to his feet using a rock for support and let his weight fall again upon Kenoch's shoulder. Fiery pain rushed back, muted somewhat by the birch-bark pills. Locked step for step, they crashed through thick brush, Kenoch struggling under his weight. He tried to ease Kenoch's burden some by using his sword as a third leg. The sky brightened as they moved out from under the jumpers and away from the cave.

They had gone only a few hundred spans when one of the jumpers launched a proj. A whoosh filled the air and a blast rocked the ground, pitching them into a sarberry bramble. He hardly felt the prickly thorns stabbing at him as a rush of heat blew past them. A black cloud of smoke and debris soared upward, and they covered their heads as it began to rain down on them.

A second explosion blotted out what little remained of the sunlight. Stones and dirt and bits of timber crashed into the ground for a while, and then slowly the forest went silent. Thore uncovered his head to see the three jumpers retreat from the treetops, rotate their noses skyward, and in a flash of light shoot out of sight.

"Gone," he breathed.

"They think they've killed us." Kenoch struggled to extract himself from the thorny bramble then lent Thore a hand.

Thore levered himself up onto one foot and leaned onto the hilt of his sword. "You all right?"

Kenoch looked down at himself and nodded. "Think so. You?"

He shook his head. "I'll not be going any farther." His brain reeled from the loss of so much blood, and now that the essence of valor was slowly ebbing from his system, he became painfully aware of the weakness in his one good leg. "This is as far as I'm going."

Kenoch looked dismayed, but there was now a spark of reality in Thore's eyes. "We'll fix you a place to stay while I go for help."

Thore nodded.

"And a fire, too. That will keep the Turnlings away."

He nodded again and swayed. Kenoch managed to catch him before he hit the ground.

"Oh, Thore." Kenoch's muted words reached him distantly. Past them he became aware of another sound. With what little was left of his failing strength he grabbed for Kenoch's arm. "Someone's coming."

Kenoch went rigid beneath his urgent grasp. "Not again! Not now!" The Lee-lander grabbed for the sword from his hand.

He couldn't let Kenoch face this new threat alone. He struggled to rally his strength, but the effort was too much, too late. The forest around him whirled, fading swiftly into a soft, black, blessed, pain-free oblivion.

28

Da-gore's Return

We weren't expecting them." Majiah's eyes glazed. "They were in the main tunnel before we knew it. No stopping them. A few of us made it out." She brushed quickly at her eyes. Sitting cross-legged on the floor opposite him, Majiah struggled to hold onto the self-control Noah knew she was famous for. Her eyes hardened once again to sparkrock.

"My father was killed defending the tunnels. I led a group to the drainage tunnel. Some drowned as we fled. Maybe they were the lucky ones. A few of us made it out." She glanced around at the handful of people seated about the jumper's wide, empty floor.

Noah put a hand on her shoulder. Her muscles flinched and went taut. "I'm sorry, Mistress Majiah. Is this all that is left?"

"All who managed to get away. We hid among the rocks and watched as the Nephs led the others away."

To Nod City. Like Sheflah. To be forced to renounce the Creator or become broodbloods or male prostitutes. Most would be dead within a few months. He didn't want to think about that. Others would end up in the growing Neph colony on Oric. Like Zinorah. He glanced at the hatch to the control room. She hadn't come out. He could see her just sitting there, alone, staring at the panel before her.

"But how did you find us?" He looked at his father standing off to one side, listening, his expression dark and at the moment unreadable. Nearby, Grandfather Methuselah sat upon one of the many scattered blankets, his thin, bony back pressed against a wall-mounted pad. Noah's mother, Naamah, and a woman whom he recalled seeing in the mines were bent tenderly over Noah's little niece. The child was awake, lying upon a padding of blankets, Mishah tending to her burns. Kitah appeared more alert. His mother had given her medicine, which Majiah kept onboard the jumper, to ease the pain. The medicine seemed to be helping.

"We were searching for you, Master Noah."

He looked back at Majiah. "Me? Why?"

"Nephs don't usually pursue those who flee the villages they overrun. That they came after us was a surprise. Then I began to put the pieces of the puzzle together. It wasn't our people they were looking for. It was you. It had to be. They'd tried to delay your arrival and then were waiting for you in Quinal-ee. When they missed their chance there, they came after you in the mines."

Her words hit like a fist. "If that's true, then your people suffered and died because you showed friendship to me." He glanced at Naamah who sat listening at his side.

"I'm sorry," Naamah said softly.

"Perhaps." She folded her arms. "But you can't blame yourself. We chose to help you. You didn't come looking for it."

He appreciated her generosity. Just the same, the burden of their suffering settled squarely on his shoulders.

"Since they didn't find you with us, we—Zinorah and I—figured the next place the Nephs would strike would be the Lee-lands. We wanted to warn you and your villages, but we couldn't reach the jumper. The Nephs had set up a camp in the valley below the mines. We were forced to stay hidden until they finally departed, about a week later."

He tried to imagine these people hiding in the rocks all those days—so close to their means of escape, but not able to reach it. How it must have frayed their nerves knowing at any moment the Nephs might discover the jumper's cloaked presence.

"We arrived too late," she continued. "New Eden was a smoking heap, the farms around it destroyed. Vera-logia fields ablaze in every direction. The air black with the smoke of them."

"What did you do?"

"Prayed."

"And that's how you found us?" The Creator must have had a hand in all this, but Noah was trying to see it.

"No. The urging we all received was to return to the mines. We figured we'd be safe there, now that the Nephs had already attacked them and left."

"And that's where you were heading when you stumbled upon us?" Naamah asked.

She nodded. "That explosion nearly blinded our sensors. Curiosity drew us, but Zinorah's keen eyes spotted your party fleeing over the pass."

"So, some good came out of their deaths after all," Lamech noted.

Majiah's frown tightened.

His father nodded gravely and looked at her. "The Creator heard your prayers after all."

Her brown eyes iced over. "I suppose you can look at it like that." She shoved her fingers through her short, dark hair a couple times and then shook it out.

"But you don't?"

His father was probing. Noah sensed a sermon coming on. He frowned. Now was probably not the appropriate time.

"I've seen too much evil in our land to know what I think anymore, Master Lamech."

"And still you don't see the Creator's hand moving?"

"Do you? My father is dead and so are many of the people I love most. Your family has suffered too. I don't see the Creator in that."

"Sometimes it is a difficult thing." His voice thickened in a way Noah knew foreshadowed what his father considered a gem of insight. "Sometimes we never see it." He drew in a breath and went on more briskly. "But you are here. You are in possession of this vehicle. Evil has been with us since the fall. And it will remain with us until the Creator's Strong Man comes back to us to make all things new again."

Her lips drew tight. "And when will that be?"

He shrugged. "His timing is not our timing, Mistress Majiah."

"That, Master Lamech, sounds like a convenient excuse to do nothing." She rapped the metal floor beneath her. "You're right. We have this jumper, and its weapons. And I for one plan on making that count for something."

"And perhaps that's been the Creator's plan all along."

Noah shifted his view from his father to the young woman. It was time to intercede. Majiah's eyebrows hitched together, and she was about to shoot back another challenge when Zinorah's face appeared in the hatchway. "They're gone."

Majiah cut off her retort and rose instantly to her feet with the fluid grace of a cat rising from cover at the scent of prey. "Strap yourselves in." She turned back to his father. "We can finish this discussion later." Then to Noah, "Better secure that canic somehow. We may not be completely out from under their guns yet."

He rose too, his effort not nearly as smooth, his knees a little creaky. "Where to now, Mistress Majiah?"

Her lips scrunched as her forehead creased slightly. She exhaled sharply. "Somewhere away from here."

"Atlan," Methuselah said, tottering to his feet. "Atlan is where we are to go next."

She stared at him, then cast an inquiring look at Noah.

He thought of Thore, and Uncle Kenoch. He ached for them, for his family taken captive or lost back in the Lee-lands. And especially for Sheflah. Naamah watched him with glazed eyes and he felt guilty at his own self-pity. She'd lost not only Sheflah, but her mother and father. There was nothing they could do about Uncle Kenoch and Aunt Cerah, but there was something they could do about Sheflah, and the others. And sitting here wasn't going to get any of them back. "We must return to Atlan. High Councilor Rhone has to be told what's happened."

Majiah nodded. "Atlan." She ducked through the low hatch, and disappeared.

Noah couldn't seem to stop pacing. The others, meanwhile, remained more or less in their own places—Lamech with a hip perched upon a corner of the long dining table, Zinorah standing with martial rigidity before the green and gold marble pillar, Majiah stiff-backed in the soft chair, and Naamah and Leenah holding onto each other as though to stand apart in their grief was more than either of them could manage. But Noah kept stalking the floor.

Rhone understood his anxiety. He felt it too for Thore. Each of them felt it and each dealt with it in his or her own way. The news had been a blow to him. He had sensed Thore's danger, but even prepared as he had been, the news had rocked him.

It had been two days since the appearance of the jumper had sent Atla Fair into a frenzy as it came to rest on the Meeting Floor below the rooftop garden.

Their discussion had momentarily hit an impasse. In the brief seconds of silence, Rhone debated his next move.

All at once Noah halted his marching and spun on his heels toward him. "The longer we delay, the longer Sheflah is in their hands. It drives me crazy imagining what might be happening to her!" He stormed forward, his eyes narrowing. "You have to do something, Rhone!"

"What I have to do is protect you, Noah."

"Forget me! It's my daughter we're talking about, and everyone else who was taken." He pointed a finger at Majiah. "Her family. My family. And what of Thore? His blood is on the Oracle's hands as well."

Leenah stiffened. A barb sank deep into Rhone's heart. Still, he was High Councilor—ruler of Atlan. He had more to think of than the lives of a few hundred people. "I understand your impatience, but I can't just fly off and attack Nod City, Noah."

Noah opened his mouth to speak, then turned away with a sweep of his arm, rejecting the remark.

Naamah's quiet weeping punctuated the momentary silence.

"Might there be diplomatic channels to investigate, High Councilor?" Lamech stood off the edge of the table and approached him. "An emissary from Atlan, perhaps?"

Rhone didn't expect that from Lamech, always the impetuous one to take matters into his own hands. "Atlan and Nod City have no diplomatic ties, Master Lamech."

Noah turned back. "We don't have time for this. We have to go in and take them. Rhone, you have a thousand Makir at the ready to move. Amass them and take the city. Take it for the Creator's sake!"

Lamech shook his head. "Noah, the Creator has no need for us to fight His battles. He asks us only to be witnesses for Him, and to spread His good news of a coming Redeemer. Nothing more. You know as well as I this world is beyond saving, even if Nod City could be taken. You're asking Rhone to send Atlan to war with the Known World over our children. Although they are precious to us, what you ask is beyond even the High Councilor's ability to grant. It is only a few years more, and the Creator will deal out His own wrath. Would you jeopardize all you have worked for, the commission the Creator has given you, because of this?"

Pyir Chrone, standing a few paces behind Rhone, stepped forward. "There is another matter you are not considering, Master Noah."

Noah seemed to deflate.

Chrone inclined his head toward the wall of the council room where they were gathered, indicating the jumper outside, resting upon the red-stone Meeting Floor. "That craft out there is far beyond anything we have in our arsenal. At this very moment my men are crawling all over that thing, trying to determine its nature, and how we might defend ourselves against them should the Oracle and Lodath decide to use them to attack Atlan. Now is not a wise time to provoke Nod City's wrath."

"Hide here from the world, if you wish," Noah growled. "You're right. There's more at risk in this than just our families. You may have to live your lives by the rules of politics, but I don't!" His dark eyes glared and his jaw was set in fierce determination. "I'm going to Nod City to free them—free them all!"

❧

"You can't, Noah."

Noah glared at him. "You intend to stop me, Rhone? Will you throw me in chains down in the Deep Chambers below the Keep?" His foot stomped the marble floor.

"I'm not going to chain you. You know better than I that you have a job to finish, Noah." Rhone wondered why he had never seen this side of his lifelong friend before. This easygoing man had become a hook-tooth tiger.

"How can I finish it while my child is in the Deceiver's hands?"

"And that's exactly what he wants," Rhone shot back. "To distract you from doing the Creator's work. If he can do that, he's won."

Noah went silent as he digested that. "Perhaps, but this is something I must do." His voice lacked some of its fire.

Lamech stepped to his son's side. "I agree, High Councilor, this may not be a wise thing to do." He smiled thinly. "But then as my dear wife is wont to point out, I've been known to do some pretty stupid things. It's my family as well as his. I helped build that Temple, and I'm partly responsible for what is going on in it now." He paused and cast a smile at Naamah, then looked back at Rhone. "When Noah leaves, I'll be going with him, High Councilor."

The situation was turning impossible. He couldn't let Noah and Lamech go off on their own. That venture was destined for failure. And he couldn't permit Noah to go unprotected. Somehow he had to dissuade both of them. "You have no plan. To rush into Nod City and invade the Oracle's Temple is folly, Noah. Doomed to failure from the start."

"I do have a plan," Noah said. "The Temple site is riddled with tunnels. Many of them enter the Temple from far below it. I'll find my way into the Temple through one of them."

Rhone drew in a breath to cool his impatience. "Tunnels terrify you."

"I'll force myself to endure."

"And you'll die trying to find your way through them." The words came from outside the chamber, followed immediately by the brisk click of footsteps. All heads turned as the man strode into the room. Slim, white-haired, face incised by the passage of time, the ex-captain of the Lodath's Guard looked trim and fit for all his seven-hundred-plus years.

"Da-gore!" He was the last man Rhone expected to see. It had been years since his old comrade in arms had showed up at the Sanctuary of Justice. He crossed the room and clasped hands with Da-gore. "Where have you come from?"

With ingrained military training, Da-gore carefully took in the room and the people. His eyes lighted momentarily upon Lamech and he smiled and gave a brief nod of recognition. "You've aged well, Master Lamech."

"As have you."

It had been over five hundred years since Da-gore had been Lamech's overseer in the Temple Prison.

Da-gore looked back at Rhone. "Within the last few weeks I've been off the coast of Beri-lior. Hunting."

Rhone detected a subtler meaning in that. The last he'd heard, Da-gore had been earning a sizable stack of glecks as a freelance bounty hunter. The soldier in a man never completely goes away.

"I just put into the harbor not half an hour ago. The place is abuzz with word of that thing sitting out on your patio, Rhone." He laughed. "How in Dirgen's name did you manage to steal a jumper from under the Lodath's nose?"

"I claim no responsibility. Mistress Zinorah is the culprit." He introduced him to all of them.

Da-gore took Noah's hand in both of his. "You were but a child when I left the service of Pyir Rhone."

"I remember you, First Statre Da-gore."

"You're the one responsible for me being here, you know."

"I thought it was my father."

He smiled at Lamech. "He was responsible for me coming to the Creator, but ultimately, you were the one who set the wheels in motion. Before you were born." He turned back to Rhone. "So, I gather from the snippets of talk I heard on my way in here that you are planning an assault upon Nod City?"

"No."

"Yes," Noah rejoined nearly on top of it.

Da-gore considered both of them. "Tell me what has happened." He glanced at Rhone. "If you don't mind, High Councilor."

After the brief recounting, Da-gore scowled off into the distance. "From a tactician's point of view, you are not holding defensible ground."

"But with the element of surprise?" Noah offered hopefully.

"Surprise can help only so much. You mentioned the tunnels."

"And you said I would die in them."

"You'll never find your way."

"But you could," Lamech said.

Da-gore's lips lifted in a tight grin. "Could I?"

Lamech's expression remained serious. "You built them, with a little help, if you recall."

"They've been sealed," Noah said. "I know. I was in them."

"Were you?"

"Another story, at a later time."

Da-gore nodded. "I know of a few ex-prisoners who have said the job was done hastily, and that if one knew the way, it is still possible to reach the Temple through them."

"Will you show me the way?" Noah asked.

Da-gore slid a glance at Rhone, then back, a smile pulling up his lips. "It's hell to get old. Your mind begins to go, and you start to do things that, years earlier, you'd disregard as pure folly."

Rhone knew then that any attempt at keeping Noah from rescuing his child was gone. Short of locking him in chains, there would be no way now to keep him in Atlan.

He looked to his son. "Chrone, put together a Kal-ee-hon. The best Makir we have."

"I'm going with you." Zinorah came forward a step.

"I am too." Majiah crossed her arms.

Rhone hitched a thumb over his shoulder. "How many Makir can we fit inside that thing?"

"Thirty ... thirty-five," Zinorah answered without hesitation.

He nodded to Pyir Chrone. "Thirty of our best."

"When?"

He thought a moment. He needed a good long session with the Katrahs and Kimahs, and an even longer one on his prayer bench. He glanced at Leenah and saw the worry in her eyes.

"Three days, Chrone."

Da-gore asked, "Might I suggest a later date?"

Rhone considered him. "When?"

"If we delay five weeks, we can arrive at the annual Appearing Ceremony. Nod City will be filled with pilgrims from around the Known World. We can move undetected in such a crowd."

From a tactical standpoint, it made sense. And the extra time would give him a chance to convince Noah to stay in Atlan. Rhone nodded. "All right. We'll begin preparations at once. In the meantime, I want to know what makes that jumper tick. Take it apart piece by piece if you have to. Only, make sure it's all properly back together again before we leave."

His son nodded. "I've got Kev-nn working on it already. If anyone can figure that puzzle out, he can."

29

Wildlanders

*T*he sounds seemed far away at first ... oddly disconnected—the ringing of little bells, the thudding of drums, the whoosh of a wave rolling up against Atlan's black Rim-wall, and then drawing back out to sea. Disjointed images, coming together gradually until they began to make some sense within his foggy brain.

He fought his way up, up, up, as if from a deep black pit, faintly aware of the clean forest air hiding somewhere above. He reached out impossibly long arms and drew himself ever upward. A faint light played against his eyelids. The sounds, growing stronger, came together into vague patterns that he began to recognize ... words. With a heaving draught of forest-scented air, he won consciousness.

"Thore?"

Blinking from the light, he slid his view sideways. "Kenoch." His voice was gravel in his throat.

Kenoch gave a thin, sad smile. "I was really worried about you."

Worried about him? The memories came back—the fireball, the smoke, even more vivid images of the pain, and Kenoch's last words before he had blacked out ...

He sat up, his heart pounding. "Nephs?"

Kenoch's hand pressed his shoulder. "No Nephs. You should remain still."

He cast about for his sword, not seeing it, but taking in the details more carefully. They were still in the forest, but now he lay beneath a silken green canopy. Here and there the shapes of tents emerged from the background. As his eyes adjusted to the light, he noted the tents were constructed of a mottled green and brown fabric that blended in with the forest colors.

"Where are we?" he asked cautiously.

"Among friends." A woman's voice answered from the other side of his cot.

He turned.

Her long gray hair was bound up in a single braid, wrapped in a leather thong that encased its full length. Her eyes were blue, her cheeks almost gaunt. She didn't smile, her lips presently pursed in a look of concern, her eyelids slightly lowered.

Kenoch said, "This is Mistress Selicah. She took care of your leg."

He remembered that, too, and glanced down at the splints and wrappings. "You're a healer?"

She nodded.

Her dress was made of shiverthorn and hemp—the sturdy material of people who dwelled in what was left of the Wild Lands. Nowadays, these folk were mostly fugitives from the law.

He looked back at the leg. "It doesn't hurt anymore."

"It shouldn't." Her expression remained stoic. "I set the bone properly, and the flesh no longer burns with fever."

Burns! He turned to Kenoch. "The jumpers?"

"Haven't come back. They think we're dead."

"So, it was the pledge pendant they were following?"

"You've taken the Oracle's Pledge?" Mistress Selicah's eyes narrowed with concern.

"No—well, not intentionally, at least."

"He's rid of it now."

She looked at Kenoch. "You didn't tell us."

He gave a lame smile. "I guess I must have overlooked that point."

The snap of a twig brought Thore's head around. A man bent under the lowered edge of the canopy and then stood. "Awake are you? Good." He glanced at Mistress Selicah. "It's not safe to stay long in one place."

"How long have I been here?"

He looked back at him. "Two days Master Thore, son of Rhone. I'm Garv'ik."

"You know who I am?"

"I told them." Kenoch shrugged. "I felt they ought to know. They were drawn off their course when the jumper exploded. They found us and helped. The Creator was watching over us."

"Half of Morg'Jalek heard the explosion." The man scowled. "The Creator must have been watching over you for you to have escaped that inferno alive." He was dressed in the stout shiver-thorn britches and vest of wildlanders of old. But the fistproj at his side was a grim reminder to Thore that he hadn't somehow stepped into the past. Garv'ik had the bearing of a man of impor-tance—the leader of this group, perhaps?

The healer stood. "The medicine I've packed around your leg will speed the knitting, but you'll be off your feet for two or three weeks. It was a bad break."

Garv'ik gave her a quick look. "I'll break camp. Be ready to move out in a sixth."

She nodded and looked back at Thore. "We've readied a litter."

"They were planning to leave later today whether you woke or not," Kenoch said.

"Where we going?" He directed the question to Garv'ik.

"No place in particular. We just keep moving." He stabbed a finger upward. "The Oracle's jumpers might come back at any time." He turned to leave.

"Why is the Oracle after you?"

Stopping to look back, Garv'ik worked his mouth into a thoughtful knot. "Let's just say he was not pleased when we refused to take his pledge." He ducked under the canopy's edge and began hustling the people into action.

⚜

The small, shielded fire cast its muted light in only one direction, toward the semicircle of tents. Since Garv'ik's people had cooked their evening meal on small 'gia stoves, the fire was probably meant only to give a semblance of civility and comfort to an otherwise primitive camp.

"You all right?" Kenoch stepped from the deeper shadows and hunkered by his side. His eyes appeared swollen in the low light—thinking about Cerah, no doubt.

He put a consoling hand to Kenoch's shoulder. "I'm feeling well." Mistress Selicah had tended to his leg earlier, rewrapping the neatly stitched incision in a poultice of distilled oils and herbs. "The healer says I'm doing fine." He didn't quite know where to go next. The adventure of the past several days had helped Kenoch keep his thoughts off of Cerah, but now that the fighting and the fleeing were over, the ache in his heart was raw and evident. "Thanks for sticking with me."

Kenoch forced a smile. "Think I would have left you back there? Never." He went silent a moment. Thore saw that something was on his mind.

"Where is my sword, Kenoch?"

"It's around somewhere. I'll ask Master Garv'ik."

"I'll need to grind a new point on it."

"Yeah. It sort of … disappeared."

That was probably the biggest puzzle.

Kenoch went to his haunches, his face earnest. "Garv'ik's been to Nod City."

"So have we. And the last time, we almost didn't make it out."

Kenoch grinned, and Thore again sensed that Kenoch had something on his mind, but didn't know how to say it. "Master Garv'ik and these people escaped from the Temple."

Thore raised his eyebrows. "That's quite a feat."

Kenoch's view seemed to drift out of focus, then all at once his fingers made a fist and he stood. "I'll find out about your sword. I'll check back later to see how you're doing." He strode off into the shadows. A little while later he was hunched near the campfire in earnest conversation with Garv'ik.

※

They traveled with Garv'ik's people for the next three weeks until the healing poultice of oils and roots and mosses, which sped the knitting of his broken bones, had done their job, and the leg was once again bearing weight. Inactivity had weakened him, and now that he was able to stand unaided again, he worked daily on rebuilding his strength, falling into his regular routine of morning and evening Katrahs and Kimahs, and bearing extra weight throughout the day to accelerate the strengthening process.

During the weeks while on his back, Thore had seen no reason for the little group's existence. At first it made sense to keep on the move to avoid detection, but to live out one's life like this seemed futile.

Once fit to travel, he was anxious to be on his way. Although he was thankful for their help, being among these people grated on his nerves. Perhaps it was his Makir training that gave him short patience with running and hiding.

"We should leave in the morning, Kenoch." He broached the subject one evening, late after most of the sojourners had retired to their tents and only Garv'ik and an old man named Orm'el remained with them around the small campfire. "The others back in Atlan will be wondering of us, of our safety."

Kenoch didn't speak. Instead he cast a glance at Garv'ik, and seemed to become uneasy.

Garv'ik began poking the sputtering coals with a willow branch.

Thore looked at Kenoch, a feather of suspicion lightly stroked up his spine. "What?"

Kenoch squirmed under his unwavering stare. "I'm not going back to Atlan, Thore." He still didn't look up at him.

At first Thore thought Kenoch intended to stay with Garv'ik's little troop of nomads. He could see no reason for it. Then Kenoch's comment that first night after he'd regained consciousness came back to him. "You're going to Nod City."

Kenoch glanced up. "You know?"

Garv'ik's stick snapped against a stone.

Thore looked at Kenoch. "I should have guessed it. Why?"

"Thore. The Oracle took my family." Kenoch's eyes filled with emotion. "They killed Cerah and then herded my nieces and nephews, cousins and sisters off to who knows what fate."

"How will your going to Nod City change any of that?" That Kenoch could help them in any way was preposterous.

He took in a breath, his body giving a tremble. "I don't know. All I do know is that I have to try. I can't go running off to Atlan when everyone who is important to me is in danger."

"What of Mistress Mishah and Lamech? Noah and Methuselah? They're waiting for us in Atlan."

"We don't know that, Thore. The last we saw of them, they were fleeing from the jumpers. Just because we stayed behind doesn't mean they made it out safely."

The notion that Noah had not made good his escape was just as preposterous as Kenoch single-handedly rescuing his family from the Oracle's clutches. Thore refused to accept it. He'd already convinced himself that he had.

"Noah and the others must have made it safely back to Atlan by now."

"Why? Because you want it to be so? Because if they didn't, you would have failed in your avowed task to protect him?"

Kenoch's accusation gave substance to a concern that for weeks he had refused to let take root. Now seeds of doubt, so long denied water and sunlight, sprang to life, weaving a thorny wall of concern around him. "That makes our return even more imperative."

Kenoch shifted his view back to the fire, his voice low and firm. "I'm going to Nod City, Thore. And you are too."

Garv'ik shifted uneasily. Orm'el watched them with a wariness that made Thore think of a caged hook-tooth, as if the man had spent a lifetime looking over his shoulder.

Thore took three of four breaths, reorganizing his thoughts, mentally standing back to look at the situation from all sides. Could Kenoch be right? Could Noah have been captured? The possibility loomed large and frightening.

Kenoch said, "You will come with me, Thore, because you don't know. I don't know. Even if Noah did make it out of these mountains and somehow found passage to the Border Sea, how long do you think he would stay there knowing that Sheflah is in the Lodath's hands?" Kenoch fixed him in a narrow gaze. "If by the slightest chance Noah is back in Atlan, he has Rhone, who shares your vow, to protect him. But because you can't know that for certain, there is only one choice you can make."

Kenoch had thought it out carefully and planned his line of attack perfectly. If Noah was in Atlan, he wouldn't stay there. Once in Nod City, he'd be in deadly danger. Would Rhone permit it? It didn't seem likely, yet he couldn't risk a delay of several weeks to find out.

"How would we find him?"

"He'd be in the Temple complex," Garv'ik said.

"But where in the complex? It might take weeks of searching it, even if we could move freely."

Garv'ik glanced at the older man beside him, then back. "If Noah has been taken, and if he had bent to the Oracle's demands and accepted his pledge pendant, he'd be in the retraining camp."

Thore bristled at the thought. "Noah would never do that. He could no more bend a knee to the Oracle than sprout wings and fly."

Orm'el pulled at his tangled gray beard. "Then he'd be in the Purification Temple, awaiting the sacrifice at the Appearing Ceremony." It was the first words the old man had spoken. His voice grated as if his throat had been injured at one time.

"Sacrifice?"

"Master Garv'ik explained it to me, Thore. The Temple was designed to offer sacrifices to the Oracle."

"It's an immense structure," Garv'ik added.

"I know that." His impatience surprised even himself. Now that it was just possible Noah was in danger, it had boiled to the surface.

"It was built to sacrifice swine and three-points, gerups and pocket dragons," Garv'ik continued

"Unclean animals," Kenoch said. "The ones the Creator instructed us not to sacrifice. The Oracle chose to defy the Creator in even this."

"That hardly seems unusual for the Deceiver. How do the Creator's Kinsmen figure into all this?"

Garv'ik said, "Years ago, he instituted the Appearing Ceremony, to celebrate his appearance on Earth. Gradually he phased out using unclean animals. Now the sacrifice is those Kinsmen who refuse to accept his pledge."

Thore took a moment to digest that. Then he whispered, "Noah would never take the pledge."

"And neither would my family, Thore," Kenoch said.

The reason for Kenoch's determination became clear. The Appearing Ceremony was only a week off. Thore's view narrowed at Garv'ik. "So how do we get inside the Temple?"

Garv'ik leaned forward and poked the broken stick back into the coals, stirring a shower of sparks among the tendrils of smoke. "The same way I and my people got out of there. You see, we were marked for sacrifice too. That's how I learned all this. It's not something the Oracle wants to become widely known—at least not yet—outside of Nod City."

Orm'el said, "There's an ancient passage from the old Temple Prison to the Temple itself. I can show you the way."

"How do you know this?" Thore asked.

"Because," said Orm'el, "I spent a lifetime in that prison under the scowling eyes of more'n twenty different quort whips, shoveling behemoth girt, feeling the teeth of wet leather in my back, and the grinding ache of hunger in my gut when someone bigger and faster and meaner than me got to the food tray first. That's how I know of the tunnel. When the walls of the Temple complex pushed out into the Old Nod City and the prison was swallowed up and closed down, the passages were sealed, but the Lodath's Guards didn't know all the passages. No one did except a few of us. Some of the prison captains knew, but they weren't in charge of sealing the place. A few lifers like me knew of them. And that's all."

30

A Plan

The slash of sunlight through the window set off Grandfather Methuselah's features in sharp contrast. His breathing was so shallow, his thin chest hardly moved. He was leaning forward upon his cane, his long bony fingers wrapped about the stick, his frail body unnaturally stiff upon the chair, his eyes focused upon something. Noah recognized that far-off stare at once when he and Shem came into the house.

Shem sensed Methuselah's deep pondering too, and quietly excused himself. "I want to see how Kitah is doing."

Noah nodded. He was interested in Kitah's healing also, and particularly curious in how Naamah was coming along. Naamah had latched onto his mother in a desperate rush to learn all that she could about the healing arts, cramming years' worth of knowledge and experience into her head, and taking copious notes. She should have begun her training a long time ago.

"I'll be along in a little while, Shem."

Shem hurried off to the back bedroom where they had put the girl.

Noah cleared his throat and took a chair across from his grandfather. "I sense a troubled spirit."

The old man didn't move at once, but like a cat who'd found a sweet spot of sunlight, he closed his brown eyes and lifted his chin as though to take in more warmth.

"Have you noticed all the animals, Grandfather? They are everywhere. Keli visited the construction site yesterday and said they are coming across the new land bridge. Deepvale is overrun with them. They're stripping the qwall trees bare and ruining the gardens. The Kleimen villages have begun putting up fences."

Noah waited, wondering if Grandfather had heard him.

Grandfather swallowed, his throat making a long slow rise and fall. His brown eyes opened and slid toward him.

Noah's smile flattened with concern. "What is it?"

"You must not go to Nod City."

He stiffened his spine and scowled. "I can't not go. You've been a father so many times; surely you must know how I feel?"

Methuselah's view narrowed. "They are my children as well as yours, Noah."

"If you were younger, you'd be going after them too." He didn't intend for the anger in his voice; it just came out that way.

Methuselah considered him a long moment. "I would, but you must not."

"I have to."

"Then you give the Deceiver what he seeks. You shun the Creator's commands, hide from His light, and go over to the darkness."

"I have no intentions of going over to the Deceiver's darkness." His eyes filled and he ground the tears away with the palms of his hand. "I only want to get my child back!"

The old man nodded. "Then let men trained to fight go. You have work to complete here." His walking stick rose and pointed. "The ark is your only responsibility now. You are amazed by the animals?"

Grandfather had heard him after all.

"They come because He has called them. Soon Atlan will be overrun with animals, and the people will despair. Once it is understood why they are here, you will become even more unpopular. You must finish your work while the days continue."

"But Sheflah?"

"Sheflah may not come back to you, Noah. If she doesn't, then it was not the Creator's will for her to come back. Do you think all this has taken Him by surprise? He knows. He knows all. Sheflah is better off in Adam's Bosom than on this stone to face the wrath to come." The walking stick lowered and Grandfather gripped it in trembling hands.

Noah wanted to cry , but held himself in check. He had never considered the possibility that all his children may not be with him safely in the ark when the wrath came. He couldn't accept it now. "My father will be going with them, and I will be at his side."

Methuselah closed his eyes and turned his face back to the warmth of the sunshine. "Nod City is Lamech's destiny." His voice cracked. "Your future lies down another road, Noah." A tear seeped from the old man's eye and streaked his wrinkled cheek.

※

He didn't expect to find so many people there. When he stepped into Kitah's sickroom, Shem was at the girl's side, holding her hand. Shem had rushed to her the moment they had arrived here from Atla Fair and he'd heard of her injuries, and Noah had gotten very little work out of the man since. Watching his son now, he realized there was more involved here than the simple concern for a cousin. Noah was surprised at the revelation, and wondered why he hadn't noticed it before.

Majiah was standing with Mishah, watching Naamah blend a concoction of oils. He recognized the strong scent of lavender and chamomile, but there were others, too. Naamah glanced up at him as he entered, then went back to work. Mishah watched her every move like a good teacher letting her student find her own way, yet never allowing her to stray too far off the proper path. Once the solution was mixed up, Naamah soaked a piece of soft cotton cloth in it, looked to his mother, and at Mishah's small nod, gently applied it to a particularly angry-looking burn on Kitah's arm, draping it like a second skin.

"How's our pretty patient?" Noah forced an upbeat tone, even though his heart was breaking. Grandfather's words had sliced it deeply, had opened it up to a possibility that he didn't want to entertain, but one that he was forced to, now that it had been dragged out into the open and dangled before his eyes.

"It doesn't hurt anymore," Kitah said in a voice that had grown up since the wedding, more than four years earlier, when she had danced carefree with Shem and the other older boys.

He smiled at his mother and Naamah. "You have two of the best healers around." He walked around the foot of the bed and stood by Majiah. "How goes the preparations?"

"All is ready, Master Noah. Zinorah has explained the jumper to High Councilor Rhone's artificers—as much as she understands. They've climbed through every square span of the craft. They understand the principal, but the power that propels it is still a mystery."

"No doubt. The question is, can Atlan defend itself against the Oracle's jumpers should they attack?"

Her mouth cocked to one side in a skeptical frown and she shrugged. "I don't know. But we are running out of time. The Appearing Ceremony is only one week away, and there is little more that can be accomplished."

One week. She was right. There was not much time left. He, too, had to make preparations. The work on the ark had to go on in the event he didn't come back. He shoved his hands into his pocket and headed for the door.

Naamah looked up from her handiwork. "Where are you going?"

"Back to the ark. So much to do. So little time."

"Will you be eating with us?"

"I don't know." He turned his footsteps out the doorway.

"Master Noah?" Majiah crossed the room. "Might I walk with you?"

"Certainly." They went back through the house. In the gathering room, Grandfather hadn't moved. He appeared in deep thought, or was he praying? The sunlight warmed his cheek, and he seemed not to hear them cross to the door and step outside.

"I would like to see what you are building, if you don't mind."

"I'd be happy for the company." Since arriving back home, Naamah had been constantly at his mother's and Kitah's side. And Grandfather had not been much company. Lamech had remained with Rhone and Da-gore, in the thick of the preparations, while the boys had stayed at the construction site—all but Shem. Wend stopped in from time to time, but he was occupied with the vineyard. He had never taken any interest in the ark anyway.

They headed toward an old cyclart, Vaul falling in at his heels.

"Does he always stay so close to you?" Majiah reached down to pet him, but the canic shifted to the other side. "He's a strange one."

"Strange? In some ways. He doesn't like to be touched, yet he seems to crave companionship."

"At least he craves yours."

Noah grinned. "It does seem that way."

"How long have you had him?"

He stepped over the low side and settled in the cyclart's seat while she went around the other side and slipped gracefully over the padded edge.

"Let me think. I can't remember exactly. A long time. He just showed up one day and latched onto me." He glanced at Vaul in the seat behind him and gave a short laugh. "That'll teach me to feed strays." But his elevated spirits lasted only a moment, and as he drove off, he thought about what Grandfather had said. Rebellion reared its head and he resolved he would be going. And he would bring Sheflah home. He would bring all his children with him!

The ark was only a fifteen-minute drive from the house, and in that short distance he had to stop four or five times as small herds of animals crossed the road, or lingered at its edge nibbling sarberry.

"They're all over the place." He recalled Grandfather's words. If these new arrivals were a gauge as to how little time was left, he wanted them all to go away.

As he rounded a corner, and the trees parted, Majiah sucked in a breath. "It's huge."

"Bigger than anything afloat. Master Jerl-eze said so."

Her dark eyes had locked upon the vessel stretching across what might have been two city blocks in Atla Fair, wider than a good size house, and taller than the wall encircling Hodin's Keep. He pulled to a stop among other cyclarts and watched a moment as Ham's rolling crane, straddling the ark, crawled along on its sixteen wheels toward the crew of men atop the roof, a bundle of lumber dangling overhead from a chain.

"Is it almost finished?" She didn't seem able to take her eyes off of it.

"The outside is … almost. A lot of little details to complete. That roof being one of them. Once it's in place, we'll pitch it then tackle the inside where there still remains much work." He climbed out of the cyclart and came around the other side to give her a hand.

Atop the ark, Ham saw them approach, waved, and started for the ladder.

"That ramp will have to be improved." He pointed at the long, sloping walkway that leaned against the ark's side and topped out at the large door, two-thirds of the way up. Along the handrail, bright parrots and shiny green kesers perched and preened. A silvery gray pocket dragon soared low over the ark, scanning the roof for cast-off keelit rinds sometimes left behind by the workers.

"We built the ramp to move supplies and people, but once we begin loading the animals, it'll have to be widened."

They started up the ramp, their feet thumping hollowly upon it. The scent of sawn wood and thick pitch were so familiar, Noah could hardly remember a time when he wasn't here in this valley, working on the Creator's ark.

As they reached the top of the ramp, Ham careened out the door and halted, grinning. "You've come to see it," he said, beaming at Majiah.

"Your father was kind enough to bring me."

"Let me show you around."

"All right."

He took her arm and the two of them disappeared inside the ark.

"Well, hello to you, too, Ham." Noah leaned against the railing and laughed, startling a flock of ruby finches to flight.

※

"The memories are old, but I don't think I've forgotten anything." Da-gore looked up from the paper spread across the table. A maze of passages crisscrossed each other at different levels. He smiled thinly at Rhone. "At the very least, I hope I haven't forgotten anything important."

"Nor I." Rhone studied Da-gore's drawings, amazed at the complexity of the underground prison labyrinth. He'd been in it only once, and at that time the Messenger-warrior Sari'el had been his guide. "And what of the sealed portions?"

"From what I understand, the Lodath had all the passages leading off of the main prison sealed." He put a finger on an L-shaped building that stood aboveground. "He also filled the ones entering the Temple here."

"The Temple is where we'll need access," Rhone pointed out.

Da-gore nodded. "Before the Temple was built, this tunnel here was used to drain the site to the River Idakla—the Hiddekel, as it's more commonly called these days. It was left in place to keep the foundations dry."

"Could men enter it from the river?" That seemed a more direct route.

"No. It's a clay conduit a little less than a span in diameter. Even if you could squeeze through it, at this point it takes a vertical drop of eighteen spans. No way to ascend it, even if it should prove free of obstacles. But after so many years, I suspect it's been invaded by a mass of tree roots."

"What do you propose?"

Da-gore's finger shifted across the chart. "About sixty years into the construction of the Temple, a seep occurred at the north corner of the foundations. Sor-dak and the others hadn't detected it because when work began the site had been dry. The solution was simple. We excavated a second drainage tunnel, but rather than running it to the Idakla, we tapped into the drain already in existence. Here."

Rhone, Lamech, Zinorah, and Pyir Chrone bent closer for a look.

"To do the job, we had to build a tunnel large enough for men to work in. We excavated a side tunnel off of this passage at the third level, intersected the drain, and built a chamber around it just west of the Temple foundation. The chamber and the drains still exist. It's about fifteen spans outside the foundation wall. A man can crawl from there into the Temple. Once inside the foundation, we'll have access into the Temple."

Lamech said, "The suntracer mechanism is a level above the drains."

Rhone glanced over. "And you built the mechanism?"

"I wasn't part of the work quort. Master Sor-dak and I did most of the design work, but others actually built it."

Zinorah said, "Where do I earth the jumper, and where do we enter the tunnels?"

Pyir Chrone glanced at Da-gore. "And once we do, can you find your way through this maze?"

"I think so."

Chrone crossed his arms and frowned. "This is all well and good, but the people we're trying to set free will not be in the Temple."

"No, they are kept in separate quarters. Here." Da-gore indicated a long building east of the Temple. "There is a period of isolation and purification before the sacrifice. If we are to use the crowds as cover for our men, our time will be short."

Rhone said, "There are several underground passages still in use. Once we penetrate the Temple, we'll take this one into the building where Sheflah and the others are being held. The Appearing Ceremony takes place just after dawn. The prisoners will have been assembled and ready to march to the Temple well before that. We need to get in and out before their guards come to assemble them. No later than the first of the second quartering."

"There's still the question of entering the tunnels," Zinorah pressed, not having been answered the first time.

Lamech said, "Fifteen years ago or so, Noah, Thore, and I found our way into them through a breech beneath the Oracle's Image."

Rhone winced at his son's name, yet the pain was not as sharp as it had been. He couldn't explain it, but he sensed that Thore was still alive. Call it wishful thinking. Call it the undying hope of a father for his child. Whatever the reason, the feeling was strong, and growing stronger.

Da-gore said, "I wouldn't count on it being there anymore, Lamech. From time to time passages open up, and the Lodath is always swift to permanently seal them once they do." He glanced at Zinorah. "You'll earth the jumper in the forest beyond Nod City—in a clearing or a farmer's field—and hope it isn't discovered. The nearest place is about a league's journey. Any closer, those creatures—those gathering spirits, as you call them—might sense its presence."

She nodded. "A league will suffice, more would be even better."

Pyir Chrone said, "Too far, and we won't make it back with the prisoners."

Rhone exhaled loudly. "The people are going to have to make it on their own once we free them. We can't take them all. We'll take Sheflah, a few of the older ones."

Da-gore gave him a concerned look. "They won't make it very far."

"They will have a better chance fleeing through the forest than chained together upon the Temple altar."

Everyone nodded at that.

Da-gore turned back to Zinorah. "We enter here." He drew a circle around a building outside the Temple-complex wall, the only one labeled on the map.

She looked at it, then quizzically back at him. "The Quort Whip Festival Hall?"

Da-gore winked at her. "Sometimes even the Captain of the Guards needed to get away—privately."

31

Change of Heart

*H*er fitful turning and quiet gasps awoke him in the middle of the night. In the soft glow of a moonglass night light, Lamech sat up and looked at Mishah. Her hair had come undone and lay across her face, catching in the corner of her mouth. Her breathing was now a panting, her head twisting upon the pillow.

"Mishah?" he whispered. She was dreaming, and the night horrors had taken hold of her. It had been almost a lifetime ago when dreams would come to torment her.

"Mishah, wake up!"

Muffled cries of pain rattled in her throat. He touched her shoulder.

With a gasp, she bolted awake and scurried up against the headboard, her wide eyes casting about the darkened room.

"It's all right, Mishah. I'm here."

Seeming to come to her senses, she threw her arms around him, trembling.

"It was only a dream." He held her until the trembling stopped, her cheeks and forehead moist with beading perspiration. Slowly she released her hold, but her breathing was still uneven and quick, as though she couldn't get enough air.

"What was it?"

Her wide eyes held his. "A dream. A very old dream."

The words chilled him. "Like you used to have?"

She swallowed and nodded. "It was Noah."

"What about Noah?"

"He was being pursued by something dark, and evil. I was trying to help, but I couldn't run fast enough, and then thorns rose up all around me." She paused, staring into space.

"Go on," he urged.

A long, deep breath seemed to help settle her. "The evil was about to pounce upon Noah, when ... when the Creator's hand that held Rahab released its hold."

Her view narrowed. "The stone shattered, and bits of it hurdled toward Earth. Then fire fell from the sky, striking the earth between the evil and Noah. The earth split apart and water shot upward to heaven. The evil was engulfed in a flood, and Noah was swept away too, and the water that exploded forth fell back to Earth as ice." She trembled again. "The sky turned black, the sun disappeared, and it was so cold ... so very cold." She rubbed her arms, peering at the remembered vision.

Her words stirred long-dormant memories. Finally he looked at her. "That was the same dream you had before Noah was born."

She nodded, staring at him. "I remember. And after we were in the Cradleland, safe from this world, the dreams went away." Her tongue moistened her dry lips. "What does it mean, Lamech?"

Rahab, the fifth stone out from the sun, whirling in its faraway course beyond Oric. Rahab was the key, and now, for some reason, the Creator was reminding them of it again.

❈

"Can't sleep?" Rhone looked over at Leenah who'd been tossing and turning for most of the quartering.

"I can't stop thinking of Thore." Her voice went brittle, and in the light of the moon streaming through the high, arching portals of their room, he saw the tears. "There was so much left to say. And now he's gone."

He took her hand. "Thore is alive."

Her head came up. "How do you know?"

"The same way I knew he was in danger."

Her grasp tightened. "Are you sure, Rhone?" Her voice filled with hope.

"Nothing is sure, Leenah. Yet when I reach out, there is a connecting, but the binding is so weak, and I can't be sure. And since I am not certain, I choose to believe he's still alive."

"Then why hasn't he contacted us?"

"I don't know, Leenah."

She went silent, then slipped quietly out of bed and walked out onto the rooftop garden. He lay there a moment before following her. Gur, nesting in a corner of the garden, lifted his long neck and leveled his head with hers, sniffing her hair. She put a hand to his broad, scaly head, on the wide place between his blinking red eyes. Rhone paused a little way back, not wishing to disturb them.

She and the dragon remained still for a long while, and then Leenah lowered her hand and stepped back. Gur stretched out a hind leg, curled his tail around a merlon, and rose to his feet, shaking himself. Ruffling his wings and flexing his neck as if working out the kinks, he hopped all at once to the top of the battlement, perched there, examined the dark, empty meeting floor below, then with a flap of his immense wings, took to the air.

She watched him flap slowly, easing higher, as if pacing himself, until he was but a spot in the night sky, fading against the blacker Rim-wall.

"Where is he going?"

She turned at the sound of his voice. "I'm not sure." Her voice was thoughtful ... distant.

"What did you tell him?"

"Only that I'm worried about Thore."

"And?"

"I felt ... sympathy. That's all."

He went to her and took her into his arms, watching the dragon disappear against the star-filled sky.

❦

Although a dull, lingering pain persisted in Thore's newly healed leg, the march from the wilderness camp in the mountains of Morg'Jalek to the nearest TT terminal had brought back much of his strength. The fare to Nod City had taken all the money that Garv'ik had generously given them.

Kenoch had not spoken much after leaving Garv'ik's camp. He spent most of his time staring out the open carriage at the landscape rushing past. They passed through occasional stands of primal forest, but most of the journey consisted of skipping from one village to the next, rushing over wide farmland and broad rivers. They paralleled the Hiddekel for most of a quartering.

Orm'el told them how as a youth he'd stowed away on a berdeniex barge after escaping the rage of a cuckolded husband. The disgraced man had sent two killers after him, but Orm'el bribed a festival-hall hostess, got the killers drunk, and waylaid them in an alleyway, killing them both. The murders put him in chains in the Temple Prison where he'd spent much of the rest of his life. His sentence was continually extended due to many attempts at escape. Thore found the story amusing, and strangely appealing to his warrior instinct.

"Won't be long now," Orm'el said, watching the barges and ships upon the broad water. "Never thought I'd come back here on my own." He laughed. "Always figured it would be the Lodath's chains hauling me back."

"So why are you coming with us?" Thore had wanted to

broach the subject, but until now, the timing hadn't been right.

Orm'el's gray eyes narrowed. "You ever hear voices, Master Thore? Only, not really there?"

He shook his head. "No."

Orm'el glanced from him to Kenoch then stared at the river beyond the open-sided carriage. "When we found you like we did, I swear I heard this whispering voice in my ear. It said, 'Orm'el, your destiny lies on the same road as theirs.' Well, not exactly those words, but that was the meaning." He laughed again. "I ignored it of course, but as the days passed and you grew stronger, those words kept coming back to me. And then Master Kenoch began inquiring of the Temple, and how to get into it to save his people, and suddenly I knew I was supposed to be the one to show him the way. Sounds crazy, don't it?"

"No, not crazy," Kenoch said, pulling himself out of his deep thoughts for the first time in over a sixth of a quartering.

They fell silent as the rumble of the overhead wheel whisked them nearer and nearer to Nod City. Thinking it over, Thore decided it did sound a little crazy ... except that his father had once told a similar story.

※

Noah watched the sky brighten beyond the bedroom window. He exhaled sharply. *Today we leave for Nod City.* Rhone and the others were ready. The Makir were assembled. His father had been up and about for a long time. He'd heard him quietly praying earlier and knew Lamech was waiting for him in the gathering room.

Naamah came up behind him, her quiet breathing the only noise inside the room. Outside the window, the day had awakened to a chorus of chirping birds and pocket dragons.

"You know Grandfather is right," she said quietly.

And that was the whole problem. His heart had become a stone, each breath an effort.

"That I stay behind?" The last few days he had tried to run and hide from the Creator's clear leading. Grandfather Methuselah's admonishment had been the catalyst.

"You'll only make matters worse by going. Rhone will have the extra burden of protecting you." She touched his arm. "Noah, I grieve for Sheflah as much as you. I desperately want her to come back to us. But what can you do that a kal-ee-hon of Makir Warriors cannot?"

Going to Nod City was important! If he had failed as a father when they had been young, wouldn't bringing Sheflah back now prove how much he really loved his children? His eyes stung, and he turned from the window.

Naamah drew him into her arms … and he sobbed into her shoulder.

Am I going on this rescue for Sheflah's sake, or for my own? Will I really be a hindrance to her safe return?

Lamech was waiting for him in the gathering room. His father's mouth tightened to a stern line as he entered. Methuselah and two Makir stood there as well. Grandfather's narrowed eyes suited his taut face. Beyond the window in the hazy morning light was an official cyclart from Rhone to carry them to Hodin's Keep.

His mother looked as though she'd been crying. Shem stood in the hallway, quietly watching. Ham had gone to Hodin's Keep the previous night to spend time with Majiah before she left with the rescuers, or he would have been here too. Over the last couple weeks his son's friendship with Majiah had blossomed into full-blown romance.

Why was Majiah going at all? What did she have to prove?

"Are you ready?" Lamech asked matter-of-factly.

"I'm not going."

Grandfather's eyes widened. His mother seemed relieved. Noah's father studied him. "What changed your mind?"

"Grandfather. Naamah. My own heart. I'll be too much a distraction for High Councilor Rhone. I'd only make matters worse." He glanced at the stern-faced warriors dressed in their black sutas—the traditional battle garb of Makir Warriors. Likely they were wearing swords under their capes—again traditional—although Noah knew when they went into battle, it would be with projers and fistprojs. "It is best if I leave this task to warriors—to Makir. The binding is useless to people like you and me. I will only be in the way."

Lamech nodded. "I understand."

"But you must go!" He turned to glance at Grandfather, recalling his words. "My destiny lies along another path."

His father nodded again, as if he, too, had had that talk with Methuselah.

Lamech gave him a hug.

The hugging, the tears, the encouraging words all spoken, they watched the cyclart drive away.

"Your father will be back, Noah," his mother said hopefully after they were out of sight.

He didn't reply.

Grandfather turned stiffly and tottered back into the house, his walking stick lightly tapping the stepping-stones.

32

Into the Oracle's Stronghold

Zinorah earthed the jumper in a forest clearing about a league north of the Temple complex. As the jumper faded from view, Rhone watched his son take command of the kal-ee-hon. If he had known that Noah was going to remain, he'd have taken himself out of this mission, but by the time word of it came, the plans had been set, and he was part of them.

Pyir Chrone organized his men into qwats and led them in the Katrahs and Kimahs, mentally preparing them for the task ahead.

Da-gore glanced at him. "Ready?"

It had been decided that he and the ex-captain would make sure the old festival-hall building with the secret passage was secure before the Makir arrived. Zinorah and Majiah would accompany them. Their presence should not raise suspicious eyebrows, unlike a kal-ee-hon of thirty Makir. Pyir Chrone's Makir would show up after nightfall, singly and in pairs so as not to draw undo attention.

Rhone cast a final look to the Makir. He longed to be a part of a kal-ee-hon again, but that was no longer his life.

Da-gore grinned at him. "It stirs the blood, doesn't it?"

Rhone understood—one warrior to another. He inclined his chin toward the Makir gathered in the clearing. "That stirs the blood." The weaving threads of the binding had already begun to gather about his heart as the Makir went through the routine.

Da-gore slung a small pack comfortably over his shoulder. "The binding. It's something I will never understand."

"No. Probably not." With a sigh, Rhone fastened a faded blue cape over his shoulders. "Let's move."

Zinorah, her face flat, her eyes unreadable, strode at Da-gore's side. Majiah, apprehensive, remained near to him. He would have preferred she stay behind. Her thoughts clearly were not focused on the mission. The women wore plain shiverthorn traveling dresses over their dark outfits. Each carried a fistproj, out of sight. To the casual eye, the four of them easily passed for a company of travelers, come for the Appearing Ceremony.

They headed for the nearest road, and soon they were in traffic shoulder to shoulder with other pilgrims. Rhone stooped a bit to disguise his stature. Hodinites weren't generally admirers of the Oracle, and he wanted no unpleasant stares or questions.

Early in the second quartering they entered Nod City. Its stone buildings soared high, the gleaming bronze rails crisscrossing overhead. The noise and smell of people, of food venders, and the rat-tat-tat crackle of poppers tossed from overhead windows, assaulted Rhone's senses.

Zinorah's face remained hard, as though carved of a block of saubor wood, but her wary eyes kept in constant motion. Majiah's shoulders appeared too taut, her lips compressed, her breathing shallow and quick. Rhone noted how her view would often follow children, and when it did, the corners of her lips would slide up.

"This way." Da-gore turned down another street where three-points bedecked in green and red silk, with golden caps upon the points of their horns, marched in a parade. Gerups and horses, small dragons, and brightly dressed people whirled past them. Naked men reenacted ritual mating dances and Temple prostitutes plied their wares. Drums, tambourines, and rikat horns throbbed out a sensual rhythm.

Majiah glanced away from it, but Zinorah glared at the passing display, as if the pain of its sight was therapy to her tortured soul.

They drew nearer the tall walls of the Temple complex. The commerce in this part of Nod City was mostly vendors of Temple objects, sacred books, and thought-shifting herbs. The road ended abruptly at some ancient buildings that seemed to merge with the hewed stone Temple complex wall.

Da-gore, following a map inside his head, a duplicate of the one given to the Makir, halted on the corner of a narrow lane. "Down this way."

The passage between the buildings was deserted. At the end of it stood an abandoned building with boarded windows and door. Glancing cautiously around, Rhone quickly pried off the board and forced the old door open.

Dusty spiderwebs hung from the ceiling and filled the shadowy corners. Here and there lingered the signs of recent visitors— a straw mattress in the corner, empty bottles of wine scattered about, the charred remains of a small cook fire beneath a window.

"Homey." Majiah's eyebrows hitched together in a scowl.

"It was at one time." Da-gore turned a slow circle in the empty room, the remnants of its past evident in a long, curving bar, a few tables, some ancient moonglass that no longer gave off any light.

It reminded Rhone of festival halls he'd known years earlier here in Nod City, in Marin-ee, and other places he'd traveled while collecting Web. But his Webmastering days were only a far-off memory. Another life ... another world. A world before the Oracle's arrival.

Zinorah showed no emotion one way or the other, that part of her having been torn out of her soul. Rhone could hardly imagine what she must have endured as a Neph captive. He grimaced at the thought of what Sheflah and the others might face if they failed in their mission here.

"Where is it, Da-gore?"

The ex-Captain of the Lodath's Guard stared a moment longer at a corner of the room, then shook himself from his reverie and pointed down a dingy corridor. "This way."

Rubble filled the floor of a storeroom at the rear of the building. Part of the wall had collapsed. Da-gore stepped across a small pile of broken stone to what appeared to be an outside wall. "We'll have to clear this away."

Once they had the rubble cleared, Da-gore examined the wall where the ancient stones had been set. Using his dagger, he cleaned out one of the seams and felt deep inside it. His lips screwed together in concentration as he examined the crevice. The quiet metallic click brought a quick grin to his face. He tugged. The wall shifted a little, then stopped.

"A hand, please?"

Rhone found the recess within the seam, and his fingers folded into the handhold. His muscles strained against the resistance of years of disuse and the stone wall groaned open a half a span.

"It's a fake." Rhone examined the edge of the door. The stone was a mere plaster veneer.

"Real enough to keep away curious eyes all this time." Da-gore removed an energized moonglass from his pocket. They squeezed through the gap and stood upon a small landing with stone steps descending deep beneath the city.

Da-gore shone the light down the steps, but the bottom remained in darkness. "These connect to the passage. A hundred spans beyond the complex's wall, it branches. One goes to the old prison. I suspect it's sealed by now. The other connects with the lower tunnels. Most of those are still passable."

"What about water?" Rhone noted the moist walls not very far below them.

"We may have to deal with that."

He remembered the flooded tunnel beneath the wall of Chevel-ee. "Let's hope we won't have to hold our breath."

Da-gore played the light along the seeping walls. "I'm not much good at that anymore."

Rhone grimaced. "Me neither."

They backed out of the tight doorway to await the arrival of Pyir Chrone and his Makir.

❧

The TT had been crammed with worshippers en route to the Appearing Ceremony. The crowd made it easy for them to blend. Although his Hodinite heritage was hard to hide, upon scanning the masses as they stepped off the TT in Nod City, Thore noted many other men and women who could very easily have come from Hodin's line, not to mention the rabble of Nephs and nephlings who were even taller.

Once away from the teaming TT terminal, they crossed town to the wide Temple Walk, which led into the complex—it, too, was jammed with people. The Oracle's Temple loomed in the distance, past the wide portal in the wall. Thore recalled a much closer view of the Temple ... and the Oracle's Image. How many years had passed since the day their stolen wing-sailer had crashed into it? Fifteen? More?

❧

Kenoch said, "How will we get inside the old prison? It's sealed up, isn't it?"

Orm'el gave him a gap-toothed grin. "We get in like everyone else. We pay our shaved gleck."

"And a shaved gleck apiece is about all we have left," Thore noted.

Kenoch blinked. "I don't understand."

Thore said, "It's been turned into a gallery, filled with artifacts and building models and histories. It tells how the Temple was built, and how the Oracle came to Earth."

"A museum?"

Orm'el scratched his scraggly beard. "You might call it that."

Within the complex, orange tiles stretched away in a vast sea of pavement, reflecting the day's heat. The Temple's size alone was enough to take one's breath away. Nearby, the Oracle's Image peering skyward gleamed in the late sunlight. Beyond it squatted a row of three four-sided temples, shaped the same as the Oracle's crystal-capped dwelling, but much smaller. To the left stood the old prison building. A little farther away was a long, low structure. The far distance held more buildings. There didn't appear to be a tree in the entire complex.

Orm'el started toward the prison. "Those buildings beyond the prison are for the sacrifice purification. If your people are here at all, they'll be held in there."

Thore inclined his head toward an ornate, vaulted gateway of white marble clad in gold, standing between the Temple and the purification buildings. "What's that?"

"The Triumphal Arch. It represents the Oracle's Appearing in our world. The sacrifice is marched through the arch, bound with chains, during the Ceremony. Then they enter the Temple."

"That will be at the next dawn." Thore frowned. "We didn't give ourselves any slack time."

"We're lucky we got here when we did," Orm'el said flatly.

"Will we make it on time?" Kenoch asked.

Orm'el cast him a quick glance. "If not, it was a long walk for nothing."

They approached the queue for the prison museum. Thore stopped and looked around.

"What is it?" Kenoch cast a wary glance about.

He let his mind reach out. It was there, a subtle stirring; the faint strings of the binding coming together—the Katrahs and Kimahs. "Makir."

"Here?" Kenoch's eyes widened.

"Nearby."

Orm'el said, "That can be good, or bad. This Makir stuff gives me the shakes whenever I think of it."

Once inside the old prison, they browsed the displays depicting the early days of Nod City. Working their way deeper into the converted prison, eventually they were alone and out of sight. They dashed up a narrow flight of stairs to the roof. Orm'el crossed to a stone vent shaft, and slipping over the edge of it, disappeared.

Thore hurried Kenoch after him, wary of their exposed position, and immediately followed. The fit was almost too tight for his broad Hodinite shoulders. The iron handholds were ancient and rusty. Descending into the darkness, his feet came upon a stone floor. "Where are we?"

"The old baths." Orm'el's outline slowly emerged from the darkness as Thore's eyes adjusted. It seemed the room with its empty pools ended abruptly at a place where a passage once stood, but was now walled over.

"This way."

Kenoch hesitated and seemed to be having second thoughts about this rescue scheme. Thore nudged him ahead.

Orm'el led them into a second bathing chamber where the light from the vent did not reach. Thore switched on his light and shone the pale beam around the room. Their footsteps echoed in the darkness. The musty air hung heavy. Something scurried in the dimness and vanished into a crack. Orm'el went to a trough that once flowed with fresh water, crawled into it and, lying upon his back, reached into the black orifice that long ago had provided the water. "Follow me." He slipped away into the blackness.

Kenoch gave Thore a concerned look.

"You heard the man."

Hesitating a moment, Kenoch crawled into the trough, reached back into the hole, and pulled himself in after Orm'el.

Thore peered into the bleak opening where the ancient iron bars had long ago rusted away. "You didn't tell me I had to be Kleiman size."

From inside the wall came Orm'el's muffled chuckle.

Grimacing, he squeezed himself into the trough, reached back behind his head, and felt around for a handhold on an old hunk of iron. Emptying his lungs, he pulled himself in, his shoulders crimping as the walls of the ancient aqueduct closed in around him.

※

With the coming of night, Rhone posted himself at the door, peering into the dark, watching the moon creep above the rooftops. He breathed a heartfelt sigh of relief when Pyir Chrone and his Makir Warriors finally began arriving, singly and in pairs.

"The streets are crawling with green-cloaks," Chrone said.

"You raised no eyebrows, I hope," Rhone replied.

"I don't think so." Chrone took a quick inventory of his warriors.

Once all the Makir had arrived, they entered the passageway, closing the secret door behind them to cover their trail.

With Da-gore in the lead, they quickly and silently traversed the corridor under the Temple Site. Their lights played off the ancient stone walls and poked into long-abandoned prison cells. That there was recent rubbish here warned Rhone that there was more than one place of entry still open. And that meant they might not be alone down here.

Here and there a collapsed wall slowed them while the Makir cleared the passage. Some of the turns ended abruptly at recent masonry walls. Da-gore seemed to know a way around each obstruction, but the detours cost them time, and the night was running thin.

33

The Temple

Orm'el scratched his head and then pulled at his beard, squinting into the darkness ahead. "Something's wrong here."

Kenoch cast Thore a worried look.

Thore shone his light down each of the two converging corridors. "Right or left?"

"That's the problem. I don't remember a branch like this."

"You'd have been coming the other direction. Things look different."

"I know that." He tromped down the left-hand corridor, stopped, and peered back. Shaking his head, he did the same in the right-hand one. "Should have never come back," he mumbled. "There were a lot of us, and I was kind of distracted." He rolled the hair at his chin between his thumb and finger, considering. "I think it was the other one."

They forged ahead down the left tunnel. The floor angled slightly downward. Here there were no side doors, and the walls pressed closer together. The ceiling was low enough to touch. After a few moments Orm'el picked up his pace, whispering, "I remember this now. It connects to the lower passages. There's some water down here. Not deep."

A few minutes later they splashed to their knees along a wider passageway with dungeons off to either side. The binding felt stronger here, but Atlan was hundreds of leagues from here. Whatever it was Thore was sensing, it couldn't be Makir.

Orm'el stopped at a small tunnel and gave a whoop of triumph.

Thore ducked his head as he followed Kenoch into the tight passage. "Where are we?"

"It's the old drainage system. The only way left into the Temple. The Lodath would have sealed this one for sure, if he'd known about it. And they can't seal the drains or the Temple's foundation would flood."

The room wasn't much bigger than the three of them, filled with water waist deep. Thore felt the tug of a small current down around his feet, rushing through what must have been a grating of some kind. Several conduits pierced the wall at different places, spilling water into the chamber.

"Lucky the grating rusted away years ago." Orm'el pulled himself up into one of them.

"In there?" Kenoch shone his light into the aqueduct.

"In there." He crawled out of sight.

Thore motioned Kenoch ahead. "After you."

"Hope it doesn't get any narrower."

"I'll be right behind you to push should you get stuck."

"You?" Kenoch's nervous laugh echoed above the spilling water. "And who will push you?"

"Fear, my friend … fear."

Kenoch frowned. "I didn't think Makir were ever afraid."

"You have a lot to learn about Makir." He pointed. "In you go."

Kenoch hoisted himself into the tube.

Thore took a breath. Fear came in many forms. Failure was only one of them. If Noah was being held, and he failed to save him … he put the notion out of his head and crawled in after Kenoch. It was even tighter than the passage in the ancient baths.

His cloak snagged a hook of rusted iron. He gave a yank and heard a rip. Grimacing, he dragged his way against the flow of water.

Kenoch and Orm'el were waiting at the other end, standing in a dark stone channel that collected water from the underground seeps.

"This way." Orm'el started up a flight of steps. At the top, he halted to listen, then crept out into a vast chamber filled with immense cogwheels, spinning bronze disks, and clicking escapements, the size of sten-gordons. Iron wheels as high as he was tall rested in wide channels cut into the stone. The air hummed with magnetic power, and the odor of 'gia wafted out from the dark bowels of the machinery.

"It's one big suntracer." Orm'el shone his light at a shadowy, stair-stepped assemblage of gears within tall bronze frames, larger than a house. "Keeps the altar pointed at Oarion, the Oracle's home world."

"This machine moves the Temple?" Kenoch bent his head back to study the great iron disk high overhead that rode upon the gigantic wheels.

"The Temple and the altar both move," Orm'el said. "Not much, mind you. Just enough to keep it pointed in the right direction."

"Lamech told me about this, but even his vivid description hadn't prepared me for the sheer massiveness of it."

"Lamech?" Orm'el eyes slowly narrowed.

"My brother-in-law."

Orm'el thought a moment, peered around the room. "Everything here is built to a dimension that dwarfs even the mighty behemoth. This suntracer took the longest to build. It was Master Sor-dak's project."

Kenoch looked at him. "You knew Sor-dak, the stargazer?"

"I'd seen him lots of times wandering the Temple grounds like a lost boy, dressed in red faded robes with pockets stuffed with scrolls and whatnots." Orm'el started them moving again. "An odd character, Sor-dak was. I personally didn't have any part in building this suntracer, but I knew a lot of men and women who did."

"I knew Master Sor-dak too ... after he left the Temple Project."

Orm'el studied Kenoch. "Small world."

Thore wondered at the note of caution he had heard in the old-timer's voice, but now was not the time to worry about it. He needed to keep focused, and the steady humming and clicking of the machinery made that difficult at best as they headed for another flight of stairs.

Up on the next level, more machinery thumped and whirred. Another staggeringly immense platen stretched just above their heads into the dim distance. The floor was cut into concentric grooves. Orm'el pointed at the man-size wheels that rode back and forth in the grooves. "The Tubal-Cain Company built a special forge to cast 'em."

At a sound, Thore grabbed their arms, and hustled them behind one of the wheels. Six Nephs strode into view, heading for the distant staircase.

Once the workers had passed, Orm'el whispered, "They keep the suntracer running."

Kenoch let go of a breath. "How much farther?"

"Not much."

The next tunnel tilted downward for a little way, then bent sharply to the right. Few people were about this late at night, and they made good time through the lower levels of the sacrifice purification building. A pair of strolling guards appeared suddenly at the end of one long corridor. Once they had passed by, Orm'el guided them up two more levels.

At the hallway's end, Thore peeked around the corner. "More guards." He pulled his head back. "Any alarms?"

"Alarms?" Orm'el grinned. "Naturally. It is a prison, after all."

There had to be another way. He motioned them back down the hall and slipped into a dim room, leaving the door slightly ajar to hear if anyone should approach. "I counted six Nephs.

Unless we move swiftly, they're sure to raise an alarm before we take them."

"We?" Kenoch's eyes rounded.

Orm'el shook his head and jabbed a thumb into his chest. "This old man's not fighting no Nephs, no way—not so long as he's still got two good legs and a clear run for the door." His view narrowed. "I already broke out of this place once. Don't know why I agreed to come back."

Kenoch and Orm'el—two old men who should have stayed home. Thore understood what drove Kenoch ... but Orm'el? Maybe it was as simple as voices in his head, as he claimed.

"Well you did, and you're here ... and we need a plan."

Kenoch nodded, his former resolve returning. "How much time do we have?"

Thore checked his suntracer. "Less than two hours before dawn."

"They'll be coming for the sacrifice soon," Orm'el warned.

"Who?" He shoved the suntracer back in a pocket.

"The gatherers. They collect the sacrifice, give 'em the robes to wear, and put the collars around their necks—for the chains."

Thore had a glimmer of a plan. "Where do the gatherers come from?"

"The Temple." Orm'el nodded in the direction they had come. "That's it."

"That's what?" Kenoch asked suspiciously.

"Our way to the prisoners."

Orm'el's scowl deepened. "And once we get in with the prisoners, how're we going to get back out again? We've got no fistprojs, and all you have is a broken sword."

He didn't need the grim reminder. "One problem at a time." Thore went to the door and peeked out. The hallway was clear. They moved out and quietly returned to the underground passage to the Temple.

❧

"There are intruders, Master. Kinsmen."

"Kinsmen?" Lucifer despised the term and all it stood for. He drew his thoughts from the glorious feast of blood awaiting him at the morning's Appearing Ceremony.

Ekalon rested the end of his battle staff upon the crystal floor. "Three. They are attempting to reach the sacrifices."

"Where are they now?"

"The Temple passage, moving back toward the Temple."

His brilliance shifted from pale blue to purple as he considered the irony of it. "A fitting trap for Kinsmen."

"What are your orders?"

"Send in a contingent of guards. Since these Kinsmen are interested in reaching the sacrifices ... help them along. There will be three more in the morning's procession!"

"Yes, High Prince Lucifer." Ekalon bowed briefly and left.

❧

Ducking his head low, Rhone slogged though the knee-deep water. If not for their lights, the tunnel would have been dark as a tomb. The ancient moonglass panels embedded in the equally old walls didn't seem to shed any light at all. At one time they would have bathed these deep passages in a soft glow.

Lamech looked like a man remembering a bad dream. Rhone could only imagine what memories filled his head. "The past rubs shoulders with the present?"

Lamech glanced at him. "I was recalling the look on Klesc's face when Sari'el and you arrived in our dungeon that night."

Rhone nodded, the event as clear in his memory as if it had happened only last week. "The beginning of the adventure."

Lamech gave a wry smile, then frowned. "And somehow, I feel, it draws to an end—here. Where it began."

"Fitting."

Da-gore stopped, then stepped down into a tight room. Water rose to his waist. He shifted his light. Six large tubes entered in various places; from each flowed a small, steady stream. "The chamber we built for the drains." He looked around. "These go to various parts of the Temple."

Rhone followed the beam. "Which one takes us inside the Temple?"

"They all will, eventually." Da-gore studied the pipes, pointing his light. "But this is the one we want to take."

Pyir Chrone squeezed in for a closer look. "How long is it?"

"Not very."

Chrone motioned his Makir into the pipe.

Rhone spied something hanging from a rusty snag and shone his light on it. "A piece of cloth. Recently left behind."

"A few people still know of these tunnels." Da-gore poked his light beam into a dark conduit. "They're home to indigents and runaways."

Zinorah whispered, "But it means something to you. I see it in your eyes, High Councilor."

"The weave—it's an Atlan pattern."

Chrone looked closer. "Its color is"—his eyes hitched up at him—"Makir."

Rhone crushed the scrap in his hand. "Thore." His heart filled with renewed hope. If Thore was alive and here, he'd know soon enough! Squeezing himself into the conduit last, he groped his way forward.

Hands reached in to help him out, and silently, they ascended a dark flight of steps.

※

Thore stiffened to a halt, casting a wary glance around the shadowy corridor.

"What's wrong?" Kenoch asked worriedly.

"Makir. Nearby. I'm sure of it."

"What would Makir be doing in a place like this?" Orm'el whispered.

"I don't know." The Temple tunnel was the last place he would have expected them as well. "I sensed them earlier and dismissed the feeling, but the binding is strong here."

Orm'el gave a shudder. "Makir. Binding. Makes my skin crawl. Let's hope they're friendly."

Thore's eyes narrowed at him. Friendly? What else could they be ... unless the Oracle had drawn some over to the evil side? He shook that notion from his head. That would never happen.

Quietly, they continued moving down the long, deserted corridor. Up ahead was a cross-passage that he recalled passing earlier. The Temple was only a short distance beyond it.

❧

"It's a suntracer, only very specialized." Lamech peered at the towering bronze and iron cage of precision gears. The slow, steady tick of the movement merged with other sounds Rhone could not identify. The odor of 'gia was strong here.

"You built this?" Rhone kept his voice low.

Lamech pulled his eyes off the old machinery and matched the quiet tone. "Sor-dak and I designed it. The hard engineering was provided by the Oracle's Messengers, but we put it all together, made it work." He looked around. The room was filled with gigantic wheels, immense cogs, and slowly moving bronze chains. "I know every square span of this place. Never thought I'd see it again." He shivered, his face hardening. "To think I had a hand in building this perversion, this affront to the Holy Creator."

"You had no choice."

"I could have refused."

"The Creator had His purpose in all this, even if we don't see it clearly now."

Lamech grinned. "You're beginning to sound like me."

He smiled. "You rub off on people."

"Which way, Da-gore?" Chrone's voice was barely audible above the noise of the machinery.

"Up those stairs."

The metallic clatter of metal hitting the floor brought them to a halt. Chrone signaled his kal-ee-hon into the shadows, and as the black-clad Makir seemed to disappear before his eyes, Rhone drew Lamech, Majiah, and Zinorah against the suntracer. He put a hand to the sword under his cloak, rather than the fistproj— partly because of instinct, born of a Makir training—and partly because an edged weapon made little sound.

In a moment five Nephs strolled out from a narrow corridor that cut through the machinery—maintenance workers, not warriors. Rhone remained motionless and the five passed by him, unaware. As the giants started up the steps, the Makir leaped upon them, swiftly flinging ropes about their necks, silencing their screams before they had a chance to escape.

Da-gore took them up the steps and through another vast chamber filled with towering wheels set into grooves cut into the stone floor. A dull iron plate large enough to hold a Kleiman village stretched overhead.

"The sacrifice floor." Lamech jabbed a finger at the iron ceiling. "Part of aligning it to the star, Oarion."

At a corridor, Da-gore signaled them to wait. He peered cautiously around it, then waved them forward. The low tunnel slanted downward, carrying them far beneath the Temple complex.

34

An Unlikely Reunion

*T*he Creator had His purpose in all this, even if we don't yet see it clearly.

Rhone's words troubled Lamech as they started into the tunnel. A purpose in building this? The notion went against his gut feelings, yet it must be true. To deny it would be to diminish the Creator's ultimate control over His Creation. And if true, then there must be a purpose in him being back here, a grander purpose that went beyond freeing Sheflah and the others.

The more he pondered it, the more convinced he became this was true. And if he had a purpose, the Makir's reason for being here must run deeper than a rescue mission.

Then it came to him, as clearly as if the Creator had drawn back a curtain and showed him a picture of what he must do. It all made sense now. He glanced over his shoulder at the opening they'd come through. How could they have ever hoped to penetrate the very heart of the Oracle's stronghold and rescue Sheflah and a hundred or more others? The attempt had been doomed from the start, yet they had been compelled to try—somehow blinded to the futility of the adventure. Why?

Rhone had seen the futility plain enough in the beginning,

but because of Noah's stubbornness, he had agreed. And then curiously, Noah had a change of heart. This was not Noah's destiny, Methuselah had said.

But it was his destiny!

He slowed, dropping farther behind as the others hurried ahead, his heart pounding faster with the idea taking on shape and substance. Drawing in a determined breath, he turned back toward the suntracer room.

As he approached the intersection, the hair at Thore's neck tingled. He stopped. In the distance, boots thumped the stone floor with a heavy cadence—a contingent of Nephs!

Kenoch and Orm'el cast him worried glances as he reached for his broken sword.

"Company." Quickly they backtracked, surprising a pair of the Lodath's green-cloaks who were no match for Makir speed. Unfortunately, there was no place to hide the bodies. Thore collected their weapons from the floor—two projers and two fistprojs. He passed them around.

The drumming of boot steps from the tunnel grew louder, forcing them back toward the preparation building they'd just left. The marching halted briefly. Thore whispered, "They've found the bodies."

Orm'el gulped. "I should have stayed in the forest."

By the look on Kenoch's face, he was thinking the same thing.

The steps resumed, a quick trot now. Thore hurried down the corridor, but came up short when a reinforcing contingent of green-cloaks barred their way.

The guards' weapons snapped to their shoulders, and Orm'el turned to stone. Kenoch, too, froze at the sight of so many Nephs filling the hallway. Squeezed between the two forces, Thore dropped his projer to the floor.

The contingent from the tunnel arrived a moment later. "Two dead," a Neph commander said.

"They'll pay the Oracle's price for this," another growled and drove the butt of his projer at Thore. Thore shifted his chin at the last instant and the blow stunned the guard holding him. Bedlam broke out, and when it was over, Thore staggered from the beating he'd received, his thoughts muddled and foggy.

Kenoch and Orm'el were unconscious. Slung over the guards' shoulders, they were marched back toward the tunnel.

Thore ached all over, but he managed to keep on his feet. As they left the preparation building, he caught a glimpse out the window at the graying sky. It wouldn't be long now. He'd failed to find Noah or Sheflah.

They hadn't gone far when a familiar surge of energy sent a current of electricity down his spine. The binding! No mistaking it this time. Makir ... nearby. Their presence emboldened him. Why they were here was a question that no longer mattered.

Drawing on the Katrahs and Kimahs, he reached out to them. His strength renewed, the fog lifted from his brain, and his thoughts sharpened.

As they again neared the intersection in the tunnel, his muscles went taut.

※

Pressed against the side of the tunnel, the kal-ee-hon seemed to blend with the shadows. Rhone glanced down the line of warriors toward the two women at the rear of the company. Zinorah's flat, expressionless gaze worried him. *Expect the unexpected from that one.* Majiah, on the other hand, showed a natural fear—one that would keep her from rash actions. But Zinorah ... it was almost as if she relished a confrontation.

His view traveled round the waiting Makir, lurched to a stop, and leaped back.

Lamech! Where was Lamech?

But it was too late to go looking for him. The sounds of approaching Nephs grew louder. His hand went naturally to the long Makir sword at his side, and in his mind's eye he saw the emblem etched into its bright, hardened steel; the crest of the House of Khore—twin dragons, tails entwined, grasping the sword of Hodin between them while their other hands, upturned, held the Flame of the Creator.

Before reaching its hilt, he stopped himself and instead drew out his fistproj. Klesc would have snarled and called it a coward's weapon. A small, wistful smile came to his face at the memory of his old friend. The fistproj was not the traditional weapon of a Makir, it was true, but realistically, it was a much more practical one. Even so, no Makir would consider going into battle without the sword.

Wryly, he reminded himself he was no longer officially a Makir. He'd grown too old and had relinquished that life after taking over the High Councilor's seat on the Council of Ten—too many years ago to count. But no matter how the road of life twisted and turned, the training of the Katrahs and Kimahs never went away.

Once a Makir, always a Makir.

The pounding of Neph footsteps drew closer. All at once a stirring in the binding made his heart skip faster. Thore?

Could it be that his son was among them? A fist of questions leaped to his brain. A moment later a contingent of Nephs turned into the dark corridor, still unaware of their presence.

Among them strode his son. Thore's head turned, caught his eye, and winked. Rhone's heart raced. Chrone would wait until they were all within the tunnel and cut off their avenue of retreat—

And then a fistproj barked, its muzzle flash lighting up the corridor.

Zinorah!

She stepped into the middle of the tunnel and five rapid shots dropped as many Nephs, and sent the others diving for cover. Heedless of her safety, Zinorah drew out a second fistproj and methodically emptied it into the Nephs rank until she went down beneath a wall of giants.

Their surprise thwarted prematurely, the Makir opened fire.

In the close-in fighting, fistprojs fired at random and the floor grew slippery with blood. Rhone emptied his weapon and drew his sword. Steel flashed in the dim light. The Makir's preferred weapon allowed more control in the confinement of the tunnel.

He backed up to Thore. "We thought you were dead."

Thore grinned, wielding a sword missing its point. "Noah! Is he safe?"

"He made it back to Atlan."

Thore looked relieved.

As Rhone swung and stabbed, the tide turned in favor of the Makir, and shortly they drove the Nephs to their knees. The battle seemed to erase the years, though his burning muscles reminded him he was over seven hundred years old.

"Who fired that shot?" Pyir Chrone surveyed the carnage then, spying his brother, clasped him by the arm. "How did you get here?"

"It's a long story. And you?"

"The same."

Many had fallen, and many more were wounded, but Neph bodies clearly outnumbered the Makir. Rhone slowly lowered his sword as Thore rushed to Majiah and then went to his knees over Zinorah's crushed body.

"I'm sorry," Thore said.

Majiah lifted teary eyes to him. "Don't be. She welcomed death, and this is how she would have wanted to die."

Rhone sheathed his sword, understanding why Zinorah might feel that way.

Majiah held her cousin for a moment, stroking the short golden brown hair, trying to keep her sobs from showing. Then she reached inside one of Zinorah's pockets, retrieved something, and shoved it into her own pocket.

Thore helped her to her feet. "What's that?"

"The key that brings the jumper into phase."

Rhone glanced around at the bodies strewn about and suddenly his heart squeezed. Da-gore. He dropped to the ex-captain's side, lifted his head, and felt for a pulse. Its slow throbbing was barely detectable; his breathing was shallow. Blood covered Da-gore's chest and gathered in a pool beneath his left arm.

"Da-gore."

Heavy eyelids opened and glazed eyes shifted toward Rhone's face. "Fitting, don't you think?" Da-gore's words came out in a hiss. "It should end where it began."

"What can I do for you?" He wouldn't offer empty hope. Da-gore was a warrior. He understood.

Da-gore's hand gripped his forearm weakly. "A prayer, my old friend. To ease me over to the other side."

Rhone nodded, and when he finished, Da-gore smiled serenely. "Give Lady Leenah my thanks."

"For what?"

He coughed. "For her trust in me. For taking the effort to explain it all." His eyes traced a slow arc toward the dark ceiling. "Because of her concern, I'm assured of what's up there, waiting." Another cough brought a wince of pain to his lips. As it passed, Da-gore whispered, "Until we meet again."

"Fair journey, my friend."

A smile lifted Da-gore's lips even as his grasp weekened and slipped from Rhone's arm. Gently, he laid his old friend's head back to the cold stone floor.

"Rhone?"

He blinked away the moisture at the sound of the familiar voice. "Kenoch?"

"Over here." Kenoch's voice came thickly from someplace in the shadows.

Rhone found him entangled in a knot of arms and legs, helped him to his feet, and looked him up and down. "You and Thore ... alive?"

Kenoch probed the back of his skull and winced. "You're not the only one who finds that rather incredible." He glanced around. "Where's Orm'el?"

"I'm over here," a grizzled old man said, clawing up from a pile of Neph bodies. "What happened?" He looked at the Nephs and the blood, and frowned. "Maybe I don't want to know."

Some of the Nephs had fled back down the corridor. Pyir Chrone ordered a defensive line across the junction of the tunnel. "The ones who escaped will be returning with reinforcements."

Rhone said, "I've got to find Lamech. He was behind me when we entered the tunnel."

"Lamech is with you?" Kenoch asked and helped Orm'el from beneath the Nephs.

"He was a few moments ago."

Chrone said, "Better find him before he gets into trouble."

Thore moved to Chrone's side. "Sheflah and the others are in the preparation building up ahead, third floor. I take it they are why you're here?" Chrone nodded. "They're heavily guarded. And now every available green-cloak in the Lodath's Guard will be descending upon our position."

Chrone blew a worried breath. "We've lost the element of surprise. Best we can do is hold a line."

"Or fall back." Rhone's view shifted between his sons. "Our plan has come apart."

Chrone narrowed his view toward the tunnel. "We can't penetrate their defenses—not now that they know we're here."

"What about Sheflah?" Kenoch said.

"Yes, what about Sheflah?" Thore stooped to help Majiah with a wounded Makir. "We didn't come all this way to fail now."

Rhone noted stubborn determination on both his sons' faces. He knew what he'd do if he was still Pyir, but now that decision fell upon Chrone's shoulders.

Kenoch scowled. "Well, I'm going to find her."

"I ... I think I'll stay back," the old man said.

Chrone shot a look at him. "Who are you?"

"Orm'el, sir." He tugged at his tangled beard. "I brought Thore and Kenoch here." Orm'el gave a quick, nervous smile. "See, I know all these tunnels under the Temple."

Kenoch started off. Rhone snagged him by the arm.

Wheeling around, Kenoch growled, "Don't try to stop me, Rhone."

"I'm not." He slapped a fistproj into Kenoch's hand. "You'll need this."

Kenoch looked at the weapon, then back at Rhone, his scowl softening. "Sorry. Thanks." He started off.

"Kenoch." Rhone stopped him again.

His back stiffened.

"I heard about Cerah. I'm sorry."

Kenoch turned back. "Thank you."

"Hold, Kenoch." Chrone looked at Orm'el, "You say you know these tunnels. Is there another way to the outside?"

"Yes. Many. But you'll be exposed. And the crowds for the Ceremony have already gathered."

"Show me."

Orm'el hitched his head toward the tunnel from where they had come. "Back that way."

Chrone ordered a double fist of Makir to secure the tunnel back to the Temple, and tend to the wounded. Taking the rest of his men, they followed Orm'el.

❧

Lamech stopped and cocked his head. The projfire had ceased. He scowled. That could be good ... or very bad. Drawing in a breath to calm himself, he whispered a prayer and rushed on. No way to know what fate Rhone and the others faced out in the passage, but he did know his time was running short. He hurried on across the wide, dark floor and headed for the stairs down into the heart of the Temple. Pulling his suntracer from a pocket, he glanced at the hour. Almost five of the second quartering.

Nearly sunrise. His heart raced. Time was short!

Flying down the stairs as fast as his old legs would carry him, Lamech staggered to a halt in the suntracer chamber and bent to catch his breath. Before him loomed the huge bronze and iron works. With a wry smile, he straightened, recalling the musings he and Sor-dak had shared on occasion about the possibilities that the Creator had now laid before him.

His eyes slowly traveled the caged gears as he searched his memory for long-forgotten details. Getting his feet moving again, he dusted off ancient diagrams, recalled hoary calculations, and groped for obscure points of construction.

Wending his way through the machinery, he found a panel he recalled designing. The sight of it released more memories. Nearby, one whole apparatus, the size of his home back in Morg'Seth, kept the suntracer supplied with power. Its energy came from a crystalline shaft that connected with the Rahabian Crystal capstone. Another vast chamber held thousands of baked clay jars filled with lead plates and deadly acid. Conduits of copper wires, as thick around as a tree, connected the various parts.

He moved purposefully among the pieces of machinery spread out like a gigantic puzzle, keeping one eye on the crystal shaft. So long as it remained dark, he had time.

Then he spied the Star Room. He started for it, but a nearby commotion drew his attention. Hurrying down a corridor of machinery, he flattened against a warm, gleaming copper tube, and peeked around the corner. Black-clad Makir rushed off the steps and started across the floor. He let out a breath. What were they doing back here? Their clothes showed dark stains, their numbers diminished. The battle must have gone poorly. He looked hopefully for Sheflah among them, his hope slowly fading. And then he spied Kenoch!

He had intended to remain hidden, but at the sight of his brother-in-law alive, he stepped from cover.

The Makir lurched at his movement, then relaxed.

"Lamech!" Kenoch rushed to him and they embraced.

"Never thought I'd see you again this side of Adam's Bosom!" Lamech looked Kenoch up and down again to make sure his eyes hadn't deceived him. "How did you survive?"

Kenoch shrugged. "The Creator's hand must have been on us."

"Us? Thore is alive too?" As he spoke, Rhone and Thore approached.

Pyir Chrone seemed impatient at the interruption. With a quiet motion, he ordered the Makir to spread out in a defensive ring.

A man he didn't recognize made his way over too.

Lamech glanced at Thore. "Your good health pleases me."

"Me, too." Thore smiled. "We'll tell you all about it … later."

Lamech winced at the pang in his heart.

Rhone looked perturbed. He folded his arms across his broad chest, his dark eyes narrowed; his gray hair was tangled and spotted with blood. "What are you doing here? You were supposed to stay with me."

"I know how you might be upset, Rhone, but I understand why everything has happened as it has. And what I have to do."

"What do you have to do?"

"All these years I struggled with why the Creator had forced me to have a hand in building this Temple. Now I know, and I know why we are here—all of us." He paused. It was hard to say what he had to. "And it isn't to rescue Sheflah or the others."

Rhone's eyes widened a little.

"I know how to take it down."

"Down?"

"The Temple. I put it up, and I can take it down. The Creator has given me this chance, and it's what I must do." His view shifted to the stranger. Should he know this man?

From far away came a burst of projfire.

Pyir Chrone approached them. "We can't delay."

Rhone took Lamech by the arm. "You can tell me later."

He pulled from Rhone's grasp. "I have to stay, Rhone." He hoped his tone would convince him. He wasn't prepared to argue the point.

"Can you really do it?"

"I can."

The sounds of battle drew nearer.

Rhone hesitated, then turned to Chrone. "Go without me. I'll catch up."

Chrone clearly didn't like that idea, but he didn't refuse his father.

"We'll talk later," Kenoch said. "I need to go with the Makir."

If only that could be so. "Please save Sheflah."

"We will." He and Thore hurried away.

"You go too, Rhone."

"You'll need help. If the Lodath's forces overrun the Makir, they'll stop you before you can finish."

He couldn't ask his friend to sacrifice himself. That was too much. This was his mission, not Rhone's.

"You've gotten old, Preacher." The stranger studied his face.

Preacher? The way he said it brought back a flood of memories. "Who are you?"

The man laughed. "Don't tell me you've forgotten your old

cell mate. Quort nineteen. We shoveled behemoth girt together, you and me."

He studied the face, recalling the men he'd been imprisoned with five hundred years earlier. "Orm'el?"

Orm'el grinned. "That's me. You explained the Creator's message in the stars, remember?"

"How can I ever forget? I was whipped for it."

Orm'el eyes saddened. "My fault."

"You were the one?"

"They promised me an early release. They lied. I'd have done anything to get out of that filthy hole. We all would have."

It was an unexpected revelation, but now was hardly the time to nurture a grudge. Projfire grew louder. Pyir Chrone had regrouped his warriors. "Orm'el," he barked. "Now!"

"Got to go, Preacher."

Stunned, Lamech nodded.

As Orm'el backed away, he said, "Never thought I'd get the chance to thank you."

"Thank me?"

Orm'el winked. "Whatever happens here today, I know where I'm going. Then we'll have plenty of time to talk."

"You're a Kinsman?"

"Craziest thing, ain't it?" Orm'el grinned and hurried off with the others.

"Father?" Thore urged one last time.

Rhone motioned them ahead. "I'll catch up."

"You won't, Rhone," Lamech said.

His face showed no emotion as he turned back. "They'll try to stop you, Lamech."

He attempted to sort through his jumbled feelings, but a burst of projfire from the chamber above drew his attention to the doorway at the top of the stairs. When he looked back, everyone was gone except for Rhone. "You really need to leave too."

Rhone checked the chamber of his projer. "Do what you have to. Make it quick."

"Rhone, if you stay, you will die with me."

"If I don't, you'll fail." His eyes narrowed. "Why do you think I'm here when I should have stayed in Atlan?"

How well he knew the answer. "Because the Creator moves men to do His will."

Rhone's lips quirked in a tight smile. "Then let's get busy doing it."

35

A Warrior's Passage

Orm'el found the way with no trouble. Thore doubted many people could have led them so precisely. It was more than luck that he and Kenoch had met just the man they needed in the deep forests of Morg'Jalek.

The gray haze of dawn hung low over the ground as they left the Temple by a small door at the end of a long tunnel. Under Pyir Chrone's lead, the Makir hurried along the side of the Temple. The distance felt vast, not being able to see much beyond fifty spans in any direction. The morning mist was at its heaviest and their timing couldn't have been better. Thore heard the crowds gathering out beyond his range of sight. The low torrent of so many voices could only mean that half of Nod City had showed up for the Appearing Ceremony. That could work for them. His brother would have already considered that.

They halted against the Temple's corner. The sky had brightened and soon the new sun would burn off the fog. Chrone signaled for Orm'el.

"Once we free her, which direction to the nearest way out of this cage?"

"The main entrance will be clogged with people. We won't

want to go that way. The crowds usually line up east to west. The way north will be open. Once we reach the wall, there will be several bronze gates spaced along it. Not usually guarded, but always locked."

"We can blow the gates," Thore said.

Chrone ordered Dor'vk to see to the task. "Wait until you see us coming before detonating." He told Majiah to go with the Makir.

She screwed her lips together in a frown. "I didn't come all this way just to leave when the going gets tough."

Chrone said, "Our plans have changed. Zinorah is dead. We'll need you to fly the jumper back to Atlan."

She apparently hadn't thought of this. Reluctantly, she nodded. "All right."

"I'll go with you?" Orm'el offered hopefully.

"You'll stay near me." Thore clamped a big hand on the old man's shoulder.

Orm'el gave a wan smile as he looked up at him. "Reckon I'll be staying here after all."

The warrior shouldered a sack, and then he and Majiah melted into the haze.

Once they were gone, Chrone turned to Orm'el. "Explain the Ceremony."

"The Oracle arrives first, led by a troop called the Separated Guards. They'll march under the Triumphal Arch. You can't see it from here. Next comes the sacrifice procession. They'll be chained—neck to neck."

Thore hefted his sword, its weight reassuring in spite of its shortened length. "Will this split the chains?"

Orm'el considered the sword, then him. "In my hands, probably not. But if I had big Hodinite shoulders like yours ..." He grinned. "Likely anything would be possible."

The sound of marching feet echoed through the lifting mist.

At the edge of his vision, Thore glimpsed a movement of green.

Pyir Chrone signaled. Hunkered low, the Makir silently overwhelmed the patrol of the Lodath's Guards before they knew what had hit them. Hauling the bodies up against the Temple's foundation stones, they quickly stripped off the uniforms and donned them over their black sutas, fixing the green cloaks over their shoulders.

"The way will be lined with more green-cloaks and dignitaries of the Oracle," Orm'el warned as they prepared to move out.

Chrone nodded. "Spread out, but not too far. Everyone is on their own afterward; make for the jumper."

The binding was tightest when they were close together. Thore's muscles drank in the energy of the ties growing stronger as they moved out. The prelude to a battle always made it so.

Once among the gathering crowds, onlookers gave way to their green uniforms. No one questioned their presence, and Thore figured that so long as they didn't run into another patrol of the Lodath's Guards, they'd go unchallenged.

And then they were near the Triumphal Arch. Through the misty air, the arch blazed beneath the powerful light beams that emanated from the Temple—from the Rahabian Crystal capstone. Here the crowds were thickest, held back by golden chains stretched on either side of the procession route along the Grand Temple Way, and by ranks of green-cloaks. Within the chained corridor stood the dignitaries. Thore noted how they whispered among themselves. They fidgeted, and laughed lowly, and overall seemed anxious for the Ceremony to begin.

Moving boldly through the crowds, Pyir Chrone made his way toward the chain unchallenged. Thore kept close to Kenoch and Orm'el; in the dim light and dressed as guards, the two old men managed to pass by without close scrutiny.

Orm'el touched Chrone's arm, and as the tall Hodinite leaned closer, Thore overheard Orm'el whisper, "You'll not want to get too close until after the Oracle passes by. There are likely no other

Kinsmen here, and we don't want him to catch our scent. I'm hoping the crowds will distract him."

Chrone nodded.

The music of leolpipes burst from somewhere up ahead and the crowds grew more agitated. Then the sound of marching feet lifted above the murmurs.

"The Separated Guards," Orm'el whispered.

The Guards came into view, marching at stiff attention. The light beams from the Temple blazed off their bronze helmets and emphasized the rich green of their uniforms—similar to the uniform Thore had pulled over his own dark clothes, but of a brighter hue. Once again the leolpipes chortled. Thore leaned his head toward the shorter man as Orm'el said, "Here he comes."

Thore's heart pounded a little harder at the prospect of seeing the Deceiver, the one who had invaded the world and changed it forever, and harder yet because standing as close as they were, a being like the Oracle might very well sense their presence. That would end the mission—their lives—in a hurry. Thore gave a wry grin at the prospects, but the binding was strong and he drew strength from the nearby Makir, just as they drew strength from him.

As the Separated Guards marched past, the crowds around Thore hushed. His view latched onto the golden throne, passing beneath the Triumphal Arch. The Oracle, borne aloft upon the shoulders of eight Nephs, appeared to radiate light. His startling white clothing shimmered in an aura of colors beneath the Rahabian Crystal's glare. Before him, the crowds cast palm fronds onto the Way.

There upon his golden throne, the Oracle seemed oblivious to the accolades, almost as if in a trance. Thore held his breath as the Oracle passed by. He released it as the throne and its Neph bearers continued onward.

Now the crowds roared with delight. The procession of the sacrifice came into view. When he saw their great numbers, Thore understood now how he and the others had escaped detection. The presence of so many Kinsmen must be overwhelming to someone who hates them so. He scanned the faces of the pitiful Kinsmen, dressed in simple brown robes, chained neck to neck by several spans of chain that might have been gold. It was hard to tell. But they weren't heavy, and Thore reenacted in his head how he would drive the hard Makir steel of his sword through those soft links.

"Sheflah," Kenoch whispered excitedly near his ear and pointed.

He spied her in the midst of a row, eight abreast. As she passed by he tried to catch her eyes. Sheflah's frightened stare remained focused upon the person ahead of her.

Thore signaled Chrone, and the word traveled quietly through the Makir ranks. As the sacrifice marched by, the Makir slipped under the golden chain and began moving with the procession. They still met with no resistance, and if it was unusual protocol for green-cloaks, at least no one tried to stop them—yet.

❦

Rhone's head snapped up at the approach of marching feet from the level ahead. "What do we have to do?"

Lamech glanced at a tall crystalline column that had begun to brighten faintly. "We haven't much time left." He started toward it. "Years ago, Sor-dak and I built a machine that would calculate the correct angle of the mirrors."

"What mirrors?" The floor beneath Rhone's feet throbbed from some immense power source.

Lamech hurried on. "At dawn the Rahabian Crystal captures the sun's light, reflecting its energy within itself, amplifying it to unimaginable power until it bursts through a lens at its base and pours into the sacrificial chamber."

Lamech stepped into a small chamber and studied the levers and pointers with markings unfamiliar to Rhone. "In an instant the sacrifice is consumed." His hand swept before the dials. "But the mirrors must be adjusted just so, or the energy will dissipate and not find its way out of the chamber and through the Homing Portal."

"And that will be bad?"

Lamech glanced at him. "It would destroy the sacrificial chamber, and everyone inside the Temple, but not the Temple itself." His view shifted out the small door at the sounds of footsteps pounding down the stairs, scattering in different directions.

Rhone said, "They're searching."

Lamech began moving dials. "To do the most damage, I need to readjust the mirrors to reflect the energy back up into the crystal." Lamech looked at him. "The overload should do the trick."

"When?" Footsteps drew nearer.

"Timing has to be precise. When that crystal column over there," he inclined his head out the door, "fully lights up ..." He touched a bronze lever that stood up from the floor at his knee. "I need to push this all the way over."

"How long after that?"

He frowned. "A few moments for the mirrors to move. That's all."

At least it would be over quickly. Rhone grimaced as he cradled the projer in the crook of his arm. "I'll give you the time you need." He glanced out the door at the crystal column, slowly growing brighter. He cleared his thoughts. It did no good to think about it. Leenah's beautiful face filled his thoughts as he slipped out into the narrow corridor. That was not helpful, and he called on the training of the Katrahs and Kimahs to keep his attention focused as he slid out the door.

The vastness of the place meant Lamech might well finish his task before he was ever discovered. But why hadn't the Nephs followed the others? He frowned. Unless something had alerted them. He knew the connection Nephs had with the other realm. Fallen Malik may have alerted them. He suspected that if he could peel back that flimsy veil that separated the two worlds, he might see a fierce battle going on even now between the Creator's warriors and the Fallen Ones who had followed Lucifer after the Rebellion.

He couldn't worry about what was beyond his reach. The here and now—the flesh and blood of Nephs—were what should concern him.

As he crept toward the sounds of footsteps, a chill raked his spine. Spinning around, he saw the Neph worker, not a guard, come around a corner. Rhone ducked as a heavy iron wrench whirled past his ear and clanged up against an iron pipe, ringing like a bell in the narrow corridor through the machinery. Growling, the huge man clenched his six-fingered fist and charged.

Rhone's projer came up, but at the last instant he drew his sword instead. He easily danced aside from the groping arms and ran the giant through. The Neph's bellowing howl as he fell to the floor alerted the warriors scouring other areas. Their heavy footfalls grew louder in his direction.

Rhone flattened against the machinery. Three guards bounded around the corner, halted, glancing about, then approached cautiously. His heart pounding, he cast a quick glance at the crystalline column, brightening with the growing light of a new dawn.

❦

Borne up the Temple steps on Neph shoulders, the Oracle disappeared through the towering Temple doors. Thore caught his breath as the sacrifice started up the stairs. His eye fixed upon his brother, and the bands of muscles across his chest and in his arms and legs tensed. Chrone would wait until the last moment. Once his signal was given, confusion would ensue. Their only hope for success lay in using the bedlam to free Sheflah and as many other Kinsmen as they could.

The sacrifice neared the door. Chrone's hand disappeared beneath the green cloak. Thore's grip tightened upon the hilt of his sword....

Steel flashed in Chrone's hand as he swept around. Two giants were dead before they hit the ground, and pandemonium erupted as Makir swords leaped to hand.

Thore shoved through the stampede of onlookers and pushed Sheflah to the stone Temple steps. "Hold still!"

Her eyes sprang wide with recognition as a swipe of his sword parted one of her chains, and then the other end.

"Uncle Thore!"

He freed two of the Kinsmen nearest to her, then wheeled and severed the arm of a Neph as it raised a fistproj. Snatching up the fallen weapon, he scooped Sheflah under an arm and plunged through a swath in the green-cloaks' ranks that the Makir had mowed open.

Shots rang out and a proj burned across his forearm. He fired into a knot of green-cloaks tightening around him, then plunged down the Temple's steps and across the wide orange pavement.

Sheflah's grip tightened about his arm as he sprinted across the grounds. Projfire cracked all around him and projlets whined past his ear and zinged off the pavement. He winced with a sting of pain as the binding began to fail. Warrior brothers were falling beneath crushing numbers, and with each passing, the binding loosened just a little more. He sensed several, like himself, breaking free and fleeing toward the far gate where Majiah and the Makir with the explosives waited.

More green-cloaks moved in from the left to cut him off. Thore swerved back toward the Temple. At least fifty more guards rounded the corner. The staccato bark of projers stitching a line in the pavement turned him again. Surrounded, he emptied his fistproj into the advancing ranks, then drew his sword. As a Makir, he would rather die with a sword in hand than any other weapon.

They had him boxed in and were in no hurry, closing their ranks cautiously. Why didn't they shoot and be done with it?

Perhaps the Oracle had ordered them taken alive. A vague stirring in the binding said that a few Makir remained, but the ties had weakened considerably. The mission had failed, but so long as he held a sword, he'd not be taken alive.

The sun crested the horizon casting its soft glow across the orange pavement, glinting off the green raiment of the circle drawing tighter. Sheflah whimpered into his chest.

A shadow flickered past. It circled and grew larger. Green-cloaks looked skyward and went rigid.

Thore glanced. Gur!

The scarlet dragon swooped low, and his great head coiled back then sprang forward, sending a fireball rolling through the green-cloak line. The dragon banked, dived back, and scorched another score of the Lodath's Guards, then stretching out its immense talons, dropped swiftly toward him.

Caught beneath his arms, Thore lurched off his feet and his sword went tumbling to the pavement. It was all he could do to keep Sheflah from following it. Her fingers dug into his arm while, below, projfire crackled. Thore winced as a hot poker stabbed his side. Gur strove ever upward, his wings going out of sync. Sheflah's fingers loosened upon Thore's arm. He tightened his hold on her. The wall that encircled the Temple complex grew nearer. Below, he had a glimpse of men fleeing afoot.

The binding had broken, and he prayed his remaining warrior brothers would escape the complex, now swarming with green-cloaks.

Gur staggered again, his powerful wings failing. Struggling to stay aloft, the dragon strove for the wall. As they passed over the wall, the projfire diminished, and the forest loomed ahead. Looking back, the Temple gleamed in the midst of a sea of people, the sunlight creeping up its walls, nearing the crystal capstone. The ache in his side burned hotter. He had to concentrate on keeping Sheflah in his grip. She seemed so much heavier.

Had his father and Lamech managed to flee the Temple, or were they still inside?

Before he had a chance to ponder that, the ground whirled unexpectedly and rushed up to meet them.

※

Standing motionless within a nest of bronze tubes, Rhone pressed back into the shadows as the three Nephs crept along the corridor. In spite of their closeness, his concentration was difficult. He tried not to think of Leenah, or the future, or anything except giving Lamech the precious few moments he needed to readjust the mirrors and throw the lever. But still, regrets pushed their way into his thoughts. Leenah, of course, and his children, his country … Noah, who was connected as close as any of his children … and Bar'ack. Bar'ack? Why should Bar'ack trouble him now? Because of a promise made many years ago—a promise unfulfilled?

He sent up a speedy prayer for the man who'd once been his ward, and now was a prisoner of spirits, and then squeezed his eyes shut and forced his thoughts back on task. What he was doing now was right and true. This Temple—this icon to evil— had been an affront to the Creator and a source of suffering to the Kinsmen for too long. Maybe Lamech was right. Maybe Lamech's whole life had been arranged for just this very moment. And maybe so had his.

The quiet, carefully placed footsteps grew nearer.

Rhone cleared his thoughts and focused. As the giants passed by, one happened to glance over. His eyes widened, but before he could bring the projer in his hands to bear, Rhone drove his sword through the giant's heart. Rhone's fistproj cracked three times, dropping the two remaining Nephs. As the reverberation of the shots faded, the sounds of rushing boots filled the void.

From the door of his cubicle, Lamech's head poked out and looked around.

"Finished?" Rhone barked.

"Almost." Lamech went back to his task.

Rhone collected a projer from one of the dead Nephs and tossed it through the door to Lamech as he hurried past. Ahead, the corridor filled. He hit the floor and emptied his projer into their ranks. Nephs tumbled back while others scrambled over their fallen bodies. He cast aside the empty weapon and steadied his fistproj upon the broad chest of the nearest Neph. It cracked and recoiled in his fist. At the sound of approaching feet behind him, he swung around and dropped another Neph. Projlets ricocheted off the floor and clanked into the machinery.

A proj hit him in the side. Another, like the stinger of a keber wasp, found his leg. Rhone pressed up against the machinery and emptied his fistproj into the charging enemy, then grabbed for his sword. They were almost on him when Lamech stepped from the small room and opened fire.

"All ready!" Lamech shouted over the noise.

The distraction gave Rhone a moment to get to his feet.

The crystalline column had begun to glow brightly. Time was running out.

He dived across the corridor to Lamech's side. His leg buckled, but the Essence of Valor coursing through his blood gave him the strength to run his blade through a Neph's throat, and the breast of another … and then the battle blurred. The Makir within him took over and his sword struck, and struck again, dropping the giants that grabbed for him.

Through a bloodred haze, Lamech fell, clutching his chest.

A proj knocked the breath from Rhone. Another punched him back inside the room. His vision blurred. The doorway filled with Nephs. Lamech hauled himself to his knees.

Rhone threw himself in front of Lamech, and as the projlets slammed into him, he no longer felt their pain. The crimson haze before his eyes dissipated to a gentle blue light. Sari'el stepped through the wall and stood by him.

The projfire dimmed to a strange hiss. As if no longer a part of the battle, Rhone watched with fascination as Lamech reached for the lever. His hand missed, but as he fell, his riddled body slammed into it, shoving it forward.

The sound of projfire ceased and a flash of light brighter than anything he'd ever seen briefly filled his vision, and then it was gone, and it was just he and Sari'el.

Sari'el extended a hand and helped him to his feet. They stood upon a vast expanse of pearlescent white and were enveloped in the sweet scent of lilacs. His senses came alive as never before—not even in the Creator's Garden where everything was more vibrant. When he turned, Lamech smiled at him, radiant, a young man, as he had been that first day they met on the Meeting Floor in Nod City.

Myriad Messenger-warriors of the Creator surrounded them. A golden light bloomed before his eyes, and from the light the voice of the Gardener boomed. "Well done, my good and faithful servants."

⁂

Thore hadn't yet untangled himself from the heavy, leathery wings that covered him when the explosion shook the ground. Through the thick hide of Gur's protective wing, the flash of light stung his eyes. The roar seemed to go on and on forever as debris fell from the sky and pummeled the wing and ground all around them.

He clutched Sheflah tighter until it was over. The silence was chilling. He forced his way from under the lifeless wing. Once free, he tilted his head back at the tower of smoke rising from beyond the Temple complex wall.

Sheflah hadn't moved. He laid her upon the grassy berm of the road upon which Gur had fallen. His heart wrenched and moisture stung his eyes. He looked at the blood upon his hands, noticing it for the first time.

"At least you didn't suffer the indignation of the Temple sacrifice, Sheflah." He gathered her into his arms, hardly aware of the sting of his own wounds. He would have gladly taken the projlets for her, if it could have saved her life.

The mission had been a failure all the way round.

People were streaming from the gates, fleeing the Temple site. Chrone staggered free of the crowd, as did four other Makir and Majiah who looked dazed.

Chrone rushed to his side, his eyes saddening as they fell upon the broken body in his arms.

"She didn't make it." Thore collected his emotion.

Majiah hugged him. "I'm sorry."

Chrone grimaced. "We lost many warriors today."

"Father?"

Chrone nodded. "Far as I know, he and Lamech were still inside the Temple when it exploded."

The pain of so much loss twisted inside him. He hardly noticed his own wounds. He glanced around. "Orm'el? Kenoch?"

Chrone shook his head. "We need to leave now."

Thore swallowed down the lump in his throat, and carried Sheflah with him. After a few paces, he stopped and looked back.

Gur's bright ruby scales had begun to fade. He thought of his mother. They had all lost so much. His arms tightened about Sheflah's body as they hurried back to the hidden jumper.

36

Methuselah's Blessings

*F*ive years later.

"It's"—Naamah thought a moment—"almost as if they're waiting for something."

Noah leaned his forearms upon the windowsill. The breeze bore the musty odor of animals. The sight beyond the ark was enough to take a man's breath away. "Where can they all be coming from?" Everyone knew of the herds of animals arriving in Atlan since the earth-shaking and consequential uplifting of the Atlan Ridge, but the numbers staggered the eye as over the weeks they had begun to gather in the valley where the ark sat high and dry.

"You know what brings them, Noah?" Her voice held quiet awe.

It had been a rhetorical question.

She looked at him. "It can only mean ..."

"Time draws short."

Her green eyes searched his face. "When?"

He gazed back at herds of oxen and three-points, the packs of sten-gordons and flops of pocket dragons. Behemoths and lions mulled about as if oblivious of each other. Flocks of gulls and golden spikers roosted in tree branches and upon the leftover stacks of lumber. Osters, grunties, and lop-hoppers were all over the place, jostling with black, scurrying jinkloos, molkies, and bisneks. Emerald kesers, gray kormens, green divers, blue parrots, scarlet dragons … even ominous mansnatchers! And a thousand others. Many of them Turnlings, yet none aggressively attacking the other. It went against everything he'd come to know as truth. In the midst of all of these milling animals sat the ark. Afloat in a sea of wildlife.

They left the room that one day would be their home and refuge through the coming flood. Noah paused and looked with a heavy heart down the row of apartments, each intended for one of his children. Some would remain empty. A tear stung his eye as he took Naamah's hand, walking slowly along the deck with sunlight streaming in from the long overhead row of windows. Vaul trotted ahead of them toward the wide door standing open to the late-day sun.

The potted trees in a neat row were thriving, their branches reaching up to the sunlit gallery overhead where earth-filled planters waited for the seeds that would see them through the ordeal ahead.

Outside, on the ramp's wide landing, they stopped and peered again across the herds of animals. Somehow they knew time was drawing to a close. Somehow they understood that here, in this valley, was where they needed to be. He sniffed. They knew, yet his own children couldn't see it.

He and Naamah walked down the ramp and headed for the road, beasts of the fields moving out of their way—docile, yet intractable. Days earlier he had tried coaxing some of them into the ark, but they had resisted his efforts. All he could hope was, when the time was right, their attitudes would change.

On the way back, they spent a few minutes over the graves in the family plot. Sheflah's grave was framed in pure white stone. They held each other and let their tears flow.

His mother's grave was also framed in stone. Mishah hadn't lasted but a few years after Lamech's homegoing. He hadn't realized until after his death how much his mother had relied on his father. How she must have pined for him all those years in the Creator's Garden. But he had been only a child. How could he have known then, as he knew now, the pain of a broken heart?

When? Naamah had asked him earlier. The Creator's timetable couldn't be sped up or slowed down. Not yesterday, not today, and, he suspected, not tomorrow.

Naamah collected a bouquet of creamy white bayolets, placed them upon the graves, and spent a moment arranging them.

"There was so much more my mother could have taught you and Desmorah." He sighed, missing her almost as much as he missed Sheflah, and Rhone, Uncle Kenoch, and Aunt Cerah. So many gone.

And after the destruction of his Temple, the Oracle's armies had practically swept the world clean of Kinsmen; and now his forces battled at the very gates of Atlan. It seemed no amount of blood would satisfy the Oracle's wrath.

Naamah stood and brushed the soil from her hands. "Mishah was a learned healer. Look what she did for Kitah. Hardly a scar from those horrible burns. She taught me much, Noah. And the books we bring with us will help us through the beginning. It will be hard living until our numbers increase and our children"—the word caught in her throat—"relearn what will have been lost."

They started again for home, and had just rounded the last bend when Majiah came into view. Her quick pace and taunt expression set Noah's teeth on edge.

"What is it?" he asked even before she had reached them.

"Grandfather! He's having some kind of seizure!"

When they reached the house, Grandfather Methuselah was stretched out on the floor, convulsing, his bony hands flopping like fish washed up on shore. Desmorah had put a stick between his teeth, but the blood on his chin, neck, and floor showed the effort came too late. Kitah, sitting next to him on the floor, looked frightened, and both women looked to Naamah for help when they rushed through the door.

"He was just sitting in his chair when it started." Kitah's breathing came in quick gulps. "I was with him."

Naamah put a hand to her shoulder as she knelt beside the old man.

Noah watched for a moment then glanced to Grandfather's chair, bent down, and retrieved his walking stick from the floor. "Did he say anything?" He held the stick a moment, then set it against the arm of the chair.

"No." Kitah trembled at the old man's side.

He took her hand and drew her from the floor. In the five years since she'd come to live with them, she'd grown into a beautiful young woman. Little wonder Shem had taken her as his wife. Pretty, smart ... and sensitive. Each one of his daughters-in-law was wonderful, but Kitah more than any of them reminded him of Sheflah. "Go get the boys. Tell them to come home." Grandfather might not last that long, and he felt they should be here. And Kitah, in her shaken state, certainly didn't need to be here right now. "And send someone to Wend's house too."

Kitah's face was as pale as the bayolet bouquet they had just laid upon his mother's grave. She nodded and hurried from the room. He turned back to Naamah and Desmorah. "What can I do?"

"I'll need you to help us move Grandfather to his bed," Naamah said, riffling through her healer's bag for a vial of oil that she dabbed upon his temples. In a few minutes the convulsions lessened and they lifted old Methuselah into their arms and carried him down the hall.

When Methuselah's eyes opened, he didn't seem to notice that his room was filled with worried faces. The boys sat quietly in chairs dragged in from other rooms while Naamah and

Desmorah hovered over the old man with their oils. They had tried teas, but Methuselah showed no interest in drinking.

Kitah, sitting on Shem's knee, leaned forward, watching quietly. Her color looked better, but Noah saw how the event had rattled her.

Sebe and Wend hadn't said much. Sebe stood behind her husband with hands upon his shoulders. Wend, slouched in the chair, was impatient, but seemed to know that for now, his place was here, not out tending the fields.

Nearby, Majiah calmly flipped through a book of remedies. Her slowly spreading glower told that she was not having any success.

Noah understood now why a healer's training took so many years. Too bad Naamah and the girls only had three to learn it all. Everyone had known his mother was wasting away with grief, but none had expected her to go so quickly. One morning she walked out in to the forest to collect her herbs and never came back. They found her sitting against a tree in the dappled evening light, her gathering basket upon her lap, filled with mushrooms and mosses, roots and flower petals. She had looked peaceful sitting there, as if merely napping. Noah remembered how she had looked like that when Lamech was at her side. And now they were together again.

Japheth stood abruptly and stared out the window into the night. Desmorah glanced up from Grandfather, then turned back to the cool cloth soaked in some concoction that lay across his wrinkled forehead.

The tension was suffocating. How long had it been? It felt as if they'd been hovering over Methuselah forever. Noah's stomach growled and he drew in a breath. "We should get something to eat."

Kitah rose from Shem's knee. "I'll fix something." She hurried out of the room. Shem stood, stretching. "I'll go with her."

"No. Stay." Methuselah's weak voice startled them. His chest heaved and then slowly fell, heaved, fell.

Kitah drew to a halt and looked back.

The old man's eyes opened slowly and surveyed the room with renewed alertness.

"Grandfather." Noah went to him.

Methuselah's glistening eyes blinked and held him for a long moment, then shifted and stared at something. A small smile came to his lips and he nodded, as if in response to something.

"What is it, Grandfather?"

The old man looked back at him, then to the boys. "Come closer," his weak voice urged.

As they moved toward the bed, he said, "Noah." His frail hand fluttered toward him.

Noah gripped it, shocked by the chill in his grandfather's flesh. "I'm here."

"My son. You are honored above all men, the father of a new world. Pure of blood, but troubled of spirit. Keep the Creator's laws so that your days may be long and fruitful."

The Blessing and Admonitions. His heart went as cold as Grandfather's hand. Enoch's prophesy sprang to mind, and he wasn't ready yet. His children weren't ready! "You will grow strong again." Grandfather couldn't die!

"My time has come. They wait." Grandfather's view shifted, then returned. "Stay obedient, for the Deceiver will tempt you where you are weakest."

"I ... I will." The words caught in his throat.

"Japheth." Methuselah looked away.

His second son came forward. "Grandfather?"

He put a trembling hand upon Japheth's forearm. "Mighty will you become. Kingdoms will you rule. The purse strings of the world will be in your hands. Remember, the Deceiver tempts you where your heart is. Your riches will not save you."

Japheth nodded. "I'll remember."

Methuselah smiled. "When the end of day comes, you will have forgotten."

Noah cringed. Why did blessings always have dire ends?

"Shem," the old man whispered.

Shem glanced at Kitah, and knelt by the bed. Methuselah placed a hand upon the boy's chest. "You have a king's heart, and you love the Creator's sayings. From you will arise the King of Kings, but your eyes will be clouded to His coming. In your day you will be a priest and king. Your children will call you Melchizedek. But the Deceiver will know you for who you are. He will follow you everywhere, and heap great sorrows upon your children. Stay true to the Word, and listen to His prophets so that you will not be held accountable for not knowing the day of The Strong Man's coming."

"I will, Grandfather," he said softly.

The old man smiled knowingly again and merely nodded.

Noah wasn't surprised. Shem had the making of a priest. But a king? He'd never thought of his son as a ruler.

"Ham."

His youngest hesitated. Majiah touched his shoulder, stirring him from his trance. As he knelt beside the old man, Methuselah's hand went to his head.

"Clever, you are. Great ideas will spring from you—devices of wonder and power. Your children will bring many blessings to their cousins. But because the right and true words are not in your heart, your children will be servants. Their blessings will enrich Japheth and Shem. Your kingdom will rise first, but the Deceiver will sit upon its throne. Warriors will spring from your loins, and they will battle everyone, and each other. But if you draw close to the Creator and heed His words, great sages will honor your generations."

Ham scowled and stood. "That will not be my fate. I am no one's servant." He stepped back. Majiah took his arm, anger in her dark eyes too.

And then Grandfather went silent.

"What about Wend's blessing?" Sebe demanded.

Methuselah looked at her. "I have no blessing for Wend."

"Why not?" Wend stepped forward.

Grandfather peered up at him. "Your future is a dark glass."

"Give me a blessing," he demanded, forcing his way past his brothers and going to the old man's side. "Don't leave me out."

Methuselah thought a moment then took Wend's hand. "Work at the labors of this world, and the fruits of this world will be your blessings."

Noah's heart raced. What could that mean? He gripped Naamah's hand, seeing confusion in her eyes.

Wend stared at Grandfather. "Is that all?"

The old man's grip tightened in his. "It is not too late to give your heart to the Creator." The hand fell weakly to the bed.

Silently, Wend rose and returned to Sebe's side. She put an arm around his waist and held him tight. Noah would have gone to him but Naamah held him back.

Methuselah lifted his view, a gasp inflating his sunken chest. "They come for me now," he whispered, staring at nothing that Noah could discern, and then a smile filled the old man's face. "Lamech."

The single word slipped from his lips, and he died.

37

An Ancient Dream

Ekalon found Lucifer suspended upon the edge of the Pit, staring into it. Lucifer's natural brilliance was muted, his countenance downcast, his view seemingly riveted upon the distant, flickering red streams of molten rock. Ekalon purposefully did not peer into the Pit as he drifted to his side. Lucifer's dejection worried him. How would he take the news?

"I see you have heard."

Lucifer caught his eye. "Abaddon is sulking."

"All the realm is in despair now that Methuselah has entered his rest."

"Rest." Lucifer's view shifted back to the depths. "What does rest feel like?"

Seeing his master like this made Ekalon nervous. It could only portend an unthinkable eternity if Lucifer didn't snap out of it. He cast a quick glance at the yellow sulfurous fumes rising, and a chilling terror rushed his words. "We've made steady progress in spite of this setback, Master. Since the debacle in Nod City, your children have scoured the earth of Kinsmen. None is left, except the holdouts on Atlan. All the people worship you, and knowledge of the Tyrant of Old is practically nonexistent. This troublesome story-in-the-stars business was easily diverted. You were brilliant in its execution, changing just enough to alter the message. Now seers everywhere are foretelling the future—with your servants advising them from the realm. These simpleminded humans have turned completely from its original message." He realized he was babbling when Lucifer speared him with an impatient glare.

"Except the holdouts on Atlan? Those are the only humans who matter!"

A weighty despair filled him. "I understand, Master."

Lucifer turned abruptly away from the Pit, and in an instant they stood in his throne room, suspended between heaven and earth, the Deceiver's attendants bowing at their appearance.

"We waste efforts trying to breech Atlan's defenses. The Tyrant has set a hedge around the nation, and a double hedge about Noah."

"We can't cease our attack!" The notion that the Tyrant might win the battle and that the Pit might become his home for all eternity filled Ekalon with dread. "We need to muster all our forces!"

"It's too late for that."

"Then the Tyrant wins?"

Lucifer cast him a withering scowl. "I don't need you cracking now, Ekalon! There is still work to be done."

"But the prophesies ... Methuselah signaling the final days?"

"This battle is lost, but the war is not over."

"We've worked hard to move the people from faith in the Tyrant to faith in themselves. All our efforts will be lost. Once on the other side, there will be only Kinsmen to carry on, and we all know that the coming Strong Man will be from Noah's lineage."

"Not all our efforts, Ekalon. I have removed most of my children to Oric where they will be safe. After the wrath, I can return them to this world to pick up were we left off."

"Still, those remaining Kinsmen!"

"They are humans, Ekalon, and they are weak. They are easily swayed by power and vanity."

Ekalon was shaken. Visions of the Pit filled his head. "It will take generations. And still, the Tyrant will have a hedge about Noah."

"Then we must plan for it. If we can't break through to nurture the seeds of rebellion, we will begin the rebellion from the inside."

Lucifer had a plan after all! Encouraged, Ekalon shook off the heaviness of an unthinkable future. "What have you devised, Master?"

Lucifer held out a hand. A black cloud grew from his open palm, and with a hot breath he blew it away, leaving a heavy book with black wood covers, carved with the Unspeakable Symbols that decorated the Lodath's chambers. "The knowledge that man craves is in here." He handed it to Ekalon. "You must get this aboard the ark where it will escape the wrath. For the right human, this will bring great power and wealth. With those, we will have an open door to begin our work again."

Lucifer turned, crimson light streaming from him as he tilted his head heavenward. "I will be more vigilant the next time. I will study the Tyrant's prophesies, and when I know who will bear the Strong Man, I will move swiftly. I personally will see to his destruction. The Tyrant has not revealed much about the Strong Man yet, but soon He must so that his servants will know Him. And when He is brought into the realm of man, then I will strike!"

Encouraged, he took the book from his master. "Tell me how to get this aboard the ark."

"Not you, Ekalon. The Guardians would never permit such intervention. But there is someone who will accept it." His finger pointed, and the woman came in to sharp focus. She stood by her husband, gripping his arm, a tight scowl upon her lips as she stared at the sarcophagus.

"She conceals bitterness in her soul. It will take only the right words from you, Ekalon, and she will become our tool to carry the book to the other side."

"I will see that it gets done, Master."

Stepping through a curtain of rippling light, Ekalon entered the realm of man, in the shape of a man, properly attired, the book nestled under his left arm. Moving in among the crowd, the words being spoken at the open grave had a somber note to them, and he recalled his anguish peering into the Pit. The sky had taken on an angry iron gray cast. He could not remember ever seeing the sunlight so impeded by clouds before. He halted a short distance from the woman. Her black hair was a pile of curls, her eyebrows hitched together, hooding her narrowed eyes. The man at her side stepped forward to join with eight other men, each taking hold of a rope. As they lowered the stone coffin into the ground, Ekalon moved up alongside her.

"His grandfather?" He indicated Noah, who had just ended his eulogy.

She started at his unexpected appearance. He smiled. In human form, smiling came easily, and he took advantage of it, wishing Sari'el was there to see. She looked him up and down and nodded. "Yes."

"A very moving service. Master Noah had so many nice things to say."

Her lips tightened. "I suppose."

"Do you believe what has been said? That once Master Methuselah went to Adam's Bosom, the Tyr-, err, the Creator would send violent wrath?"

"They all believe it."

"But you don't?"

She thought a moment. "I do."

He shook his head dolefully. "I can see you miss him terribly already."

Her dark eyes sparked. "Hardly."

He feigned surprise. "Then why the downcast face?"

She was about to speak, then obviously thought better than to say something unkind about the dead. The sound of dirt rattling upon the coffin turned their heads back to the burial.

When it was finished, the crowd dispersed. Ekalon hurried to catch up with her as she started away.

"Master Methuselah could be judgmental. A hard man, where his faith was concerned."

She stopped and glared at him. "Who are you?"

"I met old Methuselah a few times. We had some heated debates. When I heard he'd passed on, well, I just wanted to see him off, with the rest of his family and friends."

She turned and started along the road.

He fell in stride beside her. "He obviously angered you some-how. Can I help?"

"Methuselah was a good one for spewing prophesies," she growled.

"Aye, that he was."

"As if he could know the future." She scuffed her heel as she strode onward.

"There are ways to know the future. Unfortunately, I think Methuselah, regardless of how fondly I recall our talks, became confused in his old age."

"You can say that again."

He smiled, enjoying the unfamiliar feel of it, recalling a time in his existence when smiling had been as natural as praising. "What did he say to make you so angry?"

Her hot eyes lurched toward him. "Only that all my children were going to become servants to their cousins. That we will have a wayward family which will abandon the truth and go our own ways."

He laughed. "The very argument Methuselah and I once had. Humph! As if knowledge of the Creator must seal one's fate. We have choice—we must!" He lowered his voice and glanced furtively around. "You know, there is so much knowledge in this world."

Her footsteps slammed to a halt and she stared him. "If you mean the Oracle's knowledge, I'm not interested."

"I understand. But what I'm talking about is the simple truth that you can circumvent Methuselah's prophesy." He bit his lip and glanced at the book.

She considered him, a crack opening in her resolve. Another human would not have noticed it, but he did. Humans were the most transparent of creatures.

"I'm not interested in more knowledge." Her tone said otherwise.

He shrugged. "Very well. It was nice talking with you, Mistress Majiah." He bowed and turned away.

"How do you know my name?" she demanded.

He paused, his eyes widening. "I must have heard it spoken at the funeral. Your husband, perhaps? I wish you well with your future." He smirked. "If what Noah says is true, you might be one of the few with a future. But you'll understand it if I hope Master Methuselah's prophesies are a mistake." He turned his back and walked away.

"Wait."

A small smile touched his lips. He quickly replaced it with a flat expression as he rotated back. "Yes?"

Now it was her turn to glance warily about, her view finally settling upon the thick black book. "If there was a way to change the prophesy"—her tongue flicked across her lips—"how might one go about doing it?"

"How? Money, and the power it can buy you and your heirs, that's how."

"Naturally." Impatience crackled in her voice. "But what good is any of that in a world populated only by our family?"

"How long will it be before your numbers increase? A hundred years? Five hundred years? A mere half a lifetime. You'd still be young enough to enjoy it. And if your family becomes rulers of the world, then what of that niggling prophesy?"

"And ... and the means to accomplish it is in that book?"

"All the real wisdom of the world ... and the reading is light, I assure you."

A scowl darkened her face. "And just how much is all this wonderful information going to cost me?"

"Cost?" He looked hurt. "It costs nothing." He placed the book into her hands, but held onto it. "All I ask is one thing."

She released it. "I knew there was a hook."

"Hook? Perhaps. But it is a very small hook. Merely this. You place it among your things. You hide it from the others and share the wisdom only with your grandchildren."

"Grandchildren?"

"Children will be too close to Noah's watchful eyes. You wouldn't want him learning of these secrets, would you?" He pressed the book toward her.

She peered at it, her lips twisting into a knot. "My grandchildren?"

He nodded.

She considered a moment longer, but he saw her mind was already made up. She grabbed the book from him and rotated it, looking the cover over carefully.

He pointed toward a narrow glimpse of the ark in the distance. "Now, before the others return to it. Go place it among your things. Bury it deep. Keep it for your eyes only until men once again begin to fill the earth. Then, the power will be yours. Your children will be slaves to no one, and masters of all!"

Majiah stared at him, at the book, and seemed about to speak. Then she clung it close to her chest and hurried off without a word.

Ekalon laughed. The exhilaration of mirth filled him with long-forgotten satisfaction. Stepping in among a copse of trees, the air rippled and opened up for him, and he stepped once again into the presence of his master.

❧

Days after the funeral, Naamah stood among the rows of potted plants outside her kitchen door, staring up into a morning sky, hugging her arms. Noah studied his wife a moment from the kitchen door, sensing her uneasiness.

"I had a dream last night," he whispered.

She turned and looked worriedly at him.

He gave a faint smile. "Now I know how my mother must have felt when she got them."

"What happened?"

Only the end of everything. He raised his eyes to the sky. "Rahab was destroyed."

"Mishah's dream?"

He nodded. "Very much as she described it. Grandfather's homegoing was the sign. Enoch foretold it long ago. My father after him. And the Gardener."

"We need to gather the children home."

He nodded, his stomach knotting with worry. "If they will come."

"I'll send word to the girls at once."

They turned at the sound of a cyclart stopping in front of the house. Going through the house to the front door, he caught a glimpse out the window of the gleaming cyclart and knew at once who had arrived. Pulling open the door, Lady Leenah greeted them without a smile. Her driver had remained in the cyclart. This was to be a brief visit.

"Morning peace," she said with little enthusiasm. She had lost much of her vitality since Rhone's homegoing.

"Morning peace ... morning peace." They bowed and Naamah said, "Honor our house, Lady Leenah."

Noah noted the heavy bundle she carried as she solemnly passed through. They sat in the greeting room. Lady Leenah declined the honor seat. She had always been more comfortable on the long sofa with Naamah.

They'd not seen as much of the High Counciloress since Rhone's death. There was so much for her to attend to now, in his absence. Pyir Chrone had taken over the head of the Council of Ten, and Thore was often away, his services required at the Rim-wall breech where the Oracle's forces maintained a constant threat. The uplifted Atlan Ridge had become a deadly battleground, and how much longer the Makir could repel the Neph armies was anyone's guess. Fortunately, the Lodath had pressed his surviving jumpers into service transporting Nephs to Oric, and had not sent them against Atlan as some had feared would happen.

"What brings you out?" he asked.

She glanced at the bundle on her lap, then at him. "I wish to give you something to take on the ark to preserve when," she hesitated, "when the prophecy comes to pass and the Creator's wrath is poured out." Leenah looked at Naamah, then back. "The battle is not going well at the breech." Her view flicked between him and Naamah, then to the bundle.

He leaned forward. "Certainly we will take it, Lady Leenah. What is it?"

She removed the cloth covering from a milky-white chalsoma box and set it upon the low table at her knees.

Naamah bent forward as Lady Leenah unlatched the lid and lifted it away. "A collection of mementos. Some are frivolous. Others may be of some use after the flood." She lifted out a melon-shaped black stone object.

He'd seen others like it, but none this ornate. "A puzzle box?"

"Yes. This is how it opens." She turned the three bands of gold in sequence, pressed upon the top of the "melon," and the lid popped up with a snap. "It's filled with keelit seeds."

"Always eat your keelits." He smiled. How many times had he heard that? Thore jokingly recited the admonition each time he bit into one of the fruits.

"Ela said the keelit is second cousin to the Tree of Life." She smiled with the memory.

Noah recalled how the little Kleiman had helped Lady Leenah when she first arrived on Atlan—alone, defenseless, and recovering from the effects of mansnatcher's poison. He had heard the story many times. "We'll keep it in mind," he said. "We've some keelit trees potted outside the kitchen."

"These will be in case you lose those." She sealed the puzzle box and lifted out a thick manuscript.

"What is it?" The book reminded him of Aunt Cerah's Book, which he had hidden safely away.

"I call it *Cradleland Chronicles*. It's the story of your birth, Noah—your life, and mine, and Rhone's."

"You wrote it all down?" He took the manuscript from her and rested it upon his knees, running a finger over the tooled leather cover.

"I thought it too important to let slip from the memory of man."

He opened the cover and studied the neatly formed letters, recognizing her hand in them. "I will take care of it, Lady Leenah." It choked him that she had thought enough of his life to have joined it with hers in such a manner. "It must have taken you a long time to write."

"I've worked on it on and off most of my life."

He set it upon the table next to the black stone melon.

"And the rest, well, they're frivolous mementos." She smirked. "But it would please me to know they are preserved." She lifted out the smooth yellow stone. "The piece of moonglass

Ela's husband gave me. I scratched a message on it to Rhone. You can't see it now, but once, when moonglass shone …" Her words trailed off in a breath of nostalgia. "And this …" She peered at a dagger with a claw handle. "Rhone took it off one of the Lodath's green-cloaks as we fled Nod City. It was the first gift he ever gave to me." She peered at the knife, a sheen in her blue eyes, then quickly replaced all the items in the chalsoma box, snapped the golden clasps, and slipped it back into the cloth sack.

"I will take care of these for you," he said, accepting the gift.

She couldn't stay. The affairs of state—and the war—required her immediate return to Hodin's Keep.

As they hugged at the door, Noah couldn't shed the cold dread that they were parting for the last time. He and Naamah stood at their front door watching the cyclart drive away. He heard her muffled sobs behind, and when he turned, she threw her arms about his neck and wept against his shoulder.

38

Death of Rahab

*T*hore strode along the front lines, First Statre Kelir at his side, the sea wind cutting through his cloak with icy blades. At the stone battlement that stretched across the black gash in the Rim-wall, he paused and stared out over the bleak, windswept landscape. All was quiet ... too quiet.

"I don't like this." Even the animals that had once trodden paths across the rocky bridgeway had disappeared.

Kelir nodded morosely. "It bodes no good, Captain. There's no reason for the Nephs to pull back." His deep-set eyes surveyed the misty distance. "They are planning a new strategy."

"Send out a kal-ee-hon to reconnoiter."

Kelir nodded. "We should be strengthening our forward lines as well."

He did his best with what he had. The years of fending off Neph attacks had cut deep into their numbers. To worsen matters, it was no secret that Master Methuselah had died, and every Makir there knew the predictions. Morale was at an all-time low, for even Makir were not immune to such a dire forecast. It seemed hollow now to fight a meaningless war and die upon the harsh shores of Atlan's Rim-wall when time had all but run out for them. Was it better to die here, or with wives and children?

Maybe the Oracle understood that too. Had he withdrawn his Nephs to protect them? Thore glanced skyward again. *Are you all on your way to Oric even now?*

He should be more closely watching Noah. But if the Nephs were to burst their lines here, how could he protect Noah there? He was pulled two ways.

A low-flying flop of dragons cut across the sky. He watched them disappear beyond the Rim-wall.

How much longer?

Thore bundled his cloak tight in a fist and bent his head to the gusts as he and Kelir returned to the sputtering campfires along the Rim-wall.

❦

As the sun's small orb sank toward the horizon, dipping slowly below the row of three small pyramids, Bar'ack shrugged into his coat and left his living quarters, heading toward the main hall. Even when it was warm on Oric, it wasn't warm. But at least it wasn't bitter cold either, like it was during the long, dark Bleak Season.

He trudged across the red ground, the long, evening shadows broken here and there by patches of green lichen and a low, tough grass. After so many years, his lungs still struggled for each breath. If it wasn't that his weight was so much less here than on Earth, he might not move at all.

And this was a promotion?

He'd quit counting the years he'd been stranded here with mostly Nephs for company … and the three spirits that inhabited his body, voices inside his head that never stopped.

What would life be like once he returned to Earth? He'd likely be flat on his back for months, slowly rebuilding his strength simply to walk in Earth's increased gravity.

Since his arrival here on Oric, the grass that sprang to life each year in the lee of cliffs and ridges had begun to take tenuous root alongside the barracks now housing more than a hundred thousand Nephs. It flourished next to the greenhouses that supplied their food, and grew particularly robust in the warmth of the pumping stations that sucked up warm underground water from far below the barren crust.

He'd done wonders turning this desolate stone into a sanctuary for the Oracle's children who had begun to arrive in droves. And with what thanks? He was still here! And "here" was becoming increasingly burdensome every day!

He cast a scowl at the Oracle's Image, prominent in the center of the complex, its stony eyes forever staring up at the heavens—at Rahab, closer at this point in Oric's rotation than at most other times. His view darted back to Rahab. Its milky white glow had changed to an angry reddish-purple tint, as though a vast bruise was rapidly spreading across its surface. His feet slammed to a halt. When had this happened?

Rahab, swollen like an overripe orofin, expanded before his eyes like a gas bubble being heated from within.

He wasn't the only one to notice the phenomenon. All around the complex, Nephs had stopped to stare. A short distance away where the Oracle's jumpers sat in a long line, Nephs stood upon their metal skins, pointing. A chill shook him at the sight, and the voices inside his head had momentarily gone silent.

He shook it off and continued across the grounds toward the main hall. Throughout the evening, as he went about the business of tending to the Nephs' needs, he kept one eye on Rahab.

During the night, the distant heavenly stone grew to twice its size, shooting streamers of red gas. Rahab seemed to be burning itself up. An uneasiness energized the sanctuary the next day. The eerie glow in the sky had brightened so that it was still visible at midday.

That night, while Bar'ack brooded over his lot in life, deadening the voices inside his head with his third flagon of ale, a Neph burst into the big common room, urging everyone to come see what was happening. Bar'ack followed the crowd outside and found the night was nearly as bright as the day. Rahab's immense glare filled the night, expanding at a ferocious speed.

"It's coming apart!" one of the Nephs declared.

Some hurried for the observation tower and trained the large starglass upon the spectacle.

The sight riveted their attention, and for the next hour they stared heavenward at the expanding reddish-orange aura that appeared as if it might even envelop Oric.

A Neph scrambled down from the observation tower. "It's coming!" he cried, huffing in the thin air.

"What's coming?" Bar'ack demanded.

The Neph turned and pointed. "The stone! Pieces of it flying everywhere. Some this way!"

His words started a panic, and Nephs fled for cover.

Fools! If that stone should strike Oric, no hole will be deep enough to protect you. Bar'ack stood a moment, mesmerized by the fireball in the sky, noting how its light flashed off of myriad tiny objects—tiny at this distance, but if he could see them, they must be huge.

"It's going to slam Oric!" someone declared.

The words propelled the Sanctuary into greater frenzy; Nephs fled the surface buildings and dived for the old tunnels.

Bar'ack spun on his heels and raced toward the line of jumpers, his lungs screaming with pain after the first few strides. He forced himself ahead. A hundred or more Nephs had the same idea.

His lungs burned in the thin air as he slapped the metal plate and waited for the hatch to open. Inside, lights brightened as he staggered up the metal steps. Where was the sorp to pilot the jumper? Leaping behind the controls, his fingers raced across the touch-pads while behind him came the thuds and grunts of Nephs piling inside.

The air hummed as the magnetic jump drive charged up. His fingers skimmed the pads, shutting the hatch. The view screen brightened, the metal wall behind it fading to a faint transparency. Beyond, some Nephs scattered to other jumpers—some just scattered for the burnt umber cliffs. *As if caves can hide you from this wrath!*

The voices inside his head were silent, as if they understood his need to concentrate. Bar'ack pressed a hand to the controls and focused his thoughts. The jumper lurched skyward. Beyond the clear view panel, the barren red stone dropped away. He looked behind him. The panel moved with his glance. His jumper was only one of many streaking away from Oric's doomed surface.

He just cleared the thin atmosphere when the first of Rahab's stones struck Oric on the far side. The world trembled beneath the jumper and a black plume mushroomed slowly skyward. Fear tightened a fist around his chest. Bar'ack veered toward deep space. The view panel snapped to a greater magnification, showing Rahab's pieces streaking over Oric's horizon, scouring the surface as they cratered it. Roiling dust obscured the details, but he had the clear impression—Oric's meager atmosphere had been swept away, along with the Oracle's compound, and how many thousands of his children?

His heart rattled in the bone cage of his chest as his fingers danced over the controls and the mag drive wound up, approaching jump velocity. Sweat stung his eyes, and he glanced back at the panel.

Oric's shallow seas boiled away, vaporized in an instant. Swept out into space, they froze at once into tumbling chunks of ice.

A lump caught in his throat at the sight of Oric's annihilation, at the instant death of every living creature upon it. A part of his brain registered grief; it crept down into his heart. With no voices now to fill his head, his brain began to clear. Desperate to hold onto the lucid thoughts that now filled it, his attention wavered between concentrating on flying the jumper and the freedom to think his own thoughts once again.

An image took shape within his unshackled mind, and he gave a startled blink, thinking it was real. *Rhone!* He saw his old mentor was on his knees, heard Rhone's words of bitter pleading—yet could not make out what he said.

The vision wavered, but those cryptic words somehow had knifed deep into his heart. His eyes blurred as events flashed across the screen of his brain—the Oracle whom he served, the sacrifice being led to the Temple slaughter ... his mother and father. Tears stung where an instant before hot sweat had burned. He had been a party to all of it, but why did it hurt now? Because he was finally free to feel again? Free to remember?

For the moment he was free of Per, Hepha, and Pose, and his thoughts were his own! And in that moment he knew he was guilty of a life devoted to the Deceiver! And it was too late to change that!

Then a revelation kicked a gasp to his throat. In their desire to back out of his thoughts, to give him an advantage in this escape, the invading spirits had miscalculated.

The pledge pendant about his neck burned against his chest. He had to think fast. In a little while, the voices would return.

Rhone's words drifted back, and although he couldn't decipher them, one word came clear to the groping ear of his brain.

Creator.

He'd forgotten the Creator!

He glanced at the view panel, shock turning to horror, eyes stretched wide. His heart hammered. Chunks of Rahab tumbled closer, filling the view panel. Already some of the jumpers had been enveloped. Desultory, bright flashes marked the demise of one jumper after another as mountain-size rocks overtook the retreating fleet. From behind him came the moaning fear of his

Neph passengers. Any moment, the voices would reinvade his mind, but he was certain they'd wait until he'd made the jump.

His thoughts ran in confused circles, the rising whine of the jump drive warning that a jump was only moments away. They had outrun the oncoming missiles, and to escape was to live, but to live dominated by powerful spirits and no will of his own was worse than death.

Rhone's words filled his head, stronger this time. He wasn't imagining it. This was real. This was intervention!

"Creator, forgive me!" He grabbed the thong of his pledge pendant and ripped it off, flinging it across the small control room.

His body shuddered, his brain exploded with fire as the voices came alive within him. But they couldn't take hold this time. Something stronger had entered him at that instant, something that crushed the invading spirits in a hand more mighty than the Oracle's hold on him ever had been.

The drive reached jump velocity. Bar'ack swept a hand over the control pads and bypassed it. The whining pitch fell, and the speed drained off the instruments.

In the view panel, mountains of ice and rock swept past. In the space of three heartbeats he imagined himself inside a barrel being pummeled by stones. The jumper shuddered hard, reeled end over end, and the terrifying hiss of a hull breach screamed in his ears as the air pressure plummeted.

The last thing Bar'ack remembered this side of eternity was the icy vacuum of space sucking him from the jumper … and the next was the Creator's open arms: a golden light shining all around.

In the midst of a love he'd never known, Master Rhone's smile greeted him.

❧

He couldn't sleep. Sitting up in bed, in the dark, he kept a wary eye bent toward the window, but carefully avoided looking at the moon. The distant lights of his neighbors seemed buried in the haze of the gathering morning mist that arose over the night to water the land.

He swung his legs over the edge of the bed and rose, shrugging into a robe as he went out into the dark gathering room. Vaul slunk alongside him, his ears flattened, his tail low.

"You feel it too, don't you?"

The canic peered up at him with eyes that seemed to understand.

Alone, he sat in Grandfather's chair and stared into the darkness. Faces came back to him. Rhone, gone now for five years. And Uncle Kenoch and Aunt Cerah. He thought of his father; how Lamech's zeal had burned to do the Creator's bidding. How his mother had slowly faded after his death until the stalking enemy known as Death had snatched her away too—a blessing mixed with bitter sorrow. As he thought of Sheflah, a sob wrenched inside his chest and his eyes stung. All gone now ... at rest in Adam's Bosom. Why had he been spared? It would have been so much kinder simply to fade and pass as his mother had. Together with the Creator in Glory had to be better than remaining in this world, facing what he knew must come.

Pher'el's grip tightened upon the ivory battle staff as the dark stalkers pressed nearer. He cast a glance at Jas'el, heartened that the ophannin was near to help should the Watchers and Seekers rush Noah now that his defenses were down, his faith wavering. Pher'el tried to shrug off the weight from his charge's lethargy.

"Faith, Noah, faith."

A Seeker cast a dart of doubt.

Pher'el failed to intercept it before it stuck Noah's already wounded heart.

Jas'el stirred at his side, ready to leap to the battle should he need him, but so far, he'd been able to keep the nasty Seekers at bay while Watchers advanced, their ebony battle staffs lowering menacingly.

"Don't know how much longer I can keep them from him," the Guardian said, his staff leaping to intercept another barb of doubt aimed at Noah.

"Say the word, Pher'el, and we'll send these devils to the Pit ahead of schedule."

A growl rumbled in the dark Watchers' throats.

"Stay out of this, ophannin. You belong to the other realm. Let the Guardian do his job ... if he can," Bir'or snarled.

Pher'el followed Slieor from the corner of his eye as Tormor moved in the other direction. There was a flash. Pher'el's battle staff lurched, blazing golden light, neutralizing Slieor's bolt and vaporizing the Watcher to gray ash.

The other charged.

Jas'el sprang into the realm, his battle staff blazing, energy bolts flaring all around Noah. Pher'el normally would have easily kept these dark tormentors at bay if Noah's wavering faith hadn't sapped him. But an ophannin was not so affected, being nearer to a cherub than a Messenger-warrior. Jas'el's staff filled the realm with blinding power and drove the Watcher back from Noah, sending the small Seekers tumbling toward the Pit from which they had crawled.

The smoke of the brief battle cleared and the Watchers regrouped. Pher'el glanced at Jas'el and grinned. "I could have handled that."

Jas'el gave a tight laugh. "Next time I'll wait to see the outcome."

Pher'el sobered. "Next time, don't wait so long."

The two looked up as a golden light appeared above, filling the heavens. The Watchers immediately shielded their eyes and scrambled for cover. Pher'el's breath caught, and he and Jas'el went to their knees as the Creator stood before them.

"Master," they breathed, their heads bowed low.

"Stand, My children."

Obediently, they rose to their feet. Pher'el noted that every dark and vile creature had fled and it was just them and the Creator, and Noah in the chair, staring sadly into the night.

The Creator's countenance was a blaze of gold and emerald light, His smile reassuring, filling Pher'el with a peace that removed the memory of the skirmish just past to a place far from the moment.

"Well done."

"It was difficult," Pher'el said.

The Creator nodded. "His faith ebbs but for a little while, as is common with every man."

"He grieves for his family and friends," Jas'el said.

"Noah carries a heavy burden." A tear came to the Creator's eye. "And now he must bear the heaviest burden of all."

Pher'el drew in a breath and glanced at Jas'el. "The time has come?"

The Creator touched Noah's shoulder. The human appeared to rally, scrubbing the tears from his eyes.

"It has begun. Rahab is no more."

They understood.

"Now, more than ever, he needs you two close," the Creator said.

Jas'el bowed again. "I understand. I will return now."

"Yes."

Jas'el bent low and slipped back into the realm of humans.

The Creator looked at Pher'el. "His faith will strengthen now, but his heart will be broken for a long time. Watch over him well, as you have."

"Yes, Master. I will protect him."

❧

With a ragged breath, Noah somehow managed to shrug off his grief. It surprised him how he was able to deal with the loss, whereas a few moments before he had wanted to curl up and die.

"I'm just tired," he said, rising from Grandfather's chair. "I need to get to sleep."

Vaul rose and they returned to the bedroom. As Noah sat upon the bed, he couldn't help feeling the time had come. Laying his head upon the pillow, somehow he knew—he just knew come morning, the multitude of animals milling about the ark would be more tractable. But was it still too early? Strange how a few minutes alone in Grandfather's chair had improved his mood. He watched the canic circle and settle in his place upon the floor. "Maybe it's Grandfather's spirit?"

Vaul lifted an eyebrow toward him.

Naamah turned on her pillow and groaned softly. "What?"

He looked at her and smiled. "Nothing, my love. Go back to sleep."

Lucifer raged to and fro across the stormy heavens as the air all around him filled with the suddenly disembodied spirits of Nephs and nephlings. The wispy, pathetic figures gathered, mournfully lamenting the loss of their bodies, confused, not understanding the emptiness, the insatiable longing for a tent of flesh to surround them.

To wander and never find rest was a curse placed by the Tyrant of Old upon the spirits of all Earth-Born.

In fierce wrath his voice thundered to heaven. "You've killed them—killed them and left them homeless!" Riding just below the anger was something akin to grief, but it paled compared to his outrage at the Tyrant's bold move. All his planning and scheming thwarted in a single event. It was clear the Tyrant had been planning this from the beginning.

He knew! Somehow He knew it all!

Striking back was his one burning desire now. But how?

Furious red and orange light flared off his arms and thighs as he coursed the roiling sky. His servants kept well back in trembling fear. Their timidity stirred his wrath to soaring levels.

"A body, a body," the spirits pleaded. "Don't leave us naked."

Strike back. Hurt the Tyrant as He hurt me!

Lucifer wheeled, scanning the faces of his servants. From every corner of his kingdom they had come, drawn by the shaking of the realm.

"Ekalon!"

From among the myriad warriors, the Malik who had become his adviser drifted tentatively forward, his fists clutching the dark battle staff. He bowed briefly, eyes wide with fear.

"How did this happen?"

"The Tyrant, Master. He circumvented us. He waited until you had safely removed your children to Oric before striking. A cowardly attack, it was."

Fire shot heavenward from Lucifer's clenched fist. "You will pay for this!" His fiery eyes glared at Ekalon like flaming knives. "How many of my children live?"

"None on Oric. But there are still legions left on this stone," Ekalon said quickly. "And those who are en route to Oric."

"And jumpers?"

"Several returning from Oric. A few in Nod City. A fist on their way to Oric."

"Recall them now! I will throw the full power of my anger on the pitiful humans still loyal to the Tyrant. I will personally crush them."

Ekalon's slight tremble betrayed his fear. "But the Tyrant forbids your intervention. This could doom us all."

"You dare defy me?"

"No." Ekalon scrambled back from him. "It's just that—"

With a wave of Lucifer's hand, Ekalon exploded into a burst of white energy, and he was no more. The others watching retreated as a hush filled the heavens, save for the reverberating echoes of Ekalon's scream.

"Abaddon!" Lucifer summoned, his furious voice banishing the last remnant of the despairing cry.

Far below them, the Pit opened, filling the air with sulfurous fumes. The Prince of the Pit appeared before him.

"Master?" Abaddon's low voice rumbled.

"Recall the jumpers. Once they have returned, send them upon Atlan. I want Noah and his family dead, and that ark destroyed. When you have succeeded, you may have your way with what remains of Ekalon. Now go quickly. We haven't a moment to lose!"

"Yes, Master." With a bow and remote grin he vanished.

Lucifer glared at the disembodied spirits spread out to the horizons, their keening filling the heavens. "Bodies are what you want and bodies are what you shall have. The humans upon this miserable stone belong to me and I am giving them to you. Fill them with your strength, and bend every foot toward Atlan. Leave no one not bearing a pledge pendant alive. Particularly Noah and his family. They must all be destroyed!"

He again lifted a defiant face to heaven. "You've destroyed my Temple and my children. Expect no less from me!"

In whirling vapors like black smoke, the disembodied spirits streaked toward Earth. Every human wearing a pledge pendant was an open door to them, and in a moment of time an army of invading spirits had taken up residence in new bodies ... and the march on Atlan began.

39

Countdown to Wrath

Noah was jarred awake by the pounding at his door. Naamah sat up beside him, startled. Barely dawn, the gray light gave the feel of it still being night. The pounding came again, sounding as though someone was trying to batter the door open. Vaul growled and flattened his ears. Noah got out of bed and made his way through the empty house. Past Grandfather's chair, through the window, he saw a crowd had filled his front yard.

His hand hesitated at the latch. The door's heavy panels rattled again from angry blows. He opened it.

The faces of neighbors, and people he didn't know, glared at him. Hodinites, everyone, their height adding to his intimidation.

"What's happening, Noah?" Grf'ik, his neighbor from down the road, demanded. The crowd surged through the door and filled his gathering room.

Vaul barked and his long, bared fangs brought them to a wary halt.

Noah shook his head, dumbfounded. "What are you talking about, Grf'ik?"

"I'm talking about these animals everywhere. What in Dirgen's name have you brought on us?"

"Me?"

"You!" Grf'ik growled, and the crowd rumbled their agreement. "It's because of you and that thing you're building! You've angered the gods. The Oracle sends an army to attack us and Dirgen sends a plague of creatures to trample and devour our crops."

Dirgen ... the Oracle? Rhone had managed to keep Atlan turned toward the Creator while he ruled. Gone now only five years, and already the people had turned to the ways of the world.

"I've done nothing! Go back to your homes. Turn your hearts back to the Creator, and maybe He will take away the animals."

"The Creator!" Grf'ik shook a finger at him. "It's this very talk that has caused the problem."

"It's your unbelief that brings on wrath, Grf'ik!"

The mob lunged forward. Vaul leaped and drove Grf'ik to the floor, paws on his chest, his long fighting fangs glinting from the curled-back lips. Grf'ik went rigid.

Naamah rushed into the welcoming room, anger in her eyes. "Get out of my house, all of you!"

"Call your canic off," Grf'ik pleaded as deadly fangs hovered near his throat.

"Out of my house!" she shouted again.

They were angry and confused, but they weren't ready for real violence. At least not yet, Noah told himself.

"Vaul," he said softly. The canic backed off, his fur bristling, his stance a warning to them.

Grf'ik picked himself up from the floor and wiped the saliva from his neck. "I'm telling you, Noah. It's that boat that's got the gods angry. Burn it down before war and this plague destroys Atlan!"

"You heard my wife." His narrow view moved across the men who'd come through the door. "Get out of our home."

With a low, rumbling growl, Vaul advanced. The men scrambled backed out the door. Once gone, Noah closed and locked it.

The anger in Naamah's eyes turned to tears. He wrapped her in his arms and held her.

"Some of them are our friends," she said in between gasps and sobs. "What's happened to them?"

"They're frightened. They don't understand. They've been warned for the last hundred and twenty years, but only now, when the world changes before their eyes, do they take notice."

"I'm frightened too, and I do understand."

He stroked her trembling back. "So am I."

Vaul remained staring at the door. Beyond the window, the angry neighbors broke up into groups and dispersed. Time was drawing to an end. The wearisome war ... the swarms of animals ... how much longer? He held Naamah at arm's length and looked into her green eyes—and thought of Aunt Cerah again.

"I think we should move into the ark. It's more secure than this house. The Creator won't let anything happen to it."

She sniffed and wiped her eyes. "Yes. There is so much to move. We should begin."

Later that morning he hitched a large wagon to one of his three-points and hauled a load of furniture to the ark. The loading ramp creaked beneath the weight as the lumbering beasts hauled it up and through the door. Naamah carried the Book Aunt Cerah had entrusted to him.

The animals, as always, merely stepped aside for them. They didn't seem any less tractable today as they did the day before.

Noah locked the Book in a chest in his and Naamah's quarters, then they all unloaded the furniture into various compartments and began stowing the items they'd need later down in the lower hold, toward the rear of the immense vessel.

He hadn't seen Wend for days, and he was disheartened to see that his and Sebe's compartment was empty.

"I need to talk to Wend," he told Naamah as they returned to the house for another load.

"I sent word to him when I wrote to the girls. He never replied."

Noah shook his head, worry-knots twisting inside him.

The rest of that day they moved the transplanted grapevines and more than three hundred potted plants that Naamah had been amassing into the cart. They brought them to the ark and set them into the bedding trough up high by the long row of windows along the ark's roof.

That evening he got word that a starglass upon the Rim-wall had reported something strange happening far out in the heavens. An expanding cloud of gas had been observed where the Rahab ought to have been. The news raced around Atlan as reports of mountain-size hunks of the exploded planet hurled outward—some toward Earth.

"Seven or eight days, Master Noah," Keli told him the next evening, stopping at the house on his way home to the Kleiman village of Deepvale after spending the day in Atla Fair delivering a load of Kleiman cloth.

Noah recalled his mother's dreams. Rahab had been shattered, but the Creator's hand had held the pieces together all these years. Now, it seemed, He had let go.

He saw the fear in the little man's face as Keli sat in their welcoming room, holding a cup of tea halfway between the saucer and his lips.

"What can it mean?" the Kleiman asked.

"It means it is time for you to go home to your family, Keli."

"But what can be done?"

"Trust the Creator. There is little else man can do, is there? If these flying mountains strike this stone we live upon, nothing you or I do will make a difference."

Keli gulped down the last of his tea.

"Fair journey," Noah said at the door.

"You, too, Master Noah." Keli slid into his cyclart and drove quickly away.

That night they ate their last dinner in the home he'd known for almost four hundred years. Shem, Japheth, and Ham, and their wives shared it with them, and the mood was somber. Noah served the last of the wine from the vineyard and wished fervently that Wend had accepted the invitation to join them. But he had remained away. Likely worried about his grapes. He sighed as the last few drops filled his cup.

After the boys had returned to their own homes, he and Naamah sat alone in the empty house, a small fire in the old cooking fireplace casting a bit of heat into the large welcoming room. The flickering flames threw shadows against the bare walls and reflected off the dark glass.

"What will it be like?" she said softly, cuddled against him on the sofa, one of the few pieces of furniture left in the old place. "After it's all over, I mean?"

He shrugged. "Much as it was before, I suspect." He had tried to imagine something different, but couldn't envision anything but what he had known. "I'm sure. The Creator will give us a world fit to live in."

She went silent a moment. "I don't think it will be the same, Noah."

"How will it differ?"

"I don't know. But something inside me says life will be harder."

"Undoubtedly. For a while. No ready-made steel from the Tubal-Cain Company. No barrels of refined 'gia from the veralogia farms. No paper from the mills, or cloth from Kleiman looms. No artisans or boatbuilders, no cyclarts—except for what we bring. And once they break down, well, who will repair them?"

"Once the casks of 'gia run out, what will it matter anyway?"

He nodded. "No wing-sailer. No healers but you and Desmorah. We'll have to rebuild from the beginning, but at least we will have books to show us how, and our memories. We will make it all happen again."

"Noah," she said softly after a long pause.

"Hum?"

"What if it doesn't happen? What if we wake up tomorrow and the animals have all gone away? What if the stones pass us by like some say they will? What if the judgment never comes?"

He gave a short laugh. "Then we unload our furniture and bring it all back here."

She grinned. "What would the neighbors say?"

"What they've been saying all along. 'That old Noah is a crazy fool. Look how he's spent his life—and the family's fortunes.'"

"Let them say what they want." She became quiet, introspective.

A small gleam of light beyond the window caught his eye. It seemed very far away ... perhaps a bit of reflected firelight.

"Noah?"

"Hum?"

She hesitated. "I don't think the girls are coming home."

His heart cramped. "I don't think so either." Tears burned and his throat tightened. "But maybe they will." He could hardly get the words out.

She sobbed quietly against his chest.

The light in the window grew brighter. Vaul sat up and stared. "What is this?"

Naamah straightened and brushed at her eyes. "What?"

He pointed.

She drew in a breath. "I don't know."

Suddenly Vaul stretched long upon the floor. And then Noah knew.

"The Gardener."

Naamah stared at Him. "Can it be?"

The room filled with a golden light as a blaze of gold split the darkness. Two mighty cherubs stepped from the glare, and as the cherubim positioned themselves on either side of the widening portal, the image of the Gardener became clear.

Noah and Naamah went to their knees and covered their heads as the Gardener stepped into the room.

"Noah, my son."

"Here I am."

The Gardener touched both of them. Noah slowly lifted his head, his spirit instantly unburdened of its fears and worry. Naamah's face wore a smile the likes of which he hadn't seen for years.

The Gardener helped them to their feet. "Noah, the wait is over. It is time for you and your sons to come into the ark."

"We've already begun, Master." The peace in his spirit was as he remembered it as a child in the Gardener's Garden—the Cradleland. Naamah seemed in shock, and he reminded himself this was the first time she'd ever seen the Gardener. Although he'd told her over and over about Him, the experience could be quite overwhelming.

"Tomorrow I will send the animals to you. Of the clean animals, take seven, and of all the rest, take but a single pair—male and female. Take of the beasts of the field and the earth, and from the birds of the air."

"I'll start immediately!"

He smiled. "Tomorrow. You have seven days left, and that will be time enough."

"Seven days?" There was so much left to do. He had to get word to his children!

"In seven days I will break up the fountains of the deep and bring water to fall upon the earth for forty days." His face became stern. "Everywhere I look I see the wickedness of man. His sins multiply and grow continually, and every thought in his head and heart is evil. Every living thing that I have made, I will destroy off the face of the earth. Bring your family and My creatures into the ark, so that I may seal the door behind you."

Noah trembled at the thought of the coming destruction. It was too much to comprehend.

"In the ark, you and your family will be safe."

"But my heart aches for my friends and children," he said softly, his jumbled emotions catching in his throat.

"Fear not, Noah." The Gardener's gentle smile seemed to say He understood the turmoil inside him.

But the ache remained.

Silently, the Gardener stepped back into the portal and faded from sight. A moment later the cherubim followed Him, and the light collapsed back on itself and faded from his welcoming room, leaving a persistent, lingering, sweet scent.

Naamah sat stunned for a long time afterward, while he held her, wondering what the morning would bring.

※

Japheth, Shem, and Ham were busy loading their personal belongings aboard the ark when Noah arrived the next morning and told them of the vision.

"Then it's all true!" Ham said it as if up until now the building of the ark had only been a huge, expensive game—an exercise in faith, and a pleasant way to avoid the real chores of an adult life. And maybe it had been no more than that to the boys. Noah wondered if Wend hadn't been the levelheaded one after all—even if his devotion to the vineyard and making a success of it had been misplaced.

Afterward, the boys redoubled their pace, and the furniture and crates of belongings fairly flew up the ramp. The women pitched in with renewed energy too, while Noah strode up and down the long aisles making a final inspection of all the pens and cages, the watering and the waste-removal systems.

A vitality seemed to fill the milling herds of animals that pressed around the ark. Over the last couple weeks their numbers had swelled and the land around the vineyard had been practically stripped of vegetation. People at a loss as to how to drive them away had begun killing them, but more arrived continually from the forests along the Rim-wall. The Kleiman villages had been particularly hard hit by the migrations across the Atlan Ridge, in spite of the battles being waged there between the Oracle's forces and Atlan's Makir Guard.

Up until that day, the animals had remained shy of the ark's long loading ramp, but now, unexpectedly, smaller ones began venturing up it. Noah shooed six cottontails out of the ark, then set a chair on the landing outside the door and took up his post to monitor and record their coming. Sometimes four or five would show up at once and try to sneak past him. He permitted only two, as the Gardener had instructed.

A lioness strode up with two kittens, but before entering, the kittens turned on their mother and drove her back. A pair of behemoth youngsters, not much larger than a full-grown hippopotamus, lumbered docilely into their pens while two small, rapacious kinids raced along the long deck, confused and startled by Japheth's waving arms. Birds swooped in uncounted, in spite of Noah's efforts to keep some order to the arrivals. They roosted in the branches of potted keelit trees and high up along the planting troughs beneath the long overhead windows.

For the next few days, as animals crossed the threshold, the boys and their wives led them to properly sized cages or pens. The beasts remaining outside the ark grew restive. Villagers began arriving too, watching. Noah sensed their nervousness, and that made him nervous. Word of space rocks racing toward Earth had set all of Atlan on edge.

One day a contingent of farmers stomped up the ramp demanding he make sacrifices to Dirgen. Again they accused him, the ark, and talk of the Creator, of displeasing the sea god. These animals were a plague sent to punish them for permitting it!

"They've trampled all my orofins," one groused, "and stripped my keelit trees of even their leaves! It's all your fault, Noah."

A big Hodinite raised his fist to Noah. Vaul's warning growl gave the man second thoughts.

"We'll be back with the authorities," they promised. Vaul escorted them down the ramp.

※

Hunkered near the sea-wind driven flames of a fire, pouring himself a cup of carrog, Thore rose as First Statre Rogor rode into camp and leaped from his gerup.

"What is it?"

The officer hurried toward him. "A multitude approaches."

"Nephs?"

"Yes, Nephs, and many others as well." Rogor's eyes looked perplexed. "Somehow the Oracle has mustered the people to action against us."

"I thought it had become too quiet." Thore curled his fingers into a fist. "How well armed are they?"

The officer frowned. "They aren't, as far as our advance watch has been able to tell."

"No weapons? How can the Oracle mount an army and not arm them?"

"By the reports, it makes little difference if they are armed or not. By sheer numbers they will overrun our position and sweep through Atlan, marching over the bodies of tens of thousands of their fallen comrades."

The image of so great an army was hard to comprehend. "Is this possible?"

Rogor nodded grimly.

"How long?"

"A quartering. Maybe a little longer."

He considered their alternatives. They had few left. "If we can't defeat them, we can at least delay them."

Rogor replied somberly, "Obliterate the causeway?"

"It's our only choice left." He had already ordered clay explosives to be buried across the narrowest point of the Atlan Ridge, holding the trap in reserve as a last-ditch maneuver. "We'll wait until the horde is upon the narrows. We might as well take as many of them as we can in the blast, and hope the sea will claim more."

The First Statre drew in a long breath and let it slowly out. "I'll pass the word." He started off, then turned back. "This won't stop them for very long, Pyir Thore."

Thore nodded. "I understand. Holding them is all we need to do—for a little longer."

Rogor scowled. "What is the point if it will be over in a few days?"

Indeed. But the commission had been given to him—and not only him, but his father before him, and in extension, all of Atlan. "Doing the Creator's will, First Statre."

He paused a moment, then smiled. "I'll see to the destruction of the Ridge personally."

After Rogor mounted up and rode off, Thore went through the camp alerting the Makir of the coming attack. An idea began to take shape. It turned his blood to ice, but it was all that was left.

He met with his captains and statres to make final plans, then arranged for a wing-sailer to take him back to Atla Fair at a moment's notice should their first line of defense break down here at the Rim-wall.

40

The Last Battle

Noah strode the long, familiar path to Wend's house at the edge of the vineyard, nestled upon the green verge of the forest. The stone building with its flat, thatched roof had begun to sprawl over the years as Wend and Sebe's family had grown, as daughters-in-law had moved in, as grandchildren had begun sprouting like dandelions. When he pulled the cord, Sebe appeared at the door.

Her smile seemed forced. He couldn't blame her. Family relations had been less than cordial these last few years. "Father. Come in."

He entered the cluttered welcoming room and glanced around at the children's toys and books, the schooling easels, a loom, and the musical instruments that Wend's daughters played.

"Everyone all right?" Sebe closed the door.

"Everyone is fine. We're all exhausted." He gave a quick smile, hoping to ease the stilted tension. Little Leomah slid around the corner in her stocking feet and ran to him. "Gampa!"

He caught her up and kissed her cheek as her small arms hugged his neck.

Sebe smiled. "What brings you out?"

"I came for a hug from my Leomah."

Leomah giggled. "You want to see my picture?"

"Love to see your picture." He set her down, and she scampered off.

Sebe gave him a narrowed look. "You didn't come to get a hug or see the latest artwork to come from Leomah's brushes."

"No. I came to speak to Wend."

"I thought that might be the case."

"Is he here?"

Sebe shook her head. "He spends all his time in the vineyard, chasing animals away from the vines."

Disappointed, he shook his head. "Maybe I should go look for him in the fields."

She touched his arm. "I don't think that will be wise just now. He's—" She hesitated. "He's been talking with the neighbors."

"Oh." His heart grew heavy. "And he also blames me for the infestation?"

"That, and the fighting just beyond our border."

"How about you, Sebe?" He saw the indecision in her face. "Do you blame me too?"

"I don't know. I'm worried. The war is not going well, and now these reports of rock falling upon us. And all these animals! It just isn't natural."

"No, it isn't." How many times had he told her the truth, and how many times had she denied it? But he had to keep trying. "It's the beginning of the Creator's wrath."

"There you go again." Her tone sharpened with impatience. "That's the very talk that has turned your neighbors against you. It's what has alienated you from your son."

"But it is the truth." How could he get through to them? Time had run out!

She stiffened. "There are other people who disagree. It's hard to see where you are right and they are wrong, Father. These are smart people. Philosophers and scholars."

"They are foolish."

She scowled. "They haven't squandered their family's wealth building a boat that will never see a drop of water."

That stung. "Then how do you explain the animals?"

Her face hardened. "Maybe it is a judgment, like some are saying. Maybe they were sent to ravage the land so that you will finally see the folly of all that you have done. If you repent now, then maybe they will all go away."

A chill gripped him as he stared at her. "You can't mean that. That's the wisdom of this world talking. It's the old Dirgen cult coming back! High Councilor Rhone kept these lies from Atlan up until the day of his death. How can you give credence to—"

"He might have kept the old faith at bay, but he couldn't forbid what people thought, what they felt, what they spoke about when alone."

He grimaced. So, the old ways had been infecting Atlan all along. And the Oracle had won in spite of Rhone's strong rule.

Leomah came scampering back, her smile a poignant gleam of beauty in the darkness he felt all around him.

"See my picture."

He hunkered down and looked at it with her. She painted a man standing in the sea, his arms outstretched toward dark blotches in the sky. "Interesting. What is it?"

"That's Dirgen. And these are the big rocks falling from the sky. He's making them all go away."

Tears stung as he gave her shoulders a tender hug. "You are a very good artist. But now Grandpa needs to go."

"Okay. Come back soon, Gampa."

His throat clenched as he stood and turned his view on Sebe. "There are quarters aboard the ark for you and your family, if you change your minds. Tell Wend."

She nodded. "I'll tell him."

He put a hand gently upon Leomah's curly head, then left.

A breeze off the sea drove long waves against the rugged Atlan Ridge uplift as Thore and First Statre Rogor rode through the ranks of waiting Makir. Thore knew they all faced their final battle. Word from the front estimated the advancing horde at over a million men. Although most were not trained warriors, the numbers seemed to guarantee the Oracle's success. Early skirmishes had proven their strength.

Each man in the approaching mass possessed the strength of five men, and it hadn't taken long for word to spread that these men harbored the spirits of the vanquished Nephilim that had been billeted on Oric. Incredible as it sounded, Thore recalled his father telling him of such things. Somehow, the possession turned mere mortals into superhuman warriors.

He'd set up his artillery, and brought forward fresh supplies of projers and ammunition.

"There they are," Rogor said, pointing.

Thore squinted against the lowering sun. At first he only saw a shadow that lay over the rocky causeway—until he noted that the shadow was slowly advancing.

Thore lifted his eyes to the sky. *Noah's in Your hands now.* "Ready the charges."

"At your signal," Rogor replied, eyes locked on the advancing swarm.

Thore turned to his captains, who were awaiting his orders. "Take charge of your kal-ee-hons and spread out this side of the line." He glanced back at the jagged cleft in the towering Rimwall where ranks of Makir stood shoulder to shoulder as far as the eye could see. It was unreal—hard to accept even now, that all must soon be lost. Here stood the end of Atlan, all the history of nobility, the Makir way, the ancient traditions and lore— snuffed out at this last stand.

Thore shook himself free from the allure of romantic

melancholy. The last battle was at hand. These were the final lines of defense before the hordes entered the jagged cleft that split the Rim-wall years ago. Once past these warriors, all of Atlan would lay before them. But he still had one last surprise waiting. He had talked it over with his captains, and they had each agreed it was what must be done if the enemy managed to crush their lines.

"First Statre."

"Pyir Thore?"

"You know the importance of holding the line here."

Rogor nodded. "I do."

He glanced at the cloud advancing across the land. "After we blow the ridge, they'll be in confusion. Thousands will die, and the sea will claim even more. But men like that aren't driven by fear. They will keep coming. The sea will gorge itself on their bodies, and still they will come."

"I understand."

"I know you do." He smiled generously, and Rogor returned it in kind.

Rogor was a mighty Makir, and Thore had handpicked his leaders after assuming the command of the Makir when his brother, Chrone, took over the High Councilor's seat. Even now Chrone would be directing the defenses of Hodin's Keep. But if the Oracle's forces made it through the Rim-wall … if—when. It would only be a matter of time before all of Atlan fell beneath their thundering feet.

"After I give the signal, I will leave you in charge. Once the fighting starts, I have one job left to do." He pointed to the wide cleft.

"Your surprise should whittle their numbers considerably."

"Let's hope so, Creator willing." Thore grasped Rogor's forearm as Rogor clasped his, and each understood.

Rogor grinned. "When this is all over, we'll meet in Atla Fair, at the Royal Dragon over a flagon of congar ale."

A poignant regret clenched in his chest, but Thore laughed

anyway. "And I'll buy the first round!" He shifted his view to the mass of advancing men—almost to the booby-trapped narrows. "At the Royal Dragon, my friend."

"At the Dragon." Rogor gave a brief salute. "Fair journey."

"And to you." The emotion caught in his voice, and in a single motion Thore mounted his gerup and loped to where a contingent of Makir huddled over the detonator.

They surveyed the hordes of men and Nephs that moved onto the stretch of rocky ground. Days before, the explosives had been buried there—completely across the narrows and hundreds of spans deep.

"Wait until the first of them are across."

The Makir in charge of the detonator nodded. Others watched the approach through glasses.

"They are on it now," one of the warriors advised.

Thore's heart sped up as the army drew closer. A minute passed, and then another, and as the first of the men made the crossing, he nodded to his Makir. "Now."

The roar shook the old sea floor beneath his feet and a sheet of gray smoke and shattered humans shot skyward along the entire width of the causeway. As debris and bodies rained back down, the sea, which had mounded up on both sides of the Ridge, rushed into the new channel, sweeping thousands of bodies away. Grimly, Thore watched as the smoke slowly cleared and the raft of humans that filled the choppy water washed out to sea or mounded up on the ragged edges of the new waterway.

The Makir advanced under the command of First Statre Rogor and others, and the battle was engaged as stunned survivors staggered and tried to comprehend what had happened. The momentarily confused men on the other side of the wide ditch regrouped.

"I must go now." Thore took the reins of his gerup and stepped back into the saddle.

Grim-faced, they nodded, saluted in unison, and held their

stances without a word. Thore's eyes moved from one face to the next, taking each man into his memory. Some were stony and staunch in their final resolve; a few allowed a slight smile to twitch at the corner of their mouths as his eyes fell upon them, and they broke his glance with a nod, but their salutes held firm. These were the Makir. They would each fight to the last man, experiencing each man's death as the binding slowly broke down and finally vanished when the last two had fallen.

Finally Thore broke the heavy stillness of the group with a sharp returned salute. Already the booming of artillery, the cracking of projer fire filled the causeway. The shouts of men falling before his Makir Warriors drifted from the front line. Turning his gerup away from the battle, he returned to his rear line—never looking back.

He met briefly with his captain there, then rode quickly back toward the massive rent in the Rim-wall where the wing-sailer waited.

In a moment he was airborne, winging swiftly toward Atla Fair.

※

The sailer earthed at the old compound just off of Hodin's Canal, south of Atla Fair. Hundreds of years earlier it had been a major fortress, but after his father wrested control of the land from Zorin, and peace became the rule rather than the exception, the old barracks and training fields fell into disuse. The warehouses that once held arms and supplies for the forces billeted within Hodin's Passage were now mostly empty—except for the explosives.

And after the earth had trembled six years earlier and the land rose, the shallow canal that once connected it to Hodin's Canal had become a muddy track, now mostly overgrown with new vegetation. Only a small contingent of guards patrolled the area. A lieutenant approached when the sailer set down on the little-used earthing strip.

"Pyir Thore." He saluted briskly, surprised at seeing him.

Thore read the question in the man's face as they strode toward a cyclart that had arrived moments after the earthing. "We are holding, so far, but that won't last."

"How can we help?"

Thore admired his commitment, but the few warriors stationed here could do little to swerve the Oracle's torrent of Nephs and spirit-possessed soldiers. "Hold your post here. High Councilor Chrone may very well need you and your men to defend the Keep. Take me to warehouse seven."

The cyclart sped away, and a little while later Thore himself was hefting a crate of gray clay explosives into the cyclart. "Now, take me to warehouse eleven."

"Eleven?" the man inquired, his eyes showing surprise.

Thore smiled. "Trouble with your ears, Lieutenant?"

"No, sir." Setting the cyclart into motion, he whisked Thore to the large wooden building at the far end of the compound. Thore leaped out as it rolled to a stop and hurried to the tall doors. He and the men hauled the heavy panels open, letting sunlight spill into the cavernous building for the first time in years.

"Bring the clay," he ordered, and went inside and began removing the dusty tarps from the dark jumper. The craft had been put into storage after returning from Nod City, and although it had been studied from top to bottom, its workings had eluded even Atlan's cleverest engineers. It was definitely not of this world, and some even doubted it was of this realm. Even exorcised of its gathering spirit, it still radiated a spiritual presence. It defied all the physics and even philosophies of this world.

Now, as he walked around it, its low, constant hum filling the warehouse, Thore sensed it was aware of him in some inexplicable way. He came around to the hatch and placed a palm upon the small, shiny, metal star. It did not feel like metal, but almost of flesh. It obediently opened the hatchway at his touch. If it was alive, if it was indeed spiritual energy instead of honest iron and bronze and tin, at least it was bound somehow to do his will.

The oval hatch slid open and three steps materialized from the hull as if it had changed shape. The air inside didn't smell musty as he had expected. The overhead light panels brightened a little as his feet tread the floor, the pitch of the magnetic jump drive changing very slightly.

The lieutenant lumbered up the steps with the heavy box and stopped, staring around him.

"Ever been inside?" Thore took the box from him and set it aside.

He shook his head. "No. Only seen it a time or two. No one comes here anymore."

"Have a good look, then move the cyclart."

The officer's wide view came back around to him. "Are you taking it out?"

Thore nodded.

"Do—do you know how to make it work, sir?"

He'd had a little practice after the failed rescue attempt in Nod City. Not enough to be proficient—he'd never be the pilot Zinorah had been—but he knew enough to make it move—to be dangerous. A tight grin came to his face. "I'll try not to take the tops off of any of the Keep's spires."

The lieutenant flashed a quick, nervous smile.

"But just to be on the safe side, you and your men stand well clear."

Once the lieutenant had gone, Thore shut the outer pressure hatch and then unpacked the clay. He removed a panel in the back wall and the hum of the power core grew louder. The mag drive buzzed in the air, giving off a faint odor like a launderer's whitener. The core itself pulsated behind a thick crystalline lens, making his hair rise and his skin tingle.

He worked the thick clay in his palms, softening it, then packing it around the core. One crate of explosives ... five detonator caps … he couldn't risk a malfunction. Running the detonation cord out the hatch, across the empty floor, he drew it into the control room and attached it to a small igniter, like the one used to blow the causeway.

He slid into the seat and stared at the controls and took a couple deep breaths … just to ease the nervousness. He gave a wry grin. He had once warned Kenoch against panting; now look at him. He closed his eyes and whispered a prayer for strength and peace. When he opened them, his breathing had slowed to a regular, measured pace.

Recalling his few previous flights, he placed his hands upon the pads, sized to fit a sorp's hand—or a woman's. His fingertips touched ten of the twelve small pads.

The board sprang to life and the solid view panel before him shimmered and seemed to melt before his eyes. Past where the panel had been, the warehouse's doors stood wide open. Four men stood around the cyclart parked a little way off, their attention riveted.

"Here it goes." Thore applied pressure against the pads with two of his fingertips while concentrating his thoughts on moving up and forward. The jumper shuddered, screeching on its earthing pods.

His hands leaped off the controls. He blew out a breath, shifting his fingers slightly, reset them on the pads, and tried again. The jumper lurched forward with a crackling snap of wood. The viewing screen before him shifted rearward with his glance. The warehouse's front timbers were shattered, the roof slowly sagging.

The ground dropped away in quick, looping spirals, and in glimpses he saw the men dashing for cover. Buildings whirled in and out of view and his stomach lurched and his chest squeezed tight as he fought to level the craft. Glancing left, the view port shifted. Hodin's Keep loomed below him, then the city of Atla Fair. In a few moments he got the jumper leveled and pointed in more or less the right direction. His forefinger touched two pads in sequence, phase-shifting the craft under a cloak of invisibility so as not to startle the war-weary Atlanders.

Swiftly he moved out over open farmland. Far below, Noah's ark stretched long across a valley whose forest had been hacked way back. Vast herds of animals congregated around it, spreading out far and wide. With a twinge in his heart, he realized he had not said his fair journey to Noah. They'd met briefly a week earlier after the Gardener's late-night visit. Noah had told him the Gardener's proclamation at that time, but he thought they'd have another chance to speak before the end came. That had never happened. Nor would it happen now. With a grimace of regret, he angled the jumper heavenward and skipped across the limits of the firmament where the eternal blackness sparkled with stars.

He searched among the fixed points and shortly spied the glittering chunks of rocks—the broken body of Rahab, much closer than he had expected—rushing toward him. Ponderously tumbling, the debris momentarily filled his view port. Some stargazers had said the chunks of frozen water and rocks might pass by Earth's circuit, but from this vantage point, Thore doubted it.

The Creator's judgment was coming upon the earth from the heavens. He shuddered to think that it wouldn't be long now. A day at the most, maybe only an hour, was all man had left.

But he'd not see it when it happened.

Setting his jaw in rigid determination, he pointed the jumper at the speck of land in the wide blue sea and raced toward his destiny.

41

Judgment

ather!"

The animals startled at the shout, suddenly chortling, clacking, whistling, and mooing. Noah put a hand to a furry muzzle and calmed a bellowing bear cub, then walked out into the middle deck gallery where the sunlight barely reached from the windows high overhead. He craned his neck back. "Down here, Japheth. What's the emergency?"

One level above him, Japheth leaned over the railing that encircled the long, open valley down the ark's middle.

"Well? What happened? Why are you panting like a horse?"

"Because I ran like a horse … all the way"—he hauled in a breath—"from the road. They're coming!"

"*They?* Who's coming?" *Had the Nephs broken through the Makir line at the Rim-wall?*

"People. From all around. Even Atla Fair. Ulvok stopped me on the road to pass the warning. Apparently our neighbors have decided they are going to burn the ark. They think it's the only way to appease Dirgen and stop the rock from falling upon us, and to turn back the enemy at our shore."

"Can this be true?" Naamah said from somewhere above. He heard her footsteps and a moment later she stood at the railing too.

Japheth nodded. "I have to believe it is, Mother."

Noah set aside the broom he'd been grasping. There had been threats of this for days. "If it is true, we need to get everyone inside the ark." He jogged up the stairs two at a time, and they met him at the top. He grabbed for the handrail to steady himself. At six hundred, he was getting too old to run up steps.

Desmorah came from the far end of the ark where she had been checking water spigots. She carried a bucket of grain, and a small yellow monkey rode upon her shoulder. "What has set the animals off?" She petted the creature clinging to her neck and smiled at her husband, but the smile quickly disappeared. "What's happened?"

"Trouble." Noah shed his shiverthorn apron. "Where are Shem and Kitah, Ham and Majiah?"

Desmorah shook her head. "Majiah was down below checking that the storage shelves were secured. Haven't seen Ham or the others."

He took the grain bucket from her. The monkey held on tight for a moment before releasing to his tug. "You two go find them. Japheth will explain what happened."

As they left, he looked to his wife. "Provisions all aboard?"

"Almost. I'll have to check the lists. There're a few things still stacked up outside."

"Can we do without them?"

"Without them?"

He glanced to the big door standing open to the late fourth-quartering sunlight. "We may have to shut that sooner than we planned."

Her eyes rounded with worry. "We'd be better off with them. I'll get them inside immediately."

"I'll help you." He pitched the apron over the railing, setting down the bucket and the monkey at the same time.

Vaul arose from a comfortable patch of sunlight, yawned, gave a long, languid stretch on his forepaws, and followed them out the door.

※

The island loomed before the viewing panel. Thore swooped low over the western Rim-wall and slowed his approached to the battle being waged upon the causeway. The old Atlan Ridge, once a clear shallows teaming with sea life, now looked like the bony spine of a dead behemoth, crawling with maggots. Dropping lower, the maggots took shape. Nephs and humans together. His Makir Warriors had put up a valiant fight, judging from the bodies and the red pools of blood that glistened in the lowering sunlight.

But it was plain the fight was over.

Maybe a million men streamed toward Atlan. The Atlan Ridge all the way past the Pillars of Herc was black with them. They were even now squeezing through the narrow cleft in the Rim-wall. In a few hours, Atlan—and Noah—would be overrun.

His breath seeped out. This close, Thore felt the binding breaking as the last of his mighty warriors fell beneath the crushing hordes. Tightening bands of loss clenched about him. Today the Makir would vanish from the earth. The once mighty warrior clan of Atlan would never rise again … would the Book his mother had given Noah preserve their memory?

He despaired at the thought, and with renewed resolve, he set his teeth in a tight grimace and soared upward again. He could never stop them. That final feat would be up to the Creator. But he could sure make a hole in their ranks that would bring them up short in their tracks for a good long while. Maybe it would buy Noah the time he needed.

He pulled the jumper up. The glint of tumbling stones catching the sunlight burned in the blackness of space and riveted his attention as the first of the mountain-size boulders slammed into the moon. Then others. Before his eyes, the Oracle's monument vaporized, pummeled into dust.

His lips spread into a grin. How that monument had appalled Noah, and every other Kinsman. Its destruction encouraged him.

Rotating the jumper back, he pointed it at the gash in the Rim-wall.

"For Your glory," he whispered. "Protect Noah now that I am no longer able to do so." He reached for the igniter switch to the explosive clay packed around the jumper's power core.

The ground rushed up, the land black with the Oracle's warriors. Like swarming ants, they forced their way through the Rim-wall. He remembered the conversation he and Noah had, years ago, while on their way to Morg'Seth.

Some deaths don't bring honor … *And some do. Into Your hands, Creator.*

Five hundred spans above the Oracle's invading warriors, he pressed the button.…

✖

They struggled with one end of the crate as they hauled it up the long ramp. The explosion nearly startled the heavy box from his grasp. He and Naamah stared at each other along the box's wooden side.

"What was that?" Naamah asked.

As he was going to say he didn't know, the ground trembled. Setting the box down inside the door, he and Naamah hurried back down the ramp, away from the ark where they had a wider view. The mass of animals churned nervously as they moved out of their way.

Shading his eyes to the lowering sun, Noah watched the

cloud boiling skyward, tumbling within itself. He knew what had happened. Like the last time, it seemed a living nest of writhing snakes as it climbed ever higher, mushrooming as it reached for the sky.

Shem and Kitah jogged up to them. Shem's jaw dropped. "What caused that?"

Kitah stared at Noah. "I know what that is."

Noah nodded. Like him—like Naamah—Kitah had also witnessed a similar event five years earlier. "A jumper."

Shem slowly closed his mouth.

Naamah said, "That's on the Rim-wall!"

"The battle." But what had caused a jumper to explode?

Naamah gave him a startled look. "The Kleimen! That's near their villages."

The cloud spread angrily across the sky, and he was certain that whole side of the island had been devastated. The explosion's hot breath now ruffled the treetops, its coils turning a dark orange-red, muting the sun.

Japheth, Ham, and Majiah wove their way through the milling herds, their eyes fixed upon the frightening sky-mushroom growing in the distance.

What of Thore? No one could have survived—yet, the last time, both Thore and Uncle Kenoch had managed it.

The sky darkened beneath—the smoky veil widened out at the top and expanded sideways.

Shem pointed. "Look!"

The dim circle of the moon had become visible, its surface strangely misty, as if afire, the Oracle's symbol obliterated beneath a growing mass of scars.

"The mountains of Rahab." The sight stole his breath. Noah breathed.

"They're coming at us." Majiah's low voice was tight as a harp string.

Ham said, "The moon is intercepting them."

"Some, but not all." Noah's eyes had fixed upon the tiny glints of light as chunks of the doomed stone slipped past the moon's softened edge.

❦

Lucifer's fury burned as the disembodied spirits appeared once more in his presence. Below, upon the miserable stone, the fireball raced outward, consuming over half his army. He cast a glaring eye heavenward. His mark upon the moon had been obliterated into a crated mass of nothingness.

"This is my world, my kingdom! How dare You intrude!" He roared, his anger shaking the heavens and rumbling down through the earth. Fury directed at the Tyrant did little good, he knew, but at Atlan he still had a chance. If he could kill Noah now—wipe his memory from the earth—he will have won!

"Abaddon!"

Instantly the ruler of the Pit stood before him.

"Are my jumpers prepared?"

"They await your command."

"Send them to Atlan. Leave no one alive—especially Noah and his family. And destroy that miserable ark, too. I want nothing left to remind me of the Tyrant's meddling."

Abaddon's eyebrows dipped in a worried scowl. "But will the Tyrant permit it?"

Lucifer wheeled on him.

Abaddon stiffened.

He narrowed his view at the Prince of the Pit. "Don't question me!"

"Yes, Master. I'll see to it immediately." In a moment he was gone, and an instant later a fleet of jumpers appeared in the skies above Atlan.

With fury streaming red and violet from his clenched fists, he watched the land tremble under the jumper's barrage. If only he could intervene! He'd destroy Noah in a single breath.

This is my world, yet the Tyrant ties my hands.

Yet all he was allowed to do was to influence others to do his bidding. "Then so be it. I can still win this fight!"

※

With the black cloud still climbing in the west, slowly coming apart at its edges, the skies to the south suddenly filled with the dark shapes of the Oracle's jumpers.

Naamah's startled gasp drew their attention to them. "They … they just appeared!" She gripped Noah's arm, fingernails biting into his flesh.

"Phase-shifting … decloaking." He judged the distance. The jumpers had appeared over Hodin's Keep and Atla Fair. Suddenly, violent bursts of projfire filled the darkening skies. A low, heavy rumble, muffled by the distance, followed after a long interval.

The sound of angry, frightened voices now rose nearby as people—friends and neighbors—swarmed toward them.

"Dear Creator, what now?"

"They're coming to burn the ark!" Japheth said.

"Noah!" A voice with the power of a rushing river boomed in the air.

"The Gardener!" He wheeled about, searching. It seemed to have come from inside the ark!

"Noah, you and all your house come into the ark, for I have seen your righteousness before Me in this generation."

He glanced back at the people coming toward them, shovels and hoes raised in angry fists, torches flaming in the dimming light. "Quickly, inside!" He hustled his family toward the loading ramp.

Vaul kept at their heels as if urging them. Perhaps Vaul had always intuitively understood.

They scrambled past crates and old lumber, and mounds of fodder not yet taken aboard. Noah winced as his hip struck the huge sea anchor resting upon the ground at the base of the ramp. "Move! Move! Move!" They rushed up the ramp, but Vaul stopped at its base as if waiting for them to get safely inside.

The mob had trouble getting past the animals. Sten-gordons and behemoths shouldered together. Three-points and oxen joined ranks with elephants and rhinoceroses. The hunting screech of a mansnatcher drew his view. The great winged hunter plunged into the attackers, snatched a man, and strove skyward.

The man struggled until the mansnatcher's powerful beak snipped off his head. The beasts of the forest had become Turnlings once more!

His view shifted and a choking fist seemed to take hold of his throat. "Jumpers!" The distant sky glowed red with fires burning in Atla Fair. Having devastated Atla Fair, the dark crafts were now moving toward them.

Naamah grabbed his arm, pulling him toward the ark's door. "Hurry, Noah. We must get inside."

His legs had mired at the sight, but now he got them moving. The boys had already disappeared inside.

"Father! Father, wait for us!"

Noah halted and turned back again. "Wend!"

His son was struggling to get past the barricade of animals. A flash of fire brightened the evening sky. The explosion rocked the ground.

Wend had changed his mind! Noah's heart leaped with hope. "Wend! I'm coming!" He rushed back down the ramp. At the bottom, Vaul's growling barred his way.

"Father, help us. Wait for us!" Wend, surrounded by his children, was hauling Sebe by one hand and carrying Leomah in his arm. They shoved their way through the shouting crowd, the trumpeting animals, and the roar of projs exploding all around them.

"Out of my way, canic!" Noah pushed past Vaul. He staggered as the ground shook, fighting his way to Wend.

Wend has finally seen the truth! It took all this to lift his blindness, but now he understands!

Vaul leaped to his side—an attacker one moment, a protector the next. Noah hadn't the time to wonder about it. Wend needed him. He had to reach his son and help his family aboard the ark.

"Noah! Come back!" Naamah's pleading cry was drowned out by the explosions.

He rushed toward the crowd where his son struggled to get through. A proj detonated nearby, slamming him to the ground. He rolled back to his knees, smoke and dust biting his eyes and lungs, bodies and blood all round him. He spied Leomah, twisted and broken. He managed to reach her, taking the little, lifeless body into his arms.

Animal carcasses lay scattered all around him. He hardly noticed as he cradled his granddaughter in his arms. His ears roared, his skin tingled with magnetic energy; missiles exploded around him. In his dazed state, he imagined a faint blue haze had enveloped the ark. He brushed the tears from his eyes, but the haze remained.

Clinging to Leomah, he crawled through the carnage, looking for Wend. He found him not moving, bleeding badly. Gripping his son's hand, he pulled the boy to him. "Wend!"

Wend's eyes parted, vacant at first, then gained a small spark of vitality as they found Noah's face. "Father. Sorry." The words seeped from him, hardly audible above the thundering explosion, the bellowing animals.

Noah wiped the blood from his son's face. "Nothing to be sorry for." He choked. "I love you."

A faint smile touched Wend's lips, then went rigid and froze in place. Noah closed his eyes. He was frozen—paralyzed with grief.

Vaul stood beside him. Noah saw past the canic's dark fur. The jumpers were closing in. A flash announced the launch of more missiles, and they streaked toward him.

The air took on a shimmering glow and Vaul reared up in the shape of a man, taller than a Neph, a giant warrior in gleaming golden armor, grasping an ivory and gold staff in both hands.

Vaul thrust the staff toward the jumpers. A brilliant stream of golden energy swallowed up the missiles. The staff lurched again, flinging bolts of blinding light, bursting the jumpers as they zeroed in. Faster than the eye could follow, Vaul repelled the attacks, striking as if knowing instinctively where each of the crafts would appear next.

Someone reached down and took Noah's arm and helped him to his feet. Through his tears, he stared at the tall stranger.

"Who are you?" The bombardment dimmed in his ears.

"I'm Pher'el. Come, we can't delay."

Pher'el guided him up the ramp, but Noah's eyes remained fixed on the giant warrior. "What ... what happened to Vaul?"

At the door, Pher'el stopped and looked back. "His name is Jas'el. He's an ophannin."

Noah stared. "A what?"

"Long ago Elohim sent him to protect you in this realm— even as I have been protecting you in the other."

Dazed, he stumbled through the door, into the ark where Naamah grabbed him inside and hugged him, trembling with tears and fear. "I thought I'd lost you. What happened out there?"

He turned slowly from the door. "Vaul. He ... he's a Messenger."

"At least you're safe."

"Thanks to Vaul, and Pher'el."

"Who?" She peered at him through tear-filled eyes.

"Pher'el."

The faces of his sons- and daughters-in-law, drawn in fear, registered the same confusion. He turned and pointed, but the

Messenger was not there. Maybe he never had been …

Then slowly the great door began to close.

"The Gardener is sealing us," Shem breathed as the unseen hand pushed it firmly shut. He and Ham hurriedly slid the heavy locking bar in place.

Naamah took his hand and twined her fingers in his. "We're safe now." It was meant to comfort him, but his heart ached like it had been cleaved in two, and half was left outside with his other children and his friends.

As the sound of Vaul's devastating reprisal against the Oracle's jumpers slowly ebbed, a new threat began to boom all around them, shaking the ark. They climbed to the walkway beneath the long rooftop window and peered out.

Fiery balls streaked through the night sky, and the earth rocked beneath the onslaught.

Rahab had arrived.

Judgment had begun.

42

Excerpts from Noah's Diary

Day 3: Will the cries for succor never cease? Terrified voices. I hear them in my sleep. I force myself to endure the pleas from outside, but it's about all I can stand. I want to throw open the door and save them all. Sadly, that can never be. Watching from my window, water continues to fall from the sky. It's not let up since the first of Rahab's stones crashed into the earth, shaking it as though it had been split apart. Water steadily rises ... or is Atlan sinking? The animals—those still able to stand—repelled the onslaught of panicked crowds seeking to climb aboard the ark. Some have even managed to climb the sea anchor ropes ... easy picking for the mansnatchers who somehow continue to remain aloft in spite of the pounding water from above.

Water falling from the sky. So this is what it is like. I recall speculating about it with Thore, but quickly my thoughts turn to other matters as my eyes moisten. They seem incapable of staying dry for very long.

Day 7: The cold is most unexpected. We keep a fire burning in the big cooking hearth to drive off the chill.

Sometimes Naamah and I sit immobilized by grief, staring at the quarters we'd built for our children. All but three of them are empty. It must have been what the Creator wanted, but I don't understand why. With only half a heart left, it's hard to come to grips with all that is happening.

The growing odor has compelled me to start the cycler and whirl-mag to run the fans and to power the panels of energized moonglass. The days remain unnaturally dark. We seem to be drawn silently together in the common room, shaking with fear at every chunk of Rahab that still occasionally whistles through the glowering clouds, streaking a long, fiery tail as the Fallen Ones must have when the Creator cast them out of heaven so long ago!

Day 8: The ark moved today, trembling at first, then grinding lowly as it slowly lifted from the foundation pillars. Wood groaned as the hull of the great vessel scraped back and forth upon the underpinnings, responding to the current, yet still tethered in place by the fourteen sea anchors that hang off the ark. People no longer try to climb the immense hawsers. The land has become a shallow sea, and bodies fill it.

I pray that Master Jerl-eze's design is sturdy enough to withstand the abrading. Then I remind myself that it isn't Jerl-eze's ark, but the Creator's. It will hold. It must hold. It contains the future of the world ... of mankind.

Day 14: The unnatural cold persists. Everyone bundles in blankets and gathers morosely around the fire. I have to consciously work at shaking off my despair. Even though we all hurt—there is work to be done!

"Enough of this pouting," I announced today. "There are animals to feed and clean, and this smell isn't going to get any better as we mope and cling to each other."

Day 20: At least with the ark afloat, the column of water in the "Deep Pool" has begun to rise and fall with the rolling waves. The pitching to and fro makes us all ill, but the machine functions exactly as Ham had predicted. The ark surges with air that pumps the animal smell outside. I wish I can call it clean, fresh air, but it has the bitter bite of sulfur. At least I can shut down the cycler and conserve fuel.

Will we ever see the sun again? Today I cracked open the window in our chamber. Black smoke bubbles from the wild gray seas. The earth beneath must indeed have split apart. Melted rock the consistency of oatmeal and red as the fires of a Kleiman's forge pours down mountain sides, hissing as it hits the sea. Tumulus, sulfurous clouds hang low everywhere. The stuff that pounds the ark from above is more like ice than water. Once I got a snootful of the icy water, I immediately closed the hatch.

Day 28: Up on the walkway where we intend to grow food, the bleak world beyond the windows is that of a frozen wasteland. The roof is gray with dirty ice that mounds up against the windows, further cutting off the light.

Atlan's Rim-wall is slowly sinking out of sight.

Day 29: The Rim-wall is gone. Sometime during the night the last crag submerged and the ark drifted over it, out into what had once been the Great Sea. The whole world is now—or soon will be—the Great Sea.

Through the blackness of the storm, here and there I can still spy a distant mountaintop, or a high stretch of ground. If anyone has survived upon it, I don't see them. And unless they'd been prepared with plenty of firewood and a dry place to burn it, they'd all have frozen to death long ago.

It was about the second of the third quartering today while I was shoveling dung down the chute to the composting bins, that I heard footsteps pounding down the stairs and Shem and Kitah called for me.

"I'm right here. What is it?" For the first week or so, the animals had been terrified, but by now most have settled down. Some have drifted into an odd sort of stupor—not really asleep, but not fully awake either. Two weeks ago, Shem's shouts would have startled a thousand animals into bawling.

Shem and Kitah poked their heads around the corner. "Come, you have to see this," Shem said.

Kitah took my arm and pulled me along as I set the shovel aside.

"What's so urgent that it can't wait?"

"You'll see," Kitah said. A few minutes later we all stood upon the walkway along the planting shelves, high up above the third deck, and stared out the windows. With a forearm I polished away the fog upon the glass panes, and for an instant I thought the sea had been turned sideways and stood up on end. But that couldn't be it.

A wall of water rocketed skyward as far as the eye could see—which wasn't very far through the mist and fog and bitter-smelling clouds.

"What is it?" Majiah turned worried eyes to me as though I would have the answer.

"I don't know." I tried to dredge up any knowledge of such a thing. But the phenomenon was far beyond my experience. "The fountains of the deep, maybe?" I suggested, recalling the phrase, but momentarily forgetting where I had heard it.

"From the reservoirs of water stored up under the ground?" Ham has a knack for puzzles. "I remember Grandfather speaking of such things."

Then I remembered too. So, this is what the Gardener had meant. My view moved back to the terrifying specter. It would be the end of us should we get sucked into that maelstrom. Fortunately, its outward current pushed the ark farther and farther away. I breathed a genuine sigh of relief as the great wall of water slowly faded into the mist.

But for the rest of the day I was troubled. What did it mean? All I could think was the earth had cracked and broken apart, releasing some unimaginable force. What else could launch all that water into the cold, empty firmament above the earth? That would explain why most of it fell back as ice.

What would be left of the world once the waters receded—and how would they recede? Where would it all go? I fell into prayer as my concerns mounted.

One thing was now clear. The water falling from the sky was coming from that geyser, and perhaps others like it. I'd seen floods before, when a dam had broken or a river had cut a new channel. Small as they were, they had wrought great changes. What changes might a worldwide dam burst bring? Would Atlan even exist afterward? Or Morg'Seth ... or the Known World?

Day 32: The torrents from heaven have changed. No more ice. Just water. It's an improvement, and we thanked the Creator for it.

The water continued to slacken all day.

Day 40: A mere drizzle fell most of the morning. At the beginning of the third quartering, I shoved my arm far out the hatch in my quarters and it came back dry!

We ended work early, breaking out harps and leolpipes, and celebrated long into the night.

Day 41: I spent much of today peering out the rooftop windows. Here and there a mountain peak still shows—gloomy and nearly naked. Although the water from heaven has ceased, the sea upon which we ride is still a violent place. Thankfully we haven't seen any more water-walls rocketing skyward, yet it is obvious the fountains below the surface are still spewing out water. In places the sea boils and the ark lurches like a ride at the yearly Creation Day fairs, back before the Oracle forbade Creation Day observances. But the sea level has risen above the point where the fountains are able to spew their waters into the cold firmament above Earth's atmosphere.

All power has it limits—except that of the Creator.

Day 53: Sometimes the sea's motion makes us all ill. Other times the water settles down to a relative calm. Through it all, the sky remains depressingly dark. Black fumes continue to bubble from the sea's surface, feeding the gloominess. If I never smell that stink again, it will be too soon!

The work has become routine and onerous, yet there is little else to do. The animals have no choice but to rely on us. We shoulder that responsibility in spite of the heaviness in our souls. I try not to think of the world we left behind, but it is impossible not to remember friends ... and children.

Day 64: Still no sign of the sun, or its warmth. Water fell again from the sky today; such an odd phenomenon, almost as if the heavens weep for the loss. We were all stricken with fear that the torrents would return, but the water quit after only three-fifths of a quartering. To its credit, it tends to wash the air—at least for a short while.

Days drag on and the monotony of our lives, and the never-changing gloom outside the ark, wears heavily on us. Spats break out regularly. I try my best to calm them. Shem and Ham, as usual, have begun to grate on each other. And the wives! Oy, they fight worse than the boys. Fortunately the ark is large enough for the warring parties to separate until the heat of their ire has cooled. Then peace and monotony reign again ... until the next blowup.

Day 149: It's hard to be certain, nothing to judge by, no mountaintops visible, but considering how the sea has calmed, I suspect the fountains have finally stopped giving forth their waters. Time will only tell if I am correct.

On another note, Naamah and Desmorah caught a glimpse of sunlight through a break in the clouds while tending the young plants they have been struggling to keep alive. We were all down below feeding our charges when it happened. I was fixing the automatic watering system ... again. Shem designed it well, but the last hundred days of pitching and tossing has wearied the joints, and they spurt with each cycle of the pump.

At least busy hands have kept the boys from becoming Turnlings!

Day 206: Majiah called us over to see a curious sight. At first we thought it was the top of a mountain, but as we drifted closer, we discovered it was a massive raft of floating trees. Might as well have been an island for its size. From our higher vantage point, no one could see an end to it. I grabbed the glasses and scanned the forest of naked branches for any sign of life—a bird, or some small iguana clinging yet. It is built into the human spirit to hold out hope, but there was nothing. Months of icy weather have killed any chance of survival. It struck me then just how alone we really are. Indeed, the Creator has preserved a mere remnant of life within His ark. I worry we might lose some of them. With so few, the death of even one is a disaster.

And I'm concerned a little about Desmorah. She didn't look well this morning.

Day 210: Now Kitah seems a little under the weather. It must be the confinement. It wears on us all. Although the air is still chilled, I've begun removing some of the windowpanes from the overhead skylights, to help with ventilation. From time to time water falls from the sky, but the showers are brief, and thankfully warm, not icy. The clouds break up more and more. Naamah's sprouting plants look healthy, though a few don't seem to like the cooler temperatures. Soon we will have fresh vegetables to fill our plates.

This night we had our first clear view of the night sky. Everything is different. The moon lay farther to the east, and the stars have shifted out of their places, altering the signs the Creator has placed there. Ham and Shem disagreed how this might have happened, and the arguments became heated. I kept the peace as best I could while we "debated" what might have caused the heavens to move.

The moon, three-quarters full, is dull compared to how brightly it had shone before. Its surface is terribly scarred, and Majiah thinks it resembles a man's face. I suppose if you let your imagination run loose, it does. The Oracle's symbol is gone, smashed to rubble by the mountains of Rahab. Scarred and disfigured as it is, I will happily take the "man" on the moon any day over the "Oracle" on the moon!

Day 212: My girls are pregnant! How could I be so blind? Naamah suspected long ago, but she only told me this evening. Then at mealtime Kitah and Desmorah announced the happy news! The Creator is good! He has opened both girls' wombs. Desmorah is radiant. No wonder Shem and Japheth have been strutting!

Day 226: The skies are clear, the sun is warm. Our plants are thriving, and even the trees have perked up. We've removed all the glass panels, and the air within the ark has freshened. Ham's air ventilator functions perfectly in rough seas, but in pacific water there is not enough movement. We've been running the whirl-mag for light and ventilation, and the 'gia tanks are down about halfway. I should have brought more. What good will our cyclarts be if we run out? Now that the windows are open, we won't have to run the cycler as often.

Still no sight of land, though I suspect the water is draining away somewhere—at least I hope it is. The currents prove there is movement. They have been pulling together unimaginably huge rafts of trees. We drifted in among one such raft last week. The grinding against the hull had us on edge for days until we drifted free of it.

Day 264: The sudden screeching brought us all to a halt! The ark trembled, and for an instant I feared the timbers would spring a leak and we'd be lost. My faith sometimes is like the thin, brittle leaf of an alecup fern! After a few hours of grinding and thumping, we shuddered to a stop, the sea anchors encountering some immovable object!

I released a raven. It flew about and then disappeared for a couple hours. It returned and rested upon the ark until evening.

I tried coaxing it back inside, but it refused my finger and remained outside, roosting on the edge of a window.

Day 271: The raven has been gone for two days. It must have scavenged enough food, for it seemed happy enough to stay outside, hopping about the roof. And then one day it just never returned.

The ark hasn't moved in days. It seems firmly settled in place. I sent out a dove. It didn't find a place to rest and returned to my finger. I will try again next week.

Day 278: We spied a bit of land in the distance! The water truly is receding. Such a simple thing, and we were thrilled beyond measure! All work ceased, music rang out, and we tapped into a keg of wine to celebrate. The fruit of the vine made me think of Wend and Sebe, and my grandchildren. My thoughts turned to my daughters, and my heart broke even more. But I wore a cheerful face so as not to ruin the party.

I sent the dove out again. To my delight, she returned with a young olive leaf in her beak! Somewhere nearby a bit of land has been uncovered long enough for a twig to sprout!

Day 314: The water has been steadily draining from the land. We seem to have grounded upon the peak of a high mountain. The world past the windows is bleak and barren: mud, naked rock, and a harsh sky unlike what I remember. Here and there patches of green have developed. I'm watching a ribbon of grass brighten a muddy ravine past the ark where the water cut a furrow as it drained away. The brownish monotone stretches away for leagues.

Now and then the earth trembles as it did before the flood. Each time it happens, we stop what we're doing and grab for something. The shaking never lasts long. Once the ark shuddered and slipped, then shuddered again as it hauled up against the shoulder of the ravine.

Today we opened the great door and a gust of air cleaned out the stuffiness, which was my intention. I hesitate running the cycler more than necessary. The 'gia is running low.

The world after sunset is cold, and we closed the door and burned the fire hot until we retired for the night.

Day 360: Exactly one year has passed. Desmorah and Kitah are very pregnant, and to my great joy, Majiah is beginning to show too. Soon we will be eleven! I'm anxious for the day when a hundred squealing children bring joy to our new homes and village!

I often sit at the open door, amazed. How quickly the land has greened up! The Creator's hand must be in it, urging new growth along.

The boys are preparing the ramp. Everyone is pacing the decks to be out of here. I especially have to restrain Ham who would climb out of the ark in a heartbeat if I'd let him. I tell him there is a time and a place for everything, and the Creator will let us know when. He just rolls his eyes at me.

Day 371: We fell out of our chairs at the morning meal when the Voice boomed from outside the open door.

"Noah. Bring out every living thing that is with you, of all flesh, of fowl, of cattle, and of every creeping thing that creeps on the earth; and let them swarm on the earth, and bear, and multiply."

In a flash we were at the door, leaning out, peering around. But there was no one there.

The animals roused from their curious slumber almost two weeks ago, ravenous, and we worked nonstop trying to get them all fed. We are more than ready to let them go!

We lowered the sections to the ground and assembled the ramp. Took all day, but it's complete. I examined every nut and bolt until the daylight left. We retired exhausted, and anxious for the morrow.

Day 372: Our first full day on dry ground! Japheth drove down the first cyclart. Shem the second. Then we began opening cages and lowering rails. As if knowing what was expected of them, the animals filed off two by two—except for the clean ones, which bunched up in little herds. I have kept back one of each of the clean animals to sacrifice to the Creator.

And then suddenly a sight in the sky riveted me. All of us stood there, unable to move.

"What is it?" Ham asked, awed.

"The Creator's bow. It was once in the Garden. I saw it as a child. He told me He was reserving it for some important event."

Naamah asked what it meant. She put an arm around my waist as she studied the brightly colored arc, its feet appearing to straddle two peaks.

"It's a promise from the Creator that He will never again destroy the earth with water."

"Well, that's a relief to know!" Japheth crossed his arms and grinned.

Day 389: I built an altar to the Creator and offered our sacrifices upon it. His bow seemed to glow brighter.

The ark is nearly empty. Most importantly, Aunt Cerah's precious Book is safely down among our belongings at the base of this great mountain.

Most of the animals have left … and we know we must too. We can't stay here. Every day the mountain shakes, and every night the temperatures plummet, forcing us to lower ground. It is as if the Creator is trying to tell us to get down off of this mountain, but where does He want us to move?

The cyclarts helped with the move, and without them we'd have been hard pressed to get all the plants and trees and bigger items down the mountain, but fuel has practically run out. We will have to leave them. Maybe someday I can come back for them, once we have a good stand of 'gia growing and a press in place to extract the oil.

Day 390: That was a close one. I hadn't expected the ground to shake so violently. We were down to the last few items when it struck, and the ark slipped sideways sliding partway down the ravine that has been deepening with each rumble. Naamah absolutely forbids me to return for the few remaining items.

Maybe later. I regret having to leave them, but mostly, I deeply regret losing the box. I can still see Lady Leenah's earnest face when she gave it to me. I feel a traitor to her memory. If I'd only been prepared, but the shaking began so suddenly, the stone box slipped from my arms, and I wasn't going to chase it down that dung chute!

When we come back for the cyclarts, I can fetch it. Creator be praised, we all made it safely out of the ark.

As I stared at it from afar, I couldn't help but think it may be a long time before I could return. A very strange phenomenon has begun of late. The water that sometimes falls from the sky is now turning to a frozen, white, fluffy flake. Already the ark wears a saltlike rime.

We need to hurry to a lower elevation. The air grows so cold, I can hardly stand it. And the girls need to be someplace warm as their time approaches. In the lowlands we can find a place to build homes. We will likely have to live in caves and tents until the forests have regrown. But we'll make out all right. The Creator watches over us, and we are all together.

What more can we ask for?

END

Readers' Guide

*For Personal Reflection
or Group Discussion*

THE FALL OF THE NEPHILIM
Readers' Guide

Douglas Hirt continues his compelling story about human origins in this, the third and final volume in the Cradleland Chronicles, sequel to *Quest for Atlan*. As in his previous two volumes, this account of mankind's beginnings differs sharply from much of paleontologists' common wisdom, but accords with events recorded in the Bible. We see an earth that, although fallen, retains a good deal of its former glory. We see men and women made in God's image who were meant to be in fellowship with their Creator but instead find themselves separated from Him. In just a few generations, almost everyone has forgotten the true account of creation. Most regard that story as merely myth and legend. Many also find themselves alienated—from God, others, and even themselves. Most of humanity is in open rebellion against their Creator. Only a few have remembered the old stories, or have been reached by others who have retained the ancient knowledge, and they, too, have found their way back to God.

Sound familiar? In many ways, the situation depicted in Hirt's trilogy closely resembles our own. We, too, are skeptical about creation, alienated, and often in rebellion. We, too, have lost our way. We, too, find it difficult to believe in a supernatural world that lies just beyond our senses. We, too, experience fear, distrust, enmity, hatred, family tragedy, and war. We, too, wonder why this good God—if there even is such a being—seems to have withdrawn from our world.

Just as the Christian story suggests answers to these age-old difficulties, so does *The Fall of the Nephilim*. This story speaks to faith, conviction, courage, commitment, and trust. Another great storyteller, C. S. Lewis, believed that every square inch of the universe, every millisecond of time, is a battleground over which the forces of light and the forces of darkness contend. Hirt's story shares that worldview. Every decision, every action, every commitment, every choice either promotes the kingdom of God or the kingdom of the Great Deceiver.

Does all this seem unlikely? Nevertheless, many of the essential plot elements presented in this book closely follow the pattern of Scripture. To be sure, it is good fictional fun and isn't purposed to make a case for literal history. But on the other hand, it provocatively suggests there could be scenarios that remain true to the biblical account while varying profoundly from popular theories or tradition. We invite you, the reader, to search the Word of God to see if you can find your own answers to such uncertainties. We hope that the following questions will assist you in your quest for the truth about your own world today—about faith, human origins, and the natural and supernatural worlds. Even more, we hope they will stir you to take a closer look at your own relationship to the Creator.

Chapter 1

1. Lamech is a powerful preacher, taking the message of salvation as it was
    understood before the coming of Christ in the flesh, into the very heart
    of Satan's stronghold—a city occupied by giants. Genesis 6 says: There
    were giants in the earth in those days; *and also after that*. Where else in
    the Bible does God speak of giants, and might these be the same crea-
    tures, offspring of fallen angels and human women, who filled the world
    before the flood?

Chapter 2

2. When the Gardener comes to Noah to give him the commission to build
    the ark, He is accompanied by cherubim. Cherubs seem to hold a special
    place in God's kingdom, always near to the throne of God, or guarding the
    way to the garden and the Tree of Life. Because of renaissance paintings,
    we have a false image of what a cherub is. Can you find a description of
    these most powerful created beings? Also, why would two such powerful
    beings be commissioned to guard the way to the Tree of Life? Simply to
    keep man from it? Here's a hint: Who else is a cherub?

Chapter 3

3. We see here that Lamech travels in vehicles that resemble our own con-
    veyances. Technology back then is advancing as technology advances in our
    own world. This might seem to be a stretch even for reasonable suspension
    of disbelief, but that is because we've been conditioned to think in evolu-
    tionary terms. Consider this: If man was a fresh creation from the hand of
    God, with great intellect and a lifespan of nine hundred years, what sort of
    marvels might he create? Discuss the possibilities and make a list of what
    man might develop. Keep in mind, it was only a little over a hundred years

ago, one-eighth a preflood lifespan, that we were driving horse and bug-
gies, yet today we are exploring Mars.

4. By this late date the world had become a very dangerous place to live.
    What hints at this do you see when Lamech and Kerche arrive at Kerche's
    place of business in Far Port?

Chapter 4

5. Noah is frustrated when boatbuilder after boatbuilder tells him the "boat"
    he wants to build will never work, yet the Creator has told him to build it!
    How have you felt when God has put a task before you that is seemingly
    too large? Insurmountable? What must we remember when the Lord
    gives us a task that seems to be beyond our abilities?

6. Throughout this series of books, Lamech draws upon the stars as a wit-
    ness to the promise of a coming savior: the first prophecy given in the
    Bible, Genesis 3:15. In Genesis, God tells us He made the stars for signs
    and for seasons (see 1:14). How do you respond to the supposition that in
    the world before Christ, God could have spread the message of salvation
    by using "signs" in the heavens for all to see? How has Lucifer perverted
    God's truth into lies?

Chapter 5

7. The Bible doesn't tell us if Noah had any children other than Shem,
    Japheth, and Ham; but then, the Bible genealogies seem selective. In *The
    Fall of the Nephilim*, Noah does have other children, and not all of them

choose to follow their father's faith. This is heartbreaking to a parent. Why would God permit children of godly parents to go astray?

Chapter 6

8. Here we get to meet more of Noah's family. The daughters particularly appear discontented with their lot in life. Could it be that Noah and Naamah, in their zeal to protect their children from the world, have in fact caused this rebellious attitude? How do we see this same problem in our own families? How best might we protect our children from evil, yet not stifle them?

9. What turns out to be the solution to Noah's boat-designing problem? How has the Lord provided an answer and a way for you when you were attempting to do His will?

Chapter 7

10. Have you ever considered what a massive undertaking building something the size of the ark must have been? Noah must have spent years planning the project. And what about the cost? Would God have given Noah great wealth or great resources to complete the project? Consider Jesus' teaching recorded in Luke 14:26–35; how does the truth of Jesus' message apply to Noah's situation?

Chapter 8

11. Noah recalls his Aunt Cerah who had been entrusted with the book Father Adam wrote so many years before. The book contained the very words of the Creator. Now as the flood draws near, Cerah knows she must pass the

book on to Noah. Down through the ages God's Word has endured in spite of efforts to destroy it. Down through the ages Satan has tried to destroy or discredit the Bible. How do you see that happening today?

Chapter 9

12. Rhone is an old man by now, full of years and wisdom. He is a benevolent ruler and loved by his people and friends. Yet Rhone has a heavy heart. He grieves in the spirit for his old friend's son, Bar'ack, who years ago turned from the Creator and was possessed by demons. Even though Bar'ack is out of Rhone's reach, what powerful tool is available for this once mighty warrior to save Bar'ack?

Chapter 10

13. As time draws short for the people living before the flood, Satan steps up his efforts to destroy the Kinsmen, those people who still believe in the Creator. How has this happened in more recent history? How could it happen today?

14. According to the Bible, there is coming a time at the end of our age when Satan will again seek to destroy all believers. Revelation 13:17 tells us how Satan will separate believers from nonbelievers, and Revelation 20:4 tells us how he will execute them. Why does God communicate prophesy to His people even if, like Noah, it cannot be altered? What is the purpose of prophesy?

Chapter 11

15. How easily we picture Satan with horn and tail. But the Bible describes

him as an angel of light, a prideful being of incredible beauty. It was pride that caused him to rebel. Do you think Satan retains his beauty today? How can we see evil manifesting today in beauty?

16. No doubt Satan is a powerful being, even in his fallen state. Yet he is not omnipresent nor is he omniscient. Those qualities are God's alone. Not being everywhere at once or all-knowing, what sort of network of informants can you imagine him having?

Chapter 12

17. Read Job 1:6–7 and contrast the world's traditional representation of Satan with this passage's account. Now examine Ephesians 6:10–12; contrast what Paul taught about the spiritual world with popular culture's representation.

18. Here we vividly see the three demons who have taken up residence in Bar'ack's body. Too often we lump demons and fallen angels in the same pile, but the two entities are very different indeed. In this episode, what might you surmise is one of the differences?

Chapter 13

19. In this chapter we see a wedding taking place upon the open deck of the partially completed ark. Life continued as usual in spite of God's coming wrath. Consider Jesus' comparison of the setting of His own return to that of Noah, as recorded in Matthew 24:38–44—what principle does Jesus intend for us to take away from this comparison, and how do we apply it to our own lives today?

20. Think about the ark for a moment. It had to be large enough to hold and maintain thousands of animals and eight humans, so there had to be more to it than just a big box. What sort of equipment might be needed to sustain life in the ark for a year? Why does God give us responsibilities and then call us to employ our skills and creativity to accomplish such a task?

Chapter 14

21. Do you believe there are spiritual forces that can attack you on occasion? In this chapter we get a glimpse of what may go on in that spiritual realm. Satan's emissaries are always looking for our weak points, the chinks in our spiritual armor. Even believers are not immune from Satan's attacks— Ephesians 6:13–18 calls upon believers to put on their spiritual armor. Noah has a weakness in his armor—building the ark so consumed him that he has neglected his family, especially his children. Can you identify potential weak spots in your armor? What do you make of the "helmet" described in v. 17?

22. Satan revels in the sins of man, and when he finds a tender spot, he prods at it. Noah is weakest right now concerning his family and what he perceives as his neglect of them. He feels guilty, and Satan intends to work his guilt for all it's worth. Why is guilt such a potent spiritual weapon against believers who have been forgiven?

Chapter 15

23. Understanding the destruction coming upon the world, Noah and Naamah lament for their children who have rejected their faith. Still, as parents they are not willing to give up on their children. As parents, what

can we do to reach our lost children? What has Noah done to bolster his belief that all his children will be saved through the flood?

24. Rhone and Leenah have lived long, happy lives—lives they know are drawing to an end, yet they don't despair. How can you explain a believer's lack of despair, even in the face of certain death and destruction?

25. What is Rhone's greatest regret, as he looks back over his life? Should we have such regrets?

Chapter 16

26. As the time drew nearer for God's wrath to fall upon the world, signs of its coming increased. As God's wrath, spoken of in the book of Revelation, approaches, there will again be signs. Why is God described in His own Word as wrathful?

27. After this great earthquake, much of Atlan is destroyed, but the ark of God escaped unscathed. It received divine protection. Should Noah have been encouraged by this? In our lives, when we are within the will of God, do we also receive divine protection? Why do you think God allows bad things to happen to good people?

28. Why do you think the earthquake breaks down a portion of the Rim-wall and raises the Atlan Ridge from beneath the sea? Do you see God's provision in this?

Chapter 17

29. As the end draws near, Satan steps up his attack on the Kinsmen, and arranges an ambush to try to kill Noah. Why do you think Satan is singling out Noah? What does this strategy tell you about Satan's tactics? Can you find examples of how Satan has used this narrowing process to try to thwart God's prophecy?

Chapter 18

30. How would you respond to Majiah's suggestion that it is selfish of Noah to escape the coming wrath while everyone else dies? How would you similarly respond to a contemporary accusation that Christians selfishly look to their own eternal security while most of the world will be condemned?

31. Satan and his emissaries, the fallen angels, pass themselves off as "star-beings," beings from another world come to Earth to bring enlightenment. How do you respond to the supposition that contemporary examples of paranormal and UFO activity might have evil spiritual sources?

Chapter 19

32. Throughout this book Satan claims this is "his world" and he resents the Creator's interference in his affairs. Jesus did describe Satan as "the prince of this world" (John 14:30), and Paul describes him as the "ruler of the kingdom of the air" (Eph. 2:2). When Satan tempted Jesus three times (see Luke 4:1–12) and finally showed Him all the kingdoms of the world and offered to give them to Jesus if only He would bow down and worship him, Jesus didn't question Satan's authority to do so. How do you respond to Satan's protest against God's interference in his domain?

Chapter 20

33. Rhone and Leenah keep a dragon as a pet. In the beginning God created a perfect world, but after the fall everything began to change. Genesis 9:1–3 recounts how God said animals' response to humans would change to fear. It seems that in the world before the flood, man and animals coexisted on much friendlier terms than they do today. No doubt this was at least in part because man was primarily a vegetarian in those days (see v. 3). In the context of God's declaration in this passage, how do you respond to some who would argue mankind should return to a preflood diet?

34. Why does Noah take the risk of returning to his family's homeland when he knows the Oracle is out to get him?

Chapter 21

35. Noah is represented as a frail human, with failings like any of us. His particular weakness here is inferred from an account in Genesis 9:20–21 where he struggled with drunkenness. What could it be that might drive Noah to drink in this story?

36. In Ephesians 5:18, Paul cautions not to be drunk with wine. What do you make of the alternative he affirms: "Be filled with the Spirit"?

37. Why is the book that Mother Eve gave to Noah's Aunt Cerah so important?

Chapter 22

38. Sometimes when we are caught up in the throes of a disaster, we need a

friend to come up alongside us and point us in the right direction. In this story, Noah had Thore. Today we believers also have advisers that come up alongside us and point us in the right direction. Whom does God use in your life in times of crisis? How does God Himself come alongside you as an adviser?

Chapter 23

39. The company escapes into a vast field of vera-logia, an oily plant widely used for fuel. How has God provided resources for humanity in our contemporary world?

Chapter 24

40. The Oracle's jumpers seem to be able to find the fugitives no matter how hard they try to hide or how far they flee. What do you think is guiding them? What are some examples in our culture of how evil will work into unwitting humans' lives, despite their ignorance?

Chapter 25

41. When Kenoch and Thore stay back to fight the Nephs and protect Noah and the others, they know they are about to face overwhelming odds. Does it seem reasonable that they would be willing to die for their friends? This sacrifice is a sign of great love, yet both men have their personal reasons for doing this. What could be Kenoch's and Thore's motivations?

42. In spite of overwhelming odds Thore and Kenoch are victorious. How could this have happened? (What was the last act Kenoch did before the battle began?) Can you identify similar examples from your own life?

Chapter 26

43. Makir Warriors experience something called the "binding," a drawing together of spirits that makes the one as strong as the many. Because of this, Rhone senses Thore's danger even though they are thousands of miles apart. How might this "binding" be analogous to how the Holy Spirit operates in the church?

44. We meet a new Warrior Guardian, Jas'el, in this scene. He is of a different class of angel called ophannin. As mentioned in an earlier question, there are many different classes of angels, each with apparently a different role to play. What do you think Jas'el's role might be? Why does God create people (angels and humans) to have different roles?

Chapter 27

45. Upon discovering their miraculous survival, Thore puts it off to some natural phenomena. What are some examples that you are aware of in which people have tried to explain away miraculous events by explanations of natural phenomena?

46. Thore is in a bad way and cannot travel, but Kenoch refuses to leave his side even though the enemy is about to attack again. Why would Kenoch be so foolish as to risk his own life?

47. Kenoch discovers Thore is carrying one of the Oracle's pledge pendants and at once realizes how the Oracle's forces have been able to follow them. Even though it would be an easy thing for Kenoch to take the pendant from Thore, why does he insist that Thore himself has to get rid of it?

Chapter 28

48. Once back in Atlan, Noah's only thoughts are to rescue Sheflah. Rhone points out that this distraction will keep him from completing the Creator's commission to build the ark, which is exactly what the Oracle wants. How do the worries and cares of this world work to distract us from doing God's will? Do you think this is Satan's deliberate plan?

Chapter 29

49. Thore and Kenoch are helped by fugitives hiding out in the Wild Lands, an unlikely place to find aid. God's provision often comes in unexpected ways and unexpected places. Can you think of unusual ways God has reached down and provided for you?

Chapter 30

50. Noah is determined to go with the Makir to rescue his daughter; but his grandfather Methuselah advises against it, warning that this distraction from the work of the Creator is exactly what the Deceiver wants. Then he tells Noah that Sheflah may not come back. Should Methuselah have kept his opinions to himself? How do you discern when it is best to advise and when it is best to keep it to yourself?

51. Majiah is startled at the size of the ark. According to the measurements given in the Bible (300 cubits by 50 cubits by 30 cubits), it would have been approximately 450 feet long, 75 feet wide, and 45 feet high. Based upon what God said in Genesis 6:17, what animals might have been included and what might have been excluded?

Chapter 31

52. Noah's mother, Mishah, experiences a frightening dream, an old dream she'd not experienced for many years. Throughout the Bible, God communicates with His children in many ways, dreams being one of the occasional methods. Identify three examples in the Bible where God spoke to His people through dreams.

53. Worried about her son, Leenah speaks with her pet dragon using an inborn ability that was once common among man, but by now has all but died out. Is it possible Adam and Eve could have freely communicated with animals before the fall? Interestingly, when Eve told Adam of her conversation (see Gen. 3), neither he nor she seemed amazed by this occurrence. What does man's being created in God's image (see Gen. 1:27) suggest to us about animals, even those that might be able to communicate with humans?

54. All along, Noah was determined to return to Nod City and rescue his daughter. At the end, however, he changes his mind, realizing his destiny belonged to the Creator and in completing the task given him. Sometimes we, too, have to make hard choices. What are some comparably difficult choices you've faced in your own life?

Chapter 32

55. Nod City symbolized the sinful world in the days before the flood and God's wrath. Do you see any similarities between what was happening then and what is happening now? Discuss Luke 17:26–27, and how it might relate to us today.

Chapter 33

56. Wandering through the bowels of the Oracle's Temple, they wonder at the huge, "man-size" wheels upon which an immense platen turned. Orm'el said the wheels were forged by the Tubal-Cain Company. What do we know of the preflood character named Tubal-Cain (see Gen. 4:22)? How does what the Bible says about him fly in the face of standard evolutionary and anthropological teaching? How could anthropology be wrong?

57. Marveling at the intricacy of the suntracer that controls the Temple, Lamech said the "hard engineering" was provided by the Oracle's emissaries (fallen angels). In this book the author suggests there was open communication between the spiritual and physical realm. What are some of the ways people receive such messages today, and what does the Word of God have to say about it?

Chapter 34

58. Strange reunions sometimes happen. Orm'el had been a prisoner with Lamech six hundred years earlier. During their incarceration Lamech told him about the Creator and the Creator's message of salvation written in the stars. Had he simply planted a seed—a seed that someone else obviously had watered? Now Lamech learns that Orm'el has come to a saving faith; he's a Kinsman! We may never know how our words affect someone else—for good or evil—but we all should be like Lamech, casting out the seeds and praying that some find good ground.

59. Orm'el was in the right place at the right time to help Kenoch and Thore. God's hand was clearly orchestrating all of this. How do you respond to this having been the purpose God had in mind when He arranged for

Orm'el and Lamech to be locked up in prison together in the first place? (How might Rom. 8:28 apply here?)

Chapter 35

60. Rhone and Lamech pass into eternity together and are met by angels. This is a comforting thought for us who are bound up in these mortal coils. Most everyone has speculated on this event, which eventually each of us will experience. Do you think we are met by angels? What does the Bible have to say about our passage from this life to the next?

Chapter 36

61. Before he dies, Methuselah gives a prophecy to each of Noah's sons. Who else in the Bible gave a prophecy to each of his sons before he died?

62. Why do you think the prophecy given to Ham was so severe compared to his brothers?

Chapter 37

63. Lucifer has a plan to influence mankind after the flood. He knows men well enough to understand what tempts them. But in order to get the secret knowledge through the flood, he must find a human to carry it. Majiah is his choice because she harbors bitterness in her heart. Why would bitterness be an in for Satan?

Chapter 38

64. In the last few moments of Bar'ack's life, he finds himself freed of his

demons and turns back to the faith of his father. This has been Rhone's prayer all his life, but it wasn't until after Rhone's death that the prayer was answered. Think back to prayers that have been answered in your life. Have months and even years passed before the answer came?

65. Pher'el, Noah's Guardian Angel, is in a constant battle with the unseen forces that surround and taunt Noah. When Noah's faith is strong, Pher'el is invincible, but when his faith wavers, the mighty Messenger-warrior begins to falter. Why do you think the author represents faith as having such an effect on those angels assigned to guard believers?

Chapter 39

66. In this story, the disembodied spirits of the Nephilim become what we call today "demons" and take possession of a physical body as their "tent." This may be just the creative speculation of a fiction writer, but some have suggested that Isaiah 26:14 indicates this is indeed what happened. How do you respond to this theory?

67. For hundreds of years, Rhone held reign on Atlan and kept alive worship of the true Creator. In all that time, Atlan was blessed and prospered. After Rhone dies, the nation slipped quickly back into idolatry and the worship of Dirgen, the sea god. Why might a nation's leadership have such an impact upon the people? (Compare this to what happened to Israel during the days of the kings.)

Chapter 40

68. The burden in Noah's heart in these last days is for his children, but many

of them do not believe in the coming flood. He tells his daughter-in-law that there are quarters prepared aboard the ark for her and her family. The work had already been done; all she had to do was accept what Noah had done for her. How is this like the offer of salvation through Christ?

69. Thore prepares to stop the enemy at the Rim-wall by crashing one of the Oracle's own jumpers into their advancing lines. Why would he do this, even though the prospects of his stopping the onslaught were hopeless? What does this have to say to us as we face the inevitability of prophesy in our world, or the inevitability of death in our own lives?

Chapter 41

70. Too late, Wend sees the error of his way, but the time to accept Noah's offer of safety has passed. Nevertheless, Noah makes a desperate effort to reach his son, nearly losing his own life. How many of us wouldn't sacrifice our lives for our children? Do you think this is how God feels toward us, His children?

Chapter 42

71. If water came from outer space when the windows of heaven were open, wouldn't it be icy cold? What are some scenarios that might possibly explain the frozen mammoths that have been discovered in Siberia with fresh food still in their mouths?

72. Imagine yourself sealed into a pitching, rolling boat those first few turbulent weeks of the flood. Discuss what it might have been like and what

your feelings might have been. Would you be frightened? Filled with wonderment? Seasick?

73. Stepping off the ark, the eight survivors discover a new world, completely changed from what they knew. According to this story, even the climate has changed. The weather is cold, something they probably rarely experienced. Although they brought with them many plants, could all of them have flourished in this new climate? Is it likely that "in the beginning" God created ideal plants as food that allowed man to thrive? Do you think all of these plants would survive in this new world?

74. Why might God have lifted His ban on eating meat in Genesis 9:3?

A preview
from Douglas Hirt:
the continuation of the

Cradleland Chronicles

1

The Ottoman Empire—1645

The icy splinter of wood stabbed into Gawyn's palm as he pulled himself through the ragged hole and into the shattered past … his past … Muammer's past … everyone's past. Into the very heart of God's grace.

Stepping a few paces into the dim vault, his breath caught and his eyes pulled wide. Unexpected dread clutched his throat, tightening like bands about his chest. A misty void scowled back at him where ice crystals pirouetted and coiled in filtered light like amorphous snakes slithering past dark columns of timber. Brittle phantasms. The ghosts of legends?

The gloomy distance deepened to black and stretched beyond sight, swallowed by the frozen mountainside far beneath the ice. Gawyn hardly noticed the cold air that crept under his kilt and stung his bare thighs where the long woolen stockings ended. Then Muammer's struggling grunts reached him over the brisk wind outside. He exhaled a plume of gray breath, breaking the crystal spell, and turned to help his friend over the splintered breach.

With Muammer safely through the hole, Gawyn advanced a few more paces and peered about the dim interior. *It is true … all true.* He shuddered, suddenly terrified that God could at any moment stroll out from the deeper shadows.

"This is it—it really is it," Muammer whispered, puffs of steam accompanying his words.

He nodded. "It seems irreverent to stand here." Gawyn thought of the lessons he'd learned in church. Sara should be here with him. "We stand on hallowed ground. Like the desert sand before the burning bush. I feel like …

like God will strike us dead for desecrating it." He looked back at his companion. Muammer, the forty-seventh son of the sultan, was a new friend by any reckoning, but one who over the last week had proved to be as true as any of the boys he'd known all his life back in Scotland.

"Ha! Superstition. Your God no longer dwells in this place, Red Shanks." But Muammer was still whispering. "It is an empty shell, the remains of a very old boat. Nothing more." He grinned, his narrow face even darker in the heavy gloom.

"Maybe … yet it feels like … like a cathedral." Huge timbers stood like a winter forest about them, and sharp, cold air filled his lungs. Breathing was hard work, as if this mountain they had just spent two days climbing had finally run out of air. *Maybe Kazim is right?* He thought of the timid servant waiting for them on the ridge below the cliff they had climbed to reach this place. Kazim had refused to put one foot upon this holy artifact. *How can anyone come so far, be so close, and not finish the quest?* He shook his head. He did not understand Kazim, but then the Sultan's servant was an old man. Only men with no adventure in their souls grow gray and bent. Gawyn drew himself up to his full height and cast back his shoulders. Young adventurers like him seldom grew old enough to experience the ravages of the years! He fully expected not to see his thirtieth birthday, only thirteen years hence.

They had entered upon what appeared to be the second deck. The dim outlines of two staircases, one soaring upward toward brighter light and the other descending even deeper into the gloomy bowels of the ice-shrouded relic, offered tantalizing prospects of more adventure.

The ancient stair steps, heavy and wide, were a long stretch even for his legs.

Muammer grunted. "Either we are short, my friend, or these people were giants."

The light brightened as they ascended. Ice crystals the color of Sara's eyes danced like blue faeries in the sunbeams slanting through the ceiling. He stepped out upon a wide floor, immensely huge, dazed by the sight. Animal pens and corrals; wood so old, it felt like stone. They crept past the creatures. After all these centuries, the boards didn't creak underfoot. The vessel had been built to last, to support great weight. Elephants and dragons, no doubt, and perhaps other animals, the memories of which were lost in the misty past. If any odors lingered, the air was too cold to smell them.

At one place, smaller rooms sat off either side of a wide aisle. He and Muammer explored the compartments, empty except for the ghosts of long ago. He peered cautiously into shadowed corners. Muammer opened a cupboard and held up a scrap of cloth with an interlocking design about its edge. The symbols vaguely reminded Gawyn of the ancient letters he had once seen in a book on Father Simone's desk.

Deeper into the hoary vessel a great table whose top came almost to his chest filled a space in front of a massive fireplace. A few ancient cauldrons lay on their sides near it.

The deck beneath their feet shook.

Gawyn grabbed onto the edge of the table and looked to Muammer. "The mountain trembles. The hand of God warning us to leave this place."

Muammer cast about as the shaking ceased, his midnight eyes wide, his mouth agape. "This mountain often shakes, Red Shanks. I do not think it is your God's hand—or any other god's."

Gawyn peered at the dusty table. "They left nothing behind. They took it all with them."

"Except these cooking pots. Why would they leave them?"

Muammer was right. How could the ancients think of beginning a new life—a new world—and not take items of such obvious value? "Maybe something frightened them? Forced them to flee?" Gawyn realized he was whispering.

Muammer peered inside one of the pots, then up at the ceiling, and finally back into the deeper shadows where the vast open space seemed to shrink to nothingness. "We must be under the ice."

"How far back does it go?" His skin crawled. Did unseen creatures peer at them from the dark? *It's nothing. Only your imagination. There is no one here anymore, and except for a few curious mountain folk, there hasn't been for over three thousand years.*

They explored deeper. The interior grew darker than the cellar under his father's house. Darker than a Highland night in January—and just about as cold. Something loomed up out of the shadows. He stopped, daring not to move. But the thing was not alive. Here and there it reflected some of the light from the far end of the vessel. He exhaled. "Some kind of machine."

Muammer cautiously touched a long cylinder. A metal rod extended from it. He followed it back to where it connected to a tall metal wheel. "What kind of machine?"

"It looks like a waterwheel." Gawyn circled it, fingers probing hidden nooks.

Muammer grabbed one of the spokes and pulled down, but the ages had seized the wheel long ago. The rod did not move nor did the cylinder of iron crawl deeper into the heart of the machine. "What evil has wrought this beast?"

"Evil?" He pressed a hand to the beast, seeking a heartbeat but finding only cold iron. "Something from a time long before ours. A place both marvelous and wonderful."

The Sultan's forty-seventh son nodded. "Legend says that warriors before the great flood rode iron chariots to the moon and beyond."

"I can almost believe it." He tried to conjure up a picture of a people so awesome, yet a world so evil that God had to destroy it. Sara would be fascinated when he told her. A smile tugged at his lips. Sara MacLaren, soon to be Sara Lowery, cherished nothing more than a good puzzle to unweave. Thinking of her made his heart ache with loneliness. There would be so much to tell Sara when he returned home. He imagined her bellflower blue eyes widening with wonder, and that fine line at the corner of her mouth deepening as he told her the wonders they had discovered.

Neither spoke for a while, feeling their way around the iron wonder. Finally Muammer said, "The air here grows colder. Let's return to the light."

Ice crystals glittered in the soft sunlight as they descended the stairs they had climbed earlier. Muammer started for the splintered hole through which they had entered, but Gawyn wasn't ready to give up the adventure just yet.

"Muammer, what wonders might lie below?"

"It is dark down there, my friend." Muammer burnished the cold from his arms and looked longingly to the ragged patch of daylight beyond the broken timbers. "And much colder."

Gawyn started down the dark stairs, taking unnaturally long strides, imagining the tall race of people who long ago had followed this very path. The light vanished quickly as he descended deeper into the bowels of the ancient structure. The icy air held a vaguely musty smell in spite of the cold, and shadowy mounds rose in heaps. Here and there a breach in the old timbers allowed slender shafts of sunlight to draw long, thin lines across the dark landscape.

Muammer came up beside him. "Kazim will be worried."

"Kazim is a timid old man. Worry is what he does best."

Muammer laughed. "True ... but there is nothing down here for us, my friend." He looked around. "Except stones and dirt."

"Dirt? Why mounds of dirt, Muammer? Does that not seem strange?"

He frowned. Sara would have been able to decipher the puzzle. "We need torches."

"We can come back."

"No. My father will finish his business in a few days and then I will be in a caravan heading south, back to the sea, and Scotland. No, Muammer, this is my only chance to explore the mighty ark of God."

The mountain shook again. The old boat creaked and groaned. Muammer's eyes darted. "Stay if you like, Red Shanks. I will be waiting with Kazim when you get tired of nosing about in the dark."

Gawyn watched his friend hurry back up the steps, his slender form silhouetted against the marginally brighter light above. He turned back, grasping the frozen wooden railing. What was he doing poking around in the dark—in the very heart of God's grace? He did not belong here. No man belonged here. Like the Garden, man had been expelled from the ark of God.

His grasp tightened as the old wooden floor beneath his feet lurched with the mountain. *All right. I will go!* "Muammer. Wait."

Muammer halted on the topmost step.

Gawyn started for the stairs when something caught his eye. A sliver of light drew a bright line across a pile of dirt just the other side of an open hatchway. There, half-embedded in the dirt, was a dull, pale object. He turned aside and bent through the hatch.

"Red Shanks! Where are you going?"

"A moment!" He crawled up frozen soil and reached for it. A sudden tremor knocked him off balance and he tumbled to the bottom of the pile.

"Gawyn!"

He clawed his way up again, fighting against the shaking mountain, caught hold the corner of the object, and wrenched it loose. *A box made of stone, but light as wood.* No time to marvel at it now. Whatever secrets it held rattled inside it as he tucked it under his arm.

The angry mountain slammed him against the dark wall. Stunned, he clambered out the hatch.

The ancient structure bucked and squalled like a storm-tossed ship. Muammer cast out a hand at the top of the stairs and hauled him up onto the deck. "What have you there, my friend?"

They scrambled for the hole.

"Don't know."

Daylight lurched beyond the gap like the small disks of wood his archery teacher used to fling into the sky. He remembered taking aim and missing most of the time as he now aimed for the leaping hole. "God is angry!"

Muammer didn't reply.

Gawyn reached the breech first and drew himself through it, grabbing the rope in both hands, clutching the box under his arm. His kilt billowed in the cold air as he repelled off the old timbers, glimpsing Muammer's face in the opening above him. He reached the ground and pressed against the mountain's rocky shoulder as Muammer swung from the hole and started down the rope like a monkey with a leopard on his tail. Another fifty feet below them, Kazim staggered to keep his balance, waving for them to hurry.

Dropping the last five feet, Muammer careened toward the sheer edge of the cliff.

Gawyn snagged the sleeve of his woolen coat as pebbles clattered down around them from above. Muammer wobbled a long moment on the edge, then Gawyn dragged him from the brink.

As though bowing to the shaking mountain's anger, the once-bright afternoon sky darkened, thick clouds tumbling over the ragged peaks above.

"We must hurry!" Gawyn shouted.

Muammer nodded, his dusky face pale with fright.

Starting toward the broken stair step of rocks that had lifted them to this ledge, Gawyn again took the lead with Muammer on the heels of his well-worn shoes.

A crack like a fusil shot turned his head. The ledge beneath Muammer's feet broke loose and his friend let out a cry and disappeared.

"Muammer!" Gawyn clambered to the edge of the declivity, which now permanently blocked the way to the ancient ark of God. "Muammer!" His heart went to stone, his rasping breath stilled in his knotting throat.

"Red Shanks!" came the screech that set his heart back in motion.

Falling to his knees, he bent over the edge and snatched his friend's wrist the instant Muammer's three-fingers-hold gave up the challenge. Muammer's sudden weight slammed him to the ground and the box wrenched from his grasp, landing inches from the precipice. He stretched his other hand for Muammer's groping fingers. Determination clenched Gawyn's jaw as he slowly drew Muammer toward safety, his young muscles bulging beneath his short woolen jacket.

The stone box skittered closer to the edge. That couldn't he helped. He concentrated on his friend, willing his muscles to lift the heavy weight until Muammer was able to grab a jagged outcrop.

He hauled Muammer to safety, blew out a breath, and snatched the teetering box from the mountain's maw. They scrambled down off the ledge to Kazim. By then the shaking had ceased, but fear kept them moving until the ark was but a distant rectangle upon a tiny glacier-encrusted ledge. A gray veil of clouds moved down from the peaks and hung between them and the ark, spitting chilled rain and frozen snow.

Some time later they collapsed in exhaustion.

Kazim's stricken face looked as though it had been he instead of Muammer who had nearly died. And maybe he had. What punishment might the Sultan mete out had he returned carrying Muammer's lifeless body? All at once Kazim threw his arms about him. "Thank Allah for your courage, young Gawyn Lowery!"

It was not Allah, but angels sent from the throne of the God of Abraham, Isaac, and Jacob, who had circled round them and kept them from harm. But he'd not mention that to the humble Muslim servant of the great Sultan. Yet, as they recouped and started again down the mountainside, he had to wonder why he and Muammer had been spared. Had God something grand planned for their lives?

His eyes turned down to the box he carried, seeing it now in detail. It was indeed made of some pale stone, yet light as wood. Although very ancient, the bas-relief carving that encircled it was sharply cut as if carved only last year. Four metal clasps appeared to be made of gold. Upon the lid, etched symbols, like letters of an ancient language, vaguely reminded him of something. They certainly were not Turkish, or Latin. Slightly familiar with Greek from his studies, he was certain it was not that either. Sara might know. Surely Father Simone would.

He ached to open it, to see what rattled inside it so tantalizingly as he walked, but held off, fearing Kazim would take notice and insist on giving it to the Sultan. So far the old man had shown no interest in the discovery.

No imagination at all.

Gawyn Lowery was glad he'd never grow old and gray.